TANDEM

ALSO BY **ANNA JARZAB**

All Unquiet Things
The Opposite of Hallelujah

TANDEM

THE MANY-WORLDS TRILOGY / BOOK 1

ANNA JARZAB

DELACORTE PRESS

 Published in the United States by Delacorte Press, an imprint of Random House Children's Books, a division of Random House, Inc., New York.

Delacorte Press is a registered trademark and the colophon is a trademark of Random House, Inc.

Visit us on the Web! randomhouse.com/teens

Educators and librarians, for a variety of teaching tools, visit us at RHTeachersLibrarians.com

Library of Congress Cataloging-in-Publication Data
Jarzab, Anna.
Tandem / Anna Jarzab. — First edition.
pages cm. — (The many-worlds trilogy ; book 1)
Summary: Sasha, who lives a quiet life with her grandfather in Chicago but dreams of adventure, is thrilled to be asked to prom by her long-time crush, Grant, but after the dance he abducts her to a parallel universe to impersonate a princess.
ISBN 978-0-385-74277-1 (hc) — ISBN 978-0-375-99077-9 (glb) — ISBN 978-0-307-97725-0 (ebook) [1. Science fiction. 2. Adventure and adventurers—Fiction. 3. Impersonation—Fiction. 4. Identity—Fiction. 5. Orphans—Fiction.] I. Title.
PZ7.J2968Tan 2013
[Fic]—dc23
2012046712

The text of this book is set in 10.5-point Meridien.
Book design by Sarah Hoy

Printed in the United States of America

10 9 8 7 6 5 4 3 2 1

First Edition

For Eesha, who believes in the impossible

YEA, AND IF SOME GOD SHALL WRECK ME IN THE WINE-DARK DEEP, EVEN SO I WILL ENDURE. . . . FOR ALREADY HAVE I SUFFERED FULL MUCH, AND MUCH HAVE I TOILED IN PERILS OF WAVES AND WAR; LET THIS BE ADDED TO THE TALE OF THOSE.

—HOMER, **THE ODYSSEY**

BE NOT AFRAID OF GREATNESS: SOME ARE BORN GREAT,

SOME ACHIEVE GREATNESS,

AND SOME HAVE GREATNESS THRUST UPON THEM.

—SHAKESPEARE, **TWELFTH NIGHT**

PROLOGUE

When I was a sophomore in high school, I enrolled in a Western philosophy class to fulfill a graduation requirement. On the first day of the semester, my teacher, Mr. Early, wrote three words on the board: *kata to chreon*.

The phrase, he said, was ambiguous, both in origin and meaning, but basically it was translated "according to the debt." The ancient Greeks, Mr. Early told us, believed that the universe was an ordered place, where everything had a price that was collected in due course. The universe, he said, strives for harmony and balance. All that is born will someday die. Ashes to ashes. Things fall apart.

Those guys might've died centuries ago, but they were on to something. Science tells us that matter can neither be created nor destroyed, but also that every action has an equal and opposite reaction—all debts are eventually paid in full. I don't remember much else from the class, but that particular idea stuck with me. *Kata to chreon*.

Apparently, the universe won't let you get away with anything, at least not for long.

IT WAS ALMOST MIDNIGHT.

The Castle was quiet, but through the open windows she could hear the breeze rustling the leaves and flowers in the garden below her bedroom terrace; the smell of roses and lilacs rushed inside upon those same soft winds and wrapped itself around her neck like a scarf. Up in the sky, the aurora danced; the incandescent whorls of green light usually lifted her spirits, but tonight they gave her a melancholy feeling. For days she'd been on high alert for ill omens, signs of impending disaster, something that would tell her definitively that she was making the wrong choice, heading down an unsafe path. She wasn't normally so superstitious, but anxiety buzzed beneath her skin like a fly trapped against a pane of glass, and she wondered if, maybe, the universe might intervene in some unforeseen way on her behalf and make everything clear for once. But here she was, in the eleventh hour, and no clarity had come. She was truly on her own, with nothing and no one to guide her. The door was closing on her fate.

She could turn back. She didn't have to leave at midnight. She could lie down on her comfortable, familiar bed, close her eyes, and wait for the next day to begin the same as always. She could remain who she was—Juliana, Princess of the United Commonwealth of Columbia, heir apparent to the throne. In six weeks she would be eligible to rip the regency out of her stepmother's greedy hands and step into her appointed role, the one that she'd been born for. And if that was all that awaited her, she might have stayed. But who she was, was not the whole story. There were other elements at play.

For one, there was her father, a once-great man now reduced by a sniper's bullet to little more than a body on a bed. Not long before he was shot, the king had bestowed upon her a truth she did not yet understand. The bullet that had put him at death's door, that had destroyed the very essence of him—his mind—had come from an assassin's gun. The King's Elite Service simply assumed it was Libertas, though the rebel group hadn't claimed the crime and there was no proof. In the months since it happened, she'd started to have doubts. But no matter who was behind it, someone had tried to kill her father. It stood to reason that the same person would try to kill her as well. She didn't want to die, and yet she knew that, if she stayed, she would live the remainder of her life in a crosshairs. Perhaps it was cowardly of her—in fact, she knew it was—but she had encountered nothing in her life up until now the love of which would compel her to step forward to greet her own end.

The thought of running from her obligations to her country didn't fail to shame her. If Thomas knew what she was planning to do—what she had already done—he would try to stop her. Six months ago, before her father's attempted murder, the king had broken the news that he was marrying her off to the enemy in order to secure some measure of peace and safety for the Commonwealth. He'd tried in vain to convince her that this was the only way, but she'd refused to accept his reasons, had raged against him, scowled and snapped and played the spoiled brat, anything to make him change his mind, but he wouldn't. Thomas had told her that sometimes sacrifices must be made for the good of all. She'd been so awful to him after that, had hardly spoken to him since that conversation, even after what happened to her father. All she'd wanted was to ask Thomas what she should do, but she couldn't bring herself to say a word to him. Now here she was, five minutes from betraying him, betraying everyone, all the people that depended on the royal family for strength and leadership and salvation, and she knew that whatever happened next, however and whenever her life did eventually end, like all lives do, she would regret not thanking him for his friendship, and not saying goodbye.

It was three minutes to twelve. She had to leave now if she was to meet her coconspirator at midnight. When he'd come to her a few days ago and offered her this choice, she'd been repulsed. She'd never liked him in all the years she'd known him. He'd always seemed too slick to her, slippery as an eel; he reeked of insecurity and desperation, which she especially hated because she feared she might sometimes come off that way, in her weaker moments. Her father had always told her that the things people hate most in others are likely the things that they hate in themselves. When it came to this particular person, the thought made her cringe; if she was anything like him, perhaps that was the reason she was doing what she was doing. Running away, hiding, avoiding her duty—it was what he would have done. After all, he was the one helping her to do it.

At first she hadn't understood what he was offering her. How could he, of all people, give her what she wanted—the chance to live a normal life, away from the Castle, away from her responsibilities, the chance to be who she wanted to be, whoever that was. But then he told her about Libertas, that they were willing to help her disappear for the right price. But he was only the messenger, the thief inside the Castle. It was the Monad who really wanted her. It was the Monad who would set her free.

There was one last thing to take care of before she went. She wrote her note to Thomas quickly and, knowing that it needed to look inconspicuous or it would never reach him, folded it into the shape of a star, pressing her thumbnail against its edges so that it would puff out. Then she placed it in the drawer of her nightstand. Her message was short, for there wasn't much room to write, and she didn't have much to say:

T—I'm sorry, but I can't. I wish I was better, but I'm not. –J

She closed the drawer, then crossed the room and stood beneath a painting that had been done long ago. It showed her mother's country estate of St. Lawrence, which belonged to her now. She'd spent every summer there as a child, on the banks of Star Lake; it was there that some of her happiest memories were set. It broke her heart to imagine that she might never see it again, might never see her mother again. Her mother was an exile, forced to live out the rest of her days in a northern country for the mere crime of having loved the king and not having been loved enough in return. That old wound throbbed as she took her last look at regal, historic St. Lawrence and recalled the childhood she'd lost, but then she put it aside, knowing full well that nostalgia was a phantom limb, painful but useless.

She stepped out onto the terrace to take one last, long look at the Castle gardens, her favorite place in the whole Citadel. High above her the Tower stood, blacker than the night itself. She imagined Thomas asleep in his quarters, blissfully unaware of the fact that when he woke the next morning, she would be gone. She imagined the General in his office, painstakingly plotting out a future that she would not be around to take part in. The first she would feel guilty for turning her back on; the other could rot in hell for all she cared. Above the Tower, higher still, the aurora spun and turned the way it always had, the way it always would, with or without her. It had an indifferent beauty that reminded her how minuscule she was in the face of infinity. This thought was a comfort. In the grand scheme of things, she didn't matter at all. Knowing that made it easier to do what she was about to do.

EARTH

THOMAS THROUGH THE TANDEM

It was hard to get used to the sky without the aurora in it. He hadn't given it much thought before he came through, how much he'd miss it. He wasn't overly sentimental about those sorts of things, but it was strange to look up and see only an empty blanket of black pockmarked with stars. He reached into his pocket and pulled out a handful of toggles, popping them into his mouth one by one and savoring the taste of the smooth chocolate before biting down softly upon the fruit center. It was his one vice; there was nothing on Earth to compare with toggles, so even though it was against the rules to bring something from his universe that did not exist in this one, he couldn't resist carrying a bag through the tandem. He ate them compulsively when he was anxious, and they reminded him of home. It seemed to be worth the risk.

He had entered this universe through a door that wasn't there. No one saw him do it; night had fallen several hours before, and the small, quiet stretch of South Kenwood that ran along Bixler Park was empty. His entry was undisturbed; only a small tremor that rattled the swings on the playground signaled his arrival. He'd taken up his position behind the thick trunk of an oak tree and waited for his analog to appear, twisting the gold KES ring he wore, running his thumb over the inscription on the band, the KES motto: *Surpass to outlast.* At 9:40 p.m., Grant Davis left a restaurant on Fifty-Seventh Street with a small group of friends. Thomas watched as Grant said goodbye and separated from the group, jogging across the street with his hands in his pockets. He was on his way.

Thomas considered the bizarreness of what was about to happen, what he was about to do. He did have a choice. He could let Grant pass him by, let him walk up the street and disappear into the warm yellow light of the house he shared with his mother, a law professor and amateur ornithologist who rode a bicycle to work and bought all her groceries at the neighborhood co-op. But if he wasn't going to do it, then why was he there? Yes, he had a choice, but barely. This was his mission. The General was counting on him, and, even though they didn't know it, so were all the citizens of the country he'd pledged a solemn oath to protect and serve. Tonight the fate of an entire universe rested upon his shoulders. He couldn't go back on his promises now, no matter the doubts that tugged at his mind and asked him, did he really think he was doing the right thing?

Grant's footsteps grew louder as he closed the gap between them. Thomas readied himself. This would have to be done with absolute precision. There was no room for error. At least the park was deserted. At least there was no chance of anyone bearing witness to what was about to happen.

When Grant was but a few feet from him, Thomas stepped out from behind the tree and raised his eyes to meet his analog's.

It was an uncanny thing, meeting one's analog face to face. There was a feeling of unnaturalness to it, as if it betrayed the most fundamental laws of physics—which it did. People were not meant to cross from one universe to another; that was why the tandem existed in the first place, a veil that fell between the worlds, a barrier that was supposedly impermeable. And yet, they—the scientists of Thomas's universe—had found a way to cross it. There were consequences, of course. Moving in and out of universes created disruptions, imbalances of mass and energy with destructive results. The quake that had occurred when he came through the tandem this time was just part of the process, a ripple effect caused by his sudden entry and the energy it had taken to get him there. That itself wasn't such a big deal. A small imbalance made for a small disruption, one that no one had even seemed to notice. But the second complication of moving between universes was another thing altogether.

In Thomas's world, they called it the analog problem. Put simply, analogs—doubles, for lack of a better word—from different universes could not touch. If analogs did make physical contact, one of them would be ejected from the universe they both stood in, thrown through the tandem to restore the balance. Normally, it would be the analog who didn't belong; universes knew their own, and called for them across the wilds of hyperspace. But Thomas needed to stay on Earth. He couldn't be the one thrown back. Around his wrist, he wore a bracelet, a slim, close-fitting thing of shining silver that would allow him to stay.

Thomas had prepared his world for Grant. On the other side of the tandem, three agents of the King's Elite Service lay in wait; they would take him into custody and keep him safe until the time came to return him to his home world. All Thomas had to do now was get close enough to Grant to administer the touch that would toss him through the tandem like a rag doll and deposit him on the other side to fill the slot Thomas had left vacant, if everything went to plan. But Thomas had learned long ago that such things rarely did.

Grant looked Thomas up and down, trying to make sense of what he was seeing. "Whoa," he breathed. Thomas's veins thrummed with adrenaline and power. A faint singed smell hung in the air, as if lightning had struck somewhere nearby. Electricity danced in Thomas's fingertips. This was it. The time was now. All he needed to do was take one step, and he would be close enough to touch Grant. Then it would be over, and his real mission would begin.

But Thomas was paralyzed. He hadn't given much thought to what it would be like when he finally met his analog. There were things he knew about Grant, facts and dates he'd been forced to memorize in order to ensure he could effectively impersonate him, but none of that information was relevant now. He had so many questions for Grant, and about him. He wanted to know, for the first time, what it was like to actually *be* Grant, to live in his skin and see the world—his world—the way he saw it.

Dr. Moss had tried to warn him about this. "Don't believe for a second that just because you know what he is that it won't affect you," Mossie had said, but Thomas hadn't listened. And now it was too late. There was no more time. Grant Davis had to go.

"Who are you?" Grant demanded, his voice tight with fear and anger. Thomas hesitated before replying, not sure what to tell him, knowing that he shouldn't tell him anything at all. During that moment's pause, so slight a mouse couldn't slip through it, Grant took advantage of Thomas's uncertainty and lunged at him.

Grant's fingers closed around the collar of Thomas's sweatshirt, which was identical to his own. *"Who are you?"* he shouted. There was terror in his eyes.

"I'm you," Thomas told him with grave sincerity. The answer threw Grant off, and Thomas sprang into action, wrenching out of Grant's grasp and pushing him away. The other boy stumbled backward, but only for a second, then sprang up again; this time, Grant's closed fist connected with Thomas's jaw.

When Thomas opened his eyes, he was lying flat on the concrete sidewalk, and he was alone. He was more than alone; there was no sign, none at all, that Grant had ever been there in the first place.

He picked himself up off the ground and touched his jaw gingerly. The blow had been glancing; it wouldn't leave much of a mark. Grant had some of Thomas's own strength and reflexes, but he was untrained and he certainly had nothing close to Thomas's own experience with hand-to-hand combat. If only Thomas had not hesitated, Grant wouldn't have gotten in a punch at all. Still, he couldn't help but feel a surge of pride for his analog. After all, he'd done what Thomas himself would've done. He'd fought for his life.

Bixler Park was quiet and empty. Thomas was tired, an unusual feeling for him, so he shoved his hands into his pockets and jogged up South Kenwood toward the warm yellow light of home.

ONE

"What are you reading?"

I glanced up from my book to see Grant Davis towering over me. I turned my head, trying to figure out who he was talking to, because it couldn't be me. Grant Davis hadn't spoken more than three words to me in the whole time we'd been in school together. But the room was empty except for him and me. I must've looked completely baffled; Grant laughed and flopped down into the chair beside mine. *This is weird,* I thought in passing, but I decided to go with it. How often does the most popular guy in school show up in your favorite bookshop and start talking to you?

Grant Davis was, to put it bluntly, the finest human specimen that had ever come into existence. I'd had a crush on him since I was in the fourth grade and he was in fifth. It burned pretty hot for a while there in late middle school, but over the years it had been reduced to a few smoldering coals. My heart gave a small, involuntary flutter as I took him in out of the corner of my eye. Grant was just my type—tall and broad-shouldered, with eyes the color of new spring grass, strong, perfect features, and thick blond hair that always looked slightly rumpled, as if he'd just rolled out of bed. But he wasn't just handsome; I knew a lot of cute guys I'd never in a million years want to talk to. Grant was also good-natured and charming, beloved by students, teachers, and administrators alike. He always seemed so laid-back and carefree. Even now, he sprawled in his seat, looking relaxed and comfortable, while I sat there tense and nervous, clutching a worn paperback edition of Shakespeare's *Twelfth Night* like it was the only thing in the world I owned.

"What are you looking for, Sasha?" he asked, with an amused glint in his eye.

"Whoever it is you're talking to," I told him, raising my eyebrows.

"I'm talking to *you*." He flung his arms outward, gesturing around the room. We were in the reading lounge of 57th Street Books, tucked away deep in the store's underground, labyrinthine stacks. It was my favorite bookshop in Hyde Park, a quaint old university neighborhood on the South Side of Chicago where I lived with my grandfather. I almost never ran into anyone I knew at the shop, and seeing Grant among the bookshelves was kind of like spotting a polar bear sunning itself on a Malibu beach. "Do you notice anyone else around? I think we might be the only two people here."

"That's what I like about this place," I said. "It's usually so *quiet*."

"Is that a hint?" Grant asked, his tone still playful.

"Maybe." I tried unsuccessfully to suppress a smile. "What are you doing here?" The fact that he had no books in his possession hadn't escaped my attention.

"Hey." He affected a hurt tone. "I love to read. Books are my life."

I shot him a dubious look. "The last time we took an

English class together, you tried to turn in a book report on *The Matrix.*"

"Fair enough," he replied, grinning. "In my defense, I had it on pretty good authority that *The Matrix* was *based* on a book."

"And whose authority would that be?"

"Johnny Hogan's," he admitted reluctantly. I covered my eyes in embarrassment for him.

"Johnny Hogan!" I cried. "Well, then you deserve whatever you got. I don't think Johnny's read a book since *Hop on Pop.*"

His smile faltered a bit, and I realized that he didn't have any idea what I was talking about. "The Dr. Seuss book? *Hop on Pop*?"

"I know what *Hop on Pop* is." Grant rolled his eyes.

"It sure seemed like you didn't," I teased.

Grant shrugged and leaned toward me. My heart was beating so fast I could feel it in my throat. "So, are you going to answer my question? What are you reading?"

I turned the book so that he could get a look at the cover. "*Twelfth Night,* huh? Never heard of it."

"It's for Ms. Dunne's English class. But I've read it before." Several times, actually. It was one of my favorites. I couldn't imagine Grant was interested in my schoolwork, but hey, he'd asked.

"What's it about?" Grant settled back in his chair, as if preparing himself for story time.

"Really?" He nodded. "Well, okay. It's about this girl, Viola, who gets shipwrecked in a foreign country and has to pretend to be somebody else to keep her identity a secret." That got his attention; he sat up straighter, and his eyes widened a bit. "But she ends up falling in love with this guy she's supposed to be working for, and all the while the woman her boss is courting starts falling in love with Viola, who's disguised as a boy. It's a comedy."

"Sure sounds like one."

"Believe me, it's very funny. If you like Shakespeare."

"I'm assuming you do, judging by the state of your copy," he said. I glanced down at my battered paperback. The pages were curled and yellow, the cover so tattered that it was only connected to the spine by a small tab of paper that seemed liable to rip any second. For some reason, *Twelfth Night* spoke to me, in the same way that *A Wrinkle in Time* and *Alice in Wonderland* had when I was younger. I was a lucky girl; considering the way things could have gone, I'd had a wonderful life so far. But there was always a part of me, even before my parents died, that yearned to be plucked out of my everyday life and thrust into some great adventure. My favorite heroines were girls who suddenly found themselves having to live by their wits in a world they didn't quite understand. I couldn't help but envy them; their experiences made them stronger, smarter, better—or, rather, it proved to them that they had been those things all along.

"Absolutely. *Twelfth Night* is my favorite play of his. Most girls prefer *Romeo and Juliet,* because they think it's so romantic." I fiddled with the charm I wore around my neck, a crescent moon with a little star hanging beneath it. It was a sixteenth birthday present from my grandfather, and playing with it was a nervous habit of mine.

"And you disagree?"

"It's okay. The poetry is beautiful. But I've always thought Romeo and Juliet themselves were sort of silly." Why was I telling him all this? What did he care about my opinions on fictional characters? But he gazed at me with interest, as if he was hanging on my every word, which was unnerving. The experience of sitting side by side with Grant Davis was more than a little bit surreal, like a pleasant dream in which everything was slightly off-kilter.

"How so?"

"This isn't exactly an original opinion, but it seems to me that there's almost always a better way of solving romantic problems than killing yourself," I told him. He chuckled. I glanced at my watch. "Oh, crap. I didn't realize how late it was. I've got to get home." I gathered my things and stood. Grant rose as well.

"It was nice . . . chatting with you, Grant," I said, unsure of how best to leave things. Had he come over to talk to me for a reason, or was he just killing time? And what was he doing in 57th Street Books anyway? I was pretty sure he hadn't come to browse.

"Let me walk you," he offered.

"That's okay," I said, suddenly shy. The heat of a blush rose up in my cheeks. "You don't have to." Part of me was desperate to stay and keep talking to him. I was curious, and I could feel that old crush I'd nursed through junior high starting to rekindle. But another part of me wanted to get away from him as fast as possible. Talking and joking with Grant while nobody else was around was one thing, but Grant was one of the most popular kids in school, and I was . . . not. It was hard to imagine spending time with him out in the world, as if we were friends.

"I insist," he said, taking the bag from my hand and slinging it over his shoulder. "Let's go. I don't want you to be late."

It was almost six o'clock, but it was early May and the light outside was still bright enough that I had to shield my eyes as we emerged from the dim cave of the bookshop. We started down Fifty-Seventh Street, then took a left on South Kenwood and passed through Bixler Park in awkward silence. I knew Hyde Park like the back of my hand—I'd lived there since I was seven, in a ramshackle Victorian that Granddad had bought in the early eighties—and the neighborhood just wasn't that big, fifteen blocks by fifteen blocks max. I was pretty sure Grant had lived there all his life. But as we strolled the familiar streets together, I felt like I was discovering it for the first time. Everything seemed like a much better version of itself; the grass was a little greener, the historic brownstones and houses with their painted gables seemed better cared for and more brightly colored, and the breeze that came off Lake Michigan was sweeter and cooler than it had been two hours ago. I was pretty sure this was all in my head. Nothing had changed, not really. But it still felt like something had.

Grant was strolling languidly, his face tilted toward the sky to catch the warmth of the sun, as if he was in no hurry. I, however, was. Granddad enforced a very strict dinnertime—six o'clock on the dot, every night, no exceptions.

"Where do you live?" Grant asked.

"South Kenwood, between Fifty-Second and Fifty-Third."

"Not that far from us, then. We're on Fifty-Fourth and Ridgewood." He waited for a moment, then added, "My mom and I. It's just the two of us."

"Us too," I said. "Just me and Granddad."

"Yeah, I was wondering—where are your parents? If you don't mind me asking."

"They died," I told him. That part always made people uncomfortable. They didn't know what to say, and most of the time they ended up apologizing, but even though I missed my parents every day, it wasn't painful to talk about anymore.

In fact, I preferred not having to dance around it. Hiding it to avoid awkwardness seemed disrespectful to their memory.

"I'm sorry," Grant said, as I knew he would. He kneaded the back of his neck in what I took to be a nervous gesture.

"That's okay. It was a long time ago. What's the story with your parents?"

He shrugged. "Divorced. Dad's an attorney out in L.A. I haven't seen him in a while. Your grandfather teaches at the university, right?"

"Yeah, physics. He worked there for thirty years and then retired, but when he inherited me he had to start working again. I used to feel bad about it, but actually I think he missed it. He would've used any excuse to go back."

"My mom's a professor, too, but she hates it." Grant laughed. "She's always complaining about 'office politics,' whatever those are."

I smiled. "Granddad too. He never talks to anyone in his department if he can help it. Physics, he loves; physicists, not so much."

"And what do you love?" Grant asked. I looked up at him in surprise.

"What do you mean?"

"I mean, you know, what's your passion?" He held his fist out in front of me as if he was offering me a microphone. "Sasha Lawson—what do you want to be when you grow up?"

I leaned forward as if speaking into it. "Not sure yet."

"Not sure, huh? I would've thought you had your entire future planned out by now."

"Why's that?"

"Oh, I don't know. You're really focused. Killer grades, tons of extracurriculars. You just seem like the kind of girl who knows what she's doing."

"Then my master plan is working," I said with a smile. "But no. I don't." It killed Granddad that I didn't have a major picked out yet, much less a college. He claimed he decided to be a physicist when he was six years old, but that always sounded like an exaggeration to me. "What about you?"

"I'm enrolled at Loyola for the fall," Grant said, naming a university only a few miles from where we lived. I was surprised he wasn't venturing farther away from home. "But I've got no idea what I'm going to do there."

We paused at the corner of Fifty-Fourth Street and South Kenwood. "Are you sure you want to walk me all the way home?" I asked.

"Sasha, it's only a couple more blocks. I think I'll live." He squinted at me, as if he was trying to bring me into focus. "Are you trying to get rid of me or something?"

"No, no, it's not that, it's just . . ." I trailed off as we passed Ridgewood.

"Yes?" He drew the word out slowly.

"I'm confused," I said. "You have literally *never* spoken to me before. Then today you show up out of nowhere and offer to walk me home? Was there something you wanted?"

He shoved his hands deep into the pockets of his jeans. "No, not exactly. But I . . ." He stopped and turned to look at me. I stared back, trying to read his mind, but it turns out that's pretty difficult when you don't really know a person. He seemed sincere, but guarded, too. He took a deep, bracing breath. "I graduate in like a month, and it's making me think about all the things I wish I'd done differently."

"What does that have to do with me?"

"I've been thinking about you a lot," he confessed, averting his gaze.

"Me? Why?"

"I don't know!" He seemed to be retreating further and further into himself with every passing second. I'd never seen Grant look embarrassed or uncomfortable; this was a whole new side to him, a stark difference from his big man on campus persona. The moment was strange and intimate; I was starting to feel bad for giving him such a hard time. "You seem smart and cool, and you're clearly pretty. I mean, you know you're pretty, right?"

I didn't know how to respond to that, so I just said, "Thank you."

"You're welcome." He shuffled his feet. "Anyway, I just wanted to spend some time with you. Get to know you a little better." He held up his palms in a gesture of surrender. "I'm not going to try anything funny, I swear."

I laughed, and he relaxed visibly. "I believe you, I believe you. I'm sorry for making this so awkward. I just didn't get it."

Grant smiled, and my stomach did a dramatic flip-flop. We lapsed into silence, and as we continued walking the weirdness between us began to dissipate. I kept turning his words over in my head: *I've been thinking about you. You seem smart and cool, and you're clearly pretty.* I wanted to barrage him with questions, get some more definitive answers, but even my admittedly limited experience with boys told me that wasn't a very good idea.

When we were only a few yards from my house, Grant stopped again.

"Can I ask you something?" I nodded. "Have you thought about prom at all?"

What a ridiculous question—*of course* I'd thought about prom. It was all most girls in my class could talk about, now that it was only about a week away. But I hadn't expected anybody to ask me and, sure enough, nobody had. I wasn't terribly disappointed—there wasn't even anyone in particular I wanted to go with—but I couldn't deny that there was a part of me that wanted to go, if only to see what all the fuss was about.

"In what way?" I asked. Maybe that response was dense, but this whole experience was so odd; I knew that when I walked through the door of my house I would have a hard time believing it had even happened.

"Do you, maybe, want to, I don't know, go with me?" He held my gaze so tightly that it was impossible for me to look away. His face was full of anticipation and dread, which baffled me. I couldn't believe that Grant, of all the guys I'd ever known, was standing in front of me now, worrying about whether or not I would say yes.

"Really?"

"Or whatever. You're probably going with someone else, or already have plans that night or something. You can say no, it's okay." He smiled as if to reassure me. "I promise to only be a little crushed."

"That's not fair!" I cried in mock outrage. "You're trying to guilt me into saying yes."

"Is it working?"

"No," I said. He took this as a rejection, and shrugged, as if it didn't matter, but I knew it did. I rushed to clarify, not wanting the opportunity to slip out of my hands. "I don't need to be guilted. I'd love to go to prom with you." Overcome by another wave of awkwardness, I added a stilted, "Thank you for asking me."

"My pleasure." He grinned. "It's going to be fun, I promise."

"I'm going to hold you to that," I told him, with a grin of my own. "Now I really have to go in." Granddad would be so annoyed if I was late, and the last thing I wanted after this strange but happy afternoon was to be lectured on the merits of punctuality.

"Okay," he said, handing me my bag. He started toward me as if he meant to hug me or something, then backed off just as quickly. "I guess I'll see you tomorrow."

"Yeah," I said. "See you."

I turned and walked toward the house, pausing at the top of the porch steps to look back at him. He was still standing there, hands in his pockets, the wind ruffling his hair. He waved at me, and I waved back before disappearing over the threshold into the dark foyer beyond.

TWO

When it came to prom, one week was not an ideal amount of notice. First, there was the immediate obstacle of securing my grandfather's permission. I'd never attended a school dance before, or even been on a date, so it was hard to predict how he'd react.

Granddad was at the kitchen table when I came down the next morning, hard at work on the daily crossword, a pair of rimless bifocals perched on the tip of his nose. Instead of greeting me like a normal person, he called out, "Eleven-letter word for 'button seller.' "

"Hmmm. Try 'haberdasher,' " I suggested, pouring myself a bowl of sugary cereal. I wasn't a crossword whiz or anything, but I'd encountered the word recently in a book and had to look it up. This was a thing of Granddad's. He liked to challenge me.

"Excellent," he said, pleased.

"That's a bit easy, don't you think?" I teased, taking the seat across from him at the table.

"Well, it *is* only Tuesday," Granddad muttered. He looked up, finally, and regarded me with mild suspicion. "It's seven o'clock and you're awake. Why do you look so cheerful?"

"Can't I just be in a good mood?" The rosy haze of yesterday afternoon hadn't yet completely faded. For once, I'd had a peaceful night's sleep and woken up feeling happy and well rested. Of course I was in a good mood.

"I suppose." Granddad penciled "haberdasher" into the crossword, then opened the paper, shook it, and turned to the front page. "Have you started your college applications?"

I groaned. "Granddad, please. It's *May*. Applications aren't due until the fall."

"You still haven't told me where you're applying," he pressed.

"That's because I haven't decided." I hadn't told Granddad—it would've freaked him out—but I was really struggling with the idea of picking a school, and consequently a future. I had no idea what I wanted to study, and even though I knew Granddad had his heart set on me attending an Ivy League school—or, even better, the University of Chicago, where I could get a reduced tuition and live at home—I couldn't quite imagine myself at any of those places. There was only one thing I knew for certain: I had to get out of Hyde Park. I loved Chicago, and the little neighborhood where I'd grown up, but I was starting to feel restless. Granddad was content with his compact, uneventful life, but I ached for adventure, and I wasn't going to find it if I was just following Granddad's plan for me. It was going to be hard to break that to him, which was why I hadn't done it yet.

There was something else I needed to talk to him about. Something I hadn't brought up at dinner the night before, because I'd been too busy trying to decide whether it had actually happened. "Hey, Granddad?"

"Hm?" he mumbled without looking up from his paper.

"Grant Davis asked me to prom," I said. Not that I thought

he'd know who Grant was—Granddad wasn't great with names or faces, and my best friend, Gina, was probably the only one of my classmates he actually knew.

Nevertheless, the mention of a potential date got his attention. "Who?"

"Grant Davis," I repeated. "He's . . . this guy. From my school."

"And he asked you to prom?"

"Try not to sound so shocked," I grumbled. Sometimes I wondered if Granddad assumed I was just as much of a loner as he preferred to be. "It's not completely absurd that someone might ask me to prom."

"I didn't say it was absurd." Granddad set to work quartering a hard-boiled egg, sprinkling it with salt.

I smacked his hand lightly. "You know Dr. Reingold said to cut it out with the sodium."

"Don't lecture me, Alexandra. Lecturing is *my* job." Granddad always called me by my given name when I annoyed him, which meant I heard it a lot. I'd gone by Sasha for so long, I would've been surprised to find out that anyone except Granddad knew my full name. "And don't change the subject. This boy. What's his story? Are his parents professors?"

"His mom teaches at the law school," I said. Granddad shrugged; he wasn't interested in anyone who wasn't a scientist. "His dad lives out in California."

"And is he a nice boy?" He couldn't quite meet my eyes. The conversation clearly embarrassed him. Granddad had a history of discomfort when it came to the girl stuff in my life, and I couldn't blame him, but these moments always reminded me just how keenly I missed and needed my mother.

I had to wonder how my father would've reacted to me dating. Like a dad, probably. Cautious and overprotective, like

Gina's dad had behaved when she got together with her boyfriend, Jeff. But I couldn't really know. My parents had been dead for almost a decade; I'd been seven at the time, so while I had memories of them, they were blurry and fragmented. It was hard to recall what they were like. Granddad was no help, because he almost never wanted to talk about them. Before the accident, his relationship with my parents had been distant; when I came to him, we were practically strangers. I'd never found the courage to ask him why that was, but over the years I'd pieced together what was probably obvious all along—he didn't like my father. I kind of didn't want to know why. I loved Granddad *and* my parents, and if there was something dark in their shared past that would change my opinion of any of them, I was happier not knowing the particulars. But still, the question lurked in the back of my brain. What about my dad had caused them to be estranged for so long? I couldn't even venture a guess.

"Yes, Granddad," I assured him. "He's nice."

"How well do you know him?"

"We've gone to school together for, like, ever." It was best not to tell him that I didn't actually know Grant that well; it would only feed Granddad's suspicions and lower my chances of being allowed to go to prom.

"Don't say 'like,'" he grumbled. "It makes you sound silly." I rolled my eyes. "Well, all right. But I want to meet him before you go out. Do you need money for a dress?"

I braced myself. Prom dresses were expensive, and there wasn't enough time to buy one online, so I'd have to troll the department stores for something off the rack—and on sale. At least I had Gina to help me in the search. She was aces at sniffing out good deals, and her taste was excellent, certainly better than mine. "Yeah, kind of."

"How much?"

"A hundred, maybe?" I winced. I hated asking Granddad for money, but I didn't have a lot of savings, and I'd had no reason to budget for a prom dress.

He plucked five twenty-dollar bills from his wallet, handing them over solemnly. "This is a reward for being so good and working so hard. You're not *entitled* to this. You earned it."

I took the cash and gave him my brightest smile. "Thanks, Granddad. You're the best."

THREE

The days leading up to prom passed in the blink of an eye. Gina and I gave ourselves blisters walking up and down Michigan Avenue before finding the perfect thing for me to wear: a short, strapless navy dress with a sweetheart neckline and a sparkly tulle overlay that was on clearance for $99.99. The dress wasn't exactly my style—I was definitely more of a T-shirt and jeans kind of girl—but when I looked in the mirror, I had to admit, I felt beautiful in it. I hoped Grant would like it on me as much as I did.

Before I knew it, it was Saturday evening, and Gina, Jeff, and I were gathered in the parlor of the Victorian, waiting for Grant to arrive.

"He's late," Gina said. She was sitting in Granddad's armchair, wiggling with impatience, while her boyfriend loomed over her, taking nips from a flask he kept in his inside jacket pocket. Gina had met Jeff, a freshman at Northwestern, at a concert a few months earlier. Personally, I thought he was a little morose and weird, but he was really into Gina, so who was I to judge? Jeff was tall and lanky, and usually his clothes and his hair looked like they'd never been washed. Gina had managed to wrestle him into her brother's old tux, even though it was a bit too short in the arms and legs and a bit too big everywhere else.

"He'll be here," I insisted. I paced the floor in front of the fireplace. My nerves were out of control. It was one thing to imagine this moment, to look forward to it, and quite another to find myself on the precipice of experiencing it. Plus, what if Granddad didn't like Grant? I kept telling myself it was a silly thing to worry about—after all, I wasn't *marrying* Grant, I was just going with him to one dance—but it was hard to banish it from my thoughts.

My eyes rested on the framed photographs that sat upon the mantel. Most of them were school photos that charted my evolution from a thick-haired, gawky child to a relatively pretty teenager, all things considered. There were also a few of me and Granddad together in various places, my favorite being one of us standing on a pier at Lake Okobogee, hoisting a ten-pound largemouth bass between us. I smiled at the memory. If it was possible for my parents' deaths to have a silver lining, it was that I'd gotten a chance to know my grandfather. Even though he could be gruff, I knew that he loved me, and that I was lucky to have found a home with him when mine had been ripped from me.

There was only one picture of my parents. It was from our last trip to Disney World; we were standing in front of Cinderella's castle, grinning into the sun. It'd been taken only a few months before the accident, and we looked so happy in it, oblivious to the disaster looming on the horizon of our lives. The sadness that always accompanied thoughts of my parents clanged like a bell in my heart, but my smile didn't fade. The clearest memories of my childhood were from that vacation. I'd been deep in my fairy-tale phase, demanding that everyone call me Princess Juliana, a name that bewildered Mom and Dad. I'd dragged them to the castle more than a dozen times and pranced around inside it, ordering them around like servants. I still had the princess hat they'd bought me, a cardboard cone covered in synthetic pink fabric with *Juliana* stitched on the brim and a filmy purple ribbon trailing from the top. When Mom asked me why I was called Juliana, I told her I'd heard the name in a dream.

I'd never told anyone other than my parents about the Juliana dreams, but I'd had them ever since I could remember. When I was young, they came often, three or four times a week, but as I grew up they were fewer and farther between, though more vivid. Like most dreams, however, they faded almost immediately after I woke up.

In the dreams, I was never myself, but a girl named Juliana who looked exactly like me. They had a linear, realistic quality to them, as if I was literally living Juliana's life. But things were different in her world than they were in mine. I couldn't remember all the differences—there were so many of them, and dreams were hard to get a hold on—but this one thing I recalled with absolute precision: in Juliana's world, the aurora borealis danced in the sky, not just at the North and South Poles, but everywhere. That was always my favorite part.

My latest Juliana dream had happened two weeks earlier, after months of not having them at all. I'd fallen into bed at two a.m., completely exhausted after a long and painful struggle with my physics homework. I only remembered tiny pieces of it—a painting of a beautiful country house, a small origami star that seemed significant, and, as always, the green ribbons of the aurora borealis in the night sky. The overwhelming sense of foreboding I'd felt when I woke up the next morning had stuck with me through most of the day.

The doorbell rang. I took a deep breath and hurried to answer it. My heart felt buoyant, but over-inflated, like it was straining against my rib cage.

I yanked the door open, revealing Grant in all his formalwear glory. I could hear my blood pounding in my ears, and my stomach tumbled when he smiled at me. He was clean-shaven, his hair ever-so-slightly slicked back, and he carried the scent of pine needles with him through the door. The sight of him in a tux sent a sizzle up my spine. Part of me couldn't wait to be alone with him and regretted calling in Gina and Jeff as reinforcements, but another part of me felt anxious. I had no idea what to do, or what to expect of the evening. Or, come to think of it, what would be expected of *me*.

"Sorry, I couldn't get out of the house. My mom kept trying to straighten my tie." Grant stepped back to get a good look at me, his eyes traveling the length of my body unabashedly from foot to forehead, until he met my gaze with his own. "Wow. You look amazing."

A fierce blush crept into my cheeks. "Thanks." I couldn't remember the last time someone had said something like that to me, and I knew it had never been in a tone like *that*. I still couldn't believe this was happening. Why hadn't Grant asked one of the many girls he'd dated to go to prom with him instead of me, someone he barely knew? I decided not to let that bother me. What was the point? He didn't seem disappointed with his choice, and neither was I.

He shook a plastic box with a white corsage inside. "Did you want a corsage? I didn't know, so I brought one, but it's probably dumb. You don't have to wear it." He curled his arm around it, as if to shield it from my eyes, and I realized that he was nervous, too, possibly as much as I was.

"No, of course I'll wear it," I told him, and his shoulders relaxed. He slipped the corsage around my wrist, then stepped back, the corners of his mouth quirking. As I admired the flowers—an arrangement of snow-colored roses, with some leaves and baby's breath arranged along the edges—he reached over and tucked a dark brown curl behind my ear. My hair was naturally straight, and I usually wore it pulled up in a ponytail. Gina had declared that style unacceptable for prom, and she'd spent the better part of the afternoon engaging in an all-out assault on my head with a curling iron and hair spray. It'd felt like overkill to me, but the expression on Grant's face as he looked at me now told me that Gina's instincts had been right on the money.

"I like your hair down like that," he said in a low voice.

My skin buzzed where his hand had brushed it. A wave of intense shyness broke over me, and I was anxious to get moving. "Are we ready to go?" Gina and Jeff emerged from the parlor, and suddenly the foyer felt very crowded. All three of them looked at me expectantly. "Oh, right, introductions. Grant, this is Jeff, and that's Gina." Grant had gone to school with Gina as long as he had with me, but it was possible they'd never spoken before, high school heirarchies being what they were.

"Hey, guys," Grant said, pulling a relaxed, affable tone out of his arsenal of charms and shaking Jeff's hand like they were old buddies. He smiled at Gina. "I heard about your race this week. That's awesome." Gina was a fantastic runner, and she'd won all her events at Thursday's track meet. She shot me a look, surprised that Grant knew this, but nothing about Grant managed to surprise me these days. He'd clearly done his homework. I was proud of him; I knew how hard it was to subdue Gina's cynical side. "Thanks for waiting around for me."

"No problem," Gina said. I could tell she was won over.

"So," Grant said. "Should we go?"

"You have to meet my grandfather first," I informed him apologetically.

"Of course," Grant said. "I'd love to."

"Well, don't get too excited. He's not very friendly."

Grant laughed. "Just introduce us."

I shook my head in disbelief. Grant was starting to seem too good to be true. I called upstairs to Granddad, who descended minutes later, looking less than thrilled to have been disturbed. But he *had* demanded to meet my date, so he couldn't complain.

"It's great to meet you, Dr. Quentin," Grant said, offering his hand to Granddad, who shook it cordially. "Thanks for letting me take your lovely granddaughter to the prom." Grant shot me a self-satisfied smile, and I rolled my eyes. He was trying so hard to make a good impression, and the more his effort showed, the more I liked him. "Is there a time you'd like me to have her back by?"

Granddad mulled the question over for a few seconds. "Midnight should do it."

"Granddad," I said, putting my hand on his arm. "Be cool." According to Granddad, that was something my mom used to say to him as a teenager when she thought he was being too strict. He'd told me this once in rare fit of nostalgia, something I'm sure he regretted later, because it worked every time.

"All right," he relented. "One a.m., then. But no later."

"Thank you, sir," Grant said. "We won't be late." Granddad nodded, trying not to appear pleased at Grant's politeness, but I couldn't disguise my own happiness. Granddad was the world's hardest person to impress, and if Grant was managing to charm him, it meant I had nothing to worry about.

In a gesture of uncharacteristic sentimentality, Granddad placed his hand on my shoulder and kissed me on the forehead. "Have a good time, dear. And be safe."

"Thanks, Granddad. I will."

Gina hooked her elbow with mine. "Come on, Lawson. Let's get out of here."

FOUR

Grant was a terrible dancer. When we first arrived at the hotel—where prom was already in full swing—he was shy about it, demurring every time I tried to drag him onto the dance floor. Finally, I took his hand in mine; I'd had two glasses of punch, which had most certainly been fortified by something out of a flask while the chaperones' backs were turned, and was overcome by a sudden boldness.

"Okay, Grant, what's up?" I whispered into his ear. "You asked me to prom and you won't even dance with me?"

"I don't know how," he said, confessing this secret in a voice so low I almost didn't hear it over the pounding music.

I laughed, thinking he was joking, and he looked away in embarrassment. "I'm serious," he said, his expression dark and distant.

I squeezed his hand, trying to make up for laughing and to reassure him without implying that he needed any reassurance. I felt light and fearless, due to a combination of spiked punch and the realization that Grant wasn't perfect, that he had his own anxieties and faults just like the rest of humanity. It was a relief. Much as I liked Grant, I wasn't sure how long I'd be able to tolerate someone who seemed so flawless.

"You don't have to know how," I told him. "Just listen to the music and move the way you want."

He shook his head vehemently. "I don't want to. I'll look stupid."

"Not possible," I said in earnest. I led him into the crowd of shifting bodies until we were right in the center of the ballroom. He stood apart from me, glancing around as if anticipating some sort of ambush. I reached up and put my arms around his neck. His reticence had burned mine completely away, and I didn't care what anyone else was thinking or doing, so long as Grant and I were having a good time.

"Put your hands on my waist," I commanded. He did as he was told. His fingers were like feathers on my hips, but his chest was solid, so close and so warm, which I didn't mind despite the heat of the ballroom. I swayed along with the beat. "Come on," I coaxed. "Just do what I do."

He did his best to mimic my movements. We started slow, ignoring the high-spirited flailing of our classmates, and after a few minutes I felt him begin to relax in my arms. Before I knew it, half a dozen songs had played, and Grant's nerves seemed to have entirely evaporated. Soon enough, he was jumping and spinning and pumping his fist along with the music just like everybody else.

"I love this song!" he shouted. I laughed. Though we were surrounded on all sides, it was as if the rest of the world didn't exist.

Four hours later, I collapsed into a chair, panting. My hair was a disaster, I was covered in a thin layer of sweat, and my dress had a stain down the front where Gina had accidentally spilled some punch earlier in the evening. I was having the time of my *life*. Even Jeff was cracking the occasional smile, a pretty much unprecedented occurrence in my experience.

"Come on," Grant said, hoisting me out of my chair. The lights were coming up in the hotel ballroom; prom was over. Gina and Jeff were making out two tables away. The staff was going to have to forcibly eject them.

Grant put his arms around my waist and held me close. At some point in the evening he'd undone his bow tie; it was hanging loose around his neck and I batted at it playfully like a kitten. He grinned. "Let's go somewhere. We've still got an hour before your curfew."

"Where?" I fanned myself with my fingers. "It's so hot in here."

"To the beach," he suggested.

"Which one? Fifty-Seventh Street?" That was undoubtedly where everybody else was headed, there or Promontory Point, both of which were in our neighborhood. One of the best things about Hyde Park was its proximity to the water.

"No, no," Grant said. I wondered if he was thinking the same thing; if we went to a Hyde Park beach, there was no way we'd get a chance to be alone. "There's one a few blocks from here. Oak Street Beach. It's not far."

I was a little worried about making it home on time, but the beach was close and we didn't have to stay long. Besides, what was Granddad going to do if I was fifteen minutes late? I doubted he would even be up when I got home, since his usual bedtime was ten p.m.—one of the benefits of having a septuagenarian as my legal guardian. I said goodbye to Gina and Jeff, but all I got in return were a couple of barely audible grunts. That suited me just fine—I wanted to be alone with Grant so badly, my knees shook just thinking about it. I gathered my things, including the pashmina Gina had lent me, and hobbled out of the ballroom into the hotel lobby, my feet aching from the three-inch heels I wasn't used to wearing.

I was grateful when we reached the beach and I could take the shoes off. I plunged my toes deep into the cool sand and sought out my date in the darkness. Grant looked perfectly handsome and disheveled in the moonlight. He was standing with his back to me, hands in his pockets, staring out at Lake Michigan. Behind us, the high rises and skyscrapers that made up the Chicago skyline rose up into the night, mountains of light and glass. I rested my chin on his shoulder and slipped my arm through his.

"Looking for something?" He turned at the sound of my voice and his lips brushed my forehead, right along my hairline. I shivered as he put his arms around me, pulling me in and holding me tight.

"Cold?" he asked.

"No." I laid my head on his chest.

"It's big, isn't it? Sometimes I forget how big everything is." His voice was soft and far away, as if his mind was somewhere else. A charcoal cloud sailed through the sky, blotting out the moon.

"I know what you mean." I looked up at him. He was back to gazing over the water, as if he was searching for something out there in the dense black night. I admired the line of his jaw, the slight upturn of his ski-slope nose. The moon emerged again, blanching our skin and giving Grant the stately appearance of a Renaissance statue. "Granddad always likes to tell me that the Earth in relation to the galaxy is like a single pin lost somewhere in the United States. That's how small we are."

"Not us," Grant said. His hand migrated up my arm and stroked the fine hair at the nape of my neck. I shivered again. "The *planet*."

"Right," I said. " 'A mote of dust suspended in a sunbeam.' "

Grant glanced at me. "What?"

"It's a quote. By Carl Sagan. He was my father's favorite writer—he was a physicist, too, my dad. And my mom."

"The family business," Grant said, pressing his cheek against the top of my head.

I smiled into his shoulder. My parents would've loved Grant, I was sure of it. They wouldn't have had a choice. There was no way they could've disliked anyone who made me this happy. "Something like that, yeah."

Grant looked directly at me for the first time since we'd stepped foot on the beach, and a sudden bolt of sadness flickered across his face, so quickly that I thought I might've imagined it.

"Sasha," he said, with an intensity that nearly swept me off my feet. I loved the way he said my name, like an incantation, like a magic word. *I'm falling for him,* I thought, in the space between heartbeats. I was surprised by how easy that was to admit. For a long time, I'd thought the deaths of my parents might have inured me to love—fear of losing something beloved was the reason I'd never wanted a pet—but it hadn't. In fact, it had only made me want it more, something I hadn't realized until this moment.

"Whatever happens," Grant continued, "this has been the best night of my entire life."

I laughed. "What could happen?"

"Anything," he said. My heart pounded away in my chest like a bass drum, and my hands were shaking. I clenched them into fists to keep Grant from noticing.

He took a deep breath. The air changed, as if there had been a shift in the Earth's rotation. "I have a gift for you." He dug around in the inside pocket of his jacket and pulled out a flat black box the size of his palm. "Open it."

Inside the box was a thin silver bracelet on a bed of black velvet. It was the simplest thing I'd ever seen, and because of that, one of the most lovely. Not a single engraving or gem or artistic flourish, just a plain, elegant silver band. I picked it up and tried to slide it over my hand, but it wouldn't fit. It was too small. A flush crawled up my neck and into my face. My hand was too fat for Grant's gift.

"No, not like that." He reached over to take the bracelet; I didn't quite see how he did it, but he managed to open an imperceptible hinge. He placed the bracelet around my left wrist before closing it with a firm *snap*. It was snug, but not tight, as if it had been sized just for me.

The sleeve of Grant's jacket rode up and I caught another glint of silver. I grabbed his arm.

"You have one just like it?" It was a question, but not. He was wearing a bracelet identical to the one he'd just given me on his own wrist. My brain struggled to process this information, to make some sense out of it. Grant really wasn't the type to wear jewelry. At least, I didn't think he was, but it wasn't like I knew all there was to know about him. Still, it struck me as odd.

Grant didn't explain. Instead, he cupped my face in one hand and adjusted the scarf around my neck, pulling me in by my waist and holding me close. I shut my eyes and let myself drift in his arms, forgetting about the bracelets. He leaned in, his lips brushing my ear. I thought I heard him whisper *I'm sorry,* but the words were washed away by the hush of the waves on the sand, if he even said them at all.

AVRORA

7

DAYS

THOMAS IN THE TATTERED CITY

Thomas watched the rise and fall of Sasha's chest as she slept. High above, the aurora performed its nightly dance across the indigo sky, casting a soft green glow upon her skin. After everything he'd seen, he still couldn't believe how much she looked like Juliana. The resemblance was breathtaking in its perfection, and unsettling, too; he would have called it impossible if he didn't know the truth. Thomas slid his KES ring back on; it was a relief to wear it again after two weeks of having to carry it around in his pocket. His hand throbbed with pain, and a strange sort of restlessness stirred within him; it was the same way he'd felt on the night he came face to face with Grant Davis. The universes didn't like to be messed with, and try as he might, he couldn't shake the sense that he had made a catastrophic error in bringing her here.

But it was already done.

The waters of Lake Michigan—*his* Lake Michigan—gently lapped the shore ten yards away, and the towering skyscrapers of the Chicago skyline rose behind him, nearly invisible in the dark. They called it the Tattered City; Libertas had stripped it to its bones, and the buildings were largely derelict now, places where squatters played house. Electrical power was erratic in the Tattered City these days, and the city officials had started enforcing a mandatory blackout after midnight in an effort to conserve energy. He couldn't have planned their arrival in Aurora any better; the streets would be dark and empty, and he would slip through them easily with his otherworldly cargo. Operation Starling was proceeding exactly as planned.

Something beeped in his pocket; his mobie had caught a signal. He pulled it out to send a message to Agent Fillmore, who was waiting in the wings for his summons. The mobie was about the size and shape of a playing card; this one was government-issue, made of a near-indestructible titanium alloy and only an inch or so thick, not counting the retractable cover. He pressed a button and the cover slid away, revealing the screen, which demanded a thumbprint and a numerical code to be entered before it would show him what he wanted: the time. Nearly one in the morning now. Right on schedule.

We're about to miss curfew. The thought caught him off guard. No point worrying about that. And yet, he couldn't stop imagining Sasha's grandfather waiting up for her, wondering where she was. He tried not to feel guilty about it; after all, he was just doing his job. *It's for the greater good,* he told himself. *Remember that.*

Fillmore arrived in minutes. They'd chosen this spot because it was deserted at nighttime in both worlds. That was the trouble with going through the tandem, at least the way they did it—you always landed in the exact same geographical location in the destination universe as you were in the universe you'd just left. It would've been much easier to take Sasha from the Chicago of her world straight to the heart of Columbia City, where they were ultimately headed, but unfortunately it just didn't work that way.

"How was the dance?" Fillmore asked sarcastically as he bent over Sasha's body. He was a short, squat man with the face of a troll and the smile of a Cheshire cat. How he'd come to work for the King's Elite Service, Thomas didn't know. There had to be a reason the General kept him around, and it must've been a good one in order for the General to have assigned him to Operation Starling, but Thomas couldn't imagine what it was.

"Don't touch her," Thomas said, grabbing Fillmore by his jacket collar and yanking him back. "I've got it." A wave of protectiveness surged through him; Sasha was his assignment, his responsibility—Fillmore had no business getting anywhere near her.

"Did she let you kiss her?" Fillmore teased, unfazed by Thomas's poisonous glare. Fillmore was a creep, and insubordinate to boot. Thomas was light-years above him in the KES chain of command, and yet Fillmore pressed his luck at every opportunity. This happened from time to time, older agents thinking they could jerk him around in spite of his rank and connections, but he tried not to let it get to him. He knew where he stood.

"I said don't touch her!" Thomas snapped as Fillmore bent toward Sasha once more. "You were supposed to bring the moto around. Is it close?"

Fillmore pointed. "Just up there, over the hill. What's wrong with your hand?"

Thomas realized he was cradling the bruised appendage. He shrugged. "Nothing, it's fine. Go start the moto. I'll bring her."

Fillmore, apparently sensing, finally, that Thomas was in no mood for games, nodded and, for once in his life, followed orders. He scrambled up over the grassy knoll and was gone.

Thomas lifted Sasha up into his arms, taking care to avoid putting any pressure on his left hand. Other than loss of consciousness, she seemed to have suffered no ill effects from going through the tandem. Her vitals were normal, and she'd sustained no visible injuries. Everything was as expected, which was a relief. He was used to taking chances with his own life, but risking someone else's was another matter altogether. Besides, if something happened to Sasha, it would likely mean the end of his career.

When they got her back to the safe house he would give her a sedative in the hopes that she would sleep through the majority of the tandem sickness. A first crossing could be uncomfortable, to say the least. It got a little easier every time, so it wouldn't be quite as bad when she returned home; he had done over a dozen trips through the tandem and now it didn't even affect him. Still, she would be better off if she got some rest.

This did pose a problem, though. It would be much easier to transport Sasha to Columbia City in the middle of the night, but he couldn't move her now. Thomas hated the Tattered City, and spending time in Sasha's Chicago had only made him hate it more. The Tattered City was a shadow of its Earth counterpart, with less open sky and green space, more deserted high-rises and garbage. Once it had been a major metropolis, a cultural mecca and an important financial center, but that had been eroded away by the revolutionary assault of Libertas. They'd all but seized the city; you couldn't go anywhere without having to dodge Libertas "security," commandos dressed in black who carried unlicensed military rifles and prowled the streets like panthers. The local police were useless, because Libertas controlled them from within, and KES agents like Thomas weren't exactly welcome, although the city still technically fell within their jurisdiction; everything in the Commonwealth was under KES jurisdiction.

But as much as the idea of getting into it with Libertas appealed to him, that wasn't why Thomas was in the Tattered City. No one save Fillmore could know that he was there, not even the undercover KES agents on assignment in the area, and especially not Libertas; if they caught the faintest whiff of the General's plan, they would certainly attempt to intervene, and he and Fillmore—and, worse, Sasha—could die as a result. Once he managed to get Sasha past the boundaries and on her way to Columbia City, everything would be much easier, but the next twelve hours would be tricky. He had to make sure nobody saw her. That was the most important thing.

"I WANT TO SPEAK TO THE *Monad," she insisted. She'd lost count of the times she'd made this demand, but this was the first time she was making it of* him. *She hadn't seen him since the night he brought her to the Libertas bunker, but he had appeared today, sudden as a summer storm, without warning or explanation. "You promised."*

"The Monad is a busy man," he told her. "He'll see you when he's ready, Juli."

"Don't call me that," she snapped. "You'll address me as Your Highness, or Princess Juliana. Nothing else."

"The truth is, Juli,*" he said. "The Monad isn't sure you have anything to tell us."*

"Of course I do. I wouldn't have agreed to this if I didn't. And anyway," she continued, trying to keep her voice steady, though she was visibly shaking, "I'm not the one with something to prove. You told me that if I gave the Monad all the information I had about the General's plans, they'd help me get away for good. But all they've done is lock me up in this room. They won't let me talk to anyone."

"You're talking to me," he pointed out.

"Not by choice."

"These things take time," he told her. "You have to be patient. This isn't a game."

"Well, how much more time *is it going to take?" she asked. Her*

voice quaked with desperation, and she hated herself for it. She didn't want him to know that she was afraid. And she couldn't help wondering what was happening outside these walls, what black fate was befalling her country in her absence. What would they do without their princess? But perhaps they were better off without her. She'd never been a very good princess anyway.

"Soon," he said, his voice eerily soft, like he was trying to calm a frightened child. But all he'd succeeded in doing was agitating her further. "Soon. I promise."

FIVE

In the beginning, all I knew was darkness. Darkness, and silence. There was no pain, and then, in an instant, I felt it, a deep, dull ache in every muscle and bone and joint. I couldn't move, but if it was due to the pain or something else entirely I didn't know. Panic coursed through my veins, but I couldn't even open my eyes, and I feared beyond all reason that I was dead. But the dead don't hurt, do they?

Gradually, I started to hear things. Just muffled voices at first, as if I was listening through a door, but the voices started getting clearer and I could make out words. "Is she dead?" someone asked. Clearly I wasn't the only one wondering.

"She's not dead," Grant said. "Do you think we would've brought her all this way if we thought it would kill her?"

At first I was so happy to hear his voice—low, strong, familiar—that his words didn't even register. *Grant's here,* I thought with relief. *I'm safe*. But then what he'd said sank in, and questions started to form in my mind, wriggling through layers of semiconsciousness like worms. Who was he talking to? What had happened? Where was I? What did he mean by saying that "we" had brought me here? Who were "we"?

Who—what—where—why—frantic questions, bewildered questions, clanking together like glass bottles, slamming into each other like bumper cars, tangling like Christmas lights in my frozen, frightened mind. *Grant,* I thought, willing my lips to form his name, but they wouldn't, they *couldn't.*

Help me.

Grant spoke again. "It was her first time through the tandem. It knocks the hell out of you. We just have to keep her comfortable and warm until she comes around."

Feeling was starting to return to my limbs. I tried to move, but I only managed to wiggle a finger, and even then just an inch. I wanted to cry, but I couldn't. I couldn't do *anything.* A frustrated scream ripped through my head, but there was no forcing it out of my throat. The fear was so potent I could taste it, a dark, metallic tang on the back of my tongue.

"Your timing couldn't be worse," said someone other than Grant. It was a man, and something about his voice—scratchy and deep—told me he was older than Grant by years, possibly decades. "The Libertas rally is starting soon, and the streets will be crawling with patrols. If they see her, you can bet they won't rest until they have you both in custody."

"I know that," Grant said. He didn't even sound like the Grant I knew. It was him, all right, but his tone was different, somehow. Harder. Sharper. It wasn't the voice of the boy who'd looked out at Lake Michigan and said *Sometimes I forget how big everything is.* But it *was* his voice, all the same.

"They won't know what she is," the man continued. "But they'll see she's trouble."

Trouble? How could anyone possibly think that *I* of all people was *trouble*? This had to be some kind of awful mistake, it just *had* to be. That was the only explanation. But this was Grant. We'd gone to school together forever—he *knew* me, and if the events of the last couple of days were any indication, he *cared* about me. Why was he talking about me as if I was a stranger?

Unless . . . The thought struck me like a mallet to the chest. Unless I'd been wrong about Grant all along.

No. That was unthinkable. I was a good judge of character; there was no way I wouldn't have seen deceit in his eyes. He'd been sincere. He'd carried my bag and danced with me and stood with his arm around me under a blanket of stars. Could it really all have been fake? Just a lie to get what he wanted?

And if so, what did he want?

"Everything's proceeding according to plan," Grant said. *What plan?* I wanted to shout. *What do you want from me?* I could do nothing but lie there like a corpse and wait. The waiting was excruciating; every second felt like a year, each pause between breaths like an eternity. But I was growing stronger. I could feel everything now, and I suspected that if I tried, I might be able to open my eyes. But not yet. I needed the right moment. They didn't know I could hear them; if they had known, they wouldn't have been talking so freely. Maybe if I stayed still a bit longer, I could learn something. Maybe then I would know what I was up against. Maybe then I could begin formulating my own plan.

"You should wait until nightfall."

"No," Grant said with authority. "I can't spare the time. They're not going to believe that story about the princess being up at St. Lawrence for much longer. It's been almost two weeks. The queen is starting to ask questions, not to mention the media. She's blown off three interviews with Eloise Dash. Gloria's beside herself, and the General is getting impatient."

What the *hell* was Grant talking about? It was dreamlike in its absurdity; I couldn't make sense of any of it. My head began to pound; the pain made it harder to think, like the signal was being scrambled. How was I going to get out of there if I couldn't even *think*?

"She can't go out in the city dressed like that. We should change her clothes."

The thought of being undressed by a stranger made my insides seize up, but Grant said, "She can change herself when she wakes up. I've got clothes for her to wear." I relaxed a little—but only a little. Who knew what Grant and this other man were capable of?

"You're the boss," the man said, his voice tinged with bitter resignation. A rough hand grabbed my arm and I felt the pressure of a thumb on the inside of my wrist. "Pulse is up. She's coming around."

"Finally." The bed dipped as Grant sat down next to me. I knew it was him; I could smell that same piney scent he'd been wearing the night of the prom. How long ago had that been? It seemed like a million years. "Sasha, can you hear me?"

I didn't respond. I knew I could open my eyes now, speak, maybe even sit up, but I wasn't going to do so on his command. "Sasha? Come on, you have to get up."

There was the voice of the Grant I knew. Even now it stirred up a little whirlwind of yearning. What if I was wrong after all? The idea that Grant would ever do anything to hurt me was impossible to comprehend. But there was no denying that *something* had happened, and if it hadn't been his doing, I couldn't imagine whose it would be.

I couldn't let this go on any longer. I pressed down on all those tender feelings, the echoes of what had once been. I imagined them calcifying inside of me, hardening in my chest like cement so that nothing he could say would ever affect me again. I was almost as enraged with myself for being tricked as I was with him for tricking me. And though I wasn't aware of it at the time, somewhere deep down I was unlearning to trust my own heart.

"How about a shock?" the other man suggested, his threat accompanied by the sound of electricity crackling. A Taser. But I was so distracted by Grant's closeness that I couldn't find it in me to be afraid of this man and his weapon. Grant was the true enemy. He was the one who'd lied to me, and, if I was reading the situation correctly, the one in charge.

"Don't even think about it," Grant commanded. *He doesn't want to hurt me,* I realized. But I shoved the thought away. *Yet,* I told myself savagely. *He doesn't want to hurt me* yet.

"Just get her up and out of here already if you're so determined to go," the man grumbled. "Maybe people will be so distracted by the rally they won't look twice at her."

"Sasha, I know you're awake. Open your eyes." Grant eased one of my eyelids open with his thumb. My mind went blank and I reacted on impulse, sitting straight up and slapping his hand away. He jerked back, his eyes wide, as if he was surprised to see me there. He lifted his hand as if to touch me, but I wasn't about to let him get close enough.

"Don't!" I cried. I glanced around for something to use as a weapon, but there was nothing within reach. The last place I remembered being was Oak Street Beach, but now I was in a large basement apartment. It was dim inside and practically empty but for the bed, a couple of chairs, and a large metal standing locker. There were two small rectangular windows at the opposite side of the room near the ceiling, but they had been blacked out; the only light in the room came from a few bare bulbs overhead.

An old man, hunched and bald, passed into view. He smirked at me; with his absurdly wide mouth and skin that hung off his skull in fleshy folds, he reminded me of a bullfrog. It would've struck me as comical if not for the Taser in his hand and the gun at his belt.

"What did you do to me?" I demanded.

"Take it easy," Grant warned. "You need to calm down. You've been through a lot."

"No shit!" I met his eyes with a furious glare. The coppery terror was sharp in my mouth. "What is this place?"

"It's our Chicago safe house," Grant said, glancing at the door. Though it looked heavy and industrial, he was eyeing it as if he expected someone to kick it open at any second. "But I'm not really sure how safe it is anymore, so we have to leave as soon as possible. Here." He placed a blue corduroy backpack—*my* blue corduroy backpack, the old one I'd carried to school when I was a kid, long ago consigned to the back of my closet—on the bed. It looked small and foreign in his hands, like an artifact from someone else's life. "There are some clothes inside, and a few toiletries. You can clean up and change in the bathroom before we leave."

"I'm not going anywhere," I told him. "Except home."

The sun was streaming in through the small gap at the bottom of the front door. It was broad daylight outside. Granddad was going to be out of his mind with worry, but if I was still in Chicago then I couldn't be too far away. What time was it, anyway? How long had I been gone? There was no clock in the room, and Grant was unlikely to tell me.

Grant shook his head. "You can't go home."

"Watch me," I said, dropping the backpack and making a break for the door. The old man came out of nowhere, agile as a jungle cat in spite of appearances, and blocked my path.

"Sorry, sweetheart," he said, shaking his head in mock disappointment. "Your home's not out there."

"What the hell is that supposed to mean?"

"That's going to require a little bit of explanation," Grant said, rising from the bed and picking up the backpack. He shoved it at me. "Go get changed. Then we'll talk."

I stared at him in total disbelief. "What makes you think I'm going to do anything you say? You lied to me—you *kidnapped* me—and you think—" The words lodged in my throat. The expression on his face was inscrutable.

Grant gathered himself up to his full height; at six-two he was half a foot taller, and he towered over me. He was trying to intimidate me, and, what was worse, it was sort of working. When push came to shove, I was confident I could take the old man, but if Grant wanted to stop me he could. "You're a smart girl, Sasha. You can probably tell you don't have a lot of options right now, so you might as well just listen to me."

Oh yeah? I thought. I might not have had Grant's size, or the old man's Taser, but I still had my voice. I took a deep breath and screamed as high and as loud as I possibly could.

Grant clapped his hand over my mouth. I clawed at his fingers, but he didn't seem to feel it. He leaned in, and I caught that evergreen scent of his again; it made me gag.

"Be quiet," he warned, his voice darkly serious. "You're safe, Sasha, I promise. We're not going to hurt you. Don't be difficult." I heard a note of pleading, but I didn't care. He meant nothing to me. I didn't even know him.

Slowly, he drew his hand away, though his body was still wrapped around mine and I could feel the tension that remained in his muscles. He was prepared to shut me up once more, if I chose to keep screaming, which meant it was useless to try. I wasn't even sure I could; my previous attempt had made me light-headed. My arms hung loose at my sides, like snapped rubber bands, and I was starting to wonder if I would even be able to stand for much longer.

"Mayhew," the old frog-faced man said in alarm.

"I know," Grant replied. He released me, an uncertain expression on his face. "I need you to go get ready to leave, *now*."

"Or else what?"

"I'll explain everything," Grant said. "But for now you have to follow directions."

"And then you'll take me home?" I asked, although I suspected the answer was *no*. He wouldn't have gone through all the trouble of bringing me here just to turn around and let me go.

His face betrayed nothing. "Get changed. Then we'll talk."

"First tell me why I'm here," I insisted.

He turned sharply. "Let me explain how this works," he said, in a voice so cold the temperature in the room seemed to dip ten degrees. "I give the orders, you follow them. I tell you what I want you to know, when I want you to know it. You want to go home? Then follow my instructions. Now: Go. Get. Changed."

I stared into his eyes with as much bravado as I could muster, but he didn't back down or look away. I hated to admit it, but it didn't look like I had a choice. Anger—pure and unalloyed—had rushed in to replace the fear I'd felt before, burning it away. His word would not be the last. I was going to get away. It was only a matter of time before Grant slipped up and gave me an opportunity to escape, and when he did, I'd be ready. But for now I had to play the game his way. Realizing this made me calmer, my mind sharp and alert where it had previously been foggy and muddled.

I'm going home, I thought with sudden clarity and conviction. *Nothing he can do or say is going to stop me.*

SIX

Staying as far away from Grant and his crony as possible, I took the backpack into the bathroom. The door slid open without a touch, as if it was on some sort of sensor. The place looked as though it had once belonged in one of those sleek, modern hotel rooms I'd seen in the movies, but everything was old and run-down.

The door closed by itself and I slumped against it. I wanted to cry, but I struggled not to, knowing that if I started I might not stop. A few tears escaped anyway. I covered my face with my hands and breathed deeply. At least I was alone, a small relief.

How could I have thought, even for a second, that I was falling for Grant? How could I have forgotten how little I knew him? Even though I knew it wasn't my fault, I couldn't help but hold myself partially responsible for my current situation. I'd let myself be seduced by his good looks and charm, soft words and romantic overtures. It was the stupidest thing I'd ever done.

When I'd gathered myself as best I could, I picked up the bag and began rummaging through it. My hands closed first around a stick of deodorant, half-used, from my own medicine cabinet. I applied some, feeling sticky, then tossed it back and took out a brush, which I pulled through my tangled hair. The curls Gina had so painstakingly created had fallen into limp waves. I bit my lip and kept fixing myself up; the ritual of getting ready was a soothing and welcome distraction.

When I was finished, I ripped off the corsage Grant had given me, reveling in the feeling of flower petals crumpling between my fingers as I crushed it in my fist before dropping it unceremoniously in the wastebin. It felt good to take my anger out on something, however small.

I turned the bag upside down and shook it. A bundle of folded clothes fell to the floor—jeans, a T-shirt, my navy blue zip-up hoodie, and my favorite brown leather boots with a pair of thick socks. Everything in the bag belonged to me. The idea of Grant in my bedroom, going through my drawers and touching my belongings, made me shudder. I splashed some water on my face, put my hair up in a ponytail, and got dressed.

I took another long, ragged breath and let it out again. *It's going to be okay,* I assured myself, staring at my reflection in the grimy mirror above the sink. *It's going to be okay.*

There was a knock at the door. Grant called out from the other side. "Are you almost done? Hurry up, we need to leave."

I emerged from the bathroom with my bag, now almost empty, over my shoulder and my prom dress slumped in my arms like a fallen comrade. When I'd taken it off, a stream of sand had cascaded out of the bodice. I'd been on that beach. Those memories, what I had left of them, were real.

I glanced down at my wrist to check if the bracelet he'd given me was still there and found that it was. A flare went off in my brain; I had to get free of it. I would never have imagined that it was possible to hate a *thing* as much as I hated that bracelet. Somehow I knew—beyond all reason—that it had something to do with why I was there in that basement instead of home in bed. I tugged and pulled and pressed every inch of the bracelet's slim surface, desperate to remove it, but it wouldn't budge.

"Good luck getting rid of that," the old man muttered.

"Screw you," I snapped.

"It won't come off," Grant said.

"What is it?" I demanded. It might've looked like a regular bracelet, but it obviously wasn't. It hadn't escaped my notice that Grant wasn't wearing his anymore. Sometime while I was unconscious he'd changed into a pair of sturdy cargo pants, T-shirt, and hoodie, all black. The sleeves of his jacket and hoodie were shoved up to his elbows and his bare wrists were on full display. He was wearing a ring, though, one I'd never seen before, on the middle finger of his right hand, but I didn't have time to wonder about it.

"You can leave that here," he said, indicating the dress and ignoring my question. "You won't need it anymore."

I hesitated. As stupid as it was, under the circumstances, I didn't want to give up my dress. It was *mine,* goddamn it. "What are you going to do with it?"

Grant shrugged. "Fillmore will burn it, probably."

"Burn it?"

"No one can know you were ever here," Grant said. "It's too dangerous."

"For who?" I demanded. My stomach dropped. They were going to cover up all proof of my existence. Soon there would be no trail of bread crumbs for anybody to follow.

"For all of us, including you," Grant said. "I told you nobody would hurt you, didn't I? This is for your protection."

Something went slack within me. I felt as if I was falling down a long, dark shaft; black clouds roiled in my peripheral vision and I had to sit down on the edge of the bed before I fainted. The dress slipped out of my hands and onto the floor.

"Grant," I murmured. It was the only call for help I could find the strength to make. He passed in front of me, crouching down so that our eyes were level. I searched his for any sign of tenderness and he, maybe sensing my intentions, avoided meeting my gaze.

"Just breathe," he advised, his own breath growing shallow as he sat there watching me. I gripped my knees, riding out wave after wave of nausea. *What is* wrong *with me?* I thought.

"Grant, I swear to you, if you just take me home I won't tell anybody what happened," I begged. It was the only offer I could think to make, though it was a lie. My knuckles had turned a ghostly white color. "My grandfather has incredibly high blood pressure—if I don't show up, like, yesterday, he could have a heart attack!"

My own heart buckled at the thought of what Granddad must be going through. I imagined him waking up at dawn and going to check on me, only to find me missing. In my mind's eye he was picking up the phone, dialing my cell—once, twice, fifteen times before giving up—then Gina's house, then Grant's if he could find the number, and then, finally, with a heaviness he almost couldn't bear, the police.

Grant fixed me with a hard look. "I'm going to say something that won't make very much sense to you at first, but I need you to listen. I need you to hear me say it."

"There's nothing you can say that will make me understand."

He took a deep breath, bracing himself. "I'm not Grant Davis."

Of all the lies in the world, that was the one I was least prepared to hear.

"My name isn't Grant," he continued. "It's Thomas. Thomas Mayhew."

"You must think I'm a real idiot," I snapped.

He shook his head somberly. "I don't think you're an idiot, and I'm not lying to you. I'm not Grant Davis. You don't know me. My name is Thomas Mayhew. I need you to understand that."

"This is ridiculous," Fillmore barked. "Who cares if she understands? It's not going to change anything. She'll do what you tell her to do because if she doesn't you'll shoot her and leave her here. If there's two, then there's more, am I right?"

What the hell did *that* mean? This was nonsense, all of it. I wanted to grab Fillmore and throw him to the ground. Grant, at least, looked about as sick of him as I was.

"Fillmore, shut up!" he growled. He turned to me. "Don't listen to him. He talks a big game, but he won't do anything without my permission, and I'm not going to let him touch you, all right? I'm not the guy you thought I was back . . . back there, but I have no intention of harming you."

He looked away at the oblique mention of Oak Street Beach, the prom, the living room of Granddad's Hyde Park Victorian, the quiet caverns of 57th Street Books—all those things that signified *back there*.

"If you're not Grant, then who are you?"

"I already told you," he said matter-of-factly.

"You told me your name is Thomas Mayhew," I said. "Is that supposed to mean something to me?"

"If it did, I'd be surprised." He lifted his eyes to mine. It was shocking, how familiar they were, and yet how foreign, like I'd never seen them before in my whole life.

A horrifying suspicion tugged at me: what if Grant was crazy? I'd been operating this whole time on the assumption that he was a reasonable, rational being—I'd even considered the possibility that this was all a misunderstanding, although that seemed like too much to hope for. But what if he was insane?

Because what he was proposing was ludicrous. Was he saying that Grant Davis had never existed, that since infancy he'd been someone else, this "Thomas Mayhew" he claimed to be? Or was he telling me that he—whoever he thought he was—had *replaced* Grant, pretended to be him? Of the two options, I wasn't sure which was harder to swallow, but the idea that there could be two unrelated people who looked exactly the same was so unlikely that it made my head hurt.

"So you're . . . what? Grant's evil twin?" That was the only possible explanation, if he was telling the truth, although it was very *telenovela*, and in no way easy to believe.

A short, harsh laugh escaped his throat. "Not exactly."

"Then what *are* you?"

"Sasha," he said deliberately, "what do you know about parallel universes?"

SEVEN

Now I laughed. "Parallel universes? Is that supposed to be some kind of joke?"

"Your grandfather is a theoretical physicist," Grant said. "You must have heard him talk about them at some point."

"You're not trying to tell me that you're from a parallel universe!" I considered again my hypothesis about his mental stability. *Parallel universes?* That sealed it: Grant was officially bonkers.

"Actually," he said, standing up, "I'm trying to tell you that *you* are."

"That's ridiculous!" I couldn't think of anything else to say. He'd hit it on the head when he said that Granddad was a theoretical physicist, because that's what parallel universes were—*theoretical*. No one had ever proven that they existed.

He shook his head. "I know it's a shock. But you know that it's not impossible."

"You're out of your mind," I said, folding my arms obstinately across my chest.

He rubbed the back of his neck; he was trying not to get frustrated, a battle he was clearly losing. "I don't have time for this to sink in gradually, so I'm going to be very frank with you. You're from one universe and I'm from another. This one. We're not in your world anymore—we're in mine."

"And what world would that be?" I struggled to suppress the wave of hysterical laughter that was rising up. "Oz?"

He was right about one thing: Granddad *had* told me about parallel universes. When I was young, inventing worlds was part of my nighttime ritual. I would climb into my bed while Granddad took a seat in a nearby chair and we'd spin all kinds of crazy stories about universes inhabited entirely by sentient Popsicle sticks, or talking flowers that ate cotton candy, or wizards who could only use their magic to conjure pancakes. But never this. Never universes so similar to ours that they contained doubles of people we actually knew. Because the implication of such worlds only made us remember, with sharp pangs of grief, what was missing in our own.

"That's not an easy question to answer, but I guess you could call it Aurora," he said. I took a few seconds to assess him as if I was just looking at him for the first time. There was nothing about him to suggest that he was crazy. He wasn't acting shifty or unhinged. It was precisely the opposite, in fact; he seemed alarmingly serious.

"Grant—"

"My name's not Grant," he insisted, his voice tight and agitated. "It's—"

"Thomas?" He nodded. "You want me to call you Thomas? Fine. That's fine. I'll call you whatever you want. I'll call you Rumpelstiltskin if it means you'll let me go."

"I liked her better when she was unconscious," Fillmore said.

"Fillmore!" Thomas snapped, throwing a glare over his shoulder at the older man. His jaw tensed as he gritted his teeth. He turned back to me with barely contained exasperation.

"My name *is* Thomas," he said. "I know I look like Grant. I know I sound like Grant. I know that, briefly, I pretended to *be* Grant, but I'm not him. Grant is from your world. Earth. I'm not. I'm from here."

"Aurora."

"That's right."

I shook my head, drowning in disbelief. The insanity of this conversation had even managed to distract me from how badly I still wanted to throw up.

"Okay, well, if we're in some parallel universe, *Thomas,* then how exactly did we get here? Even if parallel universes exist, there's no way to move between them."

"We found a way."

"Oh yeah? What's that?"

"You're wearing it." He pointed at the bracelet on my wrist. "It's called an anchor; it helped transport you to Aurora and, as long as you have it on, it'll keep you here."

I stared at the bracelet. That awful, stomach-turning sense of doom I'd felt earlier came rushing in again. I put my hand to my forehead. I still felt faint, and was glad to be sitting.

"Are you okay?" Thomas asked.

"I feel sick," I said softly, finding it difficult to draw breath. My chest was tight and my heart was racing; the sound of blood pumping through my temples exacerbated the pain that flashed behind my eyes. All my muscles had tightened to the point where I almost felt frozen, like I'd smash into pieces if I fell to the floor.

"That's the tandem," Thomas said by way of explanation, as if I had any idea what that meant. He hovered near me, even going so far as to reach out to steady my shoulders, which were shaking. I stiffened. "Going through is difficult the first few times. It puts a lot of stress on the body. You need to relax."

"How am I supposed to relax?" I demanded. "I'm being held against my will in a dark basement by my *prom date*. What about this situation is supposed to be relaxing?"

Thomas had nothing to say to that. "Just keep breathing."

"What the hell is the tandem?" I massaged my temples, but the headache just kept getting worse.

"It's the veil that separates the universes." I stared at him blankly. "Like a membrane, sort of, that you can pass through." Thomas sighed. "It's difficult to explain."

"Clearly," I managed to choke out. My mouth filled with bitter saliva, and I knew what was going to happen next. I leaned forward and vomited all over the cement floor, barely missing Thomas's shiny black boots.

"Okay," Thomas said, lifting me to my feet by my arm as if I weighed nothing. "Up."

"If you think I'm cleaning that, Mayhew, you're out of your mind," Fillmore said from his corner. "I'm not a janitor!"

Thomas towed me to the bathroom; I tried to resist him, but I didn't have the strength. I fell to my knees in front of the toilet and threw up again, wiping my face afterward with a towel he handed me. My skin was hot and clammy, but I was shivering all over; it felt like I had the flu. When I was ready, he helped me to stand again, stepping aside as I washed my mouth out with handfuls of tap water and handing me another towel that I wet and pressed against my face. He bent to retrieve something, but I didn't see what it was; he slipped it into his pocket with a carnival magician's deft sleight of hand.

I hunched over the sink, gripping the porcelain rim as the nausea ebbed. Thomas stood behind me, and I stared at his reflection in the mirror. I was starting to see the ways in which he wasn't like the Grant I remembered. The way he carried his body, for one thing. Grant was a sloucher, an ambler, but this boy—Thomas—stood tall and walked with purpose. Did that mean I was actually starting to believe that he was a totally different *person* than Grant? I still couldn't bring myself to accept that possibility.

"Come on," he urged. "We have to go."

"Prove it," I said, pushing a few wet strands of hair back from my face.

"Prove . . . that we have to go?" Confusion passed over his face, but only for a brief second before it was replaced by the inscrutable expression I was coming to think of as his perpetual look.

"No," I said. "Prove that you are who you say you are." He hesitated, and I kept talking, the words spilling out of my mouth before my brain had any time to filter them. "I don't know what the hell is going on, but you obviously need me or you wouldn't have gone through so much trouble to bring me here—wherever *here* is. I get that you're a big tough guy, and you can threaten me all you want, but you're not going to hurt me—if you were, you already would've done it. I don't have to make things easy, and I don't plan on it, unless I get some answers."

Thomas pressed his lips together and drew a deep breath in through his nose. He appeared to be considering my proposal. *Finally,* I thought. I was starting to feel a little bit better, too, which was an encouraging sign. If I was sick, I couldn't run.

Wordlessly, Thomas turned and left the bathroom. I followed him out on wobbly legs and leaned against a wall while he dug in the pockets of a jacket that hung on the back of a chair.

"Here." He thrust a piece of hard, folded leather into my hands.

At first I thought it was a wallet, but when I flipped it open I saw that it was a badge—gold, shaped like a shield and crested with a golden sun. The badge read:

KING'S ELITE SERVICE
SECURITY DEPARTMENT
DIVISION OF DEFENSE

I was about to hand it back and tell him that some little prop badge wasn't going to convince me of anything when I noticed that the other half of the fold held a small, rectangular certificate sheathed in plastic.

UNITED COMMONWEALTH OF COLUMBIA
KING'S ELITE SERVICE
AGENT: THOMAS W. MAYHEW
AGENT CLASS: SECURITY (S)
AGENT ID: UCC-KES-1321345589

The picture in the upper left-hand corner was Grant's.

I handed the credentials back, trying not to betray how unsettled they made me. "Fake."

"They're not fake," he insisted. "Look here, at the holographic imprint. You can't counterfeit that."

"The United Commonwealth of Columbia? The King's Elite Service? Those things don't even *exist,* Grant!"

"Not in your world, they don't. But I told you—we're not *in* your world anymore. In this one the UCC and the KES are very, very real." He stepped forward. "Now, for the last time: my name is Thomas Mayhew. You can call me Agent

Mayhew, or you can call me Thomas, but I really don't care whether or not you believe me. We're leaving. Now."

I swallowed hard. "Where are you taking me?"

"Where you need to be," he said, flipping up the hood of his sweatshirt. "Fillmore, get rid of that." He gestured to my dress, which was dangerously close to the puddle of vomit. "And clean up. We're going."

"She needs to cover her face," Fillmore warned. "People will recognize her."

"Put your hood up," Thomas instructed.

"Okay, okay," I said, following orders. I slipped my arms through the straps of the backpack and walked toward Thomas and the door. "Why would people recognize me? I thought you said we weren't in my world anymore."

"In Aurora, your face is a little bit more . . . familiar to the average person," Thomas said.

"What does *that* mean?"

"Exactly what he said," Fillmore responded. Thomas shook his head and Fillmore backed down, once again in deference to Thomas's rank. "Good luck, my boy." Fillmore offered his hand for Thomas to shake, and Thomas took it. In spite of all their bickering, there seemed to be some genuine affection—or, at the very least, respect—deep down.

It sank in then, as I watched the two of them part ways. Thomas wasn't lying, and he wasn't insane. Everything he had told me was true as far as he knew it. I was trapped in another world with no idea how to get back home.

EIGHT

It was too hot outside for all the clothes I was wearing. I started to unzip the hoodie, but Thomas stopped me.

"What are you doing?" he demanded.

"Taking off some of these layers. I'm baking."

"Keep it on," he said. He glanced up and down the street, which was mostly empty except for a few people wandering by. *What is he so worried about?* I wondered. The street was practically deserted, and anyway I was dressed like the Unabomber—surely that was much more noticeable than just showing my face.

Since he was looking around, I did, too. It was difficult to describe the Chicago of Aurora. If someone had insisted that I was standing in the city I'd grown up in, it would have been hard to point to anything definitive that would prove them wrong, but I knew instinctively that this wasn't my home.

There were some things, though, that were obviously unusual. I squinted to read a nearby street sign: West Eugenie Street. We were in Lincoln Park—or we would've been, if we were on Earth—but the neighborhood, which I knew, was unrecognizable. The surrounding buildings were taller than

I would've expected, given that we weren't downtown; there should've been houses and apartments no taller than four stories, but there were towering high-rises in their place, as far as the eye could see. The basement we'd emerged from belonged to one of three side-by-side redbrick row houses that sat in the center of the block, overshadowed by their larger neighbors, remnants of a bygone era. I wondered at their even being there; it was as if someone had forgotten about them, or they were being protected, although they were so run-down that it seemed unlikely.

The rest of the buildings were more modern-looking than they would've been in my Chicago, as if they'd just been built. They were mostly glass, with elegantly curved edges and tinted windows that reflected the light from the sun in a rainbow of colors like pools of oil. But they were more dilapidated, too, as if they'd been around for ages and not well kept up. The awning that protruded from the entrance of a nearby condominium was torn, the shreds of what remained fluttering half-heartedly in the breeze. There were no trees—I looked up and down the street for blocks without seeing one—and more trash in the gutters. It was as if I'd been transported to a slightly distant future where nobody took care of anything. Cars lined the edges of the street, but they were models I didn't quite recognize. They were sleeker and more compact, all except a large, intimidating black SUV parked a few doors down. Thomas headed in that direction and motioned for me to follow him.

"Stay close," he said in a low tone. "If anyone passes by, don't look at them." *Who is this person I look like?* I asked myself. She had to be someone important; otherwise Thomas wouldn't have gone to all this trouble.

When we reached the SUV, Thomas went around to the

trunk and pressed his thumb against a small LCD pad the size of a Post-it note near the handle.

"Yeah, this vehicle isn't at all conspicuous," I said.

Thomas didn't rise to the bait. He simply opened the cargo door and said, "Climb in."

"Absolutely not." I stared at him in disbelief. "I'm not *getting into the trunk.* Are you serious?"

"I'm serious. I don't want anybody to see you, even through the window. You don't know how recognizable your face is here. If someone sees you and reports it, it'll be all over the press boards in fifteen minutes and we'll never get out of here undetected."

I waited for him to explain further; when he didn't, I sighed and asked, "What are you talking about?"

"You've been to Times Square?" Thomas asked. "On Earth, I mean."

"No." Granddad wasn't big on vacations. He'd taken me to Lake Okobogee a handful of times, and Florida once, because he liked to fish, but that was about it. "I've seen pictures."

"Well, you know the big screens?" I nodded. "The press boards are like that, but they're everywhere, and there are people in this city who I'd prefer had no idea you were here."

"Like the authorities?" I asked sharply.

"I *am* the authorities."

"'Here' as in Chicago, or 'here' as in . . . *Aurora*?" I whispered the last word, afraid of being overheard, though there was nobody within earshot.

"Both," he said. "Now get in."

I was curled in a ball in the mostly empty cargo area of Thomas's SUV. He'd draped a blanket over me, and my back was pressed against a long chrome box; God knew what he was keeping in there, but it wasn't like he was going to tell me.

We cruised along for about ten minutes before we hit traffic. From my place in the back, I could hear Thomas's muffled swearing. In the dim quiet, I began to formulate a plan.

First things first: I had to get the anchor off. If it was the thing tying me to Aurora, then it had to go as soon as possible. I shifted to face the metal box. If Thomas really was some sort of CIA-style government agent, then I figured it was at least possible the box contained weapons and other gear—guns, night-vision goggles, a couple of hand grenades . . . knives, maybe. I was hoping to find something I could saw through the anchor with, since there was no way I was going to be able to slip out of it; it was fastened too tightly around my wrist.

But the box was locked. There was a small LCD panel on the front; it glowed blue, staining my skin with cerulean light. I'd just seen Thomas use a similar panel to unlock the car door. He'd pressed his thumb against it, so the technology was probably biometric. Was it set only to recognize his print, or would mine open the box as well? It seemed unlikely, but at the very least I had to *try.*

When I touched the panel, it changed to the red color of burning coals. I jerked back instinctively as an alarm sounded.

"What's going on back there?" Thomas called out.

"Nothing," I told him. "I just accidentally hit this . . . whatever it is, with my shoulder."

There was a pause, like he was deciding whether to believe me. "Be careful with that," he said finally. The alarm quieted and the panel turned blue again. "It's dangerous."

I'm sure, I thought. I couldn't pry it open with my fingertips and Thomas would notice if I tried to break the lock.

Whatever the box contained, it was no longer an option. But I wasn't beaten yet. If there was a way into Aurora, there was a way out. I just had to find it.

I lifted the blanket and crept up to the edge of the window, peering out. We were no longer on the sleepy side street in Lincoln Park—or whatever it was called in this universe. Thomas had navigated us onto a broad avenue; there was a line of cars behind us, horns blaring. Pedestrians gazed at the backup with mild interest. It was all so *normal,* which I found upsetting, even more than I probably would have if everything had been completely different. My mind wandered again to the goofy worlds Granddad and I had invented once upon a time. *Anything you can think of probably exists somewhere,* Granddad had said. My ears caught the drone of an airplane soaring overhead. Maybe all this would be easier if there were no reminders of home.

Then I did something bold, something I would never have imagined myself capable of doing: I unlocked and opened the back hatch, leapt out of the car, and took off running.

I had no idea where I was going; all I knew was that I had to get away. I would never be able to get back home with Thomas watching my every move, so I had to escape him, even if that meant throwing myself upon the mercy of a world in which I didn't belong.

"Hey!" Thomas was out of the car in an instant, following me at full speed. I had a head start, but the pounding of his combat boots on the cracked and broken concrete was getting louder and closer; he was gaining on me, and I was still feeling the ill effects of traveling through the—what had Thomas called it? The tandem. I wasn't sure how much longer I was going to be able to keep up my pace in the hope of outrunning him, if there even *was* a hope of outrunning him.

I sprinted down the next street, weaving through a stream of people that thickened as I pushed on. I was too afraid of breaking my momentum to stop and look back, but I couldn't hear Thomas behind me anymore.

Something was happening up ahead. There was a huge crowd of people assembling in what looked like it might've once been a park, though the only greenery that remained were the weeds that poked up out of vast stretches of dead brown grass.

I plunged into the throng, shoving my way past men and women of varying ages. Some of them were carrying toddlers on their shoulders, or clutching the hands of older children. As the crowd grew denser, I was forced to slow down, and I started to notice things. The body language of the people was decidedly negative; their faces were angry, their voices, which had congealed into a singular noise like the thrum of an insect swarm, were tense and strained. Many of them were carrying signs or banners, and as I glanced up ahead I found I could read one. It said **WE SERVE NO GOVERNMENT**.

I felt as though I'd been doused with freezing cold water. The hairs on my arms stood up despite the heat, and I felt a new layer of fear descend on me—fear of the unknown. Thomas scared me, there was no denying it, but at least with him I had some idea of what I was dealing with, or thought I did. But these strangers seemed even more threatening, though I didn't know why they were so riled up; that was the most frightening thing of all.

Someone tapped my shoulder, and I whipped around, expecting to see Thomas. But it was just a young guy, in his twenties, maybe even college age, trying to get through.

"I want to stand as close to the stage as possible!" he shouted above the churning cry of the agitated horde. I glanced behind him, but couldn't see Thomas anywhere. "There's a rumor the Monad's going to show."

"What's going on?" I asked. What was a Monad? Was that a person? What kind of a name was that for a human being? And yet I felt like I'd heard it before. Where, though? Where would I have ever heard that word? I couldn't bring myself to ask the guy. Instead, I posed a different question. "Why are all these people here?'

"It's a rally," he said, narrowing his eyes.

"I can see that. What for?" I must've looked strange to him, with the hood of my sweatshirt cinched so tightly it covered my face, especially given how warm it was. I pushed the hood back and brushed the hair out of my eyes.

"Are you kidding?" he asked in astonishment. "It's a Libertas rally."

"Oh, of course," I said with a hesitant smile. The guy was looking at me more closely now. "Good luck getting up there." I nodded at the large stage that had been erected in the center of the park. It was draped in forest-green banners; they all sported a common symbol, a pattern of ten gold stars stitched in the shape of an equilateral triangle.

I started to work my way through the crowd again, hoping to leave the guy behind, but he put his hand on my shoulder and held me back. I jerked out of his grip and turned to face him.

"Hey," he said, pointing at me. We were so close, his finger almost touched my nose. "You know, you look a hell of a lot like—"

I caught a glimpse of Thomas over the young man's shoulder. "I'm not. I have to go."

I wrenched away and kept moving, ducking my head low to keep from being seen. After what seemed like an eternity,

I finally broke through the last wall of bodies on the north side of the park. A voice began booming through the loudspeakers, but I couldn't locate them in the scrum. It was as if the voice was coming, godlike, from the sky.

"Ladies and gentlemen," the voice said. It was deep and masculine, strong but musical in tone—the kind of voice that could command an army with a word. "This is the Monad. I regret that I could not join you today, my brothers and sisters, in your homes and in your cities, but I deliver unto you this message. You all know why we're here today. You all know of the *injustice* we have suffered under the tyrant rule of this declining monarchy. You all know of the *promise* that comes with revolution. The promise of liberty. The promise of freedom. The promise of choice. Our ancestors lived under the oppressive rule of a foreign royal for centuries, before the fathers of the First Revolution raised an army against them, and yet their true and solemn purpose was hijacked by thieves and traitors, a man that would crown himself king. And now, today, his inbred, *worthless* spawn sits on a throne while we—the people of this once-great nation—bleed and toil for his benefit. The king and his advisers say that the only way to make peace with Farnham is to force two teenagers into marriage, but the true path to peace is overthrowing both monarchies and forming one republic, of the people, by the people, and for the people!"

The furious hum of voices swelled to a roar. People teemed around me on every side, pressing forward to rush the empty stage. Someone shoved me and I took a step back, grinding the toes of a nearby protester under my heel.

"Hey!" he shrieked. I turned to apologize and he got a good look at my face.

"It's you," he whispered. Then, louder, "It's her! It's the princess!"

Princess? I thought in a panic. What the hell was he talking about? I was no princess! Then I remembered what Thomas had said back in the basement. *Your face is a little bit more familiar to the average person*. People were turning and staring, and I suddenly felt very exposed. They thought I was someone else.

Someone they hated.

As I scanned the scene, I saw, for the first time, clumps of armed men dressed in black. They were carrying military assault rifles and patrolling the perimeter in groups of two or three. One of them noticed me, and we locked eyes. He pointed me out to another guard, and instinct took over. I began to run again, sprinting as fast as my legs could take me.

NINE

Trapped, trapped, trapped. The word echoed through my head, banishing any other thought as I ran past shops and homes and cars and people who turned to look at me with unabashed curiosity. I was going too fast to tell if anyone else had recognized me, but I really hoped no one had.

For a while, I didn't even look to see where I was going—I didn't know the city anyway, so what was the point? Then it occurred to me how dumb that was—I was in Chicago. The Aurora version of Chicago, but still, it was possible there were similarities, that there was something I could use to orient myself. The Sears Tower, the enduring symbol of the city on Earth, had to be around somewhere.

I scanned the tops of the buildings, trying to locate the singular silhouette of the landmark and navigate by it. There were other skyscrapers—everywhere, in fact—huge ones that disappeared into the clouds that had started to gather, including what looked to be an enormous campanile rising in the distance, but I couldn't find what I was looking for. The Sears Tower didn't seem to exist in this version of Chicago; perhaps it had never been built. I knew its shape so well, there was no way I'd ever miss it or mistake it for something else. I was completely adrift in this unrecognizable world.

My home wasn't here. It didn't matter which way I went or how fast I ran.

But I kept running. I passed several of the press boards Thomas had mentioned earlier; none of them, to my relief, were showing my picture, or his, although I could see now why he'd feared the possibility. The boards were like giant TVs, broadcasting silent news reports and advertisements in an eye-straining array of bright, dazzling colors. There was one every few blocks or so, mounted on the sides of buildings and rooftops, big as billboards. If someone had put my picture up, it would've been seen by almost everyone in the city in minutes, maybe less.

I kept time by watching the clocks on the press boards as I sped by them—it was around four thirty in the afternoon, meaning I'd been gone from my world for a little less than seventeen hours. Five minutes, ten minutes, fifteen, half an hour ticked by. The chiming of the bells in the faraway tower reached me on a breeze. Finally, I figured I'd gone long and far enough that Thomas would be hard-pressed to find me; I ducked down a quiet street and sank to the ground, panting. I'd gotten away. Now how was I going to get *home*?

The only idea that sprang to mind was to keep running, but I was so tired, and I'd stopped paying attention to my surroundings. I tucked my knees against my chest, wrapping my arms around them, like if I could get as compact as possible, no one would be able to see me. There was a press board directly across the street; I spent a few minutes mindlessly watching the advertisements go by until a news program took over. I held my breath, expecting to see my own face, but instead the picture was of a building; it had been designed in the Queen Anne style, just like my house back on Earth. The headline that ran alongside the photo said: COLUMBIA CITY, NYD—BOMB SCARE AT KING ALBERT STATION. HUNDREDS EVACUATED.

It was infuriating not to have my cell phone; I'd have been on it in a second, frantically trying to decipher the codes of this strange place, to see which parts of it corresponded to parts of my own world. Practically, that wouldn't have worked for a number of reasons, but my fingers itched to do it anyway. I'd never heard of Columbia City on Earth, though that didn't mean much; the United States was a huge country. But something about the broadcast told me that Columbia City was a big metropolis—big enough, at least, to have a fancy train station—which meant that it was important. Then I remembered Thomas's badge—United Commonwealth of Columbia, it had said. Thomas had called it the UCC. Maybe Columbia City was their capital. If so, it likely only corresponded to a few places: New York, D.C., Boston, or L.A. I stopped puzzling over it then, realizing that I was only doing it to distract myself from the task at hand, which was figuring out what to do next.

And then, out of nowhere, someone grabbed my arm and dragged me into a nearby alley.

I struggled to my feet and found that I was surrounded by three armed men dressed in black; each had a forest-green patch on his arm, ten tiny golden stars stitched on it in the shape of a triangle, the same pattern I'd seen on the banners at the rally. I knew without having to be told that they belonged to the group called Libertas. My stomach sank. They were most certainly not there to help me.

One of the men—bald, with dark gray eyes and a puckered pink scar across his forehead—took hold of my ponytail and yanked me toward him.

"Who are you?" he demanded, his breath spreading, thick and sour, over my face.

"Nobody," I whimpered. Sparks exploded in front of my eyes and a pain so bad I could hardly think swelled in my skull. "Please don't hurt me," I begged. "I'm nobody. I just want to go home!"

The bald guy laughed, tightening his grip on my hair. I winced, squeezing my eyes shut to stem the tide of tears. "Yeah, I'll bet you do."

"Let go!" I cried, my fingers scrabbling against his arm, trying for a patch of exposed skin to sink my nails into. "You're hurting me!"

He leaned in close and whispered in my ear. "Answer my questions and I'll think about it. Doesn't that sound like a fair deal?" I nodded. I was shaking like a sapling in a hurricane. "Who are you and who do you work for?"

"I'm no one," I insisted again. "I don't work for anybody. Please. I haven't done anything! You've got me confused with somebody else."

The bald guy snorted. "Well, you're wrong about that, sweetheart. I know exactly who you *aren't*." He laughed and ran the muzzle of his gun along the base of my jaw. A sob rose in my throat; to keep it from escaping I bit my lip, so hard that it started to bleed. "You haven't given me much of a choice," he went on. "We had a deal, and you didn't hold up your end of the bargain, so I'm afraid—"

Suddenly, from behind us, there came a loud crash, but before the men or I could react, a bullet whizzed through the air and found its target in the bald guy's shoulder. He released me with a guttural moan and I stumbled forward, landing hard on my hands and knees. Ignoring the pain that tore through my palms, I glanced over my shoulder to get a peek at my unexpected savior.

Thomas was crouched on a nearby Dumpster, pointing a pistol at the other two men, who had their guns trained on him. My eyes flew to the top of the building, the only place he could've come from. It had to have been a three-story drop, and yet he looked unfazed.

"Let her go," he said. His voice was tight and his face was set in an expression of such incredible focus and determination that I felt myself rescued before any rescuing had taken place.

The bald guy staggered to his feet, but Thomas didn't hesitate; he shot the man in the leg, and he was down again. One of the others—this one had long, stringy hair and was the tallest man I'd ever seen, quite literally looming over my five feet seven inches—wrapped his arm around my neck and pulled me backward toward the alley's dead end. His grip was so tight it was cutting off my breath; I choked and sputtered, swinging my elbows in the hopes of jamming one into his ribs, but all I found was empty, indifferent air. The third man, who had a black ski cap pulled tight over his ears despite the warm weather, advanced on Thomas as he dismounted the Dumpster and they faced off, guns aimed and fingers on the triggers.

"No," Ski Cap said simply. "She's coming with us. Get out of the way."

"Not without her."

My gaze zoomed back and forth between them. My heart was pounding as fast as a hummingbird's, and it was almost impossible to focus on anything but sucking in air as Stringy Hair's arm continued to crush my throat. Then he jerked me sideways, which allowed him to lift his gun and point it at Thomas. It was two against one now. Thomas was outnumbered. And yet, from the look in his eyes, I knew they had more to fear than he did.

"We don't take orders from KES scum," Ski Cap said.

Thomas laughed mirthlessly in disbelief. "Oh, *I'm* scum? I'm not the one blowing up hospitals and train stations, making traitors out of innocent people!"

Ski Cap sneered. "It's for the greater good."

"Please, spare me," Thomas scoffed. "Hand her over."

"Not a chance," Ski Cap replied. "She's ours. We'll kill you if we have to."

"Fine," Thomas challenged. "Shoot me."

Ski Cap raised his gun, but he wasn't fast enough; before he'd gotten off a single round, Thomas drew out a second pistol and pressed the trigger. The gun fired, but what came out the other end was like nothing I'd ever seen before. The barrel emitted a conical stream of blinding white light, the edge of which hit Ski Cap and sent him flying across the alley, where he came to rest, finally, completely still, his head streaming with slick rivulets of blood.

The blast shook the alley and we all stumbled backward in its wake. Stringy Hair released his grip and his gun, which clattered to the ground near my feet. I gasped, pulling in air as fast as I could. I stared at the gun, unmoving, my brain screaming at me to pick it up, to defend myself, but I was too disoriented. I'd never handled a gun before, never even touched one, and I knew I'd never be able to shoot somebody. I wouldn't even be able to hold a gun convincingly enough to make anyone think I was *capable* of shooting somebody.

Thomas charged forward, unaffected by the chaos he had wrought, but Stringy Hair managed to get to his feet and attack. He was unarmed, but he was fast and brutal. He punched Thomas squarely in the jaw; Thomas barely flinched, recovering from the recoil fast enough to knee his assailant hard in the groin. Thomas pushed him backward and kicked him in the solar plexus before spinning and knocking the man in the face with his elbow. I heard the stringy-haired man's nose crack; blood spurted out of his nostrils and he fell to the ground, where he writhed in pain, clutching his stomach.

Thomas put away his gun and retrieved another, smaller weapon from his belt. He held it steady as he shot each of the men in the shoulder, one by one. The bullets made a soft whistle as they traveled through the air, and the men were still.

I watched this unfold as if at a distance, light-headed and quivering. It was as though I was in some sort of trance. I stared at the bodies of the three Libertas commandos. Were they dead? I didn't think so. I could just barely make out the rise and fall of their chests. I must've looked horrified, because Thomas held up the small gun and said, "Relax, they're tranquilizer pellets."

I nodded dully.

"What the hell were you thinking? I told you people would recognize you—I told you to hide your face!" Thomas was shouting, but I could barely hear him over the roar of blood in my ears. I flexed my fingers and pressed them against my throat. The air tasted exquisite now that I could fill my lungs to bursting, like a never-ending drink of cool spring water. *I'm alive,* I thought, giddy with relief.

"Sasha!" Thomas shook me by the shoulder. His eyes were dark slits, his brow furrowed in something like concern.

"I—" I didn't have an excuse. He *had* warned me. But how could he have expected me to listen? Did he really think I'd be that easily managed? How could he have thought I'd give up without a fight? Is that what *he* would've done? Surely not. "I'm sorry," I said dryly, not at all meaning it.

"Don't you understand that you could've been killed? I

was trying to keep you away from them and instead you ran right for them!"

"What was I supposed to do?" I snapped. "Stay put and wait for you to do God knows what with me?"

He glowered at me. "There's more where they came from. We've got to get out of the city as soon as possible."

"I'm not coming with you." I folded my arms across my chest in defiance. I was putting on a pretty good show of being stubborn, but actually I was of two minds. On the one hand, I didn't want to submit to him, to follow his orders and obey him as if he had some sort of claim on me. The urge to resist was personal; I wanted to punish him for what he'd done to me in whatever small way I could. But on the other hand, reason was telling me to go with him, that whatever his plans were for me, they were preferable to falling into the hands of Libertas.

The emotional part of me was winning out.

"Yes, you are," Thomas said. "Those men were going to take you to an underground bunker somewhere, torture you for information you don't have, and then kill you. Is that what you want? Because if I'd known you had a death wish I would've just left you to them."

"No, you wouldn't," I said. "You need me. Otherwise I wouldn't even be here."

"I don't have time to stand around and chat about this with you. You have two choices: them or me. And if I were you, I really wouldn't choose them."

I said nothing. He made a frustrated noise.

"Look, you want the truth? That anchor brought you here, and it's the only thing that can bring you home. I have the device that controls it. The anchor is made out of a reinforced titanium alloy—you can't cut it off, and even if you could, removing it won't send you back. So we can both sit here and wait for more Libertas to come calling, or we can leave. *I strongly suggest that we leave."*

Still I didn't speak, didn't move a muscle. I knew he was right, at least about Libertas, but I was having a hard time motivating myself to go along with him. I just didn't want him to think that I was going down without a fight. Or maybe I didn't want to think that about myself.

"I have to admit," he said, his tone lightening, as if he was trying, in a small, weak way, to make nice. "I'm impressed. You got farther than I expected. It was smart of you to use the rally as cover. Even I don't have X-ray vision."

"What was that whole thing, anyway?"

"Antiroyalist rally," Thomas said with a shrug of his shoulders. "Bunch of rabble-rousers. Nothing to worry about." But his expression said it was much more serious than that. I had a million questions; the rally had piqued my interest in this strange new world, but even though I was usually quite the determined interrogator when there was information that I wanted, now wasn't the time.

"Nothing to worry about? They recognized me," I told him. "And they didn't like what they saw. Overall, I do *not* feel welcome here in Aurora."

Thomas sighed. "I did try to warn you."

But it was something else Thomas had said that really struck a chord. *I have the device that controls it.* Removing the anchor might not be possible, but if I could gain possession of the remote, I could transport myself home without anybody's help. I just had to figure out how to get my hands on it.

"How did you find me?" I asked, glancing at the motionless bodies on the ground. A gun belonging to one of the men lay only three feet from where I stood, and the sight of it gave me an idea.

"The anchor has a GPS tracker in it."

"You have GPS here?" So running away again wasn't going to work.

"We had it before you did." He walked to the end of the alley and glanced up and down the perpendicular street, giving me the opportunity I needed. I crouched down and reached for the nearby gun, slowly, trying not to attract Thomas's attention while his back was turned. "I was waiting for you on the other side of the street, figuring I'd intercept you there, but then I saw them pull you into the alley—"

When he turned back around, I had the gun aimed at his chest. He lifted his hands up in a gesture of surrender, working his jaw anxiously but saying nothing.

"Give me the device that controls the anchor and I'll never bother you again," I said. My voice sounded like it was forged from steel; if I hadn't spoken the words myself, I wouldn't even have recognized it. I was trying to make myself sound like Thomas—emotionless, untouchable. The sort of person I knew I wasn't. But he hadn't given me any choice.

"I can't do that."

"Then I'm going to have to shoot you," I said, hoping he couldn't tell how badly I was shaking.

"You won't," Thomas said calmly. He stepped forward and lowered his hands.

"Yes I will." He didn't seem afraid, which infuriated me. If he kept looking at me in that patronizing, self-satisfied way, maybe I *would* shoot him.

"No you won't." Thomas took another step, and then another, making his way toward me carefully, the way one might approach a frightened animal. He seemed so sure of himself, so confident in his ability to talk me down. With every step he took, I knew I was losing ground. "You don't even have your finger on the trigger."

That was because I didn't want to fire it by accident. But if he insisted . . . I settled the pad of my pointer finger against the slim metal curve of the trigger. "Problem solved."

"You won't pull it." He was getting closer and closer. I had to shoot him.

"You take one more step and I'll do it." It was the last gasp of my bravado. I would never be able to follow through on my threat. "Don't move."

His face went white as something on the rooftop behind my head caught his attention. "I may not have to," he said gravely.

I shouldn't have done it. I shouldn't have looked. But I was still rattled from my encounter with Libertas, so I turned to get a sense of what was coming. Of course, the rooftop was empty. We were alone.

I was completely unprepared for Thomas's speed. His hand shot out as soon as I took my eyes off him and he wrenched the gun from my grip. I watched in rage and frustration as he removed the clip and stripped the rest of the Libertas rifles of their ammunition, swearing under his breath the whole time. When he was finished, he turned his glare on me.

"Never do that again," he commanded. "You shouldn't pick up a gun unless you're prepared to use it."

"You'd rather I shot you?" I snapped.

"You were never going to," he said. "Now let's go."

"No," I said, drawing a sharp breath as my vision grew hazy. My lungs burned, and I remembered how far I'd run, and how fast, without stopping. *Something's wrong.* The thought floated through my mind like dandelion fluff, small and light.

My knees gave way and I crumpled to the ground. A dull ache throbbed in my temples, radiating through my arms and legs. My eyelids drooped. Everything around me started to go dark, as if someone had smeared my eyeballs with black paint. Thomas rushed forward to prop me up, seizing my chin.

"Sasha?" he called. I reached for something to steady myself and found his left hand. I bore down hard on his fingers, making him wince; nevertheless, he squeezed back.

"What's happening to me?" I whispered.

"It's the tandem sickness. You shouldn't have run." His voice faded in and out as I fell further into semiconsciousness. "You were supposed to rest. . . . Shouldn't have run. . . ."

The last thing I saw before the darkness overtook me completely was the bright green of his eyes and the slow, fluid motion of his lips as he spoke my name.

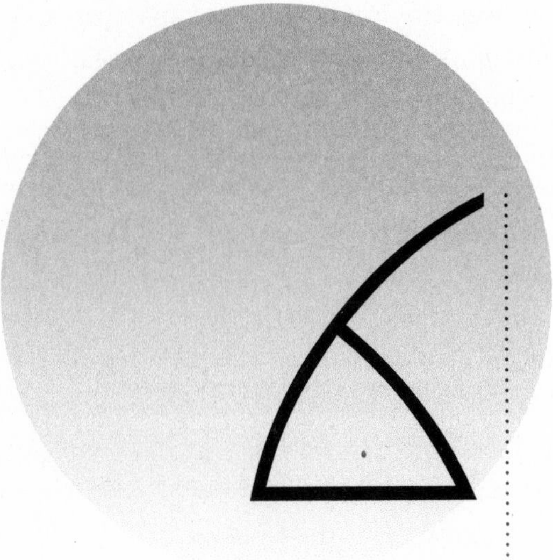

DAYS

THOMAS IN THE TOWER / 1

"Good work, Agent."

Thomas glanced to his right, startled—though he didn't show it—by the unexpected new presence in the room. "Thank you, sir. You know I do my best to make you proud."

Even he knew how shallow and obsequious it sounded coming out of his mouth. If Lucas were around, he would've scoffed at the first word; Thomas's brother had a low tolerance for brownnosing. But it was what the General wanted to hear, and Thomas always did what the General wanted, insofar as he could stand to.

"I do know that," the General said. They stood side by side, watching Sasha's inert form on the cot in the mission room through large monitors. How many times had Thomas slept on that same cot after hours and hours of meetings and briefings and research and planning sessions? Too many to count. The walls were covered with his notes, maps and photographs, charts and stratagems so calculated they were like equations. It was strange to see her there now, the centerpiece of Operation Starling, just an average girl from Earth.

Well, perhaps *average* was the wrong word. In fact, he knew it was. *Extraordinary* was more like it. *Amazing.* An analog. She had no idea how significant she was, what her presence here *meant.* She'd gone sixteen years—almost seventeen—thinking she was just a regular girl. It was remarkable how important people could be without even knowing.

"When will she come around?" the General asked.

Thomas shrugged. "That's up to you. Mo—Dr. Moss said we could wake her any time now."

He had to stop himself from using Mossie's nickname. The General disapproved of Thomas's friendship with the eccentric scientist, though the man's contribution to Operation Starling couldn't be denied. Mossie was the only reason they were able to retrieve Sasha. He'd invented the technology that allowed them to pass through the tandem, created the anchors for exclusive use by the KES. Whether he liked it or not, the General couldn't get rid of him—and he didn't like it at all. He didn't trust Mossie, and Thomas didn't blame him. Mossie was the only person in the Tower who spoke out against him, though even then it was only when he thought the General would not overhear. But the General had spies everywhere, and word had gotten out. Mossie was a liability, but he was also an asset—an asset that couldn't be wasted.

Thomas expected the General to command him to wake Sasha up immediately, but he didn't. After all the insanity surrounding Operation Starling, all the rush and the talk of running out of time, the General seemed to be relishing these last few moments of relative normalcy before everything changed forever.

"Did she give you any trouble?" he asked. Thomas always had a difficult time telling what the General was thinking, and now was no different. Only a man like the General could stand before an analog with no expression on his face. He was above it all, even this.

"Not much," Thomas said. It would be worse for Sasha if the General knew how much of a fight she'd put up, so it was best not to mention it.

The General looked over at him, but Thomas didn't turn to meet his eyes. It had taken him a long time to learn how not to squirm under the weight of the General's gaze, but he was older now, tall and broad and covered in lean muscle, not the small, fidgety boy he'd once been. He didn't scare so easily anymore. He could handle the General.

"How much?" The General's voice was dark and low.

"None," Thomas lied. "She was perfectly behaved." He didn't know what he would do if Sasha decided to become a problem in front of the General. He made a silent wish that she would sense her place and submit to him. Otherwise, they would both be in a lot of trouble.

"And if I called Agent Fillmore, he'd tell me the same thing?" The General was testing him, seeing if he'd break like metal rusted through.

"Of course." Thomas nodded, the corners of his mouth turning up ever so slightly, the widest smile he'd ever given the man. "Sir—" Then he stopped himself.

"Ask your question, Agent," the General commanded.

"Where is he?"

"Who?" The General turned to look at him, his gaze piercing behind the rimless glasses he wore on his nose. "Your analog, you mean?"

"Yes, sir. Did the squad pick him up?"

"There was an issue with the retrieval of your analog on this side of the tandem."

"An issue? What kind of an issue?" Thomas knew he should be disinterested in Grant Davis's fate; indifference to aspects outside the parameters of his mission had been a fundamental part of his training, had practically been grafted into his DNA during his time at the Academy. And yet, he couldn't help wondering. It was a strange relationship, the one between analogs. There was a natural sympathy that rose unbidden; he'd felt it when he'd met Grant Davis face to face, in the empty park back on Earth. It was a cold-hearted bastard who didn't find it in him to care about another human being who wore his face.

Besides, he didn't quite consider Grant Davis's situation to be outside the parameters of his mission. Thomas was the reason Grant was in Aurora in the first place—he'd sent Grant there himself, knowing full well what kinds of trouble there were to get into for someone who looked like them. If there had been any problems for Grant on the other side of the tandem, it was more than a little bit Thomas's fault. "Did the squad not find him? They were supposed to be waiting."

"Oh, they found him, all right," the General said, frowning at the tone of Thomas's voice, the implication that men under his command had been in any way deficient in fulfilling their duties. "About two minutes after Libertas did."

"Libertas? On the South End?" Though the Tattered City was very much Libertas's territory, their security units mostly stuck to the North End and City Center, where the majority of the remaining residents actually lived. The South End had been hemorrhaging its population for years, and these days it was mostly abandoned, so Libertas didn't waste resources on patrolling it. If there had been a unit down there, it meant one of two things: that Libertas was expanding its reach for some no doubt suspicious reason of its own, or—though Thomas really couldn't see how this was possible—they knew something was about to go down and they were lying in wait.

The General nodded, but his mind seemed far away. "Seems they're expanding."

"Why would they even want him?"

The General turned to him with an odd, inscrutable expression that Thomas had often tried to replicate, with varying degrees of success. "I assume they believed he was you."

Thomas clenched his jaw. It was unheard of for KES agents to fail in their missions. How was it possible that a team of highly trained operatives had allowed their own assignment to be captured by enemy forces? And here the General was, sedate and resigned, as if nothing could be done about it.

"So now what? We can't leave him to them." He was struggling not to raise his voice to the General, who didn't tolerate insubordination on any level. He was no ordinary KES agent, but on this point the General was as firm with him as with any other.

"They'll never believe he's not you, but eventually they'll see they can't get anything out of him," the General said. "And they'll realize that his only value is financial. I expect a ransom demand any day now."

"Will you pay it?" When it came to the General, Thomas could be sure of nothing.

"I suppose that depends on what they ask for." The General jerked his chin in Sasha's direction. "It's time."

"Sir, I—" It was unwise to oppose a direct order, but Thomas wasn't through talking about Grant. He wanted to know the particulars of what had happened that night on this side of the tandem. He needed to know if there was anything he could have done.

"Agent," the General said firmly. "It's time."

SHE SAT PERFECTLY STILL *on the bed in her tiny room. She didn't know much about this place, only that it wasn't large and it wasn't far away from the Castle, which disturbed her. Two weeks ago she'd met her coconspirator in a dark, unused corridor that belonged to a part of the Castle currently under construction. She found it satisfying that he needed her help with the actual escape. She'd taken him to the royal chapel, which had been quiet and empty, as it always was. Nobody practiced much religion in the UCC these days. They'd left the Citadel grounds by way of a secret passage that connected a trapdoor behind the altar to an exit built into the face of a large schist boulder outcropping that lined the edge of the Rambles, half a mile from the Castle. From there he'd borne her away in a moto, but not before blindfolding her, for "security purposes." And so, here she sat, a different sort of prisoner, with nothing to do but wait for her release. She was starting to wonder if it would ever come.*

The door opened, and a young girl—she couldn't have been older than twelve—entered with a tray. The girl's face blanched when she set eyes on the person she'd come to serve. Juliana smiled; she was used to this kind of reaction, especially from children. They just couldn't believe they were in her presence, after seeing her their whole lives as a two-dimensional figure on their home teleboxes or the press boards.

"Hello," Juliana said pleasantly. She'd resolved to be kind to everyone who wasn't him, *or someone who worked with him. If she'd*

learned anything these last few weeks, it was that salvation sometimes came from the most unexpected places. Then again, so did damnation.

The girl tried to return the greeting but couldn't seem to get the words out. She settled for putting the tray down on a little table in the corner. Juliana got up to examine its contents: a turkey sandwich cut diagonally down the middle, a bag of potato munchies bloated with air, an apple, an orange, and a cold bottle of sweet tea. She picked the sandwich up, a half in each hand, and offered one to the girl. "You hungry?"

The girl shook her head, though she was eyeing the sandwich somewhat keenly. Juliana shrugged and took a bite. The turkey was dry, the bread too soft and spread too thick with mayonnaise, the cheese tasteless and processed. Typical Libertas; they weren't much for luxury or comfort. After the opulence and overindulgence of Castle life, it was refreshing, but also sort of disappointing. Like it or not, she did have standards.

"Are you really the princess?" the girl asked after a time. Juliana had finished the whole sandwich and had started on the munchies, which were salty and delicious. She rarely ate junk food—she'd been on a strict diet since she was eleven, when her stepmother poked her stomach and told her that nobody wanted to look at a pudgy princess. To think she'd never have to worry about being a proper princess ever again. She could have munchies and chocolates and beer and red meat every day if she wanted to from here forward—assuming she made it out of this dungeon.

"I guess so," Juliana replied.

"Weird," the girl said, shaking her head as if to dislodge a bothersome thought.

"What do you mean?"

"It's just . . . well, some people said they saw you in the Tattered City yesterday," the girl told her. Juliana abandoned the munchies in her lap and gave the girl her full attention.

"That's impossible. I'm right here. I've been here for weeks and

it's a thousand miles to the Tattered City," Juliana pointed out. The kid was just playing with her.

"I know," the girl said, irritated at Juliana's patronizing tone. "But it was on the box at home, and then I saw it again on the press board over on Water and Broadway." The girl smiled, a wicked little gleam in her eye. "They say you were at a Libertas rally in Lake Park. There were a bunch of witnesses. Funny, huh?" She reached back to tighten her ponytail and her shirtsleeves rode up, revealing a wide fabric band fastened around her right wrist—an equilateral triangle of ten gold stars on a field of forest green.

Juliana narrowed her eyes at the girl, who seemed neither shy nor sweet anymore. A Libertine through and through, even at her age. She supposed it was to be expected; Libertas had been around for a quarter century, and they were good at planting seeds in people's heads. Made sense that they'd start with their children. But this news about the Tattered City was not sitting well with Juliana. She clearly wasn't there.

So if it wasn't her they'd seen, who was it?

TEN

I woke with a gasp and sat up like a jack-in-the-box. Adrenaline surged through my veins; beads of sweat gathered at my hairline, but other than that I felt . . . fine. Perfectly fine. I remembered the pain from before, the heavy sickness that had tugged me into darkness, but it was gone, all of it—all except for a tiny prick on my right pointer finger, which I could barely feel anyway. It was as if everything that had come before had been a dream. I didn't remember dreaming while I was asleep—unconscious—whatever—but a doomed feeling had crawled out of the darkness with me, settling like a black cloud in my chest; my mind was sticky with foreboding.

I heard a door slide closed behind me and turned toward the sound. The fluorescent lights were so intense that I had to hold my hand up to shield them; I could see at once that I was lying on a long cot in a large empty room. There was only one other piece of furniture, a wide table in the center of the floor with chairs surrounding it, but even it was dwarfed by the size of the space. The concrete walls were nearly invisible under layers of paper; the only section not plastered with maps or photographs or sheaves of notes was the wall just opposite me, the entire width of which was spanned by an enormous black shade.

This was definitely *not* a dream.

"Hello?" My voice traveled back to me on an echo. I was overcome with loneliness and dread. I almost wished the pain from before would return, just so I'd have something to concentrate on other than the ominous silence that blanketed the room.

"Hello?" I cried out again, louder now, hoping the sound of my own voice would comfort me, but instead the word came out strangled and half crazed. I was restless, my nerves thrumming; I couldn't stay in that bed one more second. I rushed to the door and began banging on it. "Let me out of here! Somebody help me! Let me *out*!"

There was a window in the door, but it was small, and there was no angle I could find that would allow me to see anything in the hallway that might give me a clue as to where I was. I thought back to what Thomas had said to me about Libertas, what they would do if they'd gotten ahold of me, and I wondered if I was their prisoner now. If that was the case, then where was Thomas? Surely his concern back in the alley wasn't for my safety alone, if he even cared about that at all; if they'd caught us, then what were they doing to *him*?

"Thomas!" I screamed. It was more likely, I figured, that Thomas had succeeded in his mission and brought me . . . where? Where I needed to be, he'd said. And where the hell was that? I shouted his name again, slamming my fist against the door. I'd pound until my hands were raw if that was what it took. He would come. He'd have to. I pressed my forehead against the cool metal and squeezed my eyes shut. I wouldn't cry. I wouldn't. I gave the door one last halfhearted thump with my open palm, then turned my back to it and let one heavy sob escape my throat, just one.

My gaze drifted around the room until something hanging nearby caught my eye. I walked over to the collage of documents tacked up to the wall. There, among the various papers, was a photograph of Granddad, a blown-up, grainy reproduction of the image that appeared on his faculty page on the University of Chicago website. Next to it hung a map of Hyde Park, with the location of my house—and Grant's—marked with big red Xs. There also was my most recent yearbook photo, my class schedule, and the Lab Schools' annual calendar with the date of prom highlighted, last semester's grade report, a picture of the Victorian and hand-drawn blueprints showing the rooms on every floor, and several other photos—me and Gina making faces at the camera, Granddad walking into the physics building carrying his briefcase, and, worst of all, a scan of the picture that sat on Granddad's mantel, the one that showed me and my parents at Disney World.

Sasha Lawson, I thought. *This is your life.*

He'd planned it all. I guess I knew that deep down, but I hadn't had much time to consider it before now. Thomas hadn't merely stumbled into my life; he'd *invaded* it, coldly calculating his entry and playing me like a fiddle until he ripped me out of my world and into his. The knowledge that I'd fallen for it hit me like a punch to the gut. Whatever my faults—and I had plenty—I'd never, ever thought I was capable of being such a fool, of not seeing what was right in front of my eyes.

On the opposite side of the room hung two huge maps. At first glance, they were almost identical; they both showed the North American continent, with its odd, familiar shape. But upon closer examination, I realized they were in fact quite different. One was a map of the United States in the present day. I located Chicago easily; it was marked by an orange pushpin on the edge of Lake Michigan. But the other map was different, to say the least. Instead of the fifty states, it depicted two countries, separated by a winding black border along the Mississippi River. The eastern half, the United Commonwealth of Columbia, was partitioned into twenty or so "King's Dominions": the original thirteen colonies, plus West Florida, East Florida, Alabama, Mississippi, Illinois, Indiana, Ohio, and Michigan. Some states had been combined, or simply never existed in the first place. Maine was annexed to Massachusetts, Virginia and West Virginia were a single Dominion, Indiana included Kentucky and Tennessee, and Michigan and Wisconsin were joined together. The western half of the map was labeled "Farnham," and it, too, was divided, by two vertical lines, creating three "Regions": Louisiana, Mountain, and California.

What had happened in this world to make it look this way? I wondered as I traced the borders idly with my fingertip. And what, if anything, did it have to do with me?

The door slid open and I jumped, shocked half to death by the first sound that wasn't of my own making. Thomas strode into the room, his expression placid but alert. Before I even knew what I was doing, I flew at him, meaning to hit him, but he caught my wrists and held me at arm's length.

"I'll thank you not to assault my employees, Miss Lawson." I heard the voice before I saw the man. A moment later, he stepped out from behind Thomas, and I got a good look at him. He was no more than two inches taller than me, with dark hair, too dark given his age; in the harsh fluorescent light his face looked dry and creased. He was in his early sixties, definitely; he wore a pair of rimless glasses that reminded me of Granddad's.

In all other ways, though, this man was nothing like Granddad. He was impeccably dressed in a pressed gray pinstriped suit with a white shirt and a silver tie, his shoes perfectly shined. He made no sound as he slowly crossed the linoleum floor.

The older man's presence in the room was unsettling, but all I cared about was extricating myself from Thomas's steel grip.

"Let go of me," I snapped. Thomas was completely unfazed and held me fast, though gently, as if he was doing his best not to hurt me. He must've been under orders not to damage the merchandise.

"Only if you stop trying to bash my face in," he said in a low voice.

"No promises," I said through gritted teeth.

"Agent Mayhew, release her," the man commanded. Thomas did so at once and stepped back, clearly believing I'd swing at him again as soon as I was able, but I no longer had the strength. Besides, it was clear that Thomas wasn't the one in charge here, and giving him a good thump on the head wasn't going to get me anywhere.

"Good girl," the man said in a patronizing tone that made my hands clench into fists. "Now, why don't you have a seat?"

"I'll stand, thanks." I wasn't really in a position to be mouthing off, but I couldn't resist.

"You'll sit," the man said coldly, gripping the back of the chair. When I hesitated, he continued, "You'll sit or I'll have Agent Mayhew strap you down."

Reluctantly, I sank into the chair, seeing that it was fruitless to argue. For the first time, I noticed just how cold the room was, like a walk-in refrigerator. Was it always this cold, or was it for my benefit, to shake me up even more than I already was? I *was* shaken, deeply. My insolence was more a reflex than a show of bravery, and I wasn't sure I had either Thomas or his nameless superior convinced. But it made me feel better, to give him a little lip.

"Who are you?" I demanded.

"My name is unimportant. Around here, they call me the General."

"Where's 'here'?"

"Where to begin?" The General stroked his chin thoughtfully. "Thomas has already apprised you of the fact that you're no longer in your home universe, I'm assuming." I shrugged, which he took as confirmation. "In that case, welcome to Aurora. You're in Columbia City, the capital of the United Commonwealth of Columbia." My eyes grew wider as I attempted to process the things that he was saying, but he wasn't giving me any time to wrap my head around them. "This the Citadel, the flagship royal military compound of the city. To be precise, you're in the Tower, which is my domain. I am the Head of Defense in this country, and you, Miss Lawson, are my prisoner."

"Your what?" Hearing myself referred to as a prisoner upset me terribly as I realized that, of course, it was the truth. I was entirely at the General's mercy. Any notion that I'd simply been mistaken for someone else—the person they really wanted—evaporated.

"I don't understand," I protested. "Why would you want to kidnap me? I haven't done anything!"

The General's eyebrows lifted. "I find it interesting that you believe this may have something to do with what you've *done,* but I assure you, that is not the case. In fact, it has nothing to do with what you've done. It has everything to do with what you *are.*"

"Don't you mean *who* I am?"

He shook his head. "No. I don't."

"What am I, then?" I said, in a voice so low it was practically a whisper. I wasn't anything but a teenage girl! Surely that was *obvious*.

"Does it strike you as curious that I keep answering your impertinent questions?"

"Not really. If I didn't think you'd answer them, I wouldn't ask them." I risked a glance at Thomas, who was standing near the door, his back straight as a pillar, hands clasped together near the base of his stomach. He stared at them as if they had something fascinating written on them, but I could tell from the tension in his shoulders and the slight incline of his head in my direction that he was paying very close attention to what we were saying. What a coward. He couldn't even meet my eyes.

"It isn't because you're particularly adept at interrogation," the General continued. "I'm telling you these things because I need you to know them. But the time for questions is over. Now it's your job to listen."

I was struck dumb. Growing up with an old-fashioned guy like Granddad had given me a healthy respect for authority, but nobody had ever spoken to me like this before. The General terrified me. My limbs felt loose and heavy, and I could barely lift my head. I hadn't realized before how much strength I'd drawn from the knowledge that I was not friendless in the world, that I had people who loved me and looked after me. In Aurora, that wasn't true, and I was starting to see just what a liability it was to be alone.

The General paused. "All right, then, I'll answer one last question. You asked what you are. You're an analog, and a valuable one at that."

"What—?" I began, but he cut me off.

"What's an analog?" The General leaned forward, as if he was about to tell me a very juicy secret. "Agent Mayhew, what is one of the most fundamental axioms of the multiverse?" He didn't look at Thomas even as he spoke to him. The General only had eyes for me, it seemed.

"Everything repeats," Thomas said, a mechanical recitation. He'd been asked this before.

"Exactly. Everything repeats. Over and over, again and again, throughout the multiverse, atoms assemble according to predetermined patterns." He said this in a philosophical way, like he really was contemplating the beauty and grandeur of the cosmos. By the time he said his next words, I had a pretty good idea what he was getting at, and I didn't like the sound of it *at all*. "An analog is a double. We all have them; if not in one universe, then in another, and in an infinite number of others besides. And as it happens, *you* have an analog in this universe who is very, very important. So important, in fact, that I have spent a considerable amount of money and resources to bring you here so that you might replace her."

"*Replace* her? Replace her how? Who *is* she?"

"Her name is Juliana," the General told me. "And she's the princess of this realm."

I drew in a sharp breath. *No,* I thought wildly. *It can't be.* The girl I'd dreamt of all these years—Juliana, the princess, the girl with my face—she was *real*. I was here because of *her*. The dreams, then—were they even dreams at all? Or were they something else altogether? Visions? Omens? Predictions? I didn't believe in things like that. Raised by a scientist, in a house without religion, I wasn't a superstitious person. Yet somehow I'd known all along. How could that be?

"Is she . . . ?" I couldn't bring myself to finish the question.

"Dead? No, she's not," the General said. "Or, rather, we have no evidence to suggest that she is."

"What happened to her, then?" I didn't know this girl, this Juliana; she wasn't me, and I wasn't her, just as Thomas wasn't Grant and vice versa. But the thought of her dead was devastating. I became light-headed with something that felt like grief. But how could I grieve for someone I hadn't even known was real until two seconds ago? How could I grieve for someone I'd never met? It was a relief to hear she wasn't dead, but that was clearly not the whole story.

"Juliana's been kidnapped," the General explained. There was no emotion in his voice, nothing to suggest he cared in the least about Juliana. But Thomas had shifted, almost imperceptibly, at his post, and I saw that he was fidgeting with the ring on his finger, looking truly anxious for the first time since he'd told me who he really was. "A revolutionary group called Libertas that operates within our borders abducted her."

"Why would they do that?"

"Libertas's goal is to destabilize the monarchy that has ruled this country for over two hundred years. Removing Juliana from these premises and holding her for ransom is their latest bid to do just that."

At the mention of Libertas, Thomas looked directly at me for the first time. His eyes widened, and he shook his head. He was telling me not to mention our run-in with Libertas to the General. Clearly he hadn't told his superiors about what had happened back in the alley. Who was he trying to protect—me, or himself?

"Just pay the ransom, then," I said. "You don't need me."

"Unfortunately, their demands are too high, and anyway, even if we acquiesced, they wouldn't return her to us. Libertas never plays fair." The General sat back in his chair. "So you see, I had no choice but to bring you here, so that you can act as princess in her stead while we search for her."

"No choice? Of course you have a choice! Just give them what they want and hope for the best!" I cried. "You can't do this! You can't just tear me away from my home."

"Obviously I *can,* Miss Lawson, because I *have.* You can scream and cry and throw tantrums and make nasty remarks all you like, but that will not change the plain fact that I have you trapped here in Aurora and there is no way for you to get home. Now," he continued, "I could be persuaded to *send* you home, and soon, provided you do everything I ask of you, without question."

"How soon?"

"Six days," the General told me. "Six days during which you give a convincing performance as Juliana and follow every order that descends from my office. That will be your ticket out of here. Do we have a deal?"

"Why six days?" It seemed like an awfully specific period of time, and something told me the General hadn't chosen it at random.

"Ah, well, there remains a part of our situation that I haven't yet informed you of. The UCC comprises the eastern half of the landmass you know as the United States, but there's another country, called Farnham, that controls the rest. Without boring you with centuries of bloody history, I can tell you that Farnham and the UCC have been at war almost continuously since our countries were founded around the turn of the nineteenth century. Six months ago, diplomatic representatives from both countries reached an agreement; a peace treaty would be signed that would prevent any further conflict, and to seal that treaty, the princess of the Commonwealth would marry one of the princes of Farnham.

And that wedding is finally going to take place—a week from today."

"You want me to get married? I'm *sixteen*!"

"So is Juliana. And yet . . ." The General shrugged. "We all must do what is necessary to fulfill our obligations. I'm sure you don't care what happens to the people of this country, and I can't blame you for that. Why should you give a damn about a place where you don't belong? However, I'm quite willing to go to the ends of the world—and beyond—to preserve the safety and happiness of the citizens of the Commonwealth to which I've pledged my life and service for the past forty years. Your presence here is proof of that fact." He sat back, hands clasped in his lap, and gazed at me. After a moment of silent contemplation he continued:

"You'll do as I say. Six days as Juliana and you'll go free. I'll return you to your home and this will all be a distant memory." He stood and walked to the door. When he reached it, he turned back to me. "Agent Mayhew will take over from here. You'll regard everything he tells you as a directive from me; you'll obey and follow him, wherever he leads you. Do I make myself clear?"

I lifted my head, my eyes burning with defiance. "What if I refuse?"

"Then I will have Agent Mayhew draw his sidearm and shoot you," the General said coolly, as if he was talking about the weather. "I caution you not to treat this as a game, Miss Lawson, because I certainly don't." He glanced at Thomas. "She's yours. Don't let me down."

"I won't, sir," he said, the weasel.

"Good." The door slid open, and the General left as quietly as he had come. When he was gone, the dam broke; I dropped my face into my hands and sobbed.

It was only later that I realized the General had said Juliana was supposed to be married in a week, yet he was only forcing me to act as her for six days. I couldn't imagine there was anything wrong with his math, which raised the question: what was going to happen in six days?

ELEVEN

Thomas appeared at my side. He reached out and I shrank away.

"Don't touch me!" I cried, my voice wet with tears.

"I was only trying to give you this." He held out a handkerchief. I ripped it from his hand and used it to wipe my face, but as soon as my eyes were dry another flood came. I couldn't believe this was happening. Just days ago, I was in Hyde Park, living out my normal, uneventful life, and now here I was, trapped in another world, being forced to pretend to be someone else under threat of death. No matter how I tried, I couldn't figure out a way to make sense of it. I just wanted to be alone, but Thomas refused to leave.

"I have to stay with you," he said. "General's orders."

"I hate you," I seethed. Every time I looked at him, all I could think was how betrayed I felt. And the worst part was, it didn't matter. He'd made me no promises, had no loyalty to me. If I'd trusted him, that was my mistake. I could be angry with him all I wanted, hate him with all the strength I had left in me; that was my right. But how could I feel betrayed by someone who had come into my life with the explicit intention of deceiving me?

Thomas nodded. "I don't blame you."

I scoffed into his handkerchief. "Yeah, right."

"Believe what you want," he told me. "But I'd hate me, too, if I were you."

I turned my back to him. He moved behind me, toward the wide black screen, and my ears caught a soft, mechanical whirring. I wanted to know what he was doing, but I was too proud to show interest. After a while, the whirring stopped, only to be replaced by a humming noise. It took me a second or two to work out that it was Thomas singing softly to himself.

"Is that supposed to be a joke?" I whirled around and glared at him. I recognized the song. The dj had played it at our—my—prom. We'd danced to it under a cheesy disco ball. A rush of memory threatened to overcome me, but I stood my ground against it; I wasn't going to be drawn back into everything I'd felt when I believed that lie, when I'd thought it was the start of something instead of the end of my life as I knew it.

Thomas shrugged, feigning innocence. "I like that song."

"You'd never even *heard* that song before . . . before then," I said, fumbling for words. I wanted to appear as aloof and untouched by our time together as he did, but I was struggling to balance detachment with bitterness. "You're just trying to upset me!"

"No, I'm not. I'm trying to get your attention. And look—it worked."

"What's *wrong* with you?" I shouted. "Don't you understand what you've done? Doesn't it bother you at all that your boss just threatened to have you *shoot* me if I don't pretend to be this—this other girl?"

"Juliana," he said flatly.

"I don't care what her name is!"

"Well, you should," Thomas told me, a little peevish, which was rich, coming from him. "You should want to know everything about her. If you're going to pretend to be somebody else, knowledge is crucial. Believe me, I know."

I almost told him then. I don't know why, but I felt an overwhelming need to tell *somebody,* and he was the only person in the room. I had to bite my tongue to keep from saying that I knew more than he thought I did about Juliana, because I'd been seeing her in my dreams ever since I could remember.

But what *did* I know? It was hard to put my finger on it, and even harder to explain it. I wouldn't have been able to name a single person that she knew. I only had flashes of her life, buried deep in my memory, pieces I had never before thought to analyze for anything significant, because I'd had no idea that the dreams were anything more than that: *dreams*. Images that my tired brain threw off like light from a dying sparkler. If I was seeing into her life, was she seeing into mine as well? Did she know I existed, like *really* existed, or did she think that I, too, was just a fantasy born of secret wishes and an overactive imagination?

"Then tell me something useful," I demanded. "What do I need to know?"

The weight of Thomas's gaze was heavy. He looked at me like I was some sort of code he was trying to decipher, as if staring at me long enough would tell him something about me, something he didn't already know. He indicated the wall behind him; the screen had pulled back to reveal a large, floor-to-ceiling picture window. The overhead lights gave the glass a mirrored effect. I stared at my reflection, trying to imagine it having a life, a name, a personality of its own. *Juliana*. It just didn't seem possible. My face was my face; it belonged to me, and nobody else. Even when I could be sure of nothing else, I knew that to be true. I was me, and me alone, something no one else could claim. The thought that there was someone out there who saw the same thing I did when she looked in the mirror was almost too much to contemplate.

But how do we get to the other universes? I'd asked Granddad once, when I was a kid.

We don't, he'd said.

But why? I knew that the worlds we invented together were silly, but Granddad seemed to sincerely believe that other universes besides ours existed. If so, where were they, and how could I get there? I wanted to know so badly.

Because, he'd said. *We were all made for one world, and one world only, Sasha. If universes were to collide, bad things would happen. They're separate for a reason.* At the time, I didn't understand what he meant, but now I was starting to get it.

"Would you like to see the city?" Thomas asked. "It's a clear night."

"I've seen a city before, thanks," I snapped. "How different could it be?"

"You'd be surprised," he said, unshaken by my tone.

I inched closer to the window, taking care to maintain a distance between Thomas and me. He reached to the side and pressed a button I couldn't see; the room went dark.

"You can see it better with the lights off," he explained.

It took a second for my eyes to adjust, but when they did I saw it: a river of undulating green light high in the sky. If I needed any more proof that Juliana's world, the one I saw when I slept, was real, this clinched it.

"I don't understand," I breathed. I was captivated by the glow of the aurora borealis, something I never imagined I'd see in person. It had always been my favorite part of the dreams. A feeling of calmness and relief flooded my body.

I had to tear my eyes away from it in order to assess the view from the window. We were more than a hundred stories up, which, aurora or not, made me feel wretched. I'd never been very good with heights; when my class had gone to visit the Sears Tower in the fourth grade, I'd had to stay inside one of the gift shops with a chaperone because I couldn't bear standing so close to such a long, steep drop. The huge window made it seem like I could step out over the edge and plunge straight to the ground below. Just standing so close to such a terrifying precipice made my palms sweat and my heart race. I stayed far away from the glass and stared off into the distance.

We were towering over a star-shaped complex of squat, dark buildings, before which was a long, tree-filled park and, beyond that, a glittering city, spread like a blanket beneath our feet, an imprecise but lovely replica of the star-filled sky above our heads, where the aurora danced and spun. Cars like insects moved through the streets below, which were laid out in a meticulous grid; elevated trains glided like eels above them, their steel roofs glinting in the moonlight. As far as I could see, we were standing in the tallest building for miles; none other even came close to half our height. The room was up so high that I could see the shadowy contours of the city, how it tapered to a point and ended on the shores of a placid river.

I heard a faint rustle of plastic and looked over to see Thomas pulling a handful of candies out of his pocket. He popped them in his mouth one by one and chewed them in a slow, rhythmic fashion that by the fourth or fifth time was pretty much annoying the *crap* out of me.

"You're eating right now?" Once I said that, I realized that I was starving.

He fished the entire bag out of his pocket and offered it to me. "Want one?"

I eyed them suspiciously. "What are they?"

"Toggles," he said. "They're chocolate with fruit jelly in the middle. Red's strawberry, purple is raspberry, blue's watermelon, although I've never seen a blue watermelon in my life so I'm not sure where they get off—"

"No thanks," I interrupted. "That sounds disgusting. Plus, I'm allergic to chocolate."

"You are?"

"What? You don't have my medical records taped up somewhere in here?"

His eyes skimmed over the paper-covered walls. "I thought I did. . . ."

"Forget it. Just stop talking to me."

I turned my attention back to the cityscape below. *It's an island,* I thought in passing. But where? I'd assumed we were in North America, but if the aurora was in the sky, we had to be somewhere very far north. The aurora was . . . there were no words for what it was. "Beautiful" felt used up, meaningless. The way the green waves moved through the indigo sky called to my mind the weightless grace of ballet dancers, the spreading of ink through water, the way ribbons spun in a breeze. It was mesmerizing, and as I watched it, fatigue began to settle over me. It was hard to believe that a place that contained something so amazing as the aurora could also be my prison, but Earth had the aurora, too, and possessed countless horrors of its own.

"Manhattan," Thomas told me. I bit my lip in frustration. When the General was giving me my marching orders,

Thomas hadn't said a word; now, he seemed incapable of staying silent.

"This can't be Manhattan," I protested, realizing I was going to have to talk to him since I was stuck with him for the next six days. "New York is too far south to see the aurora borealis."

"That's not the aurora borealis. It's the aurora universalis." He swiped a finger across the length of the sky, not quite touching the glass. "You can see it everywhere here. That's how the planet got its name. It's one of the differences." He looked over at me, as if trying to judge how this information was landing. "And I never said this was New York."

"But Manhattan is part of New York," I pointed out, although as soon as the words were out of my mouth I realized I was being a little dim. This wasn't Earth; I couldn't expect everything to be the same.

"Not here. Like the General said, this is Columbia City. It used to be New York, a long time ago, but they changed the name when the split from England was final, as a kind of symbolic act."

"What do you mean '*one* of the differences'?"

"Your planet—Earth—and this planet—Aurora—are analogs," he said. *That word again,* I thought. *Analog.*

"Why do you call them that? If they're doubles, then why don't you just say 'double'?"

"Because 'double' is an imprecise term," he said. He sounded like he was quoting someone, the words not quite his own. "A double is an exact copy, with absolutely no differences. An analog *can* be a double, but it doesn't have to be; analogs can be different in some ways, large or small, but still similar, if that makes any sense."

"Um, not really. How can something be the same, but also sometimes different?"

"Well, take this, for example," he said, gesturing toward the view from the window. "Earth and Aurora are essentially the same planet: same mass, same orbit, same axis, same natural surface geography. The only thing that makes Aurora special is that its magnetic field is two and a half times that of Earth's. That's why you can see the lights so far south. You see? They're similar, but not the same. 'Equivalent' is probably the best word. Essentially equal, but not identical."

"Is that why you look like Grant but your name is Thomas?"

He nodded. "And why you look like Princess Juliana but you have a different identity. Not copies. Not twins. Not look-alikes. Analogs."

"Analogs," I repeated. "But why?"

"Why?" He appeared genuinely confused by the question.

"Why you and Grant? Why me and . . . her? What connects us to our analogs?"

What I really wanted to ask was "Why can I see Juliana's life in my dreams?" It couldn't have been normal, otherwise he would know I could do it, and I was pretty sure he didn't suspect anything of the sort. But I didn't ask. I didn't trust him, and I wasn't ready to hear the answer.

Thomas shrugged. "Nobody knows. Not for sure, anyway. Until about thirty years ago, all this was completely theoretical—in your world it still is."

"Tell me about her." Though I'd been glimpsing Juliana's life in my dreams ever since I could remember, I didn't know much about her, but I wanted to.

"Juliana?" I nodded. "Well, she's . . . she's tough. The way she was raised, it seems like a fairy tale, but it hasn't been, at least not for a long time. Life's been cruel to her, especially recently."

"You mean the wedding?" I couldn't imagine being forced

to marry someone I didn't know just to satisfy someone else's political agenda. And if the General's explanation had been anything to go by, Juliana's fiancé was practically her enemy, the prince of a country that had been at war with her own since before she was alive.

Thomas bit back a bitter laugh. "Actually, that's the least of it."

"What's the worst?"

"A couple of months ago, her father, the king, was shot during a public event," Thomas told me. "By Libertas," he added.

I felt as though I'd swallowed a stone; a great heaviness settled in my stomach, the echoes of a grief I knew all too well. It must've shown on my face, what I was thinking, because Thomas rushed to assure me that the king hadn't died. "Although some people might think it would've been better if he had."

"How do you mean?"

"Well, he's not himself anymore. The bullet lodged in his brain, and while it didn't kill him, the surgeons couldn't remove it. He's in this strange sort of in-between state. Not a coma, really, because sometimes he's awake, but he's pretty incoherent most of the time. He doesn't talk much, and he definitely can't rule."

"So who's leading the country?"

"His wife, the queen regent. She's Juliana's stepmother, the king's second wife. Not a lot of love lost between Juliana and the queen. You'll have to watch out for her; she and Juliana have never gotten along, even before everything happened with the king, and she can be spiteful."

I closed my eyes as the enormity of my task threatened to overwhelm me. "I don't see how you and the General expect me to do this. You don't know what you're asking."

Thomas pressed his lips together. "You won't be doing it alone. I'm going to help you."

"How are you going to do that?"

"I'm not just a transporter," Thomas said. It was incredible how steady he could keep his voice, how calm he was in this very strange situation. I resented his perfect composure. It made me feel wild and untethered, entirely at the mercy of something besides my own rational mind, which wasn't like me at all. It was also not the way to be if I wanted to go home again. I had to be just like Thomas. I had to push my feelings way, way down so that they couldn't rise up and defeat me. I wouldn't let him be stronger than me.

"Then what are you?"

"I'm Juliana's lead bodyguard," Thomas said. "I know her pretty well. We've spent a lot of time together, and I can coach you through the next six days, if you'll let me."

"And if I won't?"

"I don't know," he said. "Maybe you'll do just fine."

He nodded to me as if to say goodbye and stepped back from the window, making his way toward the door. When he reached the middle of the room, he stopped and turned; I swiveled my head and our eyes locked. The room was dark, but I could still see his face, illuminated by the aurora and the moon that shone through the window like a spotlight.

"Of course," he said with a casual lift of his eyebrows, "it's not going to be easy, considering you've never met her."

I stared at him. "Where are your parents?"

The question surprised him. I felt a thrill at having caught him off guard. "My parents?"

"Yeah. If you're Grant's analog, then you're probably the same age," I said. "Right?" He nodded. "Which means you're, what, eighteen? Most of the guys I know are picking out colleges, not serving as bodyguards to a princess or running covert operations in parallel universes and kidnapping girls. Your parents just let you do this?"

"My parents are dead," he told me coldly. "I'm pretty sure they're beyond caring what I do."

"Oh." For a moment I felt bad, but my parents were dead, too, and I led a normal life. Well, I had up until recently, anyway. "I'm sorry. What . . . happened?"

"What always happens here," Thomas told me. "War with Farnham. My parents were both in the military, and we were stationed on a base near St. Louis, right along the border between Farnham and the Commonwealth. It's a heavily disputed territory, even now. They'd called a ceasefire, so things were supposed to be relatively safe, but Farnham launched a sneak attack and bombed the hell out of the base one morning. The death count was . . . substantial. Both of my parents died instantly." He closed his eyes for a second, as if experiencing a wave of intense emotion, which of course made sense, and came as a welcome relief to me. He could feel things. Some things, anyway.

"But you didn't," I said.

"No," he said. "I didn't."

We both fell silent. Finally, Thomas spoke. "I didn't tell you that story to make you feel sorry for me. You can still hate me all you want, I don't care. But I hope it gives you a sense of how important this treaty with Farnham—and Juliana's marriage to the prince—is to this world. We wouldn't have gone through all the trouble of bringing you here if we didn't have a very good reason." He shook his head, a bit sadly, I thought. "I don't know about you, but preserving the lives of hundreds of thousands of people on both sides is a damn good reason to me. I'm not going to insult you with apologies, because I'm not sorry I did what I did. Sorry it had to come to this, maybe, but that's it."

I didn't know what to do with his speech. He sounded so self-assured, and yet so conflicted. Thomas confused me. One moment he was cold and unfeeling; the next he was passionate and insistent. Much as I hated to admit it, I found him interesting. I didn't trust or like him, but I felt for him. I knew what it was like to lose your parents. I knew it was something you never got over, even though your life carried on without them. I'd been lucky; I had Granddad, who'd taken me in when I was alone, who'd made me feel loved and safe. I couldn't know for sure, but I suspected that Thomas had not been so fortunate.

"What happened to you?" We needed a different topic, and I'd noticed he was holding his hand strangely, as if it hurt. The moonlight filtering in through the window was strong and bright, and I could see that purplish bruises had started to form at the base of his thumb.

"Oh." He gave me a sheepish smile. "Well, you fell on me."

"What?"

"When we entered Aurora," he explained. "Passing through the tandem always causes a disruption—" I scrunched up my face in confusion. "It's like a ripple effect, a by-product of the energy it takes to move between universes. When we landed in Aurora, there was a small tremor, and I lost my grip on you. We fell, and . . . you landed funny. On my hand."

Part of me wished I'd broken it. "Well, sorry."

"Don't be. I didn't do myself any favors by punching out those Libertas guys." He shrugged. "One of the perks of being KES. It'd take me a week to list all the injuries I've sustained doing this job, so I'm used to it. It'll heal up quick."

"How many times have you gone through the tandem?"

"A dozen or so," Thomas told me. "Not a lot, but more than most people. Nobody knows about the tandem except a handful of KES, and the scientists who work on developing many-worlds technology, like that anchor you're wearing. It's a highly classified project. In the scheme of things, you're actually pretty special. There are probably only twenty or so people who've even passed through the tandem, and you're one of them."

"Where do I send the gift basket?" Like getting kidnapped was some kind of honor! Still, I did want to know more about how moving between universes worked.

It turned out there was a limit to what he could tell me. "I'm not so good with the physics of it," he admitted. "I know what I need to know—what happens when you pass through, and, of course, how to use the anchor."

"And how does the anchor work?"

He gave me a rueful smile. "Nice try."

"Okay, then tell me about the disruptions," I pressed. "Do they happen every time?"

He nodded. "As far as I can tell, they're proportional to how much mass you're bringing into the universe, or removing from it. The more massive the object, the more energy it takes to bring it through, the greater the disruption. When it's just you and me, the mass is tiny, especially by the universe's standards. So all you get is a little quake, something you'd barely notice if you weren't standing right at the epicenter."

"What if you wanted to bring through something bigger?"

He ran his fingers through his hair, rumpling it. He seemed tired, and all of a sudden he looked young to me, with his hair sticking up in the back and the moonlight picking up the wrinkles in his suit. "Like what?"

"I don't know. A skyscraper?"

"Not sure why you'd want to do that."

"It's hypothetical," I said.

"I'm not even certain that you *could* do that," Thomas said, after pausing to think it over. "It'd require a huge amount of energy, and unless it landed in exactly the right way, the whole thing could just fall apart. The disruption would be big, too, which would cause major structural damage to the building and those around it. Why do you ask?"

I shrugged. "No reason. I was just curious." I'd never been good enough at science to consider making a career out of it, even though, as Thomas had pointed out on the beach, it was the family business. But I knew enough to be interested, and it delayed the start of my performance as Juliana.

It was just two weeks ago that I'd last dreamt about her. I'd woken up full of apprehension. She'd been experiencing something difficult and painful, but I didn't understand what, or why, until now—she'd been busy getting kidnapped. Another question pushed its way past the walls I'd erected against these strange sensations and lodged itself in my brain: would I continue to see life through her eyes now that I was in her world? Only time would tell, but I had the distinct impression that I'd had other dreams while I was unconscious—both times—though I didn't remember them. But I couldn't count on that now. I had to dredge my memory for any lucid details that could be useful to me here, and hope for the best.

"Now what?" I didn't want to bring up the future; the conversation about the tandem and its idiosyncrasies had relaxed me a bit, and Thomas's earlier stiffness and formality had given way to something much more human, much closer to the boy he had been on Earth, when I'd thought he was

Grant. I didn't want to scare that all away by calling his attention back to the situation at hand, but there wasn't a choice. We had to move forward—*I* had to, if I was ever going to get home.

"Now," he said. "We call Gloria."

TWELVE

"Who's Gloria?" I asked. All the easiness I'd felt in talking to Thomas before dissolved in the face of meeting someone else from this world.

"Gloria is Juliana's personal secretary and aide-de-camp," Thomas explained. I tried to imagine what this person might be like, but couldn't. "She knows who you are."

"She does?"

"She has to," Thomas said. "I'm going to give you as much help as I can, but there's only so much I can do—there's only so much I know. Gloria's been with Juliana since the princess was twelve. She keeps her schedule and manages her staff. She'll be an invaluable resource for you."

"How many other people know?"

"Of the ones you'll actually meet, it's just me, the General, and Gloria. And Fillmore, of course." I grimaced. I thought I saw him smile, but it might've just been a trick of the light. "There are a few others, but nobody you need to worry about. I would save all your energy for the people who *don't* know who you are."

He pressed a button on a small console to the right of the door. It beeped and he spoke into it. "Send Gloria in."

In moments, the door slid open and a tall, brown-skinned woman entered. Her hair was pulled back into a tight French twist and she was dressed professionally, despite the hour, in a gray twill pencil skirt, perfectly pressed black blouse, sheer black tights, and a pair of high black stiletto heels. She carried a square glass tablet in her hand and wore a serious expression.

"Gloria Beach," Thomas said, stepping aside to let the woman pass. "This is Sasha Lawson."

Gloria allowed several seconds of silence to go by, fixing me with a penetrating look. "I would say it's a pleasure to meet you, Ms. Lawson, but I don't think that would be true for either of us. That said, I hope you understand that I'm here to help you. Nobody wants Juliana back more than I do, but until the General manages to locate her, I'm afraid we have no choice."

"Well, I certainly didn't." The words came out harsher than I'd intended, but Gloria nodded in understanding.

"Thomas, turn the lights on," Gloria commanded. "I want to get a good look at her." The fluorescents flickered for a moment before dousing the room in bright white light.

Gloria walked a circle around me, regarding me closely. "It's amazing, really, how much you look like Juliana."

"I'm not her," I insisted.

"No, of course not," Gloria said. "But how you look is the single most important factor in whether or not people will *believe* that you're Juliana, which is the ultimate goal. With the right clothes, hair, and makeup, even her own mother couldn't tell the difference."

"Where is Juliana's mother?" I asked. Thomas had mentioned a stepmother, the queen regent, and her incapacitated father, but surely Juliana had a mother as well? My heart burned with jealousy. It wasn't fair that she had two parents—

three, counting her stepmother—while I had none. *It's one of the differences,* I imagined Thomas saying. To me, at least, it was the greatest difference of all.

Thomas looked to Gloria, who explained. Juliana's parents had married when her mother, Alana Defort, was very young; up until then, the king was considered to be a confirmed bachelor, and everyone was shocked not only that he had decided to marry, but also that his wife was so dramatically his junior. She was from an old Commonwealth family that had made millions in textiles several generations earlier, and the only heir to their considerable fortune. Their marriage had lasted just short of ten years, and they divorced when Juliana was eight because the king had met someone else.

"Her name was Evelyn Eaves then," Gloria said. "She was a lawyer with the Royal Counsel. Everyone knew that the king had affairs, but to actually marry one of his mistresses was nothing short of scandal. Needless to say, Juliana and her stepmother don't get along, especially since the king had Juliana's mother exiled."

"Exiled?" It sounded like such an old-fashioned punishment for a woman whose sole crime was being a wife the king had grown bored with. Although, kings on Earth had done far worse than that with wives they considered extraneous. "Isn't that a little extreme?"

"Alana fought the divorce," Gloria said, pursing her lips in displeasure. She was clearly not enamored of the king or the queen regent. "It was all over the press boards for years, and everyone came out looking just awful. The king considered the bad publicity to be traitorous and forced her out of the country. She now lives just over the border in the Canadian Republic. Juliana is allowed to visit her, but Alana hasn't been back to the Commonwealth since the divorce was final. She's not even being permitted to attend the wedding."

It was hard not to feel sorry for Juliana. I missed my parents every second of every day, but even though they were gone, I was sure that they'd loved me, and each other. It was cold comfort sometimes, but other times, it actually helped to remember that.

Oh my God, I thought with a start. *My parents.*

"If I'm Juliana's analog," I said, the words coming out in a rush. "Then are her mom and dad analogs of *my* mom and dad?" It seemed like too much to hope for, but was it possible that I might be able to see my parents for the first time in a decade?

Thomas shook his head, and something inside me crumpled.

"It doesn't really work like that," Thomas said. "Our worlds . . . they're too different now. Maybe a long time ago that would've been the case, but too much has changed."

"What do you mean, too much has changed?"

Thomas took a seat, leaning forward with his elbows on his knees. He looked worn down, tired. I tried not to sympathize with him too much—after all, he'd chosen a life that had put him in the path of danger. But exhaustion didn't diminish his handsomeness, which at this point seemed to exist only to torment me. It got under my skin, how good-looking I couldn't help thinking he was, even after everything. Why couldn't awful people be ugly and good people beautiful, without exception? It would've made things so much easier.

"It might be helpful if you can manage to think of all the possible universes as many branches of a tree," Thomas began. "In the beginning, they were all the same—like a trunk. But as time goes on, changes start to happen—just small ones at first—changes that differentiate the universes, make them unique. In one world, you get up on time for school, and in another you're late. In one world you eat pizza for lunch, in another you have a turkey sandwich. No big deal, right? But change causes more change, and before you know it, the universes aren't so similar anymore. Does that make sense?"

Sense? None of this made any *sense*, really, but it wasn't so far off from things I'd heard Granddad talk about in the past. "Your basic ripple effect," I supplied.

"Exactly. At least, that was how it was explained to me." Thomas fixed his eyes on me, and I could've sworn they were brighter than before. "It doesn't even have to take that long. It's only been a couple hundred years since the Aurora-Earth LCE and look how different our two worlds already are."

"LCE?"

"The Last Common Event," Thomas said. "The moment where the timelines on Earth and Aurora fully separated."

"What was that?" Granddad would've been fascinated by all this information; so would my parents. They had spent their entire careers searching for proof of alternate universes—they would've been amazed to find out just how right their theories were.

"George Washington was killed during the Revolutionary War," Thomas said. "Or, as we call it, the First Revolution. There was a Second Revolution in 1789, this time led by a British nobleman named John Rowan who used his power as the governor of the New York Colony to raise an army against the Crown. After he succeeded in overthrowing British rule, he crowned himself king and renamed the country the United Commonwealth of Columbia, after Christopher Columbus. He established his capital in New York and renamed it Columbia City." Thomas smiled. "Aurora 101."

"So what you're saying is, even though Juliana and I look the same, we don't have the same parents, or backgrounds, or anything?"

"Juliana's a different person," he said with a helpless shrug. "Wholly and completely. I'm not a physicist; I can't explain it more than that."

"But my parents do have analogs in Aurora, don't they? Even if they're not Juliana's parents, they still exist?" Thomas drew in a deep breath. "You know who they are, don't you?"

"Your mother's analog is a schoolteacher in Virginia Dominion," Thomas told me. "She's got three kids, two boys and a girl." I blinked. Three kids? I would've given anything for just one sibling—sister, brother, I couldn't have cared less, as long as I had someone who understood, who knew what it meant to have had my parents and then lost them.

"And my dad?" I asked, trying to keep all emotion out of my voice but hearing a tremor in it nonetheless.

Thomas sat up straight and rubbed the back of his neck. "Your father doesn't have an analog in Aurora. Sometimes that happens. Nobody knows why, but it's more common than you might think. We don't all have analogs in every universe."

"Can I see her?" I asked. *Please, please, please just let me see her,* I thought desperately. Even though I knew my mother's analog wouldn't actually be my mother, I needed to know what she would've looked like now, if she had lived.

He shook his head. "Virginia's too far. There's not time."

I nodded. I should've known better than to believe something good might come from this experience. Aurora seemed to delight in crushing every faint flutter of hope I dared to have.

"All right, that's enough," Gloria interjected. I started at the sound of her voice; I'd forgotten she was even there.

"It's"—Gloria consulted her tablet—"four-thirty-seven a.m., so we don't have much time. Juliana rises precisely at seven-thirty every morning when she's at the Castle, unless she has an early engagement; I come in at eight o'clock on the nose to go over her schedule for the day and she eats breakfast while she's being prepped."

"Prepped?" I repeated, my voice hollow. "Prepped how?"

"Clothes, hair, makeup," Gloria said, as if this was all self-explanatory. It made sense; clearly, as a public figure, Juliana had to look her best every day. But the thought of being primped like some kind of life-size Barbie made me slightly ill. I already felt like an object in this world, a curiosity rather than a person in my own right. To them, Juliana was the real one; I was just a stopgap illusion they had no choice but to tolerate. "Juliana often changes several times a day, and her stylists are on call around the clock to make sure she is always perfectly presentable. I manage Juliana's staff and master calendar, and act as a sort of . . . turnstile in her life. I control access to Her Highness; nobody outside the royal family gets to her without first going through me.

"Of course, that still leaves the matter of the queen and her children," Gloria continued. "As Thomas may have told you, Juliana and her stepmother don't play well together. They never have, not even when Juliana was a child, and things have only gotten worse since the regency."

"Why?" I vaguely remembered what a regent was from my sophomore year European history class; they took over the throne of a country when the real monarch was for whatever reason incapable of ruling.

"When the king was shot, it became clear very quickly that he was never going to recover his mental faculties," Gloria said, her shoulders tensing when she said the word *shot*. "A regent had to be found to replace him." Gloria went on to tell me that, under normal circumstances, the heir apparent would automatically become regent, but at sixteen Juliana wasn't of age. She had to be seventeen to take the crown. So Congress had convened out of session to choose a regent. On paper, the queen had been the natural choice, but Juliana ran a very aggressive campaign against her, backing the president of the Congress—Nathaniel Whitehall—for the spot, and she almost succeeded. The faction that supported the queen won by a very narrow margin. "The queen has always felt threatened by Juliana, and that only made it worse. They're civil to each other in public, but in private . . . well, I suppose you'll see for yourself very soon."

"Comforting," I muttered under my breath. The last thing I needed was a woman who had known Juliana for years watching my every move with a distrustful eye. I looked over at the window and once again caught my reflection in it. "I just don't think I can do this. I can't pretend to be somebody I'm not. They'll *know*."

Thomas shook his head vehemently. "They won't. You look exactly like her, right down to the freckle on your left earlobe." I touched my ear, wondering how in the world Thomas had managed to notice that. "Sasha, I watched you for a week before I—before we first talked, back on Earth. I did my research. You can do this. People want to think you're her. What's the alternative? That you're a double from an alternate universe? I don't think we could convince anyone of that if we tried."

"Libertas has the real Juliana," I reminded him. "They'll know I'm not her. What if they go public with that information? Everything will be ruined. What'll the General do to me then?"

"They won't," Thomas assured me. "Libertas is just as in the dark as everyone else about the multiverse. If anything, they'll think we found a look-alike, someone who just happens to resemble Juliana. But who's going to believe that, when Juliana is standing on the Grand Balcony, waving to thousands of people? No one."

"You really think people are that stupid?"

"Not stupid," he said. "Ignorant. And yeah, I do."

THIRTEEN

"Oh my God," I said as I stepped inside Juliana's bedroom four hours later.

"Royalty does have its perks," Thomas said, with a trace of irritation in his voice. He was trying to teach me how to use the security device on the door. All the doors in the Citadel—including the Tower, where we'd just been, and the Castle, where we were now—were controlled by panels with biometric scanners similar to the one I'd seen him use on the car door back in Chicago; they required a handprint and a six-number code to gain access if they were locked. Juliana and I didn't have the same handprint; Thomas had replaced mine with Juliana's in the security database. But ever since the door slid open to reveal the room beyond, I was having a hard time focusing on what he was saying.

It wasn't because the room was opulent to near-Versailles proportions, although it was. In fact, Juliana's bedroom was the most beautiful, luxurious, impeccably decorated room I'd ever stood in. An enormous four-poster canopy bed with a blue satin goose down comforter and mounds of pillows took up a portion of the right wall. All the furniture was made of beautifully carved mahogany. There was a sitting area with a sofa and two armchairs upholstered in bright, cheerful cornflower-blue brocade and embroidered with tiny, perfect pink rose petals. The adjoining bathroom was done all in silver and marble, and the cavernous walk-in closet was filled with every item of clothing and accessory a girl could possibly want. Floor-to-ceiling French doors opened onto a huge stone terrace that overlooked the gorgeous landscaped garden. The sun was rising, bathing everything in a butter-yellow glow.

But it wasn't the suite's beauty that had stunned me—it was the fact that I had seen it all before. I was just as comfortable in this room as I was in my own back at home, a bizarre sensation I wasn't prepared for. It all felt like it belonged to me, and I had to remind myself very sternly that it didn't, that it never would, and that in six days I would be gone. My eyes landed on a painting hanging on the wall; it depicted a country house, large and sprawling, set against a beautiful emerald wood, with a glittering lake in the foreground.

Someone had fastened back the curtains and opened a few of the doors; the smell of roses and lilacs wafted in on a breeze, and a fountain gurgled somewhere in the distance. I stepped onto the terrace and stood at the railing; the garden was filled with sculptured topiaries, painstakingly cultivated flower beds, and rows of trimmed rosebushes. A manicured lawn stretched out at my feet like a verdant carpet. Juliana's bedroom—my new, very pretty prison—was situated in the northernmost point of the star-shaped Castle, on the third floor, facing inward toward the gardens—and the Tower. Taller than any of the surrounding buildings, the Tower was visible from practically every vantage point, a not-so-subtle reminder that wherever I went, whatever I did, the General was watching. I went back into the bedroom, letting the imposing Tower recede behind a filmy curtain.

Gloria started to say something, but was interrupted by a sweet chime emanating from the LCD panel on the inside of the door.

"Breakfast," Thomas said. He pressed a button on the panel that slid the door open, and in came an attendant wheeling a cart. The smell of eggs and toast reminded me that I hadn't eaten since prom night. It took a great deal of effort not to dive for the cart before the attendant even had time to lift the cover off the plate.

"You're excused," Gloria told the attendant. He nodded and left the way he came.

"That was rude," I said, eyeing the plate. My stomach rumbled with hunger, but I wasn't sure what I was supposed to do. Could I just sit down at the little table in the corner and start eating, or was there some sort of rule I needed to follow?

"None of that," Gloria said. "We have a system here, Sasha, protocol that must be adhered to. The domestics aren't your friends; they're your employees. You tell them if you need something and they get it for you. That's it. No chatting. Juliana wouldn't do that."

"She doesn't say thank you?" A thought struck me—if I were ever to meet Juliana in person, would I even *like* her?

"She thanks them with a paycheck," Gloria said. "What are you waiting for? Tuck in, the food's getting cold."

I glanced over at Thomas, wondering where he stood in all this. Gloria was clearly more than just a secretary to Juliana; she was a protector, a caregiver, a confidante. But what about him? As Juliana's bodyguard, it stood to reason that he would be considered an employee. But from the way he kept talking about her, I'd started to wonder if Juliana and Thomas were friends. Maybe even more than friends, although Thomas would never tell me if they were. I kept wishing I could figure him out, but whatever training he'd undergone to do this age-inappropriate job, it had been damn good.

Gloria drew out her glass tablet and used it to pull up the schedule for the day. "It's nearly nine o'clock now. Hair and makeup will arrive shortly, so we ought to get you showered. Then at ten you're going to go visit the king."

"The king? But I thought he was . . ."

Gloria nodded. "The king is ill. He was in the hospital for over a month after he was shot, but once his condition was declared stable, the queen moved him here to the Castle. His bedroom is down the hall. Juliana visits him every day. You must do the same. She usually sits with him for about an hour. After that, you have an eleven-thirty interview with Eloise Dash from the CBN, and then—"

"Hold up. An interview? With a reporter?" The familiarity of the Castle, and particularly this bedroom—which, of all the places in the visions Juliana had inadvertently sent me from her world, felt the safest and most comfortable—had started to make me feel that I might be able to do what I was brought here to do. But this new wrinkle shook my certainty, and again I was plagued with a fear of failing, and all the consequences that came with it. *Six days,* I told myself, repeating it over and over in my head like a mantra. *Just six days until I can go home.* But the more I told myself that this was all temporary, the less power the words had to console me.

The truth that I'd been trying to keep at bay swept through me like a harsh wind: I had to find my own way out of Aurora. I couldn't just go along with the General's plans in the hopes that if I fulfilled his demands I would be returned home. It was possible—even likely—that he wouldn't keep his word. I needed a plan B, in case six days turned into far more.

"Yes," Gloria said. "Juliana rarely does interviews, but Libertas may at any time decide to make an announcement regarding the fact that they have her prisoner. We can't sit around and wait for that to happen; we have to be proactive, to disprove their claims before they've even made them."

Thomas spoke up then. "Libertas has its fair share of supporters in the UCC. They're a fringe operation, but they're not unpopular across the board. There's been a fair amount of unrest in the country, and not just in the Tattered City. If they go public with the information that they're holding Juliana hostage, not everyone would be sorry to hear it."

"Are there really people who would think the kidnapping of a sixteen-year-old girl is justified?" I asked. I hadn't been talking about myself, but I couldn't help but think about it, once I said the words. Thomas's jaw tightened, and I wondered if he was thinking the same thing.

"To stop the marriage of Juliana to the prince of Farnham and the joining of our two countries with blood?" Thomas nodded. "Definitely. Not everyone wants us to stop fighting them."

"Then what do they want?"

He shrugged. "Different things. Some want a fortified wall built along the border, with no passage in and out and armed guard stations every twenty yards. Some want us to take over Farnham—the land once belonged to the UCC, and there are groups that would like nothing more than to see us roll into their capital with our tanks and occupy the whole damn country."

"And Libertas? What do they want?"

"They want to bring down both monarchies and create a transcontinental republic," Thomas told me. I remembered the Monad's speech back in the Tattered City—*the only path to true peace is overthrowing both monarchies and forming one republic, of the people, by the people, and for the people.* I realized now why it sounded so familiar—it was a bastardized version of Abraham Lincoln's Gettysburg Address. But Lincoln, being so post-LCE, probably never existed in Aurora.

"Curious," I said softly, not really meaning for anyone else to overhear.

"What?" Thomas pressed.

"Nothing. I think their methods are awful, but I can't say I disagree with the sentiment."

"Yeah, well, you're an American," Thomas said. "You would think that. But this isn't—"

"My world. I know. I've been informed."

Gloria looked back and forth between the two of us, confused. "What's an American?"

"Never mind," Thomas and I said in unison.

Gloria, who didn't seem to enjoy having less information that anybody else in the room, said testily, "While I'm sure this has been illuminating for Sasha, I think it might be time for you to leave, Thomas. The team will be here soon, and since you're not in the habit of attending the princess's *toilette,* I don't suggest you start loitering around now."

"Actually," I interrupted. "Can you both leave? Just for a couple of minutes," I added, when Gloria shot me an irritated look, although I don't know why I was expected to make apologies. After all, I was the one being held in a foreign universe against my will. Still, I was growing to like Gloria's no-nonsense, domineering way of handling this strange situation—it was comforting to know that someone had some part of this circus under control, insofar as that was even possible—and her bossiness didn't bother me. Much. But I need a little time alone.

"I suppose," Gloria said. "We'll be right outside. Just a few minutes, okay? We've got to stick to the schedule."

I nodded. It wasn't until the door had slid shut behind them that I realized I was holding my breath. I let it out in a slow stream. Then I lowered my face into my hands and massaged my temples with my fingers, which were shaking. I forced my mind to go blank and kept breathing in the steady, rhythmic way Gina had taught me when she was going through her yoga phase. *Gina,* I thought suddenly, but I beat it back before thoughts of home could provoke me to panic. If I was going to step into Juliana's life and convince a whole bunch of people who actually knew her that I *was* her, I had to stop torturing myself with memories of my own past. Otherwise, despair would paralyze me, and I wasn't about to let that happen, not while there was still a chance of returning to my real life.

Suddenly restless, I got to my feet, picking up my backpack and dropping it on the bed. I'd asked for a few minutes of alone time to wrap my head around what was happening, but I'd also wanted a chance to salvage whatever possessions of mine I could before Thomas and Gloria had them destroyed. If Thomas hadn't allowed me to keep my prom dress back in the Tattered City, there was no way they were just going to throw my dirty Earth clothes into the royal laundry. I opened the main section of the bag and dug around inside. Deodorant, hairbrush, Gina's pashmina . . . those could all go. I made a mental note to replace the pashmina when I got home. Then there was my necklace. I doubted they'd let me wear it, since it belonged to me and not Juliana; I couldn't let them get rid of it with everything else, but I needed a place to hide it.

I finished my inventory of the bag with the front pocket, which, to my surprise, contained a book.

"Oh," I said. It was my copy of *Twelfth Night.*

I sat down on the bed with the book in my lap. Thomas had packed this bag; he was the only person who could've put it in there. But why would he do such a thing? Was it a joke? A mean, nasty joke, to remind me how foolish I'd been? Maybe it was naïve of me, but I didn't think Thomas was capable of petty cruelty. The more time I spent with him, the more I was realizing that Thomas considered himself a person of upstanding moral character. I believed him when he said he'd done the right thing by bringing me into this universe; I didn't *agree* with him, but I didn't get the sense that he was lying about how he felt. So whatever Thomas's reason for sending *Twelfth Night* with me through the tandem, I didn't think it had anything to do with hurting me.

At least, not on purpose. But it did hurt, the memory of how easily I'd fallen for his ruse, and how painful the sense of betrayal had been when I discovered it was all false. The book reminded me of that. I flipped the pages, not looking for anything in particular, but it fell open to my favorite part, Viola's monologue in act 2, scene 2. *Disguise, I see, thou art a wickedness.*

No kidding, I thought.

Well, I wasn't going to just let them dispose of my favorite book, either. My eyes rested on the bedside table. It had a little drawer at the top, the perfect size to hide a few of my possessions, and close enough at hand if I needed to retrieve them quickly. I was just about to slide the book and necklace inside when a little object in the far back corner caught my eye. I reached in and pulled out a blue origami star. It seemed familiar, but I couldn't put my finger on why. I put it back where I found it, along with my own things, just as Gloria walked back through the door.

"I'm sorry, Sasha, but I can't wait any longer," she said. "The team will be here any minute, and honestly, you look like you just came in off the street. Juliana would never be caught dead in any of that. You've got to wash and change immediately."

"What are you going to do with my stuff?" I asked. "My clothes and my bag."

Gloria heaved a sigh. "We're going to have to burn them, dear. I'm sorry."

"I figured." I was glad to have rescued the items I could. Gloria gave me a sympathetic smile. She pointed at the bathroom door with her stylus.

"Shower," she commanded.

I scrubbed every inch of my body until all traces of the last two days had been washed down the drain. Afterward, I stood in front of Juliana's enormous antique dresser and looked in the mirror; with my hair wet, and my pink, clean skin, wearing only a luxurious white cotton bathrobe, I looked like a blank slate. Now that the adrenaline had worn off and weariness was setting in, I was starting to feel like a blank slate, too. Maybe that was for the best; maybe that would make all this easier. But it felt wrong.

"Wait here," Gloria said, disappearing into Juliana's enormous walk-in closet. Minutes later, she emerged carrying an armful of dresses, each of which she laid carefully on the bed. I glanced down at the dresser, which was empty but for a few framed photographs, a large mahogany jewelry box, and a collection of perfumes in cut-glass bottles that rested on a silver plate. I scanned the photographs with interest. It was easy to pick out Juliana in them; all I had to do was look for my own face. But it was the other faces that fascinated me. One picture showed Juliana around age seven with a man and a woman who I gathered were her parents. They didn't resemble mine in the slightest. The woman, a young and beautiful brunette with delicate features, had her arms wrapped around Juliana, who was beaming at the camera; the man, much older than the woman, wore a smile on his handsome, aristocratic face, but stood at a slight remove from his wife and daughter and didn't touch them.

"I'm thinking this one for now," Gloria said, indicating a one-shouldered blood orange chiffon dress with a wide black buckle and a pleated skirt. "This one for the interview." She placed a black leather pencil skirt and a sleeveless white silk blouse beside the orange dress. I squinted at them dubiously. "On those rare occasions when Juliana does give interviews, she tends to dress a little more . . ."

"Rocker chick?" I suggested.

Gloria pursed her lips. "'Mature' is the word I was looking for. And I think this one would be more than adequate for tonight's banquet. What do you think?"

The third outfit was also sleeveless, a red taffeta minidress with a huge ruffle on one side from shoulder to hem. "For a banquet?" I asked. I didn't know what that entailed, but if I had to guess I would say that it should've involved a gown of some sort.

"It's not really a banquet in the strictest sense of the word," Gloria said. "The queen has arranged a welcome-home dinner for Juliana. There will be some important political figures and high-ranking Citadel personnel there, but it won't be a huge party, and it'll be served in the formal dining room, not the banquet hall. This will be fine."

"Okay," I said. "You're the expert. I like the color."

Gloria held it up against me. "It suits you." She turned me so that I stood before the mirror. Juliana's face stared back at me. I shivered.

"Oh dear," Gloria fretted. "You're cold." The door chimed.

"That'll be the ladies. They'll do your hair and makeup. Go into the closet and get dressed while they set up. I'll let them in."

Juliana's aestheticians were waiting when I emerged from the closet. They all greeted me with a stiff, "Good morning, Your Highness," to which I took care not to respond with anything more than a head nod, as Gloria had instructed. Apparently, no staff or domestics were allowed to speak to the royal family unless they were first spoken to, except in salutation. They did their work fast. The hairdresser, Louisa, blow-dried my hair until it was stick-straight and then styled it into a waterfall of big, soft curls. Then Rochelle, the makeup artist, applied layers of foundation, powder, blush, mascara, and eye shadow to my bare skin.

"The princess is going on the box this morning, so make sure she's camera ready," Gloria instructed Rochelle. When they were finished, they left as silently as they came. Gloria gave me a bunch of shoes to choose from; they were stilettos, about three inches high. Apparently, that was all Juliana owned.

"Perfect," Gloria said. I gripped a nearby bedpost to make sure I didn't fall flat on my face. Gloria gave me a quick once-over.

"One last thing." She went to the dresser and grabbed a small gold pin. She fastened it to the dress right above my heart, careful not to damage the delicate fabric. "This is a rowan branch," she explained. "It's the symbol of the House of Rowan, to which Juliana belongs. We all wear one in the Citadel." Sure enough, there was an identical pin fastened to her shirt. Thomas had been wearing one, too—as had the General. "But this one is special. It's linked to Thomas's KES earpiece. If you press it, you'll be able to communicate with him."

"I better not lose it, then, huh?" I said, fingering it absently.

"If you do, there are more in that crystal bowl on the dresser," Gloria told me. Her mouth quirked at the ends. "Juli can be careless sometimes."

"Is that what you call her? Juli?" I liked the sound of it. My birth certificate read ALEXANDRA EMILIE LAWSON, but I'd gone by Sasha for so long that I sometimes forgot it wasn't my real name.

Gloria nodded. "Those of us who know her well." I wondered if Thomas called her Juli.

"Gloria," I said. "This interview . . ."

She pursed her lips, which, I was learning, meant she was trying very hard to think of the exact right way to put something. "It ought to be fine. We have a deal with the CBN. We approve all the questions in advance. But Eloise Dash . . . she's a more ruthless reporter than she appears to be. You'll have to be on your guard with her. Juliana doesn't like her, but then again she doesn't like any reporters."

I took one last look in the mirror. The girl I saw reflected in it looked much more like the girl in the photographs than she did me. Gloria, Louisa, and Rochelle had done their jobs well; I was starting to understand, for the first time, how someone might mistake me for a princess.

Gloria went to fetch her tablet, and as she passed through a ray of sunlight, I saw something sparkling on her left ring finger.

"Are you married?" I asked, pointing to her hand.

Gloria glanced at the ring as if it was so much a part of her that she had forgotten it was even there. "Engaged."

"Like me," I joked weakly. *Ugh.*

"Oh, I almost forgot!" Gloria rushed to a nearby bureau

and started riffling through a carved jewelry box. When she found what she was looking for, she came over and dropped something in my hand—an engagement ring. It had a thin, delicate band of what looked like platinum and a pear-shaped diamond the size of a geode sitting in the center.

"It came from Farnham a week after the engagement contract was signed," Gloria explained. "Juliana never wore it, out of protest, but I think you should. It would look bad if Prince Callum showed up and you didn't have it on. And God knows what Eloise Dash would say if she noticed your ring finger was bare."

I held the ring in between the pads of my fingers, shifting it back and forth out of the light. It was the most expensive thing I'd ever held; most of my jewelry came from the sale rack at Target.

"Go ahead," Gloria prompted. "It's not going to bite you."

I slid the ring on; it was heavy but beautiful. Even I couldn't deny that.

"Is it time to go see the king?" This was the part I was least nervous about. Thomas and Gloria had told me that the king lapsed in and out of consciousness, but that even in his more lucid moments it was unclear how much he was capable of understanding. He would probably be asleep the whole time, which meant that this was the perfect first encounter with someone who didn't know I wasn't Juliana.

Gloria consulted her tablet. "It is. Thomas will take you there."

"Hurray," I muttered under my breath, though secretly, I was relieved at not having to go alone.

FOURTEEN

"So," I said, taking a deep breath and turning to face Thomas, who was standing in the doorway. "Am I convincing?"

"Very." He nodded in approval, carefully avoiding my eyes. "We should go." He lifted his gaze to Gloria, and I followed it. She was busy scribbling away with her stylus on the glass tablet. "We must keep to the schedule."

"Yes, you must," she said, without looking up. "Get out of here."

Thomas led the way through the Castle's labyrinthine halls, but as we passed through them it occurred to me that I could've done just as good of a job. For whatever reason, Juliana's surroundings were the parts of the visions that stuck with me the most. I knew what was behind nearly every door we passed, and made a mental note to check out the library, if I ever found myself alone again.

Everything was brighter and sharper outside of my dreams. The walls were covered with paintings depicting a variety of scenes, both wartime and pastoral, portraits of long-dead kings and queens peppered throughout. French windows looked out over the lush garden, magnificent mirrors in gilded frames held our reflections as we walked, and massive crystal chandeliers hung overhead, throwing light over every surface like confetti. Our footsteps echoed as we made our way across the beautiful stone floor. None of the doors had knobs, just LCD panels to the right of each doorframe. Most of the panels were blue, but one or two were green. Thomas had mentioned what the colors meant; green for open, blue for locked. We passed several armed guards in military dress, but they didn't speak to either of us, nor did Thomas acknowledge their presence. They appeared to be part of normal life in the Castle, but they put me on edge.

"Relax," Thomas said.

"I'm relaxed," I insisted.

"You look like you're being led to your execution," he told me. "And like your spine is a steel rod—who taught you to walk?"

"These heels are three inches high. *You* try wearing them." He chuckled. "What? Now you're making fun of me?"

He held up hands in a gesture of surrender. "Never, princess. Never."

I glared at him, but didn't say aloud what I was thinking, which was: *Don't call me that.* Thomas paused at one of the doors, so abruptly that I almost walked right on past it.

Thomas pointed at the panel. I pressed my hand to it and it flashed, bringing up the now-familiar keypad. "Two, five, four, two, four, four," Thomas whispered. I input the code, committing it to memory. The door looked like it was made of wood, but as it slid open so that we could pass through I saw that the ornate carvings were merely a façade, and that the real door underneath was made of metal, just like the one to Juliana's bedroom. It was a strange place, the Castle. The old and the new mingled so closely it was as if they were part of a single organism, and I couldn't deny that the result was beautiful.

I peered into the room. It was large and brightly illuminated by several fluorescent lamps, which gave it the stark feeling of belonging in a hospital, even though it had all the trappings of luxury—intricate moldings painted white against the mint green of the rest of the room, expensive-looking paintings and tapestries hanging from the walls, antique furniture and heavy velvet drapery. The king's bed, an elegant mahogany four-poster with a rich red canopy, was in the center of the room, surrounded by machines and IV poles.

The queen was sitting next to the bed in a tall chair. I recognized her from a picture Thomas and Gloria had shown me back at the Tower, during my interminable yet somehow insubstantial briefing. The queen was tall and thin, beautiful despite the worry lines that scored her porcelain skin. I wondered if they were new, the result of her husband's illness and her country's political problems, or if she'd earned them over the course of many years. Her thick blond hair was gathered in a chignon at the nape of her neck, and she wore a simple, elegant dove-gray shift dress with almost no makeup; her only jewelry was a pair of pearl drop earrings that swung as she turned to see who was entering the room. When she caught sight of Thomas and me, she let go of the king's hand and rose from her seat.

"You're back," she said in a flat tone. She folded her hands at the base of her stomach in a ladylike manner; they were the only things about the queen that were not lovely. In fact, they were knobby and red, like she'd just gotten done washing a sink full of dishes, which I doubted.

"I am," I said. Just knowing that the queen and Juliana

hated each other made me uncomfortable. I couldn't think of a thing to say to her.

"It's about time." The queen glanced back at the king. "He's been asking for you day and night. You should have seen the look on his face when I told him you weren't here."

"Is he lucid?" Thomas asked.

The queen shook her head. "But he is talking. He's been saying the same thing over and over since you left."

"What's that?" I asked.

"Your name," she said, with a hint of nastiness. "I'll leave you alone—he doesn't seem to notice whether or not I'm here."

"I'm sure that's not . . ." But the queen held her hand up.

"Don't patronize me, Juliana, I'm not in the mood." She looked tired and drawn; I couldn't help feeling a measure of compassion for the queen, despite her incivility. "I have business to attend to in my study. Call me if something changes." She said this to Thomas, looking me over once more before sweeping out of the room and disappearing down the hallway.

"Don't let her get to you," Thomas said. "She's not as scary as she seems."

"Really? Because she seems pretty scary to me," I said. The queen had rattled me. I wasn't used to being spoken to in such a petulant way by adults. Snotty girls at school, sure, but adults tended to love me.

I gazed once more around the room. The king was lying still; the only sign he wasn't asleep was the manic fluttering motion of his right hand in the air.

"What's the matter?" Thomas asked, picking up on my anxiety.

"I don't like hospitals," I told him.

"But this isn't a hospital. There's nothing to be afraid of."

"I'm not afraid," I said. Thomas waited for me to continue. "It's just—I went to the hospital the night my parents died. Ever since then, I can't . . . I don't like it. That's all."

"Come on," Thomas said. His hand grazed my elbow and I started as if he had shocked me. He gave me a curious look but was polite enough not to mention it. "It won't be that bad. He's just lying there."

I shook my head. "I don't think I can do this." The king looked so pathetic, alone even when other people were in the room.

"It's perfectly safe," Thomas assured me. "The trick to pretending to be somebody else is to do everything exactly the way that other person would do them, even when it feels unnatural, until you get used to it."

"You would know," I muttered.

"Yeah, I would know," Thomas said. "When I was Grant, I ate peas, even though I hate them, because *he* loves them. I drank beer under the train tracks with that dumb friend of his, Ivan, because *he* would do that. I conformed to every aspect of his routine. Did you know he flosses his teeth three times a day? I read his books, I watched his movies, I listened to his music. I slept nine hours a night even though I haven't done that since I was so young I barely remember it. And you know what? *Nobody ever questioned me.* Not even when I asked you to prom. I'm an expert at fooling people into believing I'm somebody else, so you might as well listen to me."

I stared at him, my mouth agape. He had some nerve to bring up his performance as Grant. But he wasn't wrong. He'd fooled me with his act. He'd fooled everyone.

"Fine." I swallowed hard and approached the bed with caution. The king's eyes were open, but he was just staring at the ceiling. His right hand grazed the air, but it only took me a few seconds to realize that it was repeating the same rhythm over and over again, his fingers moving in the exact same way every time, his wrist rising and falling in a precise pattern.

"He does that a lot," Thomas said. "That hand thing. Ever since they moved him here he's been doing it."

"Why?"

"Not sure. The doctor said it's nothing to worry about, just a compulsion. Like his brain's stuck in a loop." But the tone of Thomas's voice said that it unsettled him as much as it did me.

I sat down in the chair the queen had recently vacated. "What do I do now?"

"Talk to him," Thomas said.

"What do I call him?"

"Try 'Dad.' "

"Hi, Dad," I said hesitantly. The word sounded strange coming out of my mouth. I hadn't called someone "Dad" in a very long time. The king showed no reaction. He didn't even blink. I tried again. "Hi, Dad, it's me—"

"Juli," Thomas prompted. I nodded.

"It's me, Juli. I heard you were asking for me. I'm sorry I was away for such a long time, I didn't know . . . Well, I'm back now. Was there something you wanted to say to me?"

Still nothing from the king. I looked to Thomas for some advice, unsure of what I was doing wrong.

"Don't be discouraged," Thomas said. "He almost never says anything real. He murmurs a lot, nonsense mostly; sometimes he parrots what people around him are saying. But usually it's just this. I know it's weird, but try not to get too freaked out. He's harmless."

I watched the king, saying nothing for a while. The poor man. I didn't know what sort of person he had been before he'd been shot, or how good a king he'd managed to be to his people. But Thomas had said that he loved his daughter, and I believed that. It was hard to see a man with three children laid up in a hospital bed, tapping out meaningless patterns in the air. That was no way to live, no matter who you were.

There was a book sitting on the nightstand. I held the volume up so that Thomas could see it. "*The Odyssey*? You have *The Odyssey* here?"

"We do," he said. "It's pre-LCE."

"Right." Still, it was odd seeing the book there, as if it, too, was marooned in Aurora, just trying to get back home.

"Why don't you read to him?"

I opened *The Odyssey* and found that someone—Juliana?—had already made significant progress. There was a bookmark on page 249, right at the beginning of Book Eleven: "The Kingdom of the Dead". It seemed a little morbid, but it was nice to have something to actually *do,* so I began to read.

"'Now down we came to the ship at the water's edge,'" I began. "'We hauled and launched her into the sunlit breakers first, stepped the mast in the black craft and set our sail and loaded the sheep aboard, the ram and ewe, then we ourselves embarked, streaming tears, our hearts weighed down with anguish . . .'"

"Juli!" the king shouted, the fingers of his left hand closing over my wrist. My muscles tightened as I tried to squirm away. I looked at Thomas in shock and saw it mirrored on his face.

"Touch and go," the king muttered. He said the words with a mysterious sort of urgency, like they meant something. I called out for Thomas's help, but he was already at my side, prying me out of the steel trap of the king's fingers.

"Are you okay?" Thomas yanked me out of the chair and clutched me by the elbows. I shook my head. I wasn't okay, I was nowhere near *okay.*

"Mirror, mirror," the king said, still distraught. "Mirror, mirror."

"Let's get out of here," Thomas said, tugging me toward the door.

"But what if he's hurt?" I protested.

"I'll call the nurse on our way out, come on."

"Mirror, mirror!" the king shouted. I couldn't tear my eyes away from him. What if he died and I was the cause? "One, one, two, three . . ."

"Come on, Sasha," Thomas urged again. I froze. I couldn't remember the last time he'd spoken my real name out loud. I hoped no one had overheard him, but Thomas didn't even seem to realize that he'd said it.

The king kept mumbling, but I couldn't make out any of the words. Thomas slammed a large red button near the door with the heel of his hand, and in a nanosecond I could hear footsteps in the hall, the sound of voices. Two nurses in pressed white uniforms burst in, checking monitors and IVs before Thomas and I had even gotten out of the room.

As we hurried down the corridor, I heard the king cry out one more time, clear as a bell: "Touch and go!"

FIFTEEN

Eloise Dash angled herself toward the camera and gave the invisible audience on the other side a winning smile. "Good morning, Columbia!" she said. "And welcome to the *Dash Report* on CBN News, hosted by me, Eloise Dash. Today I bring you a highly anticipated interview with our very own Princess Juliana, who is back fresh from her early-summer holiday just in time for her wedding to Prince Callum of Farnham, scheduled to take place in a week."

She turned, and the lights swung around, practically blinding me. It was hot as hell in the room. With all the makeup I was wearing and the silk blouse, which I was pretty sure I was sweating through, I felt encased in plastic. I was still shaken up by the incident in the king's room; Thomas had assured me it was nothing, and that it wasn't proof—as I'd suspected—that the king knew I wasn't his daughter, but it wasn't as though either of us could really know for sure. I resisted the urge to tug at the collar of my shirt, which was covered with silver pyramid studs. How did Juliana manage to breathe wearing clothes like these, let alone speak?

"Hello, Your Highness," Eloise Dash said. It took me a second to realize she was addressing me. *Focus,* I commanded myself. *Focus, and breathe.*

"Hello," I said, trying to relax. I'd been interviewed exactly zero times in my life, so I figured that the only way to get through this was to stay calm and answer Eloise Dash as best I could. Gloria had made a valiant effort to brief me earlier while I changed clothes, and I'd been able to look over the agreed-upon list of questions in order to practice my responses, so I wasn't going in blind, but I could understand why Juliana hardly ever gave interviews. I thought my heart was going to explode, it was beating so hard.

"Let me tell you what a pleasure it is to see you again." Eloise smiled. Her teeth were tiny and bright under the scorching lamps; I was sitting close enough to her to tell that she'd coated them with petroleum jelly, like a Miss America contestant.

"Thank you," I said. "It's a pleasure to see you again as well." I sounded so stilted and formal. I couldn't imagine anyone actually wanting to watch this thing.

"Wonderful. For our viewers, I'd just like to point out that we're conducting this interview in the Yellow Parlor of the Castle, which is a treat since we're rarely allowed outside the Citadel's media suite. Thank you for inviting me here with you today."

"You're very welcome," I said. Gloria was behind the camera, mouthing *Loosen up.* I took a deep, silent breath; the cameras and the lights were making me nervous and stiff. Thomas stood near the door, surveying the room with incredible alertness, despite all the noise and distractions and people crowding in and out. Having them both there made me feel a bit better. At least I knew that we shared a common goal: make this believable. And so far, it seemed, so good. I felt the tension in my shoulders release slightly, and I eased into a warm, genuine smile. *Good job,* Gloria mouthed from the back. *Just like that.*

"People are obviously curious about you, Juliana," Eloise began. "You were known for years as a party girl"—she gave a short, mirthless laugh—"but it seems as though you've settled down since getting engaged, reduced your social profile a bit. Why the sudden change?"

"Well, I guess I just came to understand that now that I'm older, I have certain responsibilities," I told her, the words tumbling out just as I'd rehearsed them with Gloria. "And I have to take them seriously. The state of things between Farnham and the Commonwealth have been tenuous for years, and I'm being given the chance, along with my new fiancé, to make a positive difference in the relationship between our countries."

"And how are you feeling about the wedding? Do you have butterflies? Not cold feet, I hope!" Eloise grinned. I wanted to smack her. This woman was the most incredible phony.

"No cold feet!" I laughed, hoping it sounded at least a little bit believable. "Definitely butterflies, but people tell me that's normal."

"You haven't met Prince Callum yet, correct?"

I shook my head. "He arrives tomorrow, and that will be the first time we've seen each other in person. But I know I'm going to love him." In fact, I had no idea what to expect when I met Callum. I'd been trying not to give it a great deal of thought; there was more than enough to get used to at the moment without driving myself crazy over what came next, but in a short time, I was going to have to face that part of my task, and I was worried about it. I hoped it didn't show on my face.

"I think I speak for most Columbians when I say we were surprised when the Castle made the announcement that you had consented to an arranged marriage," Eloise said. Her tone was light and airy, but she was trying to trap me into saying something scandalous, as Gloria had warned she might. "How did you feel when they first asked you if you wanted to be married to Prince Callum?"

Nobody had *asked* Juliana anything—she'd been *told* she was marrying Callum. But I couldn't very well say that on national television, though everybody knew it was true.

"I have to admit, at first I was stunned," I said, lowering my voice as if I was confiding something very personal to Eloise. "And uncertain. But I came to see that this was the best thing for all of us—for you, for me, for everyone in Farnham *and* the Commonwealth—and Prince Callum is a wonderful young man. I couldn't have chosen a better husband for myself if I had tried, so there was no use fighting it."

"But you're so young!" Eloise pointed out. "Wouldn't it be better to wait until you're both older before getting married?"

"I suppose," I said carefully, "that when you know you want to spend the rest of your life with someone, you want the rest of your life to start as soon as possible." It was such a cliché, but it earned me a genuine smile from Eloise Dash and I knew I'd said the right thing.

"Isn't that romantic?" Eloise asked her audience. She turned back to me with a glint in her eye. "Now, Princess, there has been a lot of controversy surrounding the Libertas movement in the UCC. My sources tell me that Libertas is stepping up their efforts to cause chaos and disrupt your wedding. Do you have any comments on that?" The tenor of her voice had changed, from flippant to dead serious.

Gloria's face contorted in fury; she leaned over to hiss in

the producer's ear. It had been part of the Castle's agreement with CBN that the interview would contain no mention of Libertas; Eloise Dash had gone off script.

I froze. I had no idea how to respond diplomatically to that question, but I couldn't simply tell them to turn the cameras off—the interview was being broadcast live. I thought back to the sorts of things I'd seen politicians say on television over the years, about terrorist attacks in the United States and abroad, trying to cobble together some sort of answer that would be both satisfactory and vague.

Finally, I said, "My most trusted advisers tell me that Libertas is nothing to fear. It pains me that there are people in this country who want to undermine the government and create panic and terror in the hearts of its citizens, but I can assure you that the wedding will go off without a hitch, and the treaty will make the UCC a more peaceful place than ever before."

"I'm so glad that you feel that way," Eloise said, but she sounded disappointed. "I find great comfort in your words, as do all Columbians, I'm sure. Thank you so much for joining us today, Your Highness. I wish you and Prince Callum a long and happy marriage."

"Thank you," I responded.

"Cut!" the director cried.

"What the hell was that?" Gloria shouted. Eloise ignored her, busying herself with removing the microphone fastened to the lapel of her fuchsia blazer. "I explicitly told you no questions about Libertas."

Eloise shrugged. "The people have a right to know how the Citadel is dealing with the Libertas crisis. If you wanted a puff piece, perhaps you should have gone with another reporter. I'm a serious journalist."

"Well, you're on *seriously* thin ice with me right now, Ms. Dash," Gloria said. "You want answers about Libertas, you contact the General's office. Do you understand?"

I stood as Thomas approached. My gaze met his as he crossed the room, and even though I knew this turn of events had angered him, the only place it showed was in his eyes, which burned bright green as he helped me remove my own microphone and steered me toward the door. He placed his hand firmly on my elbow, and for the first time I didn't shake him off. My knees felt weak, and my head was crowded with the voices rising all around me.

"She's not a child anymore!" Eloise protested. "She'll be of age in a few weeks, and soon she'll be running the whole damn country. She's got to learn to answer the tough questions!"

"That's not your call to make," Gloria said. "Get out of here, all of you. That was completely inappropriate. Don't be surprised if we give the next interview to your competitor."

It was quieter out in the hall. I was shaking, though I couldn't tell if it was from fear or exhilaration. Nerve-racking as that experience had been, it had been kind of fun, too, once I got into it. It had felt freeing to pretend to be somebody else for a while.

"I can't believe she put you on the spot like that," Thomas said. He was madder than Gloria, even, but it was the sort of rage that boiled under a calm surface. "Asking you about Libertas. As if you're in any position to comment on national security!"

"Did I do okay?" I asked.

"You? You were brilliant," Thomas said, his eyes widening at my self-doubt. I looked away, embarrassed by his obvious admiration, but I was happy he'd said so. Thomas didn't seem to care much about my ego; he would've told me if I'd failed to perform to expectation, and his approval was a pretty big relief. "That was a great answer. You did an amazing job in there."

"Only because Gloria coached me."

"No, believe me, you're a natural."

I gave him a tight smile. "I can't decide if that's a good thing or a bad thing." *Disguise, I see thou art a wickedness,* I thought.

"Well, it convinced Eloise Dash, and hopefully the entire country, so in this case, it's a good thing," Thomas said. He glanced down the hall, in the direction of approaching footsteps. "Let's go back to your room. Gloria will want to regroup, and we don't want to piss her off even more by being late."

"Got to stick to the schedule," I joked. Thomas laughed.

"You're catching on fast," he said.

SIXTEEN

A few hours later, Juliana's bedroom was the center of an enormous swell of wedding-related activity, because today was Juliana's last dress fitting. The queen was on her way, as was the seamstress with the dress, Rochelle was waiting with her ever-present trunk of beauty paraphernalia, and Gloria was standing off to one side, speaking in a low voice to someone on her mobie—which was, Thomas had explained, their slang for a cell phone. Gloria was managing the fallout from the interview incident, and I cringed in sympathy with whoever was on the other end of the line.

With nothing in particular to do, I drifted around the walk-in closet, looking for something new to wear. I didn't get the obsession with changing clothes every hour, but it was something Juliana did, so I had to do it, too. Her style was definitely different from mine; when left to my own devices, I pretty much lived in jeans and T-shirts, but the only jeans I found in Juliana's closet still had the tags on them—tags that, even though I didn't know the exact value of a dollar in the Commonwealth, gave me the impression that they *cost*. Juliana favored dresses, but her supply of them seemed infinite and I couldn't decide which to wear.

Gloria poked her head in. "That one," she said, pointing to a green silk wrap dress. I nodded and quickly changed into it.

The door slid open and the queen entered, followed by a yappy little dog and a small, stooped woman the queen didn't bother to introduce. The queen didn't greet me; she didn't even look at me, or seem to register that I was there.

"Myra," the queen said. "Bring in the dress."

"Hello, Your Majesty," I said, bowing my head to the queen as Gloria had taught me.

"Leave off with that, Juliana," the queen said, rolling her eyes. "I can't stand it when you're false to me in private."

"But I'm not—" It was difficult, knowing what to say to the queen. On the one hand, I was aware how acrimonious Juliana's relationship with her stepmother was, so if I wanted to be convincing, I ought to have snapped back, stuck up for myself. But Gloria had warned me that I needed to act as though Juliana's time at St. Lawrence had brought her to her senses. I needed to play the part of a penitent princess, one who had accepted her fate with grace and dignity, one who wouldn't fight back—someone Juliana had never actually been. And yet, if I was too good, the queen would become suspicious. It was a total minefield, and if I wasn't careful, I was liable to get blown up on the spot.

"Let's get this over with, shall we? Gloria, open the curtains. It's so dark in here." The curtains were almost completely open, sunshine pouring in, but Gloria dutifully pulled them apart as far as they would go while Myra, the small, dark-haired seamstress, summoned a porter into the room. He carried a large garment bag that almost overtook him; it looked heavy, and I was nervous about having to wear whatever over-the-top wedding dress Juliana had chosen.

The queen barely spoke as Myra hoisted and tucked and

strapped and strung me into the dress; instead, she sat on the sofa, stroking the yappy dog and quietly judging.

When Myra was finally finished, she turned me around to face the mirror.

"Wow," I said when I got a look at myself.

"It's a very lovely dress, Your Highness," Myra said.

"You're not kidding," I said. The dress was *gorgeous*. The skirt was made of white satin covered in lace, sumptuous layers of cascading fabric that seemed to go on forever. The biggest surprise was the bodice; judging by the contents of her closet, I would've expected Juliana to choose something low-cut, maybe even strapless, but it had a modest sweetheart neckline and a scalloped lace overlay with delicate capped sleeves.

"You're going to have to let the dress out a bit, Myra." The queen sighed. "I hope you've got some extra fabric. The princess seems to have gained a bit of weight since you last measured her. Don't let your mouth hang open like that, Juliana, it's very unbecoming."

"I haven't gained weight," I protested. I knew I shouldn't be taking the queen's comments so personally, since they were meant for Juliana, but I couldn't help it. It *felt* personal.

"It's too bad of you to eat so indulgently less than a week before your wedding," the queen continued. Gloria was not amused; she glared at the queen from her seat near the window, out of the queen's line of sight.

"The dress fits like a glove," I told Myra.

"It does, Your Highness," Myra admitted. Now it was the queen's turn to glare at someone.

"Don't alter it at all," I said. "But if it will make you happy, Your Majesty, I'll watch myself at meals until after the wedding."

"I told you, leave off with that 'Your Majesty' business." The queen yawned. "I see what you're trying to do, and I won't stand for it, I simply won't."

"What do you mean?"

"You're trying to pretend you've seen the error of your ways and come back from St. Lawrence a changed woman," the queen said. "This sudden meekness—it's so transparent. I don't believe it for a second. You've never been a good actress, despite your flair for the dramatic." The sound she made then was more a bark than a laugh, and she flourished her hands in the air as if she was about to conjure a dove.

"I don't know what you're talking about," I said. Myra began the process of extracting me from the complicated dress.

"Just know that I will be watching you," the queen said, getting up from the sofa and letting her dog leap from her arms onto the floor. "And if you do anything—*anything*—to upset your father or endanger the reputation of the Crown, so help me I will see to it that you are sent someplace much more tedious and remote than *Canada*. Do you understand me?"

Canada. Even I knew that was an oblique reference to Juliana's mother. I felt a sudden urge to snap back, but I couldn't—it would just give the queen another reason to jump on me, and that was the last thing I needed. I couldn't begin to imagine what would happen if the queen found out I wasn't Juliana, but it wouldn't be good.

"I understand," I said.

The queen shook her head, and I noticed something more than disapproval in her expression—there was a little bit of sadness there, too. I wondered what that was about, but it wasn't as though I could ask.

"Although," I said as Myra began to extract me from the wedding dress, "I happen to like Canada."

I'd just gotten back into the green silk wrap dress I'd been wearing earlier when two children tumbled through the door, chasing each other and shrieking with laughter. They launched themselves at my legs, giggling and snorting into the soft folds of my skirt.

That's right, I thought. *Juliana has half siblings.*

"I win!" the boy crowed. I searched through my memories of Thomas's briefing to dredge up his name—Simon, age seven. And Lillian was the little girl, age four. I put my hand on Simon's blond head, Lillian's being too far down to reach.

"Were you racing?" I asked. The little ones were completely charming. I loved them at first sight. Lillian nodded, grinning. She was wearing a lavender dress with matching shoes and white tights, her hair curled and secured by an enamel clip into a bouquet of tight ringlets.

"Yes, and I won!" Simon announced.

"Good job!" I bent down so that I was more equal to their height. "Although I don't know that it's fair, you're so much bigger than Lillian." It was easy to talk to them. They were the only people I'd met so far in Aurora who seemed to pose no threat.

"I'm fast!" Lillian pouted.

"I know, I know, of course, you're very fast," I reassured her. Lillian wrapped her arms around my neck, and when I stood she did the same with her legs around my waist. She nestled her face into my hair and sighed deeply.

The queen didn't seem as enthralled with the children as I was, but maybe that was because she was used to them. She pried Lillian off me and set her down on the floor, where she began to fuss and beg to be picked up again. The queen ignored her.

"Where is Genevieve?" she called out. "For heaven's sake,

what is the point of having a nanny if she's not even going to watch the children!"

I bent down to soothe Lillian. "Maybe they got away from her somehow."

"Yes, that's just what I need, *more* wild, uncontrollable children!" the queen cried.

"I'm not your child!" I snapped, losing control for a moment. Gloria's mouth puckered in anxiety as the queen fixed a hateful gaze on me.

"And thank God for that," she said with venom. "Simon! Lillian! Come along. Let's go find your incompetent nanny."

"Sasha," Gloria growled when everyone had gone. "You shouldn't speak to the queen like that."

"I know." I sighed and sank down on the bed.

"She's difficult," Gloria said, choosing her words carefully. "But she's under a lot of pressure. She's only doing it to get a rise out of you—out of Juliana, I mean—and if you play into it you'll only get more trouble in return."

"I don't know how Juliana does this," I said. "From the outside, her life must seem so perfect, but . . ."

Gloria nodded, sitting down next to me on the bed and putting her hand on top of mine. "I've often thought that, too. But this is the only life she's ever had. I've known Juliana for a long time, and over the years I watched as she built up walls between herself and the world, to protect herself from all the pressure and the demands of her position. Lately I've wondered if she's really made for all this."

"What do you mean?" I asked.

"Juliana's always been so stoic," Gloria told me. "She's got a quick temper, sort of like you do—"

"I don't have a temper!"

"Oh? And what was that with the queen just now?"

I conceded her point. "I'm not great at keeping my mouth shut."

"Well, neither is Juliana, but she never used to let anything get to her, deep down," Gloria said. "And yet . . . when the king informed her that he was marrying her to Prince Callum, she fought him, like everyone expected her to. And she lost that battle, like everyone expected. But I'm probably the only person who knows what she did when she came back to her room, holding the box with her engagement ring inside of it."

"What did she do?" I asked, in a voice so low it was almost a whisper.

"She wept," Gloria said, her own eyes wet at the memory. "Like a child, she wept. And my heart broke for her, as it breaks for you now. You're both so young, and you have so much resting on your shoulders. The fate of an entire nation—two nations, in fact. It just seems so grossly unfair."

She put her arms around me, and I let her. I sank my head on her shoulder and closed my eyes. I didn't know who to feel sorrier for, Juliana or myself. But at the very least, I knew that the life that belonged to me was worth returning to. And for the first time since I'd woken up in that dark basement in the Tattered City, I felt lucky.

SEVENTEEN

"So I heard you had a run-in with the queen," Thomas said, glancing at me slyly out of the corner of his eye. Gloria had returned to her office, presumably to continue ripping the people at CBN apart. They had no idea who they were dealing with; it was Gloria's new personal crusade to get Eloise Dash fired and replaced with a more obedient royal correspondent.

"You said yourself she doesn't like Juliana," I replied. "And she was awful to me at the dress fitting. She accused me of gaining weight!"

"I know she's not easy to deal with," Thomas allowed. "Believe me, I know. I've seen Juliana fight with her hundreds of times. The queen can be very petty. But if you take the bait, it just gives her more ammunition."

"That's what Gloria said." I sighed. "I've never had anyone hate me so openly before." I fiddled with the edge of a pillowcase.

"She doesn't hate you," Thomas reminded me. He stood near the door, his arms folded across his chest, his standard position. He was focused on me, but I could tell he was also on alert, as always, for anything awry, ever the soldier.

"Yeah, I know, she hates Juliana," I said. But knowing that

the queen's rancor had nothing to do with me didn't make her barbs sting any less. And how much of a difference was there, anyway, between the queen hating Juliana and the queen hating me? We weren't the same person, but we were connected. I couldn't help taking things personally on her behalf.

"No, I mean she doesn't *hate* Juliana. She's afraid of her." Thomas walked over and leaned against one of the bedposts. I glanced up and his eyes caught mine. Every time I looked at him, my brain struggled to make sense of who he was. Even now, if I encountered him and Grant together, dressed alike, I wasn't sure that I could tell the difference. But the eyes . . . they betrayed something, hidden depths of experience, intelligence, even pain. Much as I wished I didn't care, I was curious about him. I wanted to know how much of the boy he'd been with me on Earth had been a lie, but that was a question I couldn't bear to ask him.

"Afraid? Why?" The queen had all the power; she was the regent, she ran the country, while Juliana was being married off, a pawn in a game of musical countries. Just like me.

"The king loves Juliana more than anything, and the queen's always been afraid he'll leave her just like he left Juliana's mother. She knows Juliana resents her for causing her parents' divorce, and she's scared that one day Juliana will convince the king to get rid of her."

"Yeah, well, maybe he should," I grumbled.

Thomas shrugged. "Maybe. I don't know. She seems to really love him. She's just insecure."

"Thomas Mayhew, armchair psychologist." But he was probably right. In spite of the aggressive way the queen kept trying to tear down her stepdaughter, I didn't think I was imagining the sadness I'd seen in her eyes. What if, under all that ice, the queen had some affection for Juliana?

"I spend a good chunk of my days standing in the corners

of rooms, being ignored and watching people," Thomas said. "You can't help but pick up a couple of things. The personal stuff is important, but there are also a lot of political factors that make the queen behave the way she does. She sees Juli as a threat to her crown."

"Juli?" I repeated. Well, I had my answer. He and Juliana had been close, close enough for her to let him call her by her nickname—but how close was close? Close like friends? Close like brother and sister? Or close like . . . I tried not to think about it. It wasn't as if it mattered what their relationship had been. At least, it didn't matter to me.

He cleared his throat. "Juliana."

"What do you mean, 'sees her as a threat'?"

"After what happened to the king, he'll never be able to rule again. And when Juliana comes of age she can make a bid for the regency—and she might get it, since her claim on the crown is legitimate and the queen's is just a matter of momentary convenience. What will happen to the queen and her two children then? I think that's what she's worried about most."

"Not the loss of power?"

"Nobody likes to lose power," Thomas said. "But there's more than one reason why the queen would be afraid of Juliana. That's all I'm saying."

"Do you think Juliana would really do that? Just turn her out?"

He hesitated, taking time to think the question over. "No, I don't."

"That's good." I didn't like the queen much more than the queen liked Juliana, but of course she would do what was necessary to keep her family safe, even if it meant acting heinous most of the time. How could I begrudge her that while the desire to go home, and the willingness to do anything to make that happen, burned in my chest like a bonfire?

"Anyway, believe it or not, I didn't just come in here to chat with you about current political tensions," Thomas said. "I'm going to accompany you to the dinner."

"Do I have to go?" I asked, though I already knew the answer. I was dreading the dinner because I'd been informed that the General would be there. This would be the first time I'd appeared before him as Juliana, and I had no doubt he'd be watching me closely. The thought made my stomach churn. Pretending to be Juliana was one thing; pretending to be her while the architect of my situation watched, ready to pounce if I screwed up, was quite another.

"Your presence is mandatory," Thomas said. "But you don't have to worry. You can do this. You did it earlier with Eloise Dash, you can do it again."

"You keep saying that," I pointed out. "What makes you so certain?"

He hesitated for a second. "If I tell you, will you promise not to just assume I'm crazy?"

"At this point, there's not a lot I wouldn't believe," I told him. When you wake up to find you've been transported to another universe, even your most deeply rooted skepticism tends to take a major hit.

"Okay. I think—now, I don't have any proof to back this up, but—"

"Just tell me, Thomas!"

"When I was on Earth, pretending to be Grant, sometimes I felt like, I don't know, I could sense what he would do in a given situation," Thomas confided. "I prepared for my mission; I knew all kinds of facts about Grant and his life. But when you're deep undercover like that, you learn pretty quickly that facts aren't people. They're just facts. That's what makes what you're doing—what I did—so difficult. Friends, family . . . they can just tell when something's not right, even if they never figure out why. But, I don't know. Sometimes, I'd get into a sticky situation—say the wrong thing to Grant's mom, or whatever—and I'd get this feeling like I was being guided."

"You mean, like hearing voices in your head?"

"No, no, nothing like that. It was more like getting swept along with a current." He rubbed the back of his neck. "I've got this friend—he's a scientist on the many-worlds project. This stuff is his life. And he thinks that the connection between analogs runs deep. Really deep." He laughed at himself. "Forget it. You probably do think I'm crazy."

"No," I said. "I don't, not at all." I was so close to telling him about seeing Juliana in my dreams. My heart began to pound as I thought about the possible implications of what Thomas was saying. Could anyone, under the right circumstances, talk to their analogs across the tandem? What did that mean for Granddad's theory about how the universes weren't meant to come into contact?

But my lifelong visions of Juliana were a far cry from what Thomas was talking about. What if I told him and he took the information straight to the General? The likelihood of him just returning me to Earth when my six days were up if he knew I had this ability was pretty remote, and I wasn't going to do anything to jeopardize my return home. But there was a part of me—a large part of me—that wanted to talk to this friend of his, the scientist with all the theories. I wondered what he'd make of me if he knew.

Noticing my distant expression, Thomas cocked his head at me inquisitively. "What are you thinking?"

"Nothing," I told him. "It's just . . . I feel it, too. The current." Because, funnily enough, I did know what he was talking about. It was different from my visions, so subtle and incomprehensible that I hadn't even realized what it was until Thomas described his own experience as Grant. "Thomas, where *is* Grant?"

I couldn't believe the question hadn't occurred to me until now. I tried to put it down to all the craziness that had happened, that I hadn't had time to think of it when my life was in jeopardy, but I felt guilty for not asking sooner.

He sighed. "I was afraid you might wonder about that. The truth is, I don't know."

"You don't *know*?"

"There's something I haven't told you," Thomas confessed. "We call it the 'analog problem.' Analogs can't touch skin to skin. If they do, one of them gets thrown back through the tandem."

"Why?"

"When you move something out of one world and into another, it creates an imbalance. But the universes want to be equal. Usually, the analog that doesn't belong to the universe it's in gets thrown back, but not if they're wearing one of those." He glanced down at the anchor on my wrist.

"What does that have to do with Grant?" I demanded.

"He touched me," Thomas said. "Well, technically, he punched me. Right here." He tapped a spot on his jaw.

"Why would he punch you?"

"You know about Juliana, but try to imagine what it might be like to see her face to face." Thomas took a deep breath. "It's a . . . well, it's weird. I was shocked at how much he looked like me, even though that's what I was expecting. He must've thought he was losing his mind. I guess he just reacted. As soon as our skin made contact, he was thrown through the tandem."

"Are you telling me that Grant is in *Aurora*? Is he here? In the Citadel?"

"No," Thomas said, avoiding my eyes. "That was the plan, initially. I was going to send him through the tandem, and a team of KES agents in the Tattered City were supposed to retrieve him. They were going to hold him at a safe house until I brought you here, and then they were going to take him home."

"But that didn't happen," I guessed.

"Libertas got to him first," Thomas admitted. I covered my face with my hands and groaned. "They think it's me they've got in custody. The General's expecting a ransom request any day now, and when it comes, he'll pay it, and send Grant home."

"You know," I snapped, "in the battle of KES versus Libertas, you guys are totally losing. They've kidnapped Juliana, they've kidnapped Grant, and they almost kidnapped me. What is wrong with you people that you can't even do your jobs?"

Thomas opened his mouth to say something, but no words came out. Finally he said, "You're right." He sounded stunned. "You're absolutely right."

"Thomas?" I narrowed my eyes at him, trying to figure out what was going on in his mind, but I couldn't decipher his expression at all. I waved a hand in front of his face. "Are you in there?"

He nodded, blinking as if he'd just broken out of a trance. "We should go. You can't be late for dinner, the queen will kill us all."

"Not if Libertas gets there first," I muttered.

EIGHTEEN

The Castle's formal dining room was large and bright, with a long oak table that spanned its length. It was covered with candles that flickered in the slight breeze coasting in through the open windows. Crystal goblets threw rainbows of light across the place settings, each of which had more utensils than it seemed possible to use. Nathaniel Whitehall, the president of the Congress, sat near me, and he'd spent nearly the entire time telling stories from when he and the king, friends since childhood, had been young.

"And so I said to your father, if you can't ride a horse properly, how the hell are you going to manage a kingdom?" Whitehall burst into a fit of red-faced laughter, and our entire end of the table followed suit, some more sincerely than others. The queen's gaze darted to the head chair, which had been left empty in tribute to the king. I pretended to find Whitehall's anecdote amusing, more for my sake than his. The General was keeping an incredibly close eye.

The air in the dining room was clotted with tension, and not just between the General and me. The queen laughed along with Whitehall's jokes the same as everyone else, but

I could see hatred blazing in her ice-blue eyes, and remembered what Thomas had told me—that Whitehall had been under consideration for the regency the queen now held, and he almost won it right out from under her, with considerable support from Juliana. Now, watching us get on so well together, she was visibly tense, as if she expected us to launch a campaign to overthrow her right there over the fish course.

For the first time since I entered Aurora, I was truly alone among the natives. Domestic staffers came in and out to serve and clean up after each course, but the KES agents—of which Thomas was one of many—were outside the room, presumably guarding the entrances. There were even a few agents on the balcony outside; I could see them out there in their black suits, pacing back and forth on high alert for any disturbances.

I hadn't realized how much I depended on Thomas—if not for help and advice, then just as a familiar face in unfamiliar surroundings. I would've been so much more relaxed if he'd been there, watching from a distant corner while I played my part, rooting for me to succeed. I knew now why the General had trusted him with assisting me; it wasn't just that he was a respected and talented KES agent, despite his age. It was that he had both the steely-eyed composure of a soldier and the ability to speak to me like I was a real person. Maybe that was why he and Juliana had become friends. I was experiencing firsthand how people acted around her. She was simultaneously above and below them; too high born to be treated like a normal teenage girl, but too young to be taken seriously as a political force in her own right. Thomas must've been a breath of fresh air, someone she could both rely on to protect her and also confide in. Again, I wondered how deep their connection had been, and, surprisingly, found myself hoping that friendship was as far as it had gone between them.

Of all the dinner guests, Whitehall was the only person who behaved like Juliana was a regular person. Thomas had told me earlier that Whitehall was Juliana's godfather, which explained both his easy familiarity with her and the way she'd supported him when the regency was under dispute. He treated her like a beloved niece, and I did my best to act accordingly, even going so far as to call him Whit, which was apparently Juliana's nickname for him.

"You remember how bad a rider Al was, don't you, General?" Whitehall shoveled a few stalks of asparagus into his mouth and smiled amiably over at the General as he chewed. The General's eyes widened just a fraction; he took a sip of wine, swallowed, and paused before responding.

You couldn't have found two more different men than Whitehall and the General if you scoured the entire planet. Whitehall was a large man, loud and jovial and friendly. The General was smaller in height and in girth; he was lean and fastidious about his appearance, with a habit of speaking in a low voice so that you had to bend forward to hear him. Whitehall, the General, and the king had known each other since they were young, which made it all the more strange that Whitehall called the General by his title and not his name—something he didn't do for the king.

"His Majesty was a fine rider from an early age," the General said, his voice taut and dark with disapproval. "I'm surprised that you're being so cavalier with your stories about our friend, Whitehall. Can't you see how it's upsetting Her Majesty?"

I glanced over at the queen; sure enough, her eyes were brimming with tears. Whitehall hung his head, duly shamed, and apologized to the queen for his mistake.

"It's all right, Whitehall." She lifted her chin imperiously.

"But perhaps we should talk about happier things. Like, for instance, Juliana's upcoming nuptials."

I tensed as all eyes turned toward me. "What about them?"

"Prince Callum arrives tomorrow," the queen reminded me. "Surely you must be thrilled, darling." I had to restrain myself from visibly cringing at the bitter way she uttered the word "darling" and somehow managed to dredge up a smile.

"Oh yes." The General's eyes were on me, and all I could bring myself to say was, "I'm terribly thrilled."

The queen laughed. "So shy! I was all nerves before my wedding. But there's nothing to worry about, my dear."

"I'm not worried," I countered. "I hear great things about Prince Callum. I'm sure we'll be happy together."

"We've missed you here, Juli," Whitehall told me, mercifully changing the subject. "I heard you were off relaxing at St. Lawrence. What in the world were you doing there for two weeks? I'm hardly at my country house three days before I'm restless and yearning for the city."

"I like the country," I said. "It's peaceful. And I only have to change clothes once a day."

That got a huge laugh from the table; the fact that Juliana was often photographed in multiple outfits on the same day was a well-worn joke in the tabloids. Yet another gem of wisdom from Thomas, whose knowledge of Juliana's day-to-day was coming in handier than I would ever have expected.

"Fair point to you," Whitehall said, tipping his glass in my direction. Just then, a phalanx of servers bustled in carrying covered silver trays in their white-gloved hands. "What's this, then? Dessert?" He addressed the question to me with a dramatic wink.

"What . . ." A server placed a tray in front of me and lifted the lid. "Oh no."

"I was in the European Federation last week," Whitehall explained, while I stared at what was on my plate. "And our ambassador in Paris—you've met Richter Barnard, haven't you, Juli?" I nodded, not sure she had but certain nobody would question me about it. "Anyway, he ordered this for us both, and I liked it so much I twisted the chef's arm for the recipe to give to the Castle kitchen. I thought you might enjoy it. I know how much you love chocolate."

I swallowed hard. I was looking at what was probably the most delicious chocolate mousse cake ever invented, but I was never going to taste it. I hadn't had chocolate since I was three years old, when a birthday cupcake brought on a brain-splitting migraine and full-body hives. I'd been tested and sure enough—I was allergic to cacao, the main ingredient in chocolate. And now, here it was, sitting on my plate, as everyone waited for me to take a bite.

I took a deep breath and beamed at Whitehall, who seemed very proud of himself. "Thank you so much, Whit. It looks amazing, but I promised Her Majesty that I'd watch what I ate. I have to fit into my wedding dress!" My smile was so wide and tight, I thought my face might split in half. The General looked at me suspiciously over the rim of his wineglass, and the queen rolled her eyes.

"Oh, for heaven's sake, Juliana, I think you can manage a couple of bites," she said. "After all, Whitehall went to all this trouble to do something nice for you. Skip lunch tomorrow instead."

"Yes, Your Highness," the General said. "A small taste won't kill you."

I picked up my fork. It didn't look like I had a choice;

everyone at the table was waiting for me to start eating my dessert so they could dig into theirs. I'd have to eat at least a little bit, to appease them. But I wasn't sure a small taste *wouldn't* kill me, as the General so succinctly put it.

I plunged my fork into the soft, spongy cake and lifted it to my mouth. I barely tasted it; I was too worried about what was going to happen next that I wasn't even able to enjoy eating chocolate for the first time in over a decade. When I'd gotten it down, I turned to Whitehall with a grateful smile. "That is the best dessert I've ever had. They'd better take it away from me now before I eat the whole thing!"

Whitehall laughed. "Oh, just eat it, for God's sake, girl. You've only got one life, you know."

Well, I thought ruefully. *I guess that depends on who you are.*

The rest of the guests turned to their own desserts, and soon the air was full of rapturous exclamations over the cake. Whitehall grinned like a self-satisfied child as even the queen thanked him for thinking to ask the French chef for his delicious recipe and bringing it to the Castle. Only the General withheld his opinion, leaving everyone to wonder what he thought as he slowly and deliberately picked at his dessert.

Eventually, though, people got tired of praising the cake and moved on to other topics. Whitehall, desperate for the General's attention, asked him about how his sons were doing.

Sons? I thought in surprise. It had never occurred to me that the General might have children—and, in that case, a wife, or at least an ex-wife. An ex-wife seemed like a more reasonable assumption. Either way, the thought of him breeding turned my stomach. What must it be like to have the General as a father? He didn't seem like the type of person who would even want children, or enjoy raising them. I listened closer to their conversation, my interest piqued. To my relief,

I wasn't feeling any different. Maybe I'd outgrown the allergy. And not a minute too soon, it seemed.

"They're fine," the General said. He was speaking to Whitehall, but he was staring straight at me. "Lucas just got back from visiting his mother."

"Is Alice still living at the Montauk house?" Whitehall asked.

The General shrugged. He seemed irritated that Whitehall was pressing him about his family life. "She likes it better by the water. Alice has never been one for cities."

"She must miss both your boys, though," Whitehall continued, either oblivious to the General's displeasure, or in defiance of it. I mentally pocketed this piece of information—so the General had *two* sons. How interesting.

Suddenly, a shock of pain rolled across my temples.

"I'm sure she does," the queen piped up. Her voice was far away, like the sound of ocean waves inside a seashell. "It must be so difficult, having your children gone and not knowing what could happen to them. Especially in your line of work."

The General nodded. "I suppose she does miss them, but they visit regularly. Well, Lucas does, at any rate."

"Just Lucas?" Whitehall asked. "Thomas doesn't go to see her?"

A sudden crash drew all the attention in the room to me. My wineglass lay shattered on the floor in dozens of glinting pieces. The room was silent but for the sound of my labored breathing. I couldn't get enough air. Everything seemed to be closing in on me, faces pressing into my eyeballs. Blood roared in my ears and my skin was growing hotter by the second, as if someone had doused me in kerosene and then lit a match.

"Juli!" Whitehall reached out to steady me. I was listing to one side, in great danger of toppling off my chair. Whitehall's skin had the pallor of a bar of soap. "What's wrong?"

I touched my neck; I could feel hives rising beneath my fingertips. My head hurt so badly, I thought it was going to explode. I rubbed my temples, hoping to coax the pain out but failing miserably.

"I think she's having an allergic reaction. Someone call a doctor!" Whitehall shouted. He put his arm around my shoulders. I was shaking, my teeth chattering. "Close those doors! She's cold!"

The General stared at me, unmoving, his expression blank. The only indication that he might have been upset by what was happening was a slight tightness in his jaw. He didn't resemble Thomas at all, but the way they looked when they were trying to hide an upswell of emotion was something they shared. I hadn't noticed before, but now it was all I could see. Thomas was the General's son.

It made perfect sense. It explained why Thomas was in the position he was, so young and yet so uniquely placed in the agency. Nepotism had played its part well. And what about Thomas's brother, this other boy, Lucas? Was he in the KES, too? How old was he? And what was *his* reward for being the General's spawn?

But the question that kept rising to the top, the one I needed an answer to above all others, was why did Thomas tell me his parents were dead? Clearly that was a lie, and an awful one, because it had made me believe, for a few short but important seconds, that he and I might have something in common. I was so stupid. He'd only been trying to manipulate me, the way he had from the very first moment that we came into contact, and I'd fallen for it, just like I'd fallen for it back on Earth.

Hands grasped me by the shoulders and shook me to get my attention. I opened my eyes. Thomas was crouched in front of my chair, which someone had yanked away from the table with me still on it, to give me room and make way for help. I tried to wrench away from him, but I could only manage a weak shudder.

"What happened?" he whispered.

I looked over at the dessert, which was still sitting, mostly uneaten, on the plate. "I told you I was allergic to chocolate," I whispered back.

He nodded, his expression grave. "Don't worry. The doctor's on his way."

Thomas helped lay me down on a settee in the reception area that adjoined the dining room. The other guests had been shuffled off, and only the queen, the General, and Whitehall remained behind to oversee my care. The queen sat stiff as a poker in a straight-backed chair near the settee, her mouth set in a grim line. Whitehall paced back and forth. It wasn't until the General barked, "Sit down, Whitehall!" from his place near the door, that Whitehall finally gathered himself and flopped into a nearby armchair.

A wave of panic swept through me and I began to cry. I tried to staunch the tears with the backs of my hands, but I couldn't. I wanted my mother so badly. The first time I had a reaction, she took me home from the doctor's and put me to bed, then crawled in with me and curled her body around mine, holding me through the night. I missed her so much it was like a black hole had opened up inside of me, consuming everything in its path. *I want to go home,* I thought desperately, and the tears came faster, spilling down my cheeks. Thomas gazed at me with eyes full of concern, and I almost lost it.

The only thing that stopped me was the stark reality of my circumstances and fear of the General's wrath.

The door to the reception room slid open and a man walked in. I turned to look at him. He was short and grizzled, with a shock of thinning silver hair and a thick white mustache that curled over his lip like a fat caterpillar. He held a black doctor's bag in his hand and wore a pair of thick gold-rimmed spectacles that made his eyes seem overlarge and surprised.

"Who are you?" the queen demanded. "Where's Dr. Rowland?"

"Dr. Rowland is off duty tonight," the General said, before the man could speak. "Dr. Moss is one of our KES physicians."

"Your Majesty." Dr. Moss bowed low before the queen, then turned his attention to me. "Your Highness, I'm sorry to see you in this distressing state. Would you mind if I gave you a cursory examination?"

I looked at Thomas, who nodded. "Yes, of course."

"Wonderful. Excuse me, Agent, would you mind moving aside?" Thomas did as he was asked, disappearing from my field of vision.

Dr. Moss looked me over for a few minutes, then asked, "Besides the hives, do you have any other symptoms, Your Highness?"

My fingers fluttered near my temples. "A headache. And . . . it's hard . . . to breathe."

"A simple allergic reaction, then. What did you eat tonight?" I told him, and he nodded. "When did you first start experiencing these symptoms?"

"A couple of minutes . . . after . . . dessert," I said, pausing a few times to catch my breath.

"I see. Well, I'm sorry to say this, Your Highness, but it seems as though it was the chocolate that did it."

"That's absurd!" the queen cried. "Juliana isn't allergic to chocolate."

"Food allergies are mysterious creatures, Your Majesty," Dr. Moss explained. "They come and go as we age, and they can manifest quite unexpectedly."

"I suppose we'll have to do something about the wedding cake," the queen muttered.

"Don't bother," I told her. "I just won't eat any."

"Luckily for Your Highness, I can administer an antihistamine that should fix you up quite quickly. Have you any objection to needles?"

I shook my head. Under the circumstances, I could hardly protest. I squeezed my eyes shut while he gave me a shot in the crook of my elbow. "What now?" I asked when it was over.

"Now," he said, "we wait."

We didn't have to wait long. Within moments I was feeling much better; the headache had started to recede, the hives were clearing up faster than they had appeared, and in the space of fifteen minutes, I could breathe normally again. I sat up as soon as I had the strength and thanked Dr. Moss.

"Happy to be of service, Your Highness. If there's nothing else . . . ?" He looked at the General, who shook his head.

"That will be all," the General said. "You're excused."

Dr. Moss nodded. As he stood, he made eye contact with me and deliberately held my gaze. A smile quirked the ends of his mouth. *He knows,* I thought. Was Dr. Moss the same scientist friend Thomas had mentioned before, the one with all the theories about analogs?

When he was satisfied that I understood, the doctor turned and left. I wanted to call him back and pepper him with questions—Thomas had told me a lot about the tandem, but there was still so much I wanted to know, especially about the strange visions I'd been having of Juliana. Maybe Dr. Moss could explain things better.

Thomas slid his arm around my back and helped me stand. "I'll see you to your room," he offered. I shook him off, remembering another offer he'd made once, to walk me home. I didn't want him to touch me, or help me, or do anything for me. I just wanted to be alone.

Perhaps deciding it wasn't worth fighting in front of the others, he let go of me, but I hadn't gotten more than a few steps on my own before I had to stop, because the room was spinning. I reached out instinctively and he caught me around the waist.

"Are you sure you don't need any help?" he asked. I gave in, seeing as I obviously wasn't going to be able to get back to Juliana's bedroom without assistance. As we left the room, Whitehall gave me a kind smile.

"Be well, Juli," he said with affection. I nodded, wanting to appear grateful, but all I could do was wonder if I would ever truly be well again.

5

DAYS

THOMAS IN THE TOWER / 2

"Sir, I think we have a mole," Thomas said. It was early in the morning, and sun was just beginning to rise over Columbia City, chasing away the aurora. He was seated across from his father in the General's office, squeezing in this audience while the General signed off on some long-neglected paperwork. His interactions with the General had more or less always been this way, with the General only half listening as he attended to some more important matter of Citadel business. Thomas was used to it, but this morning he found it frustrating, and was doing a poor job of hiding it. The General despised signs of physical restlessness, so Thomas often had to resist pacing, drumming his fingers, tapping his feet—all those natural impulses that struck when he was agitated—but today he couldn't.

"That's ridiculous," the General said.

"No, it isn't," Thomas insisted. Most of the time, arguing with the General was a fool's errand, but Thomas wasn't going to back down about this. If someone inside the Citadel was feeding Libertas information, Sasha was in greater danger than they had foreseen. "They took Juliana out of here right under our noses, leaving behind no trace of entry or exit. How could they have done it without the help of someone with intimate knowledge of the Castle? And Grant Davis—it's not a coincidence that they had a patrol on the South End at the same time he came through the tandem. Someone told them to go there. They were waiting for him."

"And you think it's someone in the KES?" The General's tone implied that he thought Thomas was being insubordinate. He would have to tread very carefully around this issue—except that he had no interest in doing so.

"The KES isn't impervious!" Thomas gripped the wooden arms of his chair. The thought of one of his KES brothers betraying the agency and putting Operation Starling in jeopardy made him sick to his stomach, but he wasn't going to turn a blind eye and keep walking into Libertas traps. Libertas had no idea who Sasha really was—that was a secret known by so few people that unless the mole was himself, the General, Gloria, or Dr. Moss, they couldn't have any inkling as to her otherworldly origins—but that didn't mean they wouldn't find out, if the General ignored the fact that someone was funneling KES secrets their way.

"I know it isn't," the General told him sternly. "I've been part of the KES for thirty years, and I've seen many trusted agents exposed for the traitors they were. Do not presume to believe you know everything, Thomas; arrogance will betray you every time."

Thomas sighed. "I'm sorry, sir." His father was right; one of Thomas's weaknesses was his propensity to mistake passion for understanding. He was devoted to the KES and its mission, but he had only been part of it for two years. There was still so much about the agency that he didn't know.

"If you think there's a mole, then find him," the General

said. "And find him fast. Because the world is about to change, and when it does, we must be at our strongest."

"I will, sir," Thomas said, energized by the General's faith in him, grudging though it was.

"Good," the General said, turning back to his paperwork. "Now go eat something. They can hear your stomach growling all the way up at the Academy."

Thomas rode the elevator from the General's office suite, which took up the entire 114th floor of the Tower, down to the 62nd floor, which contained the KES mess hall. The King's Elite Service was a network that spread all over the country and the Tower was its nerve center. More than just a headquarters, the Tower was the workplace and residence of over twenty-five thousand agents and support staffers; they worked on the lower and upper floors of the building, but the middle floors were reserved for residential and other living spaces. Not all agents opted to take the General's blanket offer of free housing, but Thomas hadn't had a choice; when he received his assignment after he matriculated from the KES Academy, he'd been given his room number and that had been that. Housing quality was determined by years served, not by rank, so he had one of the smallest, least desirable rooms; it had a bathroom but no kitchen, so he was forced to take all his meals in the mess.

Not that he minded. The mess was one of his favorite places in the Tower, because it was where agents and staff came to socialize. He liked its noise and chaos; it reminded him of his time at the Academy. He'd only been there for a little less than six months, but they had been some of happiest months of his life.

It was a little too early for the breakfast rush when Thomas arrived at the mess, so there were only a few people scattered across the enormous dining hall, spooning oatmeal or scrambled eggs into their mouths while going over files or reading copies of the *Royal Eagle,* Columbia City's largest daily newspaper. Thomas got his food and made his way to his usual table. He was looking forward to finally being alone, because it would give him some space to think about his rapidly growing pile of problems.

First, there was Sasha. Just about everything to do with her was a problem. He hadn't realized just how much he would like her, but he had, from the moment they'd met. At the time, he'd put this down to her resemblance to Juliana, but it hadn't taken long for him to see how different Sasha was from her analog. If people were houses, Juliana was like the Citadel she'd grown up in—beautiful and well-appointed, but guarded and set apart—while Sasha was her grandfather's Hyde Park Victorian—cheerful and bright, with the windows and doors flung wide open. Sasha was curious and interested in people besides herself; she liked to laugh and didn't take herself too seriously, while Juliana, accustomed to being used and befriended for her position, kept everyone at arm's length. Spending time with Sasha on Earth had been easy and fun, and he'd meant what he said to her on the beach: it had been the best night of his life. Despite the fact that he'd been on a mission, Thomas had never felt freer than when he was on Earth; it had been such a relief to live a normal life for once, even if it wasn't—and could never be—his forever.

It was the run-in with Libertas in the Tattered City that showed him how much he'd grown to care for Sasha. He'd been so angry with her for running off, and worried for her, too, but when he saw her in that alley with that stringy-haired Libertine's arm around her neck, his blood had run cold, as if a splinter of ice had become lodged in his heart. Fear was an unusual emotion for Thomas—he'd been trained so well over his years of military education to control it, to process it into swift, precise action. He'd learned long ago how not to let it paralyze him, and it'd been years since he'd properly felt it, like a drizzle of freezing rain down his spine. But he felt it then, and he knew—she wasn't just an assignment anymore, a counterfeit Juliana. She was Sasha, and he was in big trouble.

So, then, what to do about it? There could never be anything between them besides a brief, loose friendship; the tandem was too high a hurdle, and he got the sense—silly as it would have sounded if he'd said it out loud—that the universes would disapprove. Besides, her opinion of him seemed . . . variable. She'd despised him at first, after finding out how he'd tricked her, which was understandable. He was sure he'd be able to coax her out of it eventually, and convince her to trust him at least so far as to take the help that he offered her. He'd thought it was working, but last night she was angry again, and nothing he said or did seemed to please her. In the end, he'd just stopped trying to talk to her, dropped her off at Juliana's room, briefed the night agent stationed outside, and returned to the Tower for some rest. He needed to figure out what was bothering her, and fast; if he didn't, it could compromise the entire mission.

But Sasha was only one of many things that troubled him. The Grant Davis situation enraged him, even more now that he suspected someone in the agency of funneling intelligence to Libertas, and of course there was Juliana, who he tried not to think too hard about. He wouldn't put it past Libertas to kill her if the General didn't give them what they wanted, which he never would. The only comfort Thomas had was the knowledge that Juliana would be doing her best to give them hell, because that was her way. She wasn't good at taking orders, the natural consequence of a life of privilege.

And then there was the mole. Thomas's involvement with Operation Starling didn't leave him with a lot of time to run his own covert internal investigation, and he had no idea where to start looking for the leak. The KES was a huge organization, a complicated hierarchy with a seemingly infinite set of moving parts. All missions, even Operation Starling to an extent, required the diligent work of hundreds of agents in a wide variety of fields to successfully pull off. Any one of them could be the chink in the KES armor, but ferreting him or her out would require an exhaustive search on a scale outside what Thomas could do on his own. He couldn't let that stop him, though. He'd just have to figure out a way.

Lost in his thoughts, Thomas didn't notice his brother until he took a seat across the table from him and gave him a hearty, "Hey, T."

"Lucas," Thomas said. "What are you doing here?"

Lucas was KES, too, but he was a midlevel support agent with no field duties or on-call minimums who'd chosen not to live in the Tower. Thomas knew it bothered Lucas that his younger brother was a senior-level active agent at the age of eighteen, while he'd been denied admission to the KES Academy three times. The Academy was the one place the General's favoritism didn't go very far. Potential recruits had to score above a certain level on a number of mental and physical examinations to even qualify, and despite all efforts Lucas couldn't make the grade. Thomas was sorry for that, because he knew how badly Lucas wanted to be active, and how much he hated having to settle for some mind-numbing desk job, but rules were rules, and Thomas was pretty sure the world was better off not having Lucas Mayhew on active KES duty.

"Just because I don't live here doesn't mean I'm not entitled to free breakfast," Lucas said, lunging across the table to liberate a piece of bacon from Thomas's plate.

"Actually," Thomas said, swiping at his brother with his fork. "That's exactly what it means."

"Too bad." Lucas set to work devouring Thomas's scrambled eggs. "What's on today's schedule, princess? Manicures and dress fittings?"

"No, the fitting was yesterday," Thomas said in bemusement. Lucas rolled his eyes.

"I used to be so jealous of you," Lucas said, downing half of Thomas's orange juice in one gulp. Thomas stared forlornly at his breakfast tray, the contents of which were swiftly disappearing. Lucas's very presence was growing more and more annoying. Thomas hoped he'd get to the point soon. "But if being an active agent means tea parties and fashion shows all day, forget it. I wouldn't trade jobs with you if you paid me."

Oh, yes you would, Thomas thought. He wasn't fooled by Lucas. He knew his brother would kill to be doing what he was doing, and he didn't even know about Operation Starling, or the true nature of Thomas's most recent work. The thought of how envious Lucas would be if he did know warmed Thomas's heart a little. "What do you need from me, Luke? Money?"

Lucas grimaced. "When have I ever asked you for money?" Thomas opened his mouth, prepared to launch into a long list of examples, but Lucas cut him off with a raised hand. "No, this isn't about money. It's about Mom."

Thomas sighed. "I thought so."

"She's fine, by the way. But she misses you. I know you don't believe it, but she does, and she wanted me to ask you to come out and see her. *Again*."

"I will," Thomas said, concentrating on the remnants of his breakfast in an effort to avoid Lucas's gaze. It seemed like every time he saw Lucas these days, all he wanted to talk about was what a terrible son Thomas was being, and how it broke Alice's heart that the youngest Mayhew never made it out to Montauk to visit. But it was more complicated than that, as Lucas knew full well. Alice didn't care if he came or not; she might have told herself she did, but that was only because not caring made her feel guilty.

"When? I just went out there this weekend. Would've been nice of you to come with me." Lucas eyed him carefully, and Thomas wondered if his brother knew he'd been away. By virtue of their different roles in the KES, weeks could go by without the Mayhew boys getting even so much as a glimpse of each other. But Lucas was acting shiftier than usual, and Thomas had a feeling that for all his scolding, Lucas wanted Thomas and their mother to remain estranged. It guaranteed that at least one of their parents preferred him over Thomas.

"I'm sort of busy at the moment," Thomas said.

"What, carrying Juliana's train?" Lucas scoffed. "Yeah, real important work you're doing in the Castle there, toy soldier."

"Hey!" Thomas snapped. "Don't call me that." It wasn't easy to ruffle his feathers, but that nickname got under his skin. "Toy soldier" was what they called recruits at the KES Academy, not active duty agents, and it wasn't a term Lucas was entitled to throw around in either case.

Lucas put his palms up in a gesture of surrender. "Sorry. You need to lighten up."

These days, it was as if he and Lucas were only a breath or two away from open hostility. There was nothing Thomas could do about Lucas's jealousy. He wasn't about to quit the KES, or fail in order to make Lucas look better by comparison; he couldn't help who he was, or the fact that he was good at his job. It was a shame, though. There had been a time, not that long ago, when his brother was his best friend, his most trusted confidant. He felt the loss of Lucas's affection more keenly than he would admit out loud, and he was starting to wonder if they'd ever be close again.

Thomas stood. "I'm going to go get some more food, and then I have to head over to the Castle. So . . ." He trailed off, waiting for Lucas to pick up on the hint.

Lucas nodded. "It was good to see you, T. Mom's not the only one who misses you, you know."

Thomas wanted to believe his brother was being sincere. "I miss you, too," he replied.

That, at least, was true.

THEY HAD MOVED HER THE *night before, right after the girl came in to clear her dinner tray. It didn't take long for her to get her things together; she'd brought nothing with her, just the clothes on her back and that which she was hoping to trade for safe passage into a whole new life. They'd tossed her room twice already looking for it, but she wasn't born yesterday. She kept it hidden in her bra, where they hadn't yet ventured to check, though she wouldn't put it past them to try.*

The place she'd been before had been some kind of underground bunker, but when they whipped the blindfold off her eyes this time, she saw that she was standing in front of a large and well-maintained farmhouse, in the shade of ten towering oaks, with nothing around for miles but cornfields. That was how she knew where they'd taken her. Well, that and the flag flying from the porch, the black phoenix on the red background. At first she was surprised, but then she supposed they couldn't exactly fly the Libertas banner, even here.

Her room was in the attic, but it had several windows that let in plenty of light. The place was airy and bright, and, while not up to her usual standards, it was a welcome change from the windowless cell they'd been keeping her in before. It was almost peaceful, if she could forget about the armed guards standing on the other side of the door. As soon as she was alone, she swept the room for bugs like

Thomas had taught her, but her search turned up nothing. She had to wonder what that meant—they hadn't even tried to hide the cameras in the other place.

Much as she hated to admit it to herself, she was curious about the state of affairs back in Columbia City. What had the General and the queen done when they discovered her missing? The wedding must have been canceled. Every day she prayed that even though she wouldn't be marrying the Farnham prince, the treaty and the fragile peace it had brought to the disputed borderlands would remain undisturbed. That was why it was so important to her that her disappearance look like a kidnapping—she needed the UCC to come out of the whole messy affair clean. It was her last gift to her people, perhaps the only one she had ever given them.

She tried not to think about Thomas, except to wonder whether or not he'd gotten her note. He wouldn't understand, no matter what she said; he was uncommonly steadfast and loyal to a fault, and he would never see why she'd done what she'd done. That was fine; she didn't need his approval. She just needed to know that she'd done what she could to explain her intentions and make her apologies to her only real friend. It wasn't enough, but it was something.

Her guards were infuriatingly silent on the subject of what was happening in the world outside her confines, and nobody would tell her when she was going to be allowed to see the Monad. She was starting to wonder if he even existed. It was like they were waiting for something, a perfect moment, but she didn't know what or when it was coming. Her room at the farmhouse, just like her room at the bunker, was locked from the outside at all times, but at least she could look out the windows. There was a small bookshelf under one of the slanted eaves; she picked out a slim paperback whose spine read Twelfth Night.

"Ugh," she said aloud. "Shakespeare." She'd never been much for

the Bard, whose work she found difficult and unrewarding. But she opened the book anyway, and started to read; perhaps the new Juliana, the person she was about to become, loved Shakespeare. Maybe it was the next stage in her evolution. People changed, they grew. It was possible she loved Shakespeare and didn't even know it.

NINETEEN

The Day of Prince Callum, like every other day I'd experienced in Aurora so far, was bright and sunny. I woke up at seven thirty, well-rested considering how insane the day before had been, and completely recovered from my allergic reaction. Last night had been a close call; it should have raised everyone's suspicions, because they knew Juliana wasn't allergic to chocolate, and yet they accepted Dr. Moss's justification without question. Maybe Thomas and Gloria were right; I looked exactly like Juliana, and almost any explanation was more reasonable than the assumption that I wasn't her.

Still, the incident had rattled me. I felt blurry at the edges, as if I was starting to blend in with my surroundings, evolving a Juliana camouflage. It was for the best, I supposed; it would make my job a lot easier. But I didn't want to morph into somebody else; I liked who I was. And of course, the only way I could get back to my real life was to pretend I wasn't me. The irony of the whole thing was sickening, but I had to believe that I was and always would be Sasha Lawson, that nothing could erase that.

Gloria burst in at eight with Louisa, Rochelle, and a breakfast cart, attendant attached, trailing in her wake. Gloria was impeccably dressed as always, but there was an air of harried frenzy surrounding her that I hadn't experienced before. Seeing Gloria agitated made me instantly alert. I'd forgotten how important this day was to everyone at the Castle.

"Come on, come on, Your Highness, we have a lot to do today," Gloria said. "Jump in the shower, and don't take too long!"

It was fruitless arguing with Gloria, so I didn't bother to try, but being bossed around like this was starting to get on my nerves. How Juliana could stand it was far beyond me. I was glad I wasn't going to have to deal with it forever.

"Finally," Gloria breathed when I stepped out of the bathroom, hair wet. I sat down and the attendant rolled the breakfast cart within reach. Louisa ran a comb through my hair, separating it into sections for easy drying and curling. As I ate, Gloria yelled her morning briefing over the sound of the hair dryer, until it became obvious to all parties that something had to come first—the briefing or the drying.

"First up is your visit to the king," Gloria informed me once my hair was finished. "I knew you wouldn't want to interrupt your daily visit to your father for anything, even Prince Callum, so I made room for it."

"Thanks, Gloria," I said, glancing at Louisa and Rochelle. They hardly spoke, and it was easy to forget they were there. The most dangerous moments were those in which I was in the presence of both people who knew my true identity and people who didn't. It was one thing for me to be myself, and quite another to be Juliana, but being both at once was proving to be a challenge.

Gloria moved on. "The prince arrives at three o'clock with his Farnham escort. They'll be taking him through the front gates to the main entrance, after which the escort will leave and the KES agents the General has assigned to the prince will take over his protection. You and Her Majesty will meet him at the grand staircase, you'll exchange some pleasantries and he will be escorted to his quarters. He'll have his own security briefing, then dinner. Once that's over, you'll have some time alone to get to know each other better."

"Romantic," I said sarcastically, dabbing at the corners of my mouth with a napkin. Rochelle snorted. Clearly not everyone was quite so disapproving of Juliana's antics. My chest tightened at the prospect of having to make conversation with Prince Callum. Get to know him *better*? I didn't know him at all, and I had absolutely no idea what I was going to say to him.

"Watch the attitude," Gloria warned, giving me a stern look. "Okay, Louisa, try not to make her look like a French poodle. Juliana, your outfit is on the bed; finish breakfast before getting dressed. Thomas will walk you to the king's suite at ten, then you'll be back here at eleven. You'll have from eleven to twelve to yourself, then another dress fitting from twelve to one. Hopefully we can squeeze in a quick lunch for you and then you'll meet Her Majesty in her study to go over last-minute changes to the guest list and finalize the floral arrangements. That should take you all the way up to Prince Callum's arrival. The day is tightly packed, so no dawdling and absolutely *no* wandering off."

"All right, all right," I said, waving her off with a bored little yawn. "Busy day, packed schedule, I get it."

Once I got into it, pretending to be Juliana could be fun. I was starting to see what Thomas had meant when he said you just felt it, sometimes, what your analog would do, when you were living their life. It was coming easier now. I wondered if that had anything to do with the visions of Juliana I'd been seeing in my dreams. I'd had another one last night, but, like always, I couldn't remember much, which made me nuts. If only I could figure out something, remember some pertinent detail about what was happening to her, maybe I could use it as leverage with the General, or at the very least, with Thomas. But there was nothing. Only lightning-quick impressions, small bits of imagery, remained from the dreams. I wasn't going to stop trying, but the visions were starting to feel useless, and I was getting discouraged.

"Good. Thomas will be here soon. Oh, and Juliana?"

"Yes?" I said.

She pointed at the dresser, where I'd abandoned Juliana's diamond the night before. "Don't forget to wear the ring."

I wasn't stupid; I knew I wouldn't be able to escape or avoid Thomas. He was my captor and my protector, and like it or not, I was stuck with him. But I didn't have to talk to him. It was one thing for him to pose as Grant to get me to Aurora—sure, it was screwed up and wrong, but at least it had a *point*. Telling me his parents were dead when they weren't, and hiding from me the fact that the General was his actual father, alive and well, was more than wrong—it was sick.

It took Thomas a while to notice I was giving him the cold shoulder. In fact, if I hadn't known better, I would've thought *he* wasn't speaking to *me*. He was entirely wrapped up in his own thoughts and barely even seemed to notice I was there. We walked the whole way in silence, me fuming, him totally zoned out.

There was no way around it: the king scared me. I hated his suite, with the paraphernalia of illness that crowded his bed and the choking medicinal smell of hospital that filled the room, but it was the king himself who unsettled me most. The nonsense he'd spouted the day before and the aggressive way he'd grabbed my wrist had frightened me more than they probably should have. *He's a harmless, bedridden old man,* I reminded myself. But that didn't keep my stomach from sinking when we approached the door to his bedroom.

The king appeared to be asleep when we entered; at least, his hand wasn't kneading the air in its endless pattern. Not knowing what else to do, I started *The Odyssey* where I'd left off the day before. Thomas hovered near the door, still in his own little world. I glanced up every once in a while as I read, my gaze leaping from the king, who remained motionless in slumber, to Thomas, but only when he wasn't looking at me.

"Okay," he said finally. "Are you going to tell me what's going on, or are you going to make me guess?"

I didn't answer him, keeping my eyes trained on the page. He sighed and crossed the room, pulling a chair over from up against the wall and sitting down.

"Come on, Sasha, let's hear it," he pressed. "I won't stop asking until you tell me, so you might as well quit giving me the silent treatment and say what you need to say."

"I thought you weren't supposed to use my real name," I pointed out, still refusing to look at him. He put his hand on mine and used it to close the book. My breath caught in my throat. He'd touched me before, out of necessity, mostly, but something about the way he wrapped his fingers around mine felt . . . intimate. I jerked away, wanting no part of it. I hated him. He was a liar and a coward and . . . and . . . he had the most expressive green eyes I'd ever seen. I closed mine to keep from looking into his. *What is going* on *with you?* I asked myself savagely. *It's just* Thomas, *for God's sake!*

"I think it's safe in here." Nevertheless, his eyes flickered over to the king and he lowered his voice. "Now, what's wrong?"

I shook my head. "It doesn't matter." And it didn't. He couldn't fix the problem, couldn't un-lie. He couldn't go back in time and never pretend to be Grant, never bring me here. He couldn't un-be his father's son. We were who we were, and we'd done what we'd done, and nothing was ever going to change that or make it better.

"It matters to me," Thomas insisted. "Look, if you don't trust me, you won't listen to me. And if you don't listen to me, you could get hurt. Remember the Tattered City?"

"How can I trust you when all you do is lie to me?"

My accusation took Thomas aback. "What are you talking about? I've never lied to you." I rolled my eyes and groaned. How could he even bring himself to say that to me? I couldn't believe his nerve. He conceded the point. "Okay, I let you believe I was Grant Davis. But *other than that,* I haven't lied to you, not once this whole time. I don't lie. Not unless I absolutely have to. It's just not in my nature."

"A spy who doesn't lie? Useful."

"I'm not a spy," Thomas told me. "I'm a soldier. I'm a bodyguard. I'm an interuniversal transporter. There's a difference."

"I don't care what you are," I said. "To me, you're nobody. You don't even really exist."

"What did I lie about that's got you so worked up?"

"You told me your parents were dead," I spat. "And yet, I found out last night that the *General* is your dad. You've even got a mother on top of that! Alice? Is that her name? Oh, and a brother, too. You've just got a whole crap-ton of living relatives, don't you?"

"Who'd you hear all this from?" I noticed he didn't deny it.

"Straight from the horse's mouth," I said. "In fact, I think he enjoyed it. He knew I didn't know. He knew you'd lied."

Thomas shook his head. "My parents *are* dead. My biological parents. They died when I was five, exactly how I told you before. I didn't lie. I just . . . omitted the fact that, a couple years later, the General and his wife adopted me. That brother you mentioned? His name is Lucas. He's the General and Alice's real son."

"Adopted?" I had no idea what I expected Thomas to say in defense of himself, but this definitely wasn't it.

"Yeah." He took a deep breath and looked over at me tentatively. "Do you want to know how it happened?"

I nodded. I did want to know. Here was my chance to find out something real. His story. How he'd come to be who he was.

"Other than my parents, I didn't have much family—nobody close, nobody who could take in a five-year-old kid. So I got processed by the government, and was placed in an orphanage in New Jersey Dominion called the Princeton School for Boys. I didn't think I'd ever get adopted," he admitted with a small shrug. "Older ones almost never do. So it was kind of a shock that I was—to me, and to everyone else."

"How did the General even find you? Was he just in the market for a new son?"

"I don't know, I've never asked," Thomas said. "What? Someone offers you a new home, a family, after three years of being completely alone in the world, you don't question it."

"So you were eight?"

"Yeah." He rubbed the back of his neck, his eyes trained on the ground. "The General was at the orphanage on behalf of this military school, Blackbriar. He's an alumnus, and he does voluntary recruitment for their scholarship program. He came on Field Day, where we did all these sports and activities. I wasn't great at sports, because I was too small—back then," he added, catching my dubious look. There were a lot of words I might use to describe Thomas, but "small" wasn't one of them. "But I was a fast runner. The fastest in the whole school. When the General picked me out, I thought I'd be getting a Blackbriar scholarship, but it turned out I was too young to go there. Instead, the General had decided he wanted to adopt me, officially, and I ended up going to Blackbriar anyway, two years later, as his son."

"Are you close, then? You and the General, I mean?"

"I wouldn't say that," Thomas told me. "Lucas—my brother—thinks I'm the General's favorite, and I guess, from all outward appearances, I must be. But I've never thought that. He treats me the same way he treats everyone else. It's not like having a real father. I know what *that's* like, and it's not like that at all."

I realized I'd been holding my breath and finally let it out. "I'm sorry. I didn't know."

"Of course you didn't," Thomas said. "I didn't tell you."

I nodded.

"But you should know," Thomas continued, shifting his chair so that he was facing me directly. "I'm not going to lie to you. This situation is so weird and I realize that it's a struggle. Believe me, I've done it. Stepping into the life of your analog, even for the right reasons, isn't easy. It makes you doubt all kinds of things you thought you knew about yourself. What you're willing to do. What you want. Who you can trust. I don't want you to feel as lost as I did as Grant. You have no idea how many times I wanted to tell you who I really was. I wanted someone to know." I stared down at my hands in my lap. I couldn't look into his eyes. I knew what I'd find there, and I couldn't see it, couldn't acknowledge it in any way.

"*I* know who *you* are," he told me. "And I want you to feel like you can trust me, because I know how much that means." He sat back, his speech finished.

It took me a few moments to figure out what to say. "Can I . . . Do you mind if I have a few minutes alone?" My voice cracked. It felt like I hadn't spoken in days.

Thomas indicated the king with a slight incline of his head. "He'll be here."

I let out a breathy laugh. "That's okay. He doesn't talk much."

Thomas nodded, getting up and putting the chair back where he got it. "I'll be right outside if you need me," he promised.

"I know you will," I said. "And thanks. For what you said."

"I meant every word," he told me.

When Thomas was gone, I went back to reading *The Odyssey* out loud to the king. I just didn't know what else to do. I hadn't wanted him gone so that I could think. Thinking about Thomas was the last thing I wanted to do. I needed something else to focus on, and took comfort in the familiar act of reading. There was something about saying the words aloud that was meditative and soothing. I let the cadence of my own voice, speaking words that were written thousands of years before, wash everything away like a receding tide.

"'But once your crew has rowed you past the Sirens, a choice of routes is yours,'" I read. "'I cannot advise you which to take, or lead you through it all—you must decide for yourself—but I can tell you the ways of either course.'"

The king muttered something unintelligible, startling me. I looked up at him, but his eyes were still closed. I wasn't even sure that he'd said anything at all.

I cleared my throat and kept going. Something shook inside of me, as if someone was jangling a set of keys against my rib cage. "'On one side beetling cliffs shoot up, and against them pound the huge roaring breakers of blue-eyed Amphitrite—'"

The king made another inscrutable noise. This time I was sure I'd heard it, and started to wish Thomas would come back in. The king spooked me; I couldn't explain it, but I didn't like it, not one bit.

I paused in my reading and watched him. His eyes flew open, staring straight ahead, and he raised his hand; his fingers resumed their hypnotic dance. "Mirror, mirror."

I tried to ignore it, but after a few moments I could sense him looking at me. I put the book down. *He's in a hospital bed,* I told myself. *He can't do anything to you.*

"What is it?" I didn't expect him to answer, but was it possible that he was attempting to communicate? The doctors were certain the king's mumblings were random and meaningless, but what if that wasn't true? What if he was actually trying to say something?

"Angel eyes," he said. I wondered if that was his pet name for Juliana. I smiled at the thought. It was sort of sweet. My dad had called me "Little One."

"Angel eyes," he said again, more insistent this time. "Mirror, mirror."

"On the wall," I said, playing along. "Who's the fairest of them all?"

"One, one, two, three, five, eight," he said.

"That's not how the story goes," I informed him. Not that he was listening.

"Touch and go," the king said. "Touch and go." I sighed.

The door slid open and Thomas came in. "Is everything all right?"

"He's talking again. And doing, you know, the hand thing." But the king's odd behavior didn't seem to bother Thomas.

"Oh," he said. "Well, I guess that's normal. Relatively

speaking, anyway. Are you ready to go?" All traces of awkwardness from our previous conversation had disappeared, at least on his end. He was acting as if the past half hour had never even occurred. Maybe I should've been grateful; I wanted to ignore it, too. But the fact that *he* wanted to ignore it made me want to talk about it more, which I knew was a bad idea, so I bit my tongue and said nothing.

Thomas glanced at his watch. "Sasha?"

I liked it when he said my name. It felt good to be reminded, by someone other than myself, who I was. "Yeah, I'm coming."

I put *The Odyssey* back in its place on the bedside table. The king didn't seem to notice us leaving. It was as if he had no idea we were even in the room. He looked so sad and desolate lying there alone, in an impenetrable bubble where nothing mattered except for what was going on in his head. He was older than my own father would have been if he had lived, much closer to Granddad's age. Someday, I realized with a jolt, it would be Granddad lying in that bed, or one very much like it. The thought made my heart ache. I felt the sudden urge to stay with the king, just so he wouldn't have to be alone. But I couldn't. I had a schedule to keep. And a life to live.

TWENTY

"Are you nervous?" Thomas whispered.

Of course I was nervous, and having him at my side right now wasn't helping. My thoughts were like a flock of birds being chased into flight, wheeling around inside my head, looping and gliding so fast that I couldn't sort them out, but they all came circling back to Thomas in the end. In spite of all my doubts and fears, I felt connected to him. He was my only link in this world to my past, the reality of my true life. The only one, as he had said back in the king's bedroom, who knew who I was. I wanted him close, but I wanted him far away, too.

And now, to complicate things even further, Prince Callum was coming. I hadn't had to be really intimate with anyone in my short time as Juliana, other than Gloria and Thomas. My analog was the sort of person who kept most people at a distance. But Callum was Juliana's *betrothed*. Would he expect to kiss me? To hold me? To . . . sleep with me? I had no idea what he would want, or what questions he would ask, and no one could tell me that, not even Thomas.

"You'll be fine," Thomas assured me. "He's got no reason

to suspect anything. He's never met Juliana. He's never even been outside Farnham. To him, Juliana is whoever you allow her to be."

Yeah, I thought. *But who is* that?

We'd nearly reached the head of the grand staircase, where I was supposed to meet the queen to await the arrival of the Farnham prince. I was almost as unnerved by the prospect of spending more time with the queen as I was by meeting Callum. I'd spent the last few hours in the queen's study as she discussed last-minute details for Juliana's wedding with her staff, but no one asked my opinion, or even glanced my way. The wedding was a monsoon, and all I could do was sit there while it raged all around me. It didn't bother me so much, because I wouldn't even be there to see it, but I couldn't imagine Juliana being able to stand it.

"Hey." I tugged at the sleeve of Thomas's jacket. "I was just wondering if you'd heard anything about Juliana—or Grant." It was driving me crazy that even though I was still dreaming about her, I didn't know anything about where Juliana was or what was happening to her. I wished I could force a vision, see through her eyes while I was awake. I was sick of this passive power; it wasn't helping anyone. And as for Grant—I felt responsible for him. Whatever he was going through, it never would've happened if it hadn't been for me. I had as little control over that as he did, but I couldn't get him out of my head.

Thomas hesitated. "The KES raided a Libertas hideout downtown last night on a tip, but they didn't find anything. I'll tell you as soon as I know anything more."

"You don't think— You're sure you'll find them?"

"We'll find them," Thomas assured me. "Libertas is going to hide Juliana as well as possible for as long as possible, but we're better trained and better funded and smarter than they are, and eventually they'll slip up. When they do, we'll be there. And Grant . . ." Thomas shook his head. "To be honest, I'm worried. We should've heard from Libertas already. They might not know he's not me, but he can't tell them anything. They'll have figured that out by now. If we don't hear from them soon . . ." He trailed off, but I knew what he was thinking. It was the same thing I was thinking: *If we don't hear from them soon, it means he might be dead.*

I didn't want to hear him say it. I wasn't going to give up hope that Grant was alive. I just couldn't accept that an innocent boy was dead because of me.

"I'll be standing off to the side," Thomas said. He reached out a hand as if he was going to touch my shoulder, but then he stopped, obviously thinking the better of it. He cleared his throat and continued, "This should all go according to protocol. Just follow the queen's lead."

At the grand staircase, Thomas peeled off and left me standing at the top all by myself. There was another row of KES agents already stationed at the foot of the staircase; these men would protect Callum for the length of his stay in the UCC—which at the moment was indefinite. By custom he wasn't allowed to retain his own Farnham guard.

The queen swept in from the other side of the staircase with a pair of KES agents trailing behind. Though her exterior was unruffled, the queen had to be agitated; the situation was so politically sensitive, there was no way she could be as calm as she seemed. The mere mention of Farnham and its royal family made everyone in the Castle uneasy; even Gloria had been jumpy as she helped me prepare for the meeting. What would it be like when there was a foreign element in their midst? A perverse part of me was looking forward to finding out.

"Let's get this over with, shall we?" The queen smoothed

the gold-trimmed satin sash she wore over her pale blue dress and reached up to give the rather impressive diamond crown on her head a minuscule adjustment. Gloria had given me the choice of many blingy headpieces, but I'd gone the other way, opting for a simple circlet of gold rowan leaves to wear with the beige peplum top and matching skirt she'd dressed me in. "I take no pleasure in marrying you off like this, you know, Juliana. I think it's a barbaric tradition. I thought we'd done away with it a long time ago."

I nodded. "I understand." I wondered if perhaps the queen was against it because her own marriage to the king had been so unconventional. If the king hadn't been allowed to choose his bride, the queen would still be Evelyn Eaves, a lawyer with the Royal Counsel and not much else.

"I know this is hard for you," the queen continued. "But you have to believe that it's for the best. The past is the past, but the future is still worth preserving."

Before I could respond, the doors of the front entrance to the Castle swung open, and in stepped the most beautiful young man I'd ever seen. To my surprise, this wasn't the first time I was seeing him; his analog was Will Base, an actor on one of Gina's favorite television shows. I struggled against an overwhelming starstruck feeling. This was no time to lose my composure.

Callum was shorter than I would've imagined, only an inch or two taller than my five-seven. He had a mess of curly brown hair tamed with some kind of gel, big blue eyes and soft, handsome features. He wore a gray three-piece suit with a red pocket square and carried a large black leather notebook in his left hand. The Farnham Royal Guard gathered behind him, their expressions as sober as the ones the KES agents wore.

The queen descended the staircase with me at her heels,

alighting in the main foyer with the practiced aloofness of a true royal, while I tried not to stumble in my four-inch suede cobalt heels. "Welcome to the Commonwealth, Your Highness," she said, extending her hand. Callum bowed his head to kiss it.

"Thank you for having me here, Your Majesty," he said with a polite smile. He released her hand and she stepped away so that I could greet him. I'd forgotten that this was expected of me; for a moment it was as though I'd slipped out of time and was watching all this play out from a safe distance.

"Hello, Prince Callum," I said. Gloria had coached me to address him that way, but it still felt strange, calling someone "Prince."

Callum reached out and took my gloved hand, kissing it in the exact same manner he'd kissed the queen's—polite, but removed. He was wearing a signet ring on the pinky finger of his right hand, a black bird fixed on a red stone. The symbol was familiar to me, but I wasn't sure where I'd seen it, though the ring itself reminded me a little of the one Thomas wore to signify his active duty in the KES. I resisted an urge to turn back and look at him, focusing instead on the boy in front of me. I had to say something, so I went with, "I like your ring."

"Oh," he said, after a strange pause. "It was my father's. Rick gets the kingdom, I got this." He meant his brother, Richard, who was heir to the throne and would become king when their mother, Queen Marian, died or stepped aside. Callum was the second of three brothers; the other, Samuel, who went by Sonny, was eleven. I'd learned all this from Gloria.

"I think you got the better part." I smiled at him, and he smiled back.

"I think I did, too," he said.

"Do you know what the symbol means?" I asked, struggling to make casual conversation.

His brow furrowed in confusion. "It's the Farnham phoenix . . . the one from our flag?"

I should've been panicked, but I didn't have the mental energy to worry about my mistake, because I remembered why I recognized the phoenix. *The flag.* It came to me in a flash, a red flag with a black bird on it, its wings outstretched, its mouth open in a battle cry, and midnight-colored flames licking its feet. *Oh my God,* I thought, stunned by the realization.

I knew where Juliana was.

"Well," I blurted out. "I'm glad you're here." *Okay, Sasha, calm down,* I commanded myself. But it was hard to relax, because what I wanted to do was run off to process what it was I had seen. The dreams weren't worthless after all. If I could remember seeing the flag, I could remember other things, things that could lead the KES to Juliana. I didn't know what the General had in mind for when my six days were up, but I was sure that it was something I wouldn't want to do; this was the leverage I needed to escape it. This was my ticket home.

"Thank you," Callum said. I could tell my behavior bewildered him, but he was trying hard not to show it. "I—I brought you something. A present." He glanced behind him, and one of his guards rushed forth with a gift bag, its handles tied together with a silver bow. I accepted it with as much grace and gratitude as I could muster. Because Callum seemed to expect me to open the present immediately, I reached my hand into the bag and pulled out the gift.

"A potato?" That's what it was, just a regular old potato, like the ones you could buy in the supermarket. Why would Callum give a potato to his fiancé? It was literally the most unromantic thing I'd ever heard of, and Gina's ex-boyfriend,

Noah, had once given her a bottle of hand sanitizer for her birthday.

"It's from one of our state farms in the Mountain region," Callum said by way of explanation, although it didn't illuminate the situation much for me. "I assumed you'd never had one before."

I laughed. "Of course I've eaten a potato!" It wasn't as if they were some sort of delicacy, at least . . . not on Earth. It dawned on me then that I'd committed a strange, incredible faux pas. I went rigid. After everything I'd been through in Aurora, was a potato going to be the thing to unmask me?

The queen looked at me in shock. "When have you *ever* eaten a potato, Juliana?"

"I—I'm sure I have." I couldn't remember Thomas or Gloria ever mentioning anything about potatoes. I was so stunned, I couldn't come up with an excuse that sounded halfway believable.

Callum cleared his throat. "Well, you've never had one quite like this. You should have your kitchen bake it for you with butter and salt."

"Okay. I'll, um, do that," I mumbled. "Thank you so much. What a thoughtful gift."

Nobody seemed to know what to do after that. Eventually, the queen took charge, for which I was grateful.

"I'm sure it's been a long journey for you, Prince Callum," she said. "This is Agent Bedford." A tall red-haired man in a suit stepped forward and approached Callum. "He's with the King's Elite Service and will be supervising your protection. You can dismiss your men. You won't be needing their services anymore."

Callum hesitated. "I was hoping I'd be able to keep my own bodyguard."

"Unfortunately, it's against our diplomatic policy," the queen told him. "But I assure you, the KES is second to none. You can trust them."

I couldn't blame Callum for being uncomfortable with this proposition. He'd probably been taught from an early age never to trust anyone from the UCC, just as Thomas and everyone else in the Commonwealth had been raised never to trust anyone from Farnham. Though Callum appeared nice enough, the animosity between the two countries—and between the two royal families—ran deep, deeper than I could possibly ever understand.

But Callum, overpowered by the queen's insistence, relented. He spoke with the head of his bodyguard in a hushed voice, and they left as silently as they'd entered.

"Wonderful." The queen was smiling, but I could tell she was ready to be done with this farcical show of international goodwill. "Agent Bedford will accompany you to your rooms and give you your security briefing. Afterward you will have some time to yourself before dinner."

Callum must've found the queen as intimidating as everybody else did, but he found the courage to ask a question. "I'm sorry if this is forward, but when will Juliana and I be able to talk in private?"

"We have some time scheduled for the two of you to get properly acquainted after dinner," the queen told him, with a calculated, frigid imperiousness that set my teeth on edge. Against all odds, Callum seemed pleased by this, as if the queen had wrapped her arms around him and welcomed him to the family, which meant that he was either very stupid or had resolved to be a ray of sunshine no matter what the cost—and he didn't look stupid.

Agent Bedford gestured for Callum to follow him up the grand staircase. He paused first and glanced over at me. "It's a pleasure to meet you, Juliana," Callum said. "I'm looking forward to getting to know you."

"Likewise." I nodded at him as he passed.

"I guess I'll see you later," Callum said, taking the stairs backward in order to keep looking at me. I gave him a little wave, and he returned it with a grin.

Well, at least one person was happy about the impending wedding. It surprised me. Shouldn't Callum hate the idea as much as Juliana did? Wasn't he infuriated at having to live his life the way other people wanted him to? I would've been. I guessed I would find out, because Callum clearly had a lot he wanted to say to Juliana—alone.

"What was that with the potato?" the queen hissed at me as soon as Callum was out of earshot. "You've never eaten a potato!"

"I'm sorry, I—I thought I had," I stammered.

"Where? On some holiday to Farnham? You were just trying to show off. I won't stand for it, Juliana, do you hear me? You promised me that you were going to behave yourself and I expect you to do that. This marriage is the key to peace, and if you endanger that . . ." She let the threat dangle in the air, but it seemed to me that it was the queen who was really frightened. "You should go back to your room. I'm going to sit with your father for a while."

The queen shook her head at me and left with her bodyguard. I was alone in the foyer. I sank down on the bottom step of the grand staircase and buried my face in my hands. Waves of powerlessness washed over me. I couldn't seem to do anything right, even when I tried.

Thomas took a seat beside me on the step and reached into the bag, pulling out the potato and cradling it in his palm. "Potatoes," he said softly. "They don't grow here."

"In Aurora? Then how did Callum—"

"In the Commonwealth," Thomas explained. "We can't grow them. Something about the soil . . . but they're a Farnham specialty. They import potatoes from their farms in the Mountain region all over the globe."

"But not to the UCC?"

"No. Trade negotiations keep falling through. Another thing the peace treaty will fix, which is probably why he brought you one in the first place." He stared at the spud in his hands. "This would fetch a high price on the black market. I wonder what it tastes like."

"You can have it," I said.

"Don't be silly. It was a gift." But he eyed it covetously all the same.

My chin quivered and a tear slipped down my cheek. I hated to cry, but seeing Thomas holding that potato so gently, like a baby bird, broke something inside of me. Meeting Callum had made me aware, in a way I hadn't been up until then, of the incredible realness of my situation, and how out of my depth I was. My allergic reaction the night before had been dramatic and alarming to everyone involved, but Dr. Moss's confident—if biologically suspect—explanation seemed to have done its job of banishing any suspicions it had caused. And perhaps my most recent mistake would be written off as confusion, or even bad behavior, but I couldn't keep making mistakes and drawing attention to myself. Yet that seemed to be all I was doing. Sooner or later, I was going to be found out, and thinking about what might happen to me threatened to send me right over the edge.

"Hey," Thomas said. "What's wrong?" He reached out a hand as if to touch me, then took it back, obviously unsure how I would react to such a gesture. I would've been grateful for it, but I didn't want him to know that.

"I have to tell you something," I said, struggling to keep calm. "But if I do, you have to promise not to tell the General."

Thomas shook his head. "Then you shouldn't."

"What? Why?" I demanded. "You said I could trust you!"

"You *can* trust me," he said. "But if it's a matter of national security, I have an obligation . . ."

"Screw your obligations," I snapped. "If the General finds out, he'll keep me here forever. I know he will. He'll lock me up in some cell and never let me go. Is that what you want? Me trapped here forever?"

"No, of course not," Thomas said, his voice low and hoarse. A stray hair fell across his forehead, and I had the sudden urge to smooth it back, but I didn't. I couldn't figure out what it was about him that made me so angry, and at the same time melted my insides like butter left out to soften. I wished things had gone differently between us; I wanted what had happened back on Earth to have been the real thing, and this whole experience in Aurora some sad, strange fiction. Because no matter how hard I tried to make myself see reason, all the feelings I'd started to have for Thomas when I thought he was Grant just *wouldn't go away.*

Whether I liked it or not, my relationship with Thomas was important. It had been the difference between life and death for me in the Tattered City, and it was the difference between success and failure at the Castle. I depended on him. I needed him. And despite everything, I wanted him to need me, too, if only so that we were even. If only so I knew I wasn't as helpless or desperate as I sometimes felt. I had to tell him what I was seeing. I had to know that I'd done something to rescue myself. For whatever reason, I'd been given this ability a long time ago, as if someone, somewhere, somehow knew that one day I would need it. I couldn't just ignore it and pray the General kept his word, and I couldn't abandon Juliana to her fate because it was easier to let the clock on my time in Aurora run out—if it ever would. But I couldn't do it without Thomas.

"Please," I whispered. I couldn't fathom a scenario in which the General was aware that I could see Juliana's life through her eyes and allowed me to return home. Best case, he'd keep me in Aurora and let the scientists who worked on the many-worlds project run test after test in the hopes of making more discoveries about the tandem; worst case . . . well, I couldn't even say, and didn't want to imagine. But I was certain that a man who had sunk so much money and so many resources into developing technology to travel from one universe to another wasn't going to just let me waltz out of his clutches with a direct line to my analog's mind.

I could see in his eyes that Thomas was struggling. It was against his training and his nature to keep vital information from his superiors. How could I have ever believed that he would be more loyal to me than he was to the KES, than he was to his own *father*? The worst part was, I understood it. The General had taken him in, had given him a family after his was stripped away from him. I knew what it felt like to owe someone like that. I'd go to the ends of the world for Granddad, do anything I could to protect him and make him proud, because when everything I'd come to count on had been lost, he'd gathered me in his arms and told me I wasn't alone. How could I ask Thomas to betray the person who had done that for him?

He reached for me again, and this time he made contact; his hand was a soft weight on my shoulder. "Okay," he said, a sigh carrying his words along. I jerked my head up, shocked both by his touch and his answer. He glanced around. "Not here, though."

"The library," I said. I grabbed his hand without thinking and stood, tugging him along in my wake. His eyes narrowed in surprise and his mouth hung open, as if he was about to say something, but apparently he thought better of it, because he followed me in stunned silence as I guided him by instinct to the one room in the Castle I'd always wanted to visit.

TWENTY-ONE

The library was empty. The door creaked as it slid open, and the air in the room had a musty smell, as if the windows hadn't been cracked in weeks. The surfaces were dust-free—the domestics at the Castle were nothing if not fastidious—but the library had all the hallmarks of a space that was mostly forgotten. I got the impression that the room missed Juliana. It was one of her favorite places in the Castle, after the gardens; it had featured in many of my dreams. There was an enormous vaulted ceiling covered in sky-hued frescoes and floor-to-ceiling shelves packed tight with multicolored leather spines in various states of wear. The floor was parquet with an elaborate inlaid herringbone pattern, and the whole place was illuminated with warm light emanating from hidden sources atop the bookshelves. On the opposite side of the room there was a globe tall enough to reach my waist. I went to it, eager to give it a spin. I let my fingers wander over its miniature topography as Thomas stared at me, waiting for an explanation, but the words stuck in my throat.

After a long silence, Thomas ventured a question. "How did you know where the library was?" He had that look in his eye again, the one that meant he was trying to decipher me like a code. He must have spent a lot of time doing that, trying to figure out what people were thinking and planning, searching for hidden undercurrents in their words and in their body language. It must've been part of his training; I wondered if he knew he was doing it with me, or if it was just instinct.

I took a deep breath, pressing harder on the tiny ridge of the Alps to steady myself. "I saw it," I told him. "In a dream."

"What?" He looked baffled, for which I couldn't blame him. And yet, he'd seen plenty of unlikely things, and done some pretty unlikely things as well. I didn't even consider the possibility that he might not believe me. "I don't understand."

I laughed, a sharp sound that ricocheted off the ceiling. "Me neither."

"No, seriously," Thomas said.

"Maybe you should sit down for this," I said, gesturing to a nearby armchair. Thomas's face was easy to read. All his emotions—interest, concern, and slight anxiety—showed in his eyes, in the crease of his brow, in the grim set of his mouth. He could mask his feelings, of course; I'd seen him do it. But that was a choice. This was pure Thomas, shining out from within like the beam of a lighthouse.

"All right," he said. "I'm sitting. You're sitting. Now *talk*."

"I think I know where Juliana is." The words tumbled out of my mouth before I could stop them, and I could tell that it wasn't what he'd expected to hear. His entire body pulled away and he raised his eyebrows in what could only be shock.

"What do you mean, you know where she is? How do you know? Where is she?" The last question came out strangled, and I had to fight against a wave of jealousy. Of course he wanted to know where she was. She was his assignment—she was his friend—she was his . . . Of course he'd want to know.

"I think she's in Farnham," I said.

"What makes you think *that*?" His tone was accusatory, and I found myself insulted by it.

"Because, I . . . I saw Callum's ring just now, and it was the black phoenix on a red background, and I realized I'd seen it before, at the house where they're keeping her, on a flag . . . The flag of Farnham, it must be . . . !" My voice broke under the strain of trying to say so much at once and not being able to say enough. I hadn't realized until now how much this bizarre power—this extraordinary gift—frightened me, how deeply I feared I was going insane, and how desperately I wanted him not to mirror those same fears.

"Hey, hey," Thomas said, covering my hand with his own. I looked up and our eyes caught. He smiled tentatively, as if wanting to reassure me but not knowing how, under the circumstances. "Slow down. What do you mean you *saw* it?"

I swallowed hard. "That's what I've been trying to tell you. I . . . see her. See through her, really. Mostly when I'm asleep. Okay, always when I'm asleep, and I don't usually remember very much, but sometimes details come back to me—"

"Sasha," Thomas said firmly. "I think you're going to have to start from the beginning."

I took a deep breath. I told him how I'd always had these dreams of Juliana's life, from a very early age, as long as I could remember. That I'd always assumed they were just my imagination running wild while I was asleep, that I never knew any of it was true before I came to Aurora and realized what I was seeing. And that I knew now where Libertas was keeping Juliana: in a large farmhouse somewhere in a foreign country, behind enemy lines. As I spoke, I watched Thomas's thoughts pass over his face like the aurora sweeping across the sky, one emotion after another, none lingering long enough for me to catch hold and orient myself.

When I was finished, I sat back and waited for him to say something. He rubbed his face vigorously, as if trying to bring himself back to some kind of reality he could get a firm grasp on.

"That was . . ." He paused, searching for the right thing to say. ". . . not what I expected you to tell me."

"What did you expect?"

"I don't know." He gave me a weak smile. "Not that."

"It's a lot to take in, I know," I said. "But you believe me, don't you?" I tried to ask as if I didn't care about the answer, as if I was so convicted about my story that not a doubt lingered in my mind, but the tone faltered, because I really, really needed to be believed.

"Yes," he said, with a finality that I found comforting. "I believe you. But I've got to be honest—I don't know where that leaves us. Juliana's in Farnham, but where? It's a big country. And you don't know what they're planning to do with her?" He wanted more from me, and I wanted to give him more, but I couldn't. I understood his desperation; I wanted more from me, too. This wasn't a parlor trick; it was a real thing, it came from somewhere, and if it didn't exist to help me—to help *us*, Juliana and me—then why did I have it at all?

"At least we know she's alive," I pointed out. "That's something."

"It's a relief, for sure." He kneaded the back of his neck with his fingers and I had to smile; in his unguarded moments, he was so predictable, you could set your watch by him. "Why did you tell me?"

"What do you mean?"

"I know I've asked you to trust me," he said. "But I've given you plenty of reasons not to. Good reasons. Reasons that you keep reminding me of. So why now? You've known this since when?"

"Since the Tower," I admitted. "When the General told me her name."

"And you didn't tell me then."

"How could I? I knew that something was up, but I didn't understand it. And even if I had . . . I couldn't tell you until I was sure."

"Sure of what?" he asked, his voice going soft.

"That you would help me," I said. This was the point of it, after all, the reason I'd told him. Because I thought I finally had some useful information to bargain with. But you can only barter for your freedom with someone who wants something else more than keeping you trapped.

"I see," he said, a bit coldly. "Why don't you just tell me what you were thinking, then? Get it all out in the open."

"Thomas, what if I could control it?" He looked at me as if I'd grown a second head. "Wait, listen. Obviously I'm connected to Juliana. I don't know why, but I do know that it's not an accident. It's been happening my whole life. There has to be a *reason*. If I could control the visions—if I could force them to happen instead of just waiting for them to come to me when I was asleep—I might be able to figure out where they're hiding her. And if I could do that—"

"Then we could bring her back," Thomas finished. "And you could go home." His voice was flat, and I could see him pulling away, receding behind his KES mask. The way Thomas was reacting made me feel guilty, like I was turning my back on him, which was ludicrous. I didn't owe him anything . . . did I?

"The General's not going to let me go," I said. "I need to find another way."

"You don't know that," Thomas insisted.

"Six days," I reminded him. "*Six days*. That's what he told me. That's what he promised. But you said it yourself: the KES has no idea where Juliana is. How can he be so sure he'll find her before my time is up? He's planning something, Thomas."

"Like what?"

I shook my head. "I don't know. You're the expert. You tell me."

There was a long pause while Thomas sorted through things in his head. Finally, he said, "So what do you want from me, then?" The connection I'd felt forming between us had all but vanished, and I sensed that he was creating the distance on purpose. He was talking to me like a stranger he was haggling with over a trinket, not . . . whatever I was to him. Maybe I was nothing. Maybe it was—and had always been—just in my head.

"If I can tell you where Juliana is—*exactly* where she is—I want you to promise you'll get me home as soon as possible. No matter what." I held my breath, waiting in agony for him to respond. This was it. The only chip I had to play. I hoped I'd played it right.

"Fine. You help me find Juliana, I'll make sure you go back to your own world, even if it's against my orders."

"You'd really do that?"

"It'd be worth it, to bring her back. To make things right again. Besides," he continued, with a resigned shrug, "what can he do to me? I'm his son." Something in the tone of his voice told me he didn't quite believe that, but he was trying very hard to convince himself it was true.

"Right." I stared at my hands. "Now all I have to do is figure out how the hell I'm going to do it."

"Actually," he said. "I might know someone who can help you."

"You do?"

"Yes, and so do you. Come on," he said. "We're going to see Dr. Moss."

TWENTY-TWO

"Dr. Moss . . . the doctor who treated me last night?" That incident seemed so long ago. I'd nearly forgotten it in the hubbub surrounding Callum's arrival. I glanced at Thomas's wrist, hoping to catch a glimpse of his watch, but he caught me looking and raised his eyebrows with a hint of amusement that I was glad to see.

"I'll have you back in plenty of time for dinner," Thomas promised. "I'd rather face down a squad of ten Libertines than Gloria when her schedule's been compromised."

I laughed. The tension that had gathered in my shoulders melted a bit. I took a deep breath to center myself. We'd crossed over from the Castle to the Tower via one of the glass sky bridges that connected the two buildings and were now standing in a circular elevator bank. Each elevator was marked with the floors it served, but the one we were waiting for simply said DOWN, which struck me as more than a little ominous. When it arrived I stepped into it beside Thomas and watched him hit the button labeled SUBBASEMENT F.

"Dr. Moss is your friend with all the theories about analogs, isn't he?"

Thomas nodded. "About Dr. Moss," he said cagily, tugging at the cuffs of his suit jacket. "He's not technically a medical doctor."

"What are you talking about? He gave me a shot!"

"I couldn't call a real doctor," Thomas explained. "Dr. Rowland, the royal physician, wouldn't have been satisfied with giving you a little antihistamine and going about his night. He would've been suspicious; he would've wanted to do blood work and all kinds of tests on you, and I think you know what that might've yielded."

"Would it have proven I wasn't Juliana?"

"I don't know." Thomas shrugged. "But it's possible. I knew the General wouldn't want to risk it, so I took the liberty of calling Dr. Moss instead."

"What kind of doctor *is* Dr. Moss?"

"Theoretical physicist," Thomas said with a wry smile, perhaps thinking of my "family business." My stomach dipped with the impact of a sudden sadness at the thought of Granddad and my parents, but I did my best to put it out of my mind. I couldn't allow myself to fall apart with missing them, not when I was so close to getting answers about my mysterious ability and its implications for my quest to return home. "He's completely brilliant, Mossie. He invented the anchors. He knows everything there is to know about parallel universes and analogs."

I fiddled with the anchor. Most of the time I forgot it was there. "Mossie?"

A shy grin transformed his face. "I like Dr. Moss. And you'll like him, too."

"How can you be so sure?"

"Because," he said with confidence as the elevator arrived at Subbasement F. "The General hates him."

* * *

The F level contained only a short hallway with one steel door opposite the elevator. A sign on the door read:

SUBBASEMENT F

HIGHLY CLASSIFIED

NO ONE BELOW LEVEL 6 CLEARANCE ADMITTED WITHOUT A DOD ESCORT.

The LCD screen next to the door wasn't green, or even blue, but bright red and pulsing, a very clear sign that no one was welcome down here, me included. But Thomas had Level 6 clearance; his handprint changed the screen to blue, and the code he punched in unlocked the door. It swished open, revealing a large, slick laboratory just beyond the threshold. Loud music blasted out of unseen speakers, and strangely enough, the song was one that I recognized.

"Mossie!" Thomas shouted. I glanced around the windowless laboratory, taking in several imposing machines, digital boards covered with hastily scribbled mathematical formulas, and tables cluttered with all manner of things: burbling Bunsen burners, stacks of files, and piles and piles of books. There was one thing missing, however—Dr. Moss.

"Mossie!" Thomas cried again. The elderly man popped up from behind one of the shuddering machines. When Dr. Moss saw Thomas, he grinned and shuffled over to an old-fashioned record player. An earsplitting scratch filled the air as he removed the needle from the spinning LP.

"Thomas!" He rushed forward to shake Thomas's hand. When his eyes landed on me, his grin grew so wide I thought it might crack his face in half. "And look who you've brought! Our little Earthling."

I wrinkled my nose at the term, despite the fact that it

was as accurate a description of what I was as anything else. I preferred it to "analog," but all I could think of were the alien movies I'd seen as a kid.

"Remind me of your name, dear," Dr. Moss said. "I'm afraid I've forgotten it." He tapped himself on the temple. "Mind like Swiss cheese, and growing holier by the day!"

"Sasha," I told him, gathering my confidence. It seemed like forever since I'd said my own name out loud. "Sasha Lawson."

"That's right. Ms. Lawson." Dr. Moss grinned at me. "I can't tell you how happy it makes me to find you got through the tandem in one piece." I didn't doubt it; he'd invented the anchor that had brought me to Aurora, so if I hadn't survived the journey, it would've been at least partially his fault. I shot Thomas a dubious look. This was the man who was supposed to help me? He seemed a little nuts.

"Was that Chuck Berry you were playing?" I asked.

Dr. Moss snapped his fingers, impressed. "Right you are. I was introduced to the Father of Rock and Roll by another one of your kind many years ago, and I've never lost the taste."

Dr. Moss sat down on a nearby stool and drummed his fingertips on his knee. The steel tabletop was littered with notebooks containing lines of cramped, handwritten notes. Seeing them—the whole place, in fact—reminded me of Granddad's lab at the university, except larger and shinier. On the table there stood a large glass bottle of the type that might once have contained vodka, and it was filled with tiny origami stars in a rainbow of colors. They were scattered all about, piling up in the empty spaces and peeking out from beneath his notes.

I picked up a green one and held it between my thumb and forefinger. I wondered if the one I'd found in Juliana's nightstand had its origin here, in Dr. Moss's lab. "Did you make these?"

"Actually," Thomas said, taking it and dropping it into the bottle, "they're mine."

"Yours?" Then had Thomas given Juliana the blue star, as some sort of token or memento? Was that why she'd kept it? Was that why she'd hidden it away?

He nodded. "When I was little, I was anxious and fidgety. One of my teachers taught me how to make these, and told me that whenever I felt antsy, I should just take out a piece of paper, rip it up, and make stars." He gave me a wry smile. "The habit stuck."

I smiled at the mental image of a boyish Thomas sitting at a classroom desk, making stars with his restless hands. "Aw, that's sweet."

He rolled his eyes; apparently, "sweet" was not a compliment to a soldier. He ran his fingers through his hair and dipped his head to hide a faint pinkness that colored the tips of his ears. *"Anyway,"* he said. "I spent a lot of time down here with Mossie during the planning stages of Operation Starling, which is, you know, why they're here."

"I've been keeping them safe for you, boy," Dr. Moss said, not even bothering to look up from a nearby text that had drawn his attention away from us.

"What's Operation Starling?" I asked. Dr. Moss swiveled around and Thomas lifted his eyes to mine. A moment of silence passed. "Oh," I said, my voice flat with realization. "Right. Why do you call it that?"

"It's, um . . . kind of a joke," Thomas said, with a soft snort of self-effacing laughter.

"Oh really? What's so funny about it?"

"Not *funny,*" he said. "It's just that Juliana's KES code name is 'Sparrow.' Sparrows and starlings are related, I guess."

"They're from the same biological order," Dr. Moss explained. "Passeriformes."

"Fascinating."

"It was his idea," Thomas said, pointing at Dr. Moss. "As you can probably imagine."

"Well, children, I haven't got all day," Dr. Moss said. "And I assume it wasn't an interest in ornithology that brought you here, so why don't you tell me what *did*, eh?"

Thomas drew in a deep breath. "We have a situation."

"Oh? What sort of situation?"

"Go ahead," Thomas said, putting a hand on the small of my back and pushing me forward. "Tell Mossie what you told me."

I still wasn't quite sure about Dr. Moss, but I didn't see that I had a better option, so I explained everything as best I could. This time, it came out easier, and more intelligibly. As he listened to me describe my "situation," excitement bloomed across Dr. Moss's face.

"Well," he said when I was finished, with soft but potent enthusiasm. "That *is* interesting."

Just *interesting*? "Have you heard of that happening to other people?"

"Other people?" He tapped his chin with his fingers. "Not as such." The wheels of Dr. Moss's mind were turning swiftly and energetically, fueled by a new mystery, and his eyes held that same glint of excitement Granddad used to get when he was on the verge of a particularly gratifying discovery in his own work. "What do you know about parallel universes, Ms. . . . ?"

"Lawson," Thomas and I provided in unison.

"Right." His hands flapped in the air, an impatient gesture meant to spur me to answer.

"Not a lot," I admitted. "My grandfather is a physicist, but it's not something I was personally very interested in—up till now, anyway."

"Hmmm." My lack of knowledge disappointed Dr. Moss, but he soldiered on with an air of great burden. "Then I guess I'll have to start with the basics, won't I?"

"That would probably be best," I said.

Dr. Moss nodded, rushing to a keyboard and typing a series of quick commands. There was a large screen on the opposite end of the laboratory that took up almost the entire wall. When Dr. Moss was finished, the screen, previously blank, held one inscrutable image.

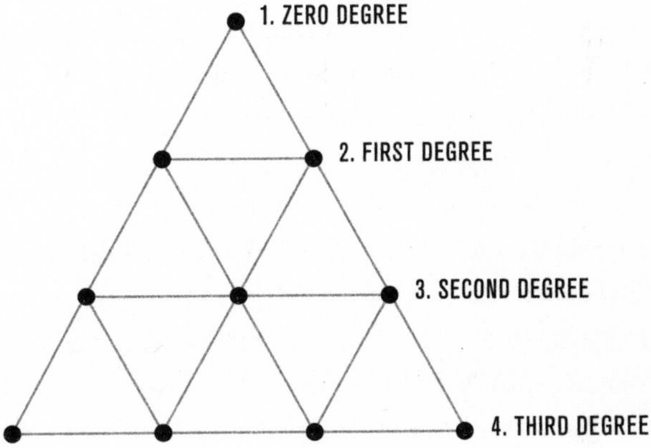

I know that symbol, I thought with a sudden, grave certainty. I struggled to remember where I had last seen it, but I couldn't. Was it something Granddad had once shown me? Then I realized—it was the Libertas insignia, except that instead of stars it was made up of dots.

"What's that?" I asked, advancing toward the screen.

"No touching the equipment, if you please," Dr. Moss scolded. I drew my hand away.

"That is a tetractys," Dr. Moss told me. "A mathematical

symbol dating back to about 500 BC. But the shape doesn't matter—it's what the tetractys represents that's important."

"And what's that?" I asked, squinting so that I could read the type.

"Universes." I could hear a grin in his voice when he said the word. If nothing else, Dr. Moss certainly had a flair for the dramatic.

"As we are all well aware, there is a large number—perhaps infinite number—of universes in existence," Dr. Moss continued. "But what you may not know is that there are many different *kinds* of universes. What you see on the screen is a method I've developed for categorizing universes in their many forms." Dr. Moss took one look at my baffled expression and said, "Allow me to explain further."

"Please do," I urged.

"For the purposes of this demonstration, let us consider Earth to be our home universe," Dr. Moss said with a nod in my direction. "At the top of the pyramid, you have Earth, and all of the universes that are separated from it by what I've taken to calling zero degrees. These are universes that are *virtually indistinguishable* from Earth itself. They are nearly identical, apart from minuscule changes that have no global consequences. For instance, Thomas is wearing a blue tie today. In a zero-degree universe, he's wearing a black tie. A small difference with no measurable impact.

"The second row is representative of all universes that are separated from Earth by one degree. These are distinguishable from Earth, but are not so different that the world appears substantially changed. For instance, if you were comparing Earth to another world with one degree of separation, at any given time the President of the United States could be a different person in each world, but there would still be a President of the United States. Do you understand?"

"I guess."

"The third row is where it gets interesting," Dr. Moss said. "It represents universes that are *substantially differentiated* from one another. At some point in time, history took a very different turn, resulting in an altered worldscape. Earth and Aurora are universes separated by two degrees."

"Because of the Last Common Event," I said, remembering what Thomas had told me—in Aurora, George Washington had died during the Revolutionary War, and the war was lost. As a result, history had forged a new route.

"Precisely!" Dr. Moss was growing more and more excited by the second.

"So what's the fourth row?" I asked. Granddad would've thought Dr. Moss was a lunatic, but he would've loved his theories, and his penchant for organization.

"Universes separated by three degrees are *highly differentiated* from each other," Dr. Moss said. "In these universes, something happened that was so major that it completely changed the worldscape. Of course, at the moment these third-degree universes are entirely theoretical. We're incapable of proving that they actually exist. And there might be other universes still, separated by four, five, six degrees, with entirely different laws of physics, perhaps! You can see how difficult it is to imagine what such universes might look like."

"What does any of this have to do with analogs?"

"Everything!" Dr. Moss cried. "People are products of their environments. The more different two universes are, the more different the analogs in those universes will be from each other, not in appearance but in *circumstance*. In a universe where the differences are subtle—universes of zero, or even one degree—your analog is much more likely to be like you. In these universes, analogs share names and genealogical backgrounds and identities, and if you were to compare the lives of analogs in these universes, you would find that they are being lived almost entirely in parallel with your own, allowing for relatively few slight variations. Of course, there are exceptions. There are *always* exceptions."

"Can I ask you something?" Dr. Moss gave me a curious look. "How come Juliana and I have different parents?"

"I'm not sure I understand your meaning," Dr. Moss said. "You're different people."

"I know that, but, if we're analogs, shouldn't our parents be analogs, too? And our grandparents? Isn't that how biology works?" This was something I had been wondering for a while, but no one seemed capable of explaining it to me. If anyone knew the answer, though, Dr. Moss would.

"Not necessarily," Dr. Moss said. "Because of the LCEs, those linchpin moments that create divergent histories, analogs in second-degree universes and higher do not, for the most part, share the same genealogical backgrounds or identities. Although, again, there are outliers; analogs in second-degree universes *can,* in unique cases, live their lives along very similar paths, but it's rare. And your analog in a third-degree universe is likely to be even more different from yourself than Juliana is."

"I don't see how that's possible," I said. I was a normal high school junior; Juliana was a *princess.* How much more different could two lives be?

"Believe me, Ms. Lawson—anything is possible."

"I still don't understand," I said. "What about DNA? If we look the same, shouldn't we come from the same parents?"

"Are you familiar with Anaximander's theory of *apeiron*?" Dr. Moss asked. I stared at him blankly. He sighed. "No, I thought not. Anaximander was a Greek philosopher in the sixth century BC. *Apeiron* means 'boundless' or, perhaps more colloquially, 'infinity.' It describes a sort of hyperreality from which everything ultimately descends. Anaximander believed that everything we see in every world originates in *apeiron*, that what exists in the universes is a mere fragment of a greater whole. As far as I can tell, that's what an analog is—a worldly fragment of one whole and perfect being that exists only in *apeiron*.

"Have you ever visited a hall of mirrors, Ms. Lawson?" I nodded. "Imagine standing in one, then. Everywhere you turn, there are multiple reflections of your own image. The mirrors are expertly arranged so that these reflections appear to multiply in every direction, stretching out into infinity. You look alike, you move in perfect harmony, but the reflections are not *you*. They simply have their origin in you. You are the primary being, and they are mere copies. That is an imperfect but adequate example of what I mean."

"And in this scenario, I'm the *apeiron* being and they're . . . analogs?" I ventured.

"In a manner of speaking. Technically, in a hall of mirrors, you—your physical self that stands before the mirrors—is a sort of source code that exists only in *apeiron*. Your DNA—and everything else that makes you look as you do—adjusts in order to deliver that predetermined result."

He turned back to his keyboard and brought up a three-dimensional rendering of ten or so human beings standing in a dispersed group, connected to each other by dotted lines. Dr. Moss indicated one of the lines.

"Dr. March and I—"

"Who's Dr. March?"

"Don't ask," Thomas muttered under his breath.

"Dr. March was my research partner," Dr. Moss said. I shot Thomas a questioning look. What was so weird about that?

"Dr. March and I developed a theory—that analogs with a single *apeiron* source are connected across the universes by what we call a 'tether,'" Dr. Moss said. "An invisible cord that binds you all together, through the tandem and beyond."

"A cord? A cord made of what?"

"Energy," Dr. Moss said. "Dark energy, to be precise. Don't worry, it's not nearly as ominous as it sounds. The word 'dark' merely implies that it's hypothetical. We believe it exists because when two analogs come into contact with one another, energy is released, which causes the destruction you witness as a disruption event."

"So this tether . . . ," I prompted, trying to get him back on point.

"It's the thing that makes you and Juliana—and countless, perhaps infinite copies of you out there in the multiverse—analogs and not identical twins, or clones, or mere coincidental look-alikes. Every analog is connected to each of their other analogs by one of these tethers, forming an intricate web across multiple parallel cosmos. Like DNA, the tether is what carries the code that informs your physical similarity to your other analogs." Dr. Moss smiled, impressed with himself. "To put it simply: you aren't connected to your analogs because you look alike—*you look alike because you are connected*. Your appearance is a kind of echo, and the tether is the medium upon which it travels. The bond is stronger than genetics; it's probably one of the strongest forces we've ever encountered. Theoretically, of course."

"An echo?" The word sounded so empty and lifeless. "Does that mean that I'm not really a person? That I'm not really me?"

"Oh, no, you're most definitely a person," Dr. Moss said. "Certainly yourself, whatever that means. As far as I can tell, you are a singular human being. Rest assured of that, at least."

"So you think that the visions I'm having of Juliana are coming to me through this so-called tether?" I asked. My head was spinning, but I was pretty sure I'd managed to follow everything the scientist had told me. Dr. Moss nodded. "But why?"

"Why what?"

"Why me? Thomas doesn't see visions of his analog," I pointed out. "As far as I know, nobody else does, either. But I've been having dreams of Juliana since I was a kid. That can't be normal."

"Well, normal is relative," Dr. Moss told me. "But it's highly unusual, I must admit."

"So why me?"

"Frankly, my dear," Dr. Moss said, "I have no idea."

TWENTY-THREE

"So that's it?" I demanded. "You just don't know?"

Dr. Moss shrugged. "I don't have all the answers. If I did, the world would be very different."

"I think Sasha was hoping to get advice about how to control what she's seeing," Thomas put in helpfully. "If she can force the visions, she might be able to lead us to Juliana."

Dr. Moss paused to consider this. "I suppose you're right. Well, the good news is that the connection has already been partially established. From what you've told me, I have to conclude that you are involuntarily witnessing events in your analog's life in your most vulnerable moments—when you're asleep, when you're unconscious. When your mind's natural defenses are at their lowest."

"Yeah, except I don't remember them clearly when I wake up," I reminded him. "If I could only have a vision when I was awake, I might be able to get some real information."

"There are other times besides sleep when your mind is similarly unguarded," Dr. Moss told me. "When you're feeling an extremely heightened emotion, for instance. Like fear, perhaps, preferably brought on by physical peril, when your mind is so busy defending your body that it can't concentrate on defending itself."

"Are you saying that if I can somehow scare myself enough, I might be able to force a vision?"

"I can't promise you that," Dr. Moss said. "But it's certainly possible. The question is, are you willing to do what it takes in order to open the floodgates?"

Thomas, ever-watchful, noticed my apprehension and shifted closer to me, putting a hand on my shoulder. "Maybe this isn't such a good idea," he said.

I closed my eyes, trying to shut everyone else out so I could think about Dr. Moss's question properly. What *was* I willing to do? This was, quite possibly, my only shot at freedom, my only chance to get home. I was *willing* to do just about anything.

"What did you have in mind?" I asked Dr. Moss.

"That depends," he said. "What are you most afraid of?"

"Er . . . I don't know," I said. "Snakes?"

"That's not it." Dr. Moss and I both turned to look at Thomas.

"Oh? What am I most afraid of, then, if you're so smart?"

Thomas said nothing, only looked up at the ceiling and raised his forefinger in the same direction. I recalled sharply the fizz of anxiety that had traveled through me when I'd realized how high up we were in the Tower two days ago. He cocked his head at me knowingly.

"I really don't think—" I began to protest, but Dr. Moss hopped off his stool and clapped his hands in a fit of excitement. *Every scientist loves an experiment,* I thought bitterly.

"You're afraid of heights?" Dr. Moss asked. He lit up like a Christmas tree with glee. "Splendid. That's it, then. Come now, hurry; I gather we haven't much time, from the way Thomas has been eyeing his watch."

"Wait," I asked, following Dr. Moss and Thomas out of the lab. "Where are we going?"

"To the roof."

I'd foolishly hoped they meant the roof of the Castle. At four stories tall, it wasn't too high, and I thought I could stand it well enough. But the Tower was one hundred and fifteen stories, which was completely unmanageable, especially if we were going to be outside.

"What if somebody sees us?" I hissed as the elevator for the subbasements arrived at the main elevator bank, where we were to switch over to the one that would take us to the roof.

Thomas peered through the open doors. "There's nobody in there. Quick, let's go."

"I really don't think this is a good idea," I said, twisting my hands at my waist as the steel elevator shaft gave way to a glass one; we were riding up at the rate of about three floors per second. I covered my face and turned away from the view. "Oh my God," I moaned. I hated heights, but I didn't like elevators very much, either, and the combination amplified by the speed at which we were traveling made me want to be sick all over Thomas's perfectly shined shoes.

"It'll be all right," Thomas said, putting a hand on my shoulder. He was trying to soothe me, but I didn't want to be touched by anyone. I just wanted to go back *down*.

"Don't comfort her, Thomas!" Dr. Moss admonished sharply. "She's *supposed* to be scared—that's the point!"

"So? I can't just watch her suffer!" Thomas cried. Then, perhaps thinking the better of his outburst, he took a deep breath and regulated his tone. "If you want to stop, we can stop. You don't have to do this. We'll find another way, or we just won't do it."

"We're doing this," I insisted. "Dr. Moss is right. Just ignore me." I was sort of hoping we'd never have to get to the top, that my immediate fear would be enough to trigger the connection I was looking for, but nothing was happening, and I could tell that mere anxiety wasn't going to cut it.

"Listen to the girl," Dr. Moss chided him. "You'd think she was more of a lionheart than you are, the way you're carrying on." That did it; in the face of having his reputation as Brave Man on Campus sullied, Thomas stopped squawking and left me alone.

The elevator came to a smooth stop. I was trembling, and a panicked sweat was gathering around my hairline. The door opened and we stepped out onto the roof, into the bright afternoon sunlight. I followed Dr. Moss reluctantly to the edge of the building.

"Look down," he commanded. After a moment's hesitation, I did so. A wave of nausea bore down on me. The ground was *so far away*. "Stay here. Thomas, come with me."

Dr. Moss led him to the opposite end of the roof. "Where are you going?" Neither answered me. I watched their conference; first, Dr. Moss proposed something, which Thomas vehemently opposed. Dr. Moss argued with him for several minutes and then, finally, Thomas's objections were subdued. As they approached me, Thomas's face was pale and drawn. Whatever Dr. Moss had told him to do, he wasn't happy about it; his fists were clenched at his sides, and his mouth was a straight, unreadable line.

"Ms. Lawson," Dr. Moss said. "Will you consent to do whatever it takes in order to force the connection with Juliana?"

I nodded, swallowing hard. "What are you going to do?" I

addressed these words to Thomas, who looked away, unable to meet my eyes.

"It's best if you don't know," Dr. Moss told me. "Look again."

I peered down and a feeling of light-headedness engulfed me. I was sure I was going to faint and began to step away from the concrete balustrade, an automatic response in the face of my worst fear.

"Now, Thomas!" Dr. Moss commanded.

In one deft movement, so swift and smooth it was almost graceful, Thomas grabbed me by my wrists, lifted me off my feet, and whipped me over the edge.

I opened my mouth to cry out, but no sound emerged. I was falling, falling, falling. I felt like I would never stop. And then I did. I was hanging off the edge of the roof, anchored only by Thomas's tight grip on my wrists. I looked up, terrified, into his face, which showed the strain of bearing my weight as I hung thirteen hundred feet in the air.

"Don't let go!" The words came out choked and broken; it was possible he hadn't even heard them over the shrieking sounds of the wind as it rushed by.

Dr. Moss's face appeared over the balustrade. "Close your eyes!" he shouted. "Channel everything you're feeling into the tether. Let yourself feel it all and focus it!"

What he was telling me to do was impossible. My mind was a frantic jumble of panicked thoughts, and my mouth tasted like copper, the metallic tang of fear I recognized from the moment I woke up in Aurora. I could hardly breathe, and was sure that I was going to pass out. *No,* I told myself, shocked that I could even manage to formulate a single coherent thought. I wrapped my fingers around Thomas's wrists, holding him as tightly as he was holding me; if I went limp, he might drop me, and I would surely die. I stared into Thomas's eyes, expecting to see fear there, but there was nothing but fierce determination to hold on. If I'd ever cursed Thomas's single-mindedness, I was grateful for it now.

Having no other option, I yielded to Dr. Moss's instructions. I forced myself to inhale deeply and closed my eyes, focusing all my attention and energy on the fear that writhed inside me. At first, nothing happened; then I felt an abrupt, almost physical snap, like that of a knuckle cracking or a shoulder being forced from its socket—except that it was in my *mind*—and after a brief, dark moment, images came rushing forth, pieces of long-forgotten dreams, one on top of each other, small fragments like shards of glass.

The black phoenix on a red background, swaying back and forth in a sweet country breeze . . .

A girl no older than twelve, wearing the Libertas symbol—the tetractys made of stars, stitched on a forest green armband—taking away a dinner tray . . .

The darkness of the secret tunnel and the bobbing yellow orb of a flashlight as Juliana followed a young man stealthily toward freedom . . .

A thin blue strip of paper being folded into the shape of a star to conceal a message and being placed in the back of a drawer where no one else could find it . . .

The painting of the lake house . . .

A face—the young man's face, older than Thomas but not by much, his lips curling up into a self-satisfied smile . . .

The images came so fast and there were so many that I only saw them for a fraction of a second. Some were old, worn, and blurry at the edges, while some were sharp, more recent. But they were all from the past, all pieces of dreams I'd had before.

There was nothing from the present. And then, another snap, and there it was—the tether. In my mind's eye, it looked like a tiny, brilliant filament of light, shifting this way and that, curling in on itself and then stretching infinitely in both directions. I stared into it as it grew larger, closer, and, summoning all the bravery I had, I let it consume me.

There was a knock at the door, but whoever was on the other side entered without waiting for permission. She sat on the tiny bed—she hadn't slept on something so small since she was in a crib—her book in her lap. She closed it as he entered and appraised him coolly, but it was a front. She'd been in the custody of Libertas for two weeks and the only people who'd come to talk to her were him, *at the beginning, though he was gone now; the girl at the previous location, who had not accompanied them to the farmhouse; and a new woman, a taciturn old country broad with a sparse mustache on her lip and a mean look in her eye, who brought her meals and did her wash, albeit begrudgingly. This man was entirely new to her. He was thin and wiry and tall, dressed in all black with no outward signs of his affiliation.*

"Who are you?" she asked him imperiously, as was her habit.

"They call me the Shepherd," he told her. He pulled the chair out from underneath the small white writing desk and sat on it backward.

"Do they," she said, arranging her face in an expression of utter disinterest. It was one of her great skills, which she'd learned from her father. She was able, through years of steady practice, to fabricate her expressions to show exactly what she wanted them to. Pretending to be sorry for some slight against her stepmother had saved her from going to bed without dinner many times as a child.

"Do you know why?" he asked.

"I don't care," she said, knowing he would tell her anyway, because he wanted her to know.

He smiled, showing his teeth, but it was a cold smile. "As you are probably well aware, Libertas is an expansive and ever-growing enterprise. It has many members at many levels and many moving parts that need attending to. I am the one who brings them all together. I am the one who gathers the sheep and makes sure that none wander from the flock."

"And you're here because . . . ?"

"Because right now, you are a wandering sheep."

She looked pointedly around the room. "That's funny, because I feel penned in."

"Oh, no, I don't mean it that way," he replied. "I mean that you haven't yet been drawn in to the flock, incorporated into our plan. There are some outstanding debts to be paid, questions to be answered."

"I've done what I was told to do," she said, folding her arms across her chest in defiance, but also to conceal her shaking hands. "The conditions of our deal were clear—I would speak only to the Monad about what I know."

"I'm the Monad's chief adviser," the Shepherd told her. "You can speak to me. I'll relay any message."

"That's not what we agreed on."

"Janus had no authority to make such a promise. He knows very well that the Monad doesn't consult with outsiders."

She laughed. "Is that what you call him? Janus?" She paused to appreciate how apt it was. "The god with two faces."

"Sometimes our names are chosen for us, and sometimes we choose our own."

"I'm not telling you anything," she insisted once more. "If you want what I have, you'll bring me to the Monad." She was no ordinary person; she was the princess of the Commonwealth, much as she loathed the position, and she wasn't going to trade secrets with a mere lackey.

"You're going back on our bargain, then?"

"And what if I did?" Sometimes she wished she could. Sometimes she felt that her freedom—or, rather, the promise of it—had come at too high a price. How could she have betrayed her country for something as transient as personal happiness—and only the potential of it, at that? Other times, she knew that she could have done nothing but what she had done. It had been her only way out.

He stared at her baldly, something she was unused to. Very few people had the temerity to look her in the eye. It had been that way ever since she was a child—even her stepmother avoided it if she could. That was one of the reasons she'd taken to Thomas; she could tell from the first day he was assigned to her detail that he wasn't afraid of her. At first, she'd thought it was because he hadn't the sense to be afraid, but after a while she realized it was because he wasn't much afraid of anything—except, perhaps, the General. Gloria was another, and her childhood nanny, Miss Bix. Her mother and her father. And the dreaded General. That was all.

"That's a very good question," the Shepherd said. "We couldn't return you, of course. Janus made it clear that once you took the bargain, there was no going back, did he not?"

"He did," she said. She felt as though she wanted to cry, but that was something she simply never did. Her mother had been very strict on this score; she considered it unbecoming of royalty to act as a flesh-and-blood mortal. It was one of the things Juliana despised about the way her stepmother was raising Simon and Lillian; either of them was liable to dissolve into hysterics, to sob and rage and carry on for hours, at the slightest provocation. She had a temper herself, but she had been taught to control it, and to channel it into more useful avenues. She had her moments, but she tried to follow her mother's advice whenever possible and keep things private.

"Then, you see, if you were to withhold the information you promised, you would leave me no choice. We'll have to dispose of you." He spoke of her death as if it was a matter of taking out the trash, and

she remembered with great clarity the fear that had washed over her when news of her father's shooting reached her, the tiny voice in her head that had whispered, You're next.

What have I done? *she thought wildly. It had been monstrously foolish to throw her lot in with Libertas, to take their devil's bargain and consent to betray her country for some small measure of personal safety. What had possessed her to do it? But even as these thoughts whirled through her head like a tornado, she knew very well why she had done it. It wasn't just that she didn't want to die. She wanted to live. And she could not call what she'd been doing for the past sixteen—almost seventeen—years living. Her mother hadn't wanted her to be a flesh-and-blood mortal, but she was one, and she couldn't imagine another sixty years of being a pawn in someone else's game.*

"You'll kill me, then." It wasn't a question. His meaning was clear. There was no use mincing words. She had always been a very straightforward person, and for some reason saying the words out loud had bled her of all feeling. She was numb.

"That would not be the ideal outcome," he told her. "But yes. It would be the only way, you see."

She'd never thought of that possibility, that they would kill her, and gladly, but it wasn't as though she was surprised by it. They hated her—not just Libertas, but the people. They hated the monarchy and what it stood for. Not all of them; she was sure there must still be some loyalists. But the Shepherd was right—Libertas was growing, their influence strengthening with every hour. She had made this deal with them to escape death, but perhaps that was her fate. Perhaps it was the only thing left for her. But she wouldn't welcome it.

"Yes," she said. "I see." That was something else her father had taught her, to know when she had been beaten, and to accept defeat with grace and dignity—if only to save her energy for the next fight. And the truth was, she had been beaten the moment she decided to leave the Castle forever and put her life in the hands of the fiends who

wanted to depose her and all of her kind. But it was done. "I'll tell you. I'll tell you everything. Just, please—help me."

The Shepherd smiled. "So you'll cooperate?"

She took a deep breath and reached into her bra, where she was keeping her bargaining chip. It was the last thing her father had ever given her. The night before he was shot, he summoned her to his office, quite unexpectedly near dawn. He'd been frantic, and he'd given her this sheet of paper without explaining, only telling her to keep it close and show nobody.

What is it? *she'd asked, yawning. Gloria had woken her from a deep, heavy sleep.*

Maybe nothing, *he'd said, although she could see from the expression on his face, the dark circles under his eyes, that "nothing" was the last thing it was.* But for God's sake, don't ever let the General know you have it, *he'd warned her.* Don't ever let him know you've *seen* it, Juli. Promise me.

I promise, *she'd said. And now here she was, handing it over to Libertas. She asked herself for the thousandth time why she was doing this.* Because the General tried to have my father murdered, *she thought. She was certain of this, as she had never been certain of anything in her entire life.* And if this is a secret he wants to protect, then it's something that can be used against him. *She didn't know how, for she didn't understand what it was she held in her hand, but she wanted the General taken down, and she was glad to let Libertas do it. They wanted the end of the monarchy? That was fine with her. Because if the monarchy crumbled, so would the General's hold on the country—and then, maybe, peace would have an actual chance. And she would have an actual life.*

The Shepherd tried to snatch the paper from her hand, but she held it back. He narrowed his eyes at her, no longer smiling. "What are you playing at?" he snarled.

"I have one more condition," she said.

"What is it?"

"You cannot hurt my family," she insisted. "You will not hurt them. My brother, my sister, my father—if he lives long enough—even my stepmother. You won't harm a hair on their heads, do you understand me?"

"Yes, yes, all right," he said, impatient. "Now give that to me!" He lunged for it, but she kept it out of his reach.

"I'm not finished," she said. "My secretary, Gloria Beach. You'll keep her safe, too. And my bodyguard. Thomas Mayhew."

"Mayhew?" The Shepherd let loose a bitter bark of a laugh. "The General's son? The toy soldier."

"Don't call him that," she snapped. She knew how much Thomas hated it.

"All right. Yes. You have my word. They'll all be safe when—when the time comes." The Shepherd held out his hand and she placed the piece of paper in his palm. He stared at it for a long time, his mouth curling in an unattractive frown.

"He was right," the Shepherd whispered. "It won't be long now."

"What do you mean?"

"Nothing," he said, standing and putting the chair back in its place. "You'll stay here for a few more days. We need time to arrange things. When we're ready, you'll know it."

"What are you going to do?"

He paused at the door, his head tilted, as if he was listening for music she couldn't hear. "It won't be long now," he repeated. And then he was gone.

Thomas hoisted me up by my arms, gathering me close and placing me gently on the concrete. My heart was beating so fast I thought it might burst out of my chest, and my head was full of so many foreign images I could hardly tell where I was or what was happening. One minute I'd been hanging off the roof of the Tower, and the next I was in the attic room of the farmhouse, everything so sharp it was as if I was actually there. I was shaking so hard it was as if my bones were rattling around loose in my body.

Thomas crouched in front of me. "Are you okay?"

I punched him squarely in the throat. He toppled backward, his hands flying to his neck, his mouth forming a tiny O of surprise.

"What the hell?" he managed to choke out.

"You bastard!" I cried. "How could you do that to me? I could have *died*."

Thomas shook his head. "I—had—you."

"Oh yeah? And what if you let go? How were you planning to explain the fact that the *princess* fell from the *roof*?" A sob rose in my chest and I fought to suppress it, knowing that I would crumble to pieces if I didn't.

Dr. Moss's cragged face hovered mere inches from mine. "We needed to push you to the very breaking point," he told me. "There is no other way. You needed to be truly afraid."

"Shut up!" I screamed. "You're crazy, you know that? You're both completely *insane*."

"You saw something, didn't you?" Dr. Moss gripped me by the shoulders, shaking me slightly. "What did you see?"

"I don't know!" I tried to fight him off, but I didn't have the strength.

"But you made contact," Dr. Moss insisted. "You saw through Juliana's eyes—you were able to force your way through to the other end of the tether. Where is she? *What did you see?*"

"Nothing!" Dr. Moss's eyes were wild, and his desperation was terrifying me. How could I have been so foolish as to think that I could use my connection with Juliana to my advantage? It was only one more way they had me trapped.

"That's not true," Dr. Moss said.

"Mossie!" Thomas shoved him away. "Leave her alone. Can't you see she's scared?"

"I need to get out of here," I said, pressing the heels of my hands into my eyes and rubbing hard, as if by doing so I could erase everything I'd seen.

"You can't!" Dr. Moss cried. "You have to process what you saw."

Thomas slipped his arms under mine, lifting me off the ground. I leaned against him, too tired to resist his help. "We're leaving. You and I will talk later," he said to Dr. Moss. "I've got to get her back to the Castle before someone starts wondering where she is."

I tried not to think about the people waiting for me back at the Castle. I would deal with them later; right then, my priority was getting the hell off that roof.

"Come on," Thomas said, guiding me back to the elevator. "Lean on me. We're almost there."

TWENTY-FOUR

By the time we'd gotten back to Juliana's bedroom, I was feeling much better. My heart rate was back to normal and I could draw full breaths again; I was calm enough to hold the glass of water Thomas had brought me, taking small sips to soothe my parched throat. I reclined on the bed, propped up by a couple of pillows; Thomas paced like a jungle cat a few feet away.

"I can't believe I did that," he said, raking his fingers through his hair in frustration.

Now that I'd recovered a little, I was less frantic and more forgiving. After all, I'd gone up on that roof voluntarily; I'd agreed to do whatever it took. I hadn't thought they'd go so far as to nearly throw me off the building, but now that the experience was over and done with, that wasn't what was bothering me. I'd achieved my goal—I'd opened the connection with Juliana, and any time I wanted to now I could dip back in, find the tether again, and travel through it to the other side, if only in my mind. But after what I had seen I wasn't sure I wanted to anymore. Because what I'd discovered was the answer to a question I'd never even thought to ask.

Juliana had been complicit in her own kidnapping. She

had walked willingly into the hands of Libertas in exchange for her own freedom. And she and I were the only ones who knew. She, and I, and the mysterious Janus, the person with whom she'd arranged her escape. But who was he? Why in the world had she done it? And—the biggest question of all—how was I going to tell Thomas? Because clearly he had no idea. He believed that Juliana had been kidnapped, and when Thomas believed in things, he did so wholly and without question.

I couldn't help but feel a burning sense of betrayal. Juliana was just as responsible for my presence in Aurora as anyone else. And not only that, but she'd turned her back on her country, abandoning her family and her responsibilities in pursuit of . . . what, exactly? What could Libertas possibly give her that was worth leaving behind the only life she'd ever known? I wished the tether allowed me to see into her private mind as well as her surroundings, but I couldn't hear her thoughts, only what she said and what was said to her. It wasn't enough. There was so much more I needed to know.

I couldn't blame her for wanting to get away. The longer I stayed in Aurora, the more I saw how lonely and trapped she must have felt. And with the arranged marriage to Callum, the fate of two countries weighing on her shoulders, maybe it wasn't so difficult to understand why she had done what she'd done. If it had been me, would I have done the same?

Thomas would be horrified when he found out. I could tell that he put a lot of faith in her, and even though I hated to admit it to myself, I was jealous of that faith. His loyalties, too, lay with Juliana, and he wanted her back as soon as possible. *Of course he does,* I told myself. It was childish for me to expect him to prefer me. But I didn't like being a placeholder, a poor substitute for someone else. It made me feel cheap and used and extraneous. More than ever, I wished that I could return to my normal life. At least there, I could be who I was. At least at home, I had people who loved me instead of people who loved the person they thought that I was. I was trying not to think of Granddad, of Gina, because I knew that if I started I would never be able to stop, that I would be consumed with missing them. But it was so hard, and I was so tired. I just wanted this all to be over.

Still, I couldn't bring myself to tell Thomas about Juliana—not just yet. My heart swelled with tenderness for him, so strong that it was almost overwhelming, and I searched in vain for something to say to him.

"How's your neck?" I settled on at last.

"What?" He glanced up in surprise. "Oh, fine. How's your hand?"

I was cradling my right hand gingerly in my left. "A little sore," I admitted.

He laughed. "Well, that's normal. You've never punched anyone before, have you?"

I shook my head. "Not really my thing."

"For a novice, you've got one hell of a right cross," Thomas told me. His eyes wandered to the foot of the bed, and then he raised them to mine in a silent question. I nodded and he took a seat, careful not to rumple the covers. "Otherwise, you're okay?"

"I guess." At least I'd stopped shaking, which was a marked improvement.

"It was Dr. Moss's idea," he told me. "I didn't want to do it. I was so afraid I'd lose my hold."

"So was I," I told him. "But you didn't."

"No," he said quietly, as if to himself. "I didn't. Thank God."

"I don't know that God had very much to do with it."

"You don't believe in God?" Thomas asked.

"Not really," I said. "I was raised agnostic."

He nodded. "Me too. But I've always thought that there had to be something out there. Something bigger than this." He gave me a wry smile. "Maybe it's just like Mossie said. There's *apeiron*—that source of all perfection—and then there's us. All our different versions, in every possible universe. And that's it."

"It's as good a theory as any," I mused. I didn't know anything about what my parents may or may not have believed, but I'd always found it interesting how Granddad talked about the universe, like it was a living, breathing organism full of intention. Even Thomas had done that: *The universes want to be equal,* he'd said. It reminded me of that phrase Mr. Early had written on the board the first day of my Western philosophy class: *kata to chreon*. But even if Thomas and Granddad and the ancient Greeks were right, it didn't mean the universes cared at all about us as individuals. At the end of the day, one analog was just as good as another. And if that was true, then what did it matter who we actually were?

"The royals used to think they were chosen by God," Thomas said. A private smile crept over his face. "Juli used to say that if that was true, they were being punished, not rewarded."

"I'm going to go ahead and agree with her." I stared at Thomas; when I told him that Juliana had left the Castle and gone with Libertas of her own free will, he'd be shocked and hurt—but would he be *surprised*? "You're close, aren't you? You and Juliana?"

He opened his mouth to protest, but I interrupted him. "I know, I know, you say that you're not allowed to have relationships with your 'assignment.' But you're not totally ambivalent about me, I don't think."

He hesitated. "No," he said finally, if abstractly. "I'm not."

"And you've only known me a little while," I pointed out. "You were her bodyguard for a year before she . . . disappeared. You can't tell me you don't care about her."

"Of course I care about her," he confessed. "I can't help it. We're all alone together, she and I. I mean, we're never actually alone, at least not very often. But we're so young compared to everyone else. And we're both, you know . . ."

"Lonely," I supplied. It was something that I'd recognized in them—Thomas just from spending time with him, and Juliana in my visions. I recognized it because I felt it, too, sometimes. I figured it was the residual effect of being parentless. Granddad had never neglected me, but as long as I did well in school and didn't have any tattoos, he pretty much stayed out of my business. Now that I was older, I appreciated the independence, but when I was growing up, I wanted so badly for someone to take more than a passing interest in the day to day of my life, to prove that they loved me by asking questions and keeping track of where I was. Maybe that was why I felt the way I did about Thomas; his mere presence, his investment in what was happening to me, made me feel less alone.

He shrugged. "Something like that. It's complicated."

"Are you in love with her?" It was an inappropriate, much too personal question, but I had to know.

"I—" The door chime stopped him, and he looked sheepishly grateful for it. His KES mask descended and I couldn't divine from his expression what he had been about to say. "That's probably Gloria. I wouldn't tell her about"—his eyes wandered up to the ceiling—"if I were you."

"Oh believe me, I don't want her to know any more than you do," I said. I arranged my hands in a more normal way, so as not to draw Gloria's hawk-eyed attention.

"Sorry, sorry," she said as she bustled in, with Louisa and Rochelle at her heels. "My mobie's been ringing off the hook with interview requests from reporters, the florist lost their permit to import tropical plants, and—" She paused, her eyes darting back and forth between Thomas and me.

"What's wrong?" she asked, suspicious. "You two seem very serious."

"Nothing's wrong," I told her, climbing off the bed.

"No," she corrected herself. "Not serious. *Guilty.*"

"Don't we have a schedule to keep?" I asked pointedly, inclining my head in the direction of Juliana's aestheticians. Even if I was going to tell her what had happened on the roof of the Tower, I wouldn't have done so in front of them. She caught the hint and backed down.

"Yes, always." She sighed. "Thomas, get out."

"I was just leaving," he said.

"Okay," Gloria said when he was gone, examining the state of me. I wasn't as disheveled as I had been when Thomas and I first arrived at Juliana's bedroom; I'd tidied myself up as much as possible, mostly so that I didn't tip Gloria off. I hadn't done as good of a job as I thought, because she seemed exasperated by my appearance. "Where do I even begin?"

Dinner was a strange, tense affair. The queen was outwardly polite to both Callum and me, but there was something dark and bitter lurking behind every word she spoke. I was used to the queen's barbed comments by this point; what bothered me was her undisguised resentment of Callum's presence. He'd done nothing to deserve her scorn except be born in a country she despised; even his presence in the Castle was outside of his control. I felt sorry for Callum, and strangely embarrassed. This wasn't the way to welcome a guest, even a foreign one from an enemy country. After all, they'd invited him in; they'd even handed over their princess for him to marry. The least the queen could do was be civil over a meal.

Callum looked miserable and homesick, but he made a valiant attempt to win the queen's approval nonetheless. I was glad when dinner was over and we could escape—so glad, in fact, that it wasn't until Callum and I were alone in the White Parlor with mugs of warm tea in our hands that I realized I had no idea what to say.

Luckily, I wasn't the only one. Callum seemed similarly tongue-tied. We were sitting about three miles apart from each other on different sofas, sipping at our tea, the silence punctuated by a ridiculous round robin of polite, throat-clearing coughs and nervous laughter. Callum smiled at me shyly, and I smiled back. I was starting to understand how deep the animosity between Farnham and the UCC went, because there was no other reason why anyone could dislike Callum. Even Thomas, who was usually so even-tempered about other people, had warned me to be wary of the Farnham prince, but by all appearances he was just a teenage boy like any other, albeit a little bashful and self-conscious. Admittedly, he didn't seem like the sort of guy Juliana would've chosen for herself. I could see why, outside of the fact that she was being forced to marry him for political reasons, she wouldn't have particularly appreciated the match.

"I'm sorry about dinner," I said, after the awkwardness had gone on so long I couldn't stand it any longer. "I'm afraid my stepmother and I don't really get along."

"I've heard that," Callum said. He seemed grateful for my attempt at conversation and latched on to it with enthusiasm. "She doesn't seem to like me much, either."

"Oh? What makes you say that?"

Callum laughed and I relaxed. He seemed determined to like me, which was going to make my job a lot easier. "You don't have to be diplomatic with me, Juliana. I get it. My mother would hate you, too. The feud is in our blood."

Well, it wasn't in *my* blood, and I thought it was awful. "It really doesn't bother you?"

"Of course it bothers me," Callum admitted. "I wouldn't be here if it didn't. That's what this is all about, right? Bridging the gap? Bringing people together? Making amends for history?"

"I suppose." I couldn't help thinking of Thomas's parents, and their deaths at the hands of the Farnham military during the last big Farnham-UCC conflict. If Juliana's marriage to Callum could prevent future bloodshed, then who was I to say it was wrong?

"This whole thing is pretty strange, isn't it? Us getting married, I mean." He ducked his head, incapable of looking me in the eye.

I breathed a sigh of relief. "Oh, good, I'm glad you think so, too."

He nodded. "I never thought that I would be married off. I didn't think things like that happened anymore. Although my mother loves to remind me that my grandparents had an arranged marriage."

"It's barbaric," I said, recalling my conversation with the queen earlier.

"Is it?" He raised his eyebrows in a questioning challenge.

"What do you mean?"

"War is barbaric," Callum said, with a seriousness that made him seem less boyish. "Letting your country get torn apart by revolutionaries—that's barbaric. This is . . . this is a civilized solution to an uncivilized problem." He sounded like Thomas, though I wasn't so sure Thomas would agree about that.

"Civilized? It's like they're offering us up as collateral!"

Callum looked me in the eyes. "That's exactly what we are," he said darkly.

I grimaced. "Well, I don't like it. No offense."

"None taken," he said. "I have to say, though—if I had to be married off to anyone, I'm glad it's you."

"Really?" I would've thought he'd hate the idea of having to live in a foreign country, to marry the enemy. Not to mention that Juliana had a reputation for being difficult and demanding and stubborn. Other than the rather unique situation they'd both been born into, it didn't seem to me that Juliana and Callum had much in common at all; while Juliana had run, Callum was here to do what was being asked of him. He would probably be disgusted if he knew what she'd done.

He nodded. "And I'm glad to be here. I don't know how much they've told you about me, but my life until now has been . . . restricted."

"Well, don't get any ideas about this place," I said. "It's quite the gilded cage."

"You don't understand," Callum said. "This is the first time I've ever left Farnham. It's actually the first time I've ever left Adastra." Adastra City was the capital of Farnham; I'd seen it on the map in the Tower room. Thomas had mentioned that the name came from the Farnham national motto: *Per Ardua Ad Astra—Through Struggle to the Stars*. "I wasn't allowed to travel anywhere or do anything. Mother wouldn't even send my brothers and me to school. She said it wasn't safe. I almost never leave our palace, I don't have any friends besides Rick and Sonny. So to me, this"—he gestured vaguely at the surroundings—"this is freedom."

"I didn't realize." I was starting to see why Thomas had such a low opinion of the queen of Farnham. She sounded like a real piece of work.

Callum waved my pity aside, clearly discomfited by the discussion of his confined—and, I'd gathered—unhappy childhood. "It doesn't matter. I'm here now."

He wandered over to the grand piano in the far corner of the room. Though it was meticulously dusted, it didn't appear to have gotten any use in years. He sat down at the bench and started randomly pressing keys. After listening for a few minutes, I realized that he was picking out a real melody, though I didn't recognize it.

"It's a little out of tune," he observed.

"What's that song?"

"Oh, nothing you would've heard." He paused, his fingers hovering over the keys. "Actually, I wrote it."

"You did?"

"Yeah," he said. "I had a great music tutor. I play a whole bunch of instruments, but piano is my favorite. After a while I got tired of all the stuff she made me practice and I started writing my own songs."

"Will you play it for me?" I asked. "I mean, really play it?"

Callum blushed and looked away. "No, that's all right."

"Are you sure? I'd like to hear it," I insisted. I'd never met anyone who could write his own music before, and the song—or what I'd heard of it—had been lovely. I had a healthy appreciation for classical music; it was the only kind Granddad ever listened to, and the sound of a piano always reminded me of quiet nights spent sprawled out on the living room rug, doing math homework while Granddad read in a nearby armchair.

"Well, how about this one? I wrote it about living at home with my mother. It's called 'I Hate This Place So Much (So Much).'" He flexed his fingers, then brought them down hard on the keys and sang, *"I hate this place so much—I'm crushed. Gotta get outta here, outta here, outta here."*

I giggled. "That's very good." He had a beautiful voice, deeper than I'd expected, a nice, strong baritone.

"I'm glad you think so." He grinned. "Maybe I'll play you another one later. We have a whole lifetime, after all."

"Yeah," I said, trying not to sound surprised. I'd almost forgotten who he thought I was, which was dangerous. I could never forget, but it was easy with Callum; he was so friendly and relaxed, remarkably unaffected. "I guess you're right."

"What about you?"

"Oh, I don't play the piano." As soon as the words left my mouth, I was seized by a sudden panic. For all I knew, Juliana *could* play the piano.

"No, I meant, what do you like? Do you have any hobbies?"

I considered the question. What *did* Juliana like to do? No one had ever told me. All I had to fall back on were the old visions from my childhood, which told me almost nothing. "Shopping?" Juliana certainly did own a lot of clothes.

Callum laughed. "Traditional royal pastime," he said. "Anything else?"

"Well, I really like reading and history," I continued. "I spend a lot of time in the Castle library." *That* was true, at least, a little gift of knowledge gleaned from my dreams, though I hadn't thought to mention it until it popped out of my mouth.

"That's interesting," Callum said. "Maybe you can teach me a few things about this place. It's much bigger than our palace in Adastra. Older, too, I'm sure. Lots of history here."

"Of course," I said. "Like you said, we have a lifetime."

Callum smiled. "Something tells me that might not be enough."

4

DAYS

THOMAS IN THE TOWER / 3

"How's our little princess?" asked Dr. Moss. He was speaking to Thomas, but his eyes were locked on his computer screen. It was driving Mossie crazy that he couldn't figure out why Sasha of all people could see through the tether, and he was determined to discover the cause of her unusual ability, even if it meant working around the clock.

"Fine," Thomas told him, picking up a slip of red paper and folding it into a star. He'd amassed a small pile of them in the time he'd been there. He paused to fish a handful of toggles out of his pocket, popping them in his mouth one by one. "No thanks to us."

"She's a strong one," Dr. Moss said, giving Thomas a pointed stare.

"Yeah," Thomas murmured. "She is." He paused. "She asked me last night if I was in love with Juliana." The question embarrassed him, but he felt like he had to tell *someone*.

"Are you?" They'd never discussed this before, but Mossie must have wondered.

Thomas shook his head.

"And did you tell her that?"

"I didn't get the chance." He wasn't sure if he would ever tell her. She might not have the nerve to ask again, and he preferred not having to talk about it at all, but he also didn't want her thinking what she clearly already thought was true.

He rubbed his eyes. He never slept well anymore. He was too worried about Sasha and Juliana, and when he wasn't thinking about them, he was thinking about his own analog, lost and trapped in a universe where he didn't belong. His mind kept wandering back to Grant's mother, who had cooked for him, done his laundry, asked him about his day, and told him every night before bed that she loved him. Thomas couldn't remember the last time someone had said that to *him,* as himself. The thought of the General saying the words "I love you" to anybody was absurd, and Alice Mayhew, though she had been kind and generous with him, was only his mother by default. Come to think of it, Thomas couldn't remember the last time that *he* told someone he loved them. Love just wasn't the sort of thing he had much occasion to express.

"Have you let the General know that Juliana is in Farnham?"

"No," Thomas said. "I don't think I can."

"Why not? Wasn't that the point of dangling Ms. Lawson off the roof of this building?"

"I promised Sasha I wouldn't say anything to the General." Even as he said it, the excuse sounded ridiculous. What did one little promise matter, when it meant the possibility of Juliana's return? And yet, he was incapable of breaking it. He put great stock in the power of a person's word, and he wouldn't break his own, especially when it came to Sasha.

"Then how do you propose to get Juliana back?"

"I have no idea," Thomas said. "I was hoping you might be able to help me with that."

"You want me to falsify intelligence?" Dr. Moss feigned disappointment, but Thomas knew full well that he enjoyed the promise and challenge of subterfuge. Plus, he hated the General, for a specific reason Thomas had never been able to pry out of him, and he looked for any opportunity to spite him, even secretly.

"Can you?"

"I can certainly try. Does Ms. Lawson know exactly where she is?"

"No. But she does know they're keeping Juliana in a farmhouse somewhere."

"Oh, wonderful. Only a handful of farms in Farnham," Dr. Moss said. Farnham, while not nearly as technologically advanced as its neighbor to the east, had a much more substantial agricultural industry than the UCC, due to the fertility of its soil. Trying to find Juliana in a farmhouse would be like looking for a needle in a haystack.

"They'll be near the border," Thomas told him. "Close enough to a major metropolis, and not far from the Tattered City. I'd say that narrows it down to the Louisiana Region, within a hundred miles of Adastra."

"Hmph." Dr. Moss was struggling to look put out, but Thomas knew he would have fun coming up with a clever way to trick the General into thinking the KES had uncovered a lead as to Juliana's location.

"You'd better watch yourself around that girl, Thomas," Mossie warned.

"What do you mean?"

"Your loyalty to her makes me nervous," the scientist said. "If I know the General—and I do—he's watching you both closely. If you give him any reason to doubt you, he'll take you off Operation Starling, or worse."

"I don't consider my loyalties compromised," Thomas said. Dr. Moss scoffed. "I'm just trying to do what's best for everyone. Sasha's afraid that if the General knows she's got a direct line to Juliana, he'll never let her go back home. I had to promise to keep it a secret so that she would feel comfortable enough to tell me about it in the first place! What choice did I have? I'm not trying to hide any information, I'm just . . . omitting how I got it."

"You know well enough the General isn't the type to split hairs," Dr. Moss said. "He won't care about any of that. And, for what it's worth, the analog is probably right—he would keep her here. He wouldn't risk sending her back to Earth knowing what she can do, and to be honest, I'd rather she didn't go back, either. Imagine what we could discover about analogs and the tandem if we could study her."

"No!" Thomas put his hands on Dr. Moss's shoulders, swiveling him around so that they were facing each other. He stared intently into Dr. Moss's eyes. "You cannot tell him. Sasha goes home in four days, maybe less if we can find Juliana before then. She *goes home*. That's what she wants. I'm not going to be the one to screw that up for her, and neither are you. We're responsible for the fact that she's even here. We owe her."

Dr. Moss sighed. "You may be right. But I won't say I haven't thought about it."

"Well, stop thinking about it, because it's not going to happen. I won't let it."

Moss regarded him for a long while. Finally, he said, "Did you volunteer for this assignment, Thomas?"

The question took Thomas aback. "What do you mean?"

"You say you're responsible for Sasha Lawson being here," Dr. Moss said. "And that's certainly true in a way. But did you want to do it? That is what I'm asking."

"Not especially." In fact, he'd fought tooth and nail against it; he'd wanted a place on Juliana's search-and-rescue team, but the General hadn't given him the option.

"And what did you do when the General told you he was sending you to Earth to seduce and kidnap a sixteen-year-old girl?"

Thomas glared at him. "Don't say it like that, you know that's not how it was."

"Wasn't it? Your heart's not in this, Thomas; anyone who's known you as long as the General has can see that. Go ahead, talk all you want about how this is a necessary evil to ensure peace between Farnham and the Commonwealth, but you don't believe it, do you?"

Thomas rubbed the back of his neck in agitation. "You really think the General knows?" Mossie nodded. "So why give me the assignment in the first place?"

Mossie hesitated, which spoke volumes. The man never missed an opportunity to express his own opinions.

"You'd better tell me," Thomas said fiercely.

Mossie took a deep breath. "Sending you through the tandem to retrieve the analog was a trial run," he said. "He needed to know that you could do it, that it could be done at all."

"What are you talking about?" Thomas demanded. "A trial run for what?"

"Much as I hate to admit this, the General is a smart man," Mossie continued. "He sees what's coming, and he has something special planned for you."

"What *is* coming?" Thomas was growing more and more exasperated. It was just like Dr. Moss to confide half truths, to speak in riddles.

"We may not be the only universe that has developed the technology to pass through the tandem," Mossie told him, avoiding Thomas's eyes. Mossie was hiding something from him, something big, but Thomas knew from experience that prying information out of him was impossible—he would have to wait for Mossie to offer it up. "And on the off chance that we are, we won't be for long. Soon enough, land disputes and treaties with Farnham will be the least of our worries. The future of war is interuniversal, and he intends for you to help him fight it."

TWENTY-FIVE

"'And then, that hour the star rose up, the clearest, brightest star, that always heralds the newborn light of day, the deep-sea-going ship made landfall on the island . . . Ithaca, at last.'"

"Angel eyes," the king said, as if in response.

I let *The Odyssey* fall closed in my lap and sat back in my chair, watching the king's fingers weave the air in front of him. His bed had been adjusted so that he appeared to be sitting up; the queen claimed he liked it that way, though how she could know that was anyone's guess. I glanced over at Callum, to see how he was handling all this; I was growing used to the king's idiosyncrasies, but I knew from experience how jarring it could be for the first time. I'd warned Callum about it, and he seemed to be handling it fine, though he was a bit on edge.

"This must be incredibly scintillating for you," I said. He gave me a nervous smile.

"It's nice," he replied. "That you do this, I mean. For him."

I shrugged. "I'm not even sure he can hear me."

"Even if he can't," Callum said. "It's sweet." He sat forward as if he wanted to touch me, but he was on the opposite side of the king's bed, too far away to take my hand. "Besides, it's a good book. Nothing wrong with the classics."

"This is my first time," I told him, realizing only after I said it that I might've found a better way to phrase it.

"You didn't have to read *The Odyssey* in school?" I shook my head. Juliana might have; Thomas had told me that she had gone to a private school in Columbia City called the Lofton Academy for Young Women, but that the king had pulled her out the year before and hired a tutor to finish out her education. Still, I felt confident Callum wouldn't have any idea what she had or hadn't studied there.

"Not that I'm an expert on what people have to read in school," he continued.

"I guess that means you did," I said, trying to draw the conversation back to him. I couldn't imagine living my whole life locked up, not being able to have friends or go places without an escort or attend school. I felt ashamed for thinking my life on Earth had been boring and confined. There were far worse ways to grow up, as Callum, and even Thomas and Juliana, were teaching me.

"Well, I had a Greek tutor for nine years, so, yeah. I read it."

"Your tutor was Greek, or he taught you Greek?" I smiled.

"He *taught* me Greek." Callum laughed. A light brown curl fell over his eye. "He was Irish, actually, I think. Seamus Ryan."

"That's a very Irish name," I teased.

"He was obsessed with *The Odyssey,* Ol' Shay," Callum said. "But I preferred *The Iliad.* More action, less time spent on boats."

"What have you got against boats?"

"I just have this feeling I'd get seasick and end up with my head hanging over the side." He patted his abdomen. "Delicate royal stomach, you know."

"Have you ever even *been* on a boat?"

"Nope. This is my first time outside of Adastra, remember?" Callum said. "Not much ocean where I come from, sad to say."

"You've never seen the ocean?" Even I'd seen the ocean, on a vacation to Florida with Granddad. I'd spent the entire time with my toes buried in the sand, the sun beating down on my pale legs, breathing in the salty air and loving every minute of it.

"Don't look at me like that," he said, pressing his lips together so that they nearly disappeared.

"Like what?"

"Poor little rich boy," he said with a small sigh.

"If you're a poor little rich boy, then what does that make me?" I asked. He smiled almost in spite of himself. It was nice to have a conversation with someone without having to second-guess everything that came out of my mouth.

"I don't know," Callum said, playing along. "What does that make you?"

Analog, a small voice whispered inside my head. But of course I couldn't say that to Callum, so I let the question slip by unanswered.

"Juli," the king said suddenly. I closed *The Odyssey* and put my hand on his. "What's wrong, Dad?"

"Touch and go!" the king shouted, startling both Callum and me. "Touch and go! Touch and go! One, one, two, three, five, eight . . ."

"Yes, yes, I know," I said wearily. I picked up *The Odyssey* and set about locating the line where I'd left off. The king always seemed calmer when I was reading to him.

"Why does he say that stuff?" Callum asked.

"Not sure," I said. "They say it's like his brain is stuck on repeat."

"So they don't mean anything, the things he says?" I shook my head. "Are you sure?"

I wasn't, but if they did mean something, I couldn't fathom what. "Who am I to argue with the doctors?"

"His daughter, for one. The princess, for another." He shifted a little in my direction. "Did he call you 'Juli' just now?"

I nodded. "It's what my friends and family call me."

"Can I call you that?" His voice was low and deep. I was trying not to notice, but Callum had the good looks of someone who ought to be on television, with his tousled brown curls and bright blue eyes. No wonder his Earth analog was an actor. Up close it was distracting how attractive Callum was.

"Are we friends?" I was flirting and I knew it, but it was hard to resist.

"I hope so."

I smiled. "Then yes, you can call me Juli. Do your friends call you Cal?"

Callum laughed. "If you mean my family, then yes. But only Sonny."

"Then that's what I'll call you," I told him. He seemed pleased by this.

Callum appraised the king. "Do you think he even knows we're here?"

"I just hope he knows he's not alone." I might not have been the king's daughter, but his condition just about broke my heart.

"I'm sorry, Juli," Callum said. He gazed at me with such tenderness that I had to avert my eyes, embarrassed by the intimacy of the look. "This must be so hard for you."

He glanced around the room at all the blinking monitors and intravenous tubes. "Almost losing your father, and then seeing him like this, day in and day out. It's so unfair." He paused. "They told me it was Libertas that shot him. Is that true?" His eyes returned to me, but this time there was a slyness in his expression that took me off guard. He was fishing for information, something I hadn't expected out of the sweet, unassuming prince. It was actually a relief to see that he had hidden undercurrents; the chances of him getting along with the real Juliana were greatly increased by this development. Still, Thomas and Gloria had both warned me not to speak to Callum about Libertas.

"It's okay if you don't want to talk about it," Callum said, when several moments had passed wherein I said nothing. "I just wanted to say I'm sorry. My father died when I was a kid, from a long illness, and I've never really gotten over it."

"I can imagine," I said quietly. I couldn't help but think of my own parents and how deeply I still felt their loss. Someday, Juliana's father would also die, sooner rather than later. At least I hadn't had to watch my parents suffer and fade away. Were Thomas and I the lucky ones, too young to remember the bad as well as the good?

"You think they're always going to be there," he continued, rubbing his jaw thoughtfully. His voice sounded lost and far away. "To protect you. To give you advice. And then they're not and they never will be again."

I dug my nails into my palm, determined not to cry. I tried to think of something else, anything else, to get my mind off my parents, but the images of their faces refused to fade.

The door to the room slid open, and I was grateful to see Thomas on the other side of it. Callum turned, and I quickly dabbed at the corners of my eyes with my fingertips.

"Is everything all right?" I asked Thomas.

"Everything's fine," he said. "The queen would like to see

you in her study; she wants to go over the seating arrangements for the wedding and the ball."

"You can tell her I'll be there in a few minutes," I said. He nodded and left the room, but not without first glancing warily over at Callum.

"The ball?" Callum shot me a questioning look. "I thought that was tonight?"

I shook my head. "That's the concert. *Your* concert." Callum rolled his eyes good-naturedly. It had been the queen's idea to bring in the Columbia City Orchestra to perform on the Rambles, the enormous park that served as something of a backyard for the Castle. Earlier, Callum and I saw the bandshell being constructed from the king's bedroom window. The orchestra was in honor of Callum's arrival in the UCC; his love and appreciation of classical music had preceded him.

"The queen is throwing us a pre-wedding gala." I'd been briefed on all this, but I was careless about wedding details and it had slipped my mind. "It's in three days. I hope you brought your tux."

Callum grinned. "Of course."

"Great. Well, I'd better go. The queen hates it when I don't come running." I put aside *The Odyssey*. "Sorry to abandon you, although I'm sure you have better things to do than sit here all day listening to me stumble over the word *Charybdis*."

He laughed. "As it happens, I don't." As I passed him, he caught my hand in his.

"In a few days this will all be over," he reassured me. I stared at his hands. His fingers were long and thin, the better to play the piano with, but his nails were short and uneven—he had a nail-biting habit. "Then we can do whatever we want. We'll be free."

"You're quite an optimist," I said with a smile. It was refreshing to be around someone so hopeful, even when I knew he was wrong.

"Can't help it." He spread his hands in a helpless gesture. "That's how I was born."

I wanted to share his faith in the future, but mine was waiting for me elsewhere, in a different world far from this one. Assuming, of course, that I was lucky enough to find my way back to it.

I emerged from the queen's study two and a half hours later, my brain liquefied by the experience of listening to the queen, Gloria, and half a dozen other wedding planners argue over outstanding details of a wedding I wouldn't even be there to experience. Not so long from now, I would be back in Hyde Park, far away from all this madness.

Except . . . I couldn't keep from imagining what it would be like when I returned. It had been several days since anyone had last seen me; there would certainly be questions, questions I couldn't answer. They would think I was insane if I'd told them where I'd gone; the only person who might believe me was Granddad, but even that wasn't guaranteed. There was also the question of Grant: could I really go home before they managed to send him back as well? The thought of leaving him to fend for himself in Aurora twisted me up into guilty knots. Much as I wanted to go back, there was no possibility of returning to my old life; Earth wouldn't be the sanctuary I desperately yearned for. And I wouldn't be the same person I was when I left.

Did I even want to leave? *Of course I do,* I thought. Why would I ever want to stay in Aurora? But I knew there would be things that I missed. After all the time we'd spent together, I couldn't wrap my head around the idea that I might never see Thomas again. He'd woven his way into the fabric of my life, of who I was, and the thought of separating from him struck me hard. *That's just because you can't live here without him,* I told myself. *Once you're home, you won't need him anymore.* But no matter how logical it sounded, that didn't seem quite like the truth.

Where was Thomas? Normally he stationed himself right outside the door of any room I was in, but as I emerged from the queen's study I didn't see him anywhere. I waited for a few moments, thinking he might just have gone off briefly and would soon return, but when that didn't happen I decided to make my way back to Juliana's bedroom myself. My visions of Juliana had taught me the layout of the Castle well, and I felt confident that I could navigate it just fine.

I'd just rounded the corner when I saw Thomas at the other end of the corridor, deep in conversation with a young man I'd never met before. He was tall, but not as tall as Thomas, lean but slight compared to Thomas's broad shoulders and muscular physique, with brown hair that had outgrown its short, cropped cut and needed to be trimmed. He was dressed in a black suit, like Thomas, which told me that he was KES, but that was all I could gather from so far away.

"What are you doing here, Lucas?" Thomas was struggling to keep his voice low, but the acoustics in the hallway were such that I could still hear him from where I was standing. So this was Thomas's brother, Lucas, the actual biological spawn of the General and Alice Mayhew. Naturally, I was very interested in this conversation.

"I'm here to see Juliana," Lucas said. The casualness of Lucas calling Juliana by her first name made me wonder just how well he knew her; I'd learned at dinner my first night that the General and the king had been friends most of their lives, so it was possible—even probable—that their children might be acquainted. Thomas had told me in passing that he'd met her a few times in the two years between his adoption and being shipped off to Blackbriar, but Lucas, being the General's biological son, would've had much more time in which to get to know her.

"Princess Juliana," Thomas reminded him sharply. Lucas rolled his eyes. "We're not kids anymore. And she's busy. Since when do you have clearance to just wander around the Castle like this? Aren't you supposed to keep to the Tower like a good little support agent?"

I wasn't really sure what all that meant, but I could tell from Thomas's tone that he was wound up and possibly baiting his brother. Lucas didn't rise to it, and I remembered that he was four years older. Maybe this was their relationship dynamic—Thomas, the younger, always acting defensive, and Lucas, the elder, looking for ways to defuse him. It didn't match up with what I already knew about Thomas's personality and character, but I was well aware of how certain people could bring out a different side of you.

"Then the General didn't tell you," Lucas said. I found it telling that even the General's natural born son didn't call him "Dad," or even "Father." "I've been promoted."

"To active?" Thomas's eyes widened in surprise, fiddling with his KES ring.

"Not yet. But maybe soon. The General said he might be able to arrange for me to take my trials in October." Thomas's jaw tightened; this information wasn't sitting well with him.

"Don't be jealous," Lucas teased. "There's plenty of action out there for the two of us. If you ever find a way to get yourself reassigned, that is."

"You assume I want to be reassigned. Maybe I like where I am."

"Oh, come off it, T, you're a glorified babysitter. You didn't blow through the Academy just to end up holding the princess's train while she traipses around the Castle, did you?"

Thomas shook his head, not in denial but in irritation. "What do you need her for?"

"I just wanted to say a quick hello," Lucas told him. "And congratulate her on her upcoming wedding. Is that so horrible? You're acting like you think I've got ulterior motives."

"I'll give her your message, okay? Just go back to the Tower and do your job, whatever that is."

"Are you angry with me, little brother?" Lucas asked. "If this is about Mom, I'm sorry I interfered, but I really think—"

"Don't start with that again," Thomas warned him.

I'd heard enough of this. I wasn't just going to hide around the corner and wait for them to come to blows over their personal issues. I stood at the head of the corridor and cleared my throat. They both looked up; Thomas tensed, but Lucas smiled as he turned to look at me and I got my first glimpse of his face.

"The truth is, Juli," I heard him say, *"the Monad isn't even sure you have anything to tell us."*

I shut my eyes tight as things I had seen in earlier visions elbowed their way back into my mind. The underground bunker where Libertas had been holding Juliana, the wide fabric bracelet with the gold star tetractys the girl had been wearing on her wrist, and then Lucas's face, peering at me smugly, his features illuminated by the harsh light of the overhead fluorescents. *Him.*

Oh my God, I thought in disbelief. *Lucas is Janus.*

"Your Highness," Thomas said. "Agent Mayhew was just leaving." He put a slight emphasis on *Agent Mayhew,* as if he was trying to inform me that Lucas was his brother.

I nodded, swallowing hard and forcing a smile. "Good afternoon, Agent Mayhew."

I held my breath, anxious to see how Lucas was going to react to me. He knew I wasn't Juliana. But then why had he been seeking me out? Was he going to expose me? Or did he just want me to know that he knew? Did he think I was just a look-alike, or was he aware of the tandem and the fact that Juliana and I were analogs, that I was from another universe altogether? And finally—how much did he know about Thomas's involvement in my presence in Aurora? He didn't seem to know anything, from the way he'd been talking to Thomas earlier, but Lucas was a double agent—*the god with two faces,* Juliana had said, a reference I now understood—and there was no way for me to tell just at a glance what he was thinking or intending to do.

Lucas bowed his head and returned my polite smile. "I just wanted to congratulate you on your upcoming wedding to Prince Callum, Your Highness."

Yeah, I'm sure you do, I thought. "Thank you," I said. I lowered my voice in a way that implied I was confiding something in him. "Although I have to tell you, I'm looking forward to having it over and done with. You can't imagine how many boring meetings I've had to sit through while the queen and Gloria argue about place settings and flower arrangements and who can't sit next to who because of what political scandal." I sensed Thomas relax at my side.

The two-faced god grinned. "But I thought women liked planning weddings."

"Well," I said with a wry laugh, "most women get to choose their husbands."

"Your Highness, we need to go," Thomas said. "Gloria wanted you back in your suite at four o'clock sharp for your fitting."

"Yes, of course. It was good to see you, Lucas," I said, extending my hand for him to shake. He took it, squeezing just a bit too hard. He looked into my eyes, and I could read his meaning in them: *I know who you are*. Or, rather: *I know who you* aren't. "Thank you for your congratulations."

"The pleasure was all mine," Lucas said. His eyes lingered on me a moment longer; then he turned, with a farewell nod to his brother, and walked away.

When the sound of his last footsteps had faded, I turned to Thomas, who was still staring after Lucas. I gave him a slight shake to get his attention.

"Sorry," he said, rubbing the back of his neck. "Lucas doesn't usually come to the Castle—support agents don't have the clearance. He said he'd just gotten promoted, but I can't think—"

"Forget that," I commanded. He narrowed his eyes, sensing my urgency. "You and I need to talk, *now*. Somewhere private."

"Library?" Thomas suggested. I nodded.

"How's it going with the prince?" he asked as we made our way.

"Good," I said, grateful for the momentary distraction from what I was about to tell him. "He's really nice. I think he's lonely. Did you know that his mother wouldn't let him go to school? This is his first time leaving the city he grew up in."

"Queen Marian gets a lot of criticism from the press hounds about that. They say she does it to make sure that they're weak and entirely dependent on her."

"I think Callum might despise his mother," I said.

"I don't blame him." Thomas looked like he was about to say something else, but he refrained. "You brought Callum in with you to see the king this morning. How do you think that went?"

"Callum lost his father when he was little," I said. "He

seems to understand what I'm going through. I mean—well, you know what I mean."

"And there weren't any problems with the king?"

"No. He just kept saying the same old stuff over and over again. You know: 'Mirror, mirror,' 'touch and go,' and that string of numbers . . ."

"One, one, two, three, five, eight," Thomas said. "It's from—"

"The Fibonacci sequence," I finished for him. "I know." After about an hour of seating charts and arguments, I'd started to tune the queen out and for some reason the numbers floated up in my memory and snagged in my mind. They wouldn't let go until I figured out what they were trying to tell me, which was that they weren't random at all.

"You're good," Thomas said. "I had to look them up."

"Granddad taught me to recite the sequence when I couldn't get to sleep," I told him. "That and the exact value of pi. I can do that one to twenty-five decimal places."

"Your granddad is quite the character," Thomas said. I smiled. My upbringing had been eclectic to say the least, but I wouldn't have traded it for anything—well, almost anything.

"What do you think it means?"

Thomas shrugged. "Not sure. Maybe nothing. Could be just a coincidence."

"I don't believe in coincidence," I said.

"Neither do I," Thomas agreed.

"The king keeps calling me 'angel eyes,'" I continued. "Is that his pet name for Juliana?"

"No, it isn't." Thomas frowned. He locked eyes with me, and without even saying a word I knew we were thinking the same thing. Something was up. The Fibonacci sequence wasn't a string of random numbers; it was an ordered progression that continued infinitely. Granddad called the Fibonacci sequence "magic numbers," and they were. They occurred in nature all the time: in the spiraled scales of a pinecone, the arrangement of leaves on a stem, the curve of waves, and the ancestry of honeybees.

This was another lesson Granddad had taught me: *The world is far less random than it appears.* Once you started paying attention, patterns emerged where before you only saw chaos. So what was it that we were missing?

TWENTY-SIX

"What's the matter?" Thomas asked, once he'd done a thorough sweep of the library for anyone who might be lurking in corners or behind bookshelves. "Did something happen with the queen?"

I shook my head, kneading my hands in my lap. I had no idea how to phrase what I was about to tell him. All I knew was that I couldn't keep this secret from him anymore. Not telling Thomas that Juliana had arranged her own kidnapping with Libertas in order to preserve his good opinion of her was one thing, but I couldn't hide his brother's treachery from him. It made him too vulnerable, made it too easy for Lucas to manipulate him, and I couldn't allow that. In spite of the fact that Thomas had brought me to Aurora, he had always tried to protect me, and I wanted to protect him, too.

"Then what?" Thomas reached out and took my hands in his, a tender gesture that made me light up inside. Why did everything have to be so difficult? Why did I have to like him so much after everything that he'd put me through? But for better or worse, I cared about him, and I knew he cared about me. So informing him that the two people he was closest to in the entire universe had betrayed him would be the hardest thing I'd ever have to do.

The hardest thing apart from leaving him when all this was over.

"Thomas," I said softly. "I know how Libertas managed to kidnap Juliana."

"You do?"

I nodded. "It wasn't a kidnapping. She wanted to escape, and Libertas helped her do it. They promised her a new life if she gave them a piece of information that they needed, something the king told her before he was shot. Lucas works for them. They planned the whole thing together."

"No." Thomas snatched his hands away. "You're wrong. Juliana would never do that. Neither would Lucas."

"She didn't want to marry Callum. You told me that yourself," I insisted. "And maybe she was afraid that what happened to her father would happen to her, too, if she stayed. I don't know if Lucas approached her first, or if she somehow figured out what he was doing and struck a deal with him, but either way—"

"Stop!" Thomas cried, rising to his feet. "Don't say anything else. You don't know what you're talking about."

"Yes, I do!" I was trying to keep calm—it wasn't like I'd expected him to take this news *well*—but I was having a hard time controlling my temper. "I saw it!"

"Then you misunderstood." His voice was cold and vibrating with anger. "You said yourself the visions were intermittent and that you didn't remember them well. You're just mistaken."

"I remember them now, and I'm telling you that this is what I saw. I *saw it,* Thomas."

"If you're not mistaken, then you're lying," Thomas accused. "You're jealous of Juliana and you're trying to get me to hate her, but it's not going to work. I *trust* her. She's my friend."

I reared back as if he'd hit me. "You really think I'd do that?" My voice was so small it would've fit inside a thimble. "You really think I'd lie about Juliana because I'm *jealous*?"

"You asked me if I was in love with her and you—you—" He couldn't bring himself to say it, but I caught his implication just fine without it. He thought *I* was in love with *him,* and that I wanted to destroy what he had left of her to get my own way. I couldn't believe that he would consider me capable of that, after everything we'd been through.

"Be careful what you say next," I warned him. "You won't be able to take it back once you do." But we both knew we had already gone past the point of no return.

"I won't stand here and listen to this," he said. "I won't."

"And what about Lucas? You think I'm lying about him, too?"

Thomas's jaw tightened. "You don't know anything about my brother, or Juliana, either. You think you do because you've been here for three days, but you don't know *anything* about this world or our lives. You're just trying to manipulate me so I'll send you back, but if you think I'm going to take your word for it that the two people I trust more than anyone have been playing me for months, you're going to be sorely disappointed."

"Thomas," I said. I'd managed to get my anger under control somewhat, and my tone was even. "I know this is a shock. I know you don't want to believe it. But I wouldn't be telling you if I didn't think you needed to know."

"You don't know what I need," Thomas snapped. "Our deal is off. I'm not going to tell the General about your little 'ability,' because I don't think it actually exists. But you'll stay here until he decides to send you back. I'm not going to stick my neck out for you anymore. From now on, you're on your own."

Back in Juliana's room, I sat immobile on the bed, trying to process the emotional runoff of what had just happened with Thomas in the library. I considered searching for him, but the Castle was huge, not to mention the rest of the Citadel—I'd never find him if he didn't want to be found. I wanted to dissolve into tears, but they wouldn't come; my entire body had frozen.

I felt like I'd been torn in half. One part of me was so angry with Thomas that I wanted to hit him until he felt even a small amount of the pain I'd felt at his unfounded accusations. *Jealous? Manipulative?* How could he believe those things of me? He knew who I was, more than anyone else, and yet it was so easy for him to just assume I was lying about Juliana and Lucas. I hated him for that. I hated him for having more faith in them than he had in me, when I was the one who'd done everything he asked, the one who'd tried to help him. How could he turn his back on me when I was the only one who hadn't turned my back on him?

But as much as I wanted to sink into my anger, there was another part of me that understood what he was going through. Thomas wasn't difficult to figure out. He was a truth-teller, a boy with scruples and dignity and an outsized capacity for loyalty. He wasn't naïve, but he trusted himself and his instincts, and those instincts had told him that Juliana and Lucas were loyal to him. Doubting them meant doubting himself, those things that he counted on every day in his job, to keep people safe, to keep *me* safe. From his perspective, I was telling him that he was a fool, that he'd let emotion override common sense and perhaps, unknowingly, jeopardized his own mission. My heart broke for him, because I knew what it was like to have your entire world ripped away, to discover that someone you cared about wasn't who you thought they were.

The two halves of me were playing tug-of-war with my brain and with my heart, and eventually I couldn't take it anymore. I needed a distraction, something else to occupy my mind so I didn't go crazy trying to figure out what I was going to do about Thomas. Because at the moment there was nothing *to* do except to hope that he would come to his senses. I opened the nightstand drawer and took out the copy of *Twelfth Night* that Thomas had sent through the tandem with me. Tears sprang to my eyes at the sight of it as I tried to reconcile the boy who'd thought to bring my favorite book into an alternate universe in the hopes that it would comfort me with the boy who'd just called me a jealous liar. No, I couldn't read it, not today. I went to put it back when the little blue origami star caught my eye. I pulled it out and held it in my palm.

I'd seen Juliana write something on the inside of the paper before she folded it up and placed it in the drawer herself, the night she had escaped. I didn't even have to open it to know what it said, because I'd seen the words in a vision of Juliana, as if I'd written them myself:

T—I'm sorry, but I can't. I wish I was better, but I'm not. —J

She'd *wanted* him to know what she had done. Or maybe she thought he'd figure it out on his own, that he'd suspect her without needing to be told, and this was her apology.

It was a sorry attempt at making things right. Maybe those words would mean more to Thomas than they did to me, but they felt insubstantial for the amount of trouble she'd already caused, and the amount that I was sure would come. I placed the star on the nightstand and stared at it. I wasn't sure yet what I should do with it. It felt obvious that I should give it to Thomas and allow him to make of it what he would, but what was the point? He'd already decided I was a liar; why would this note, which I could have easily forged, convince him of anything?

I sighed and lay back on the bed, feeling very weary. As I shifted my back, I heard the familiar crumple of paper and, reaching behind, found that someone had laid a more traditional note on the pillows for me to find.

Was looking but couldn't find you. I'm in the garden, would love some company if you're not busy.

—Callum

I walked onto the terrace and scanned the gardens; Callum was sitting on a low bench, sketching in the black notebook he always carried. There was something comforting about seeing him there, hunched over and absorbed in his task. I liked that I didn't have to perform for him the way I had to perform for the queen, and that I didn't have to answer to him the way I did with Thomas and Gloria. I could be myself with Callum, or what was passing for myself these days, even if he didn't know who that was.

I called his name to get him to look up; I waved, and he waved back. I held up a handful of fingers and he nodded. Then I went back inside, taking a brief moment to fix myself up before heading out to meet Callum among the roses.

* * *

"Hey," I said as I approached. Callum glanced up at me and smiled.

"Hey yourself."

I nodded at the agents who were hovering within earshot; they shuffled off to stand in the shadows and give us our privacy.

I joined Callum on his bench. "What are you drawing?" I asked, leaning over to take a look. "Oh," I said in surprise. "It's a window?"

To be fair, it wasn't just any window. The drawing was a simple black-and-white charcoal sketch, but it was obvious from the elaborate design that the original was stained glass. Callum had done all sorts of intricate shading to register the subtle differences in color.

He pointed ahead with the tip of his pencil. "It's that window."

We were seated about ten feet away from one of the Castle's interior brick walls and, indeed, the window Callum was putting on paper was directly opposite us. At first, I thought it was abstract, just a hundred or so different colored pieces in various shapes and sizes, but as I stared at it a more deliberate picture emerged.

"It's the Seal of the Commonwealth," I told him. I recognized it from the marble floor of the Castle's grand entrance, in which a large bronze replica of the Seal was embedded. It showed an eagle, legs and wings outstretched, holding a rowan leaf in one talon and a bundle of arrows in the other. The shield over the great bird's torso depicted a gold crown against an azure blue backing, crested by a golden sun with twenty-one rays. The sun itself was surrounded by an undulating pale green ribbon—I assumed it represented the aurora for which the planet was named. A rattlesnake wound its way around the seal's edge, making it a perfect circle. The eagle clutched a scroll in its mouth upon which the motto of the Commonwealth was inscribed: *Sic tyranno liberi sumus.*

Thus we are free from the tyrant.

"Yup," Callum said. "I'm not doing it much justice like this, but in black-and-white it's easier to see the design." He handed me the sketchbook. He wasn't wrong. Though the stained glass was beautiful, the Seal popped so much better without the distraction of color and the glare of the setting sun. Still, it wasn't quite right without those things. The starkness of the charcoal rendering gave the image a sinister quality, which was perhaps what Callum, until very recently an enemy of the Commonwealth, had intended.

"You're a really good artist," I told him. "Where did you learn to draw like that?"

"You can learn to do anything well with a lot of free time. I might not have any friends, but I do have a bunch of useless talents."

"They're not useless," I argued. "They're impressive."

"Not really." He leaned in closer and lowered his voice. "Do you want to know why I'm sketching this window?"

"Because it's beautiful?"

"No. It's because windows are all I draw." He looked away, embarrassed by the admission, though I couldn't quite see why. "Windows and doors. See?" He flipped through the notebook, showing page after page of different kinds of windows and doors. Some of them were from the Castle, sketches he'd made in the short time since his arrival, and then further back, to renderings of portals and entryways I'd never seen before. They were intricate and flawless, masterfully shaded to reflect a certain time of day or amount of lighting in the room. I was enamored of his gift, even if his chosen subject was unorthodox.

"Why?"

"I don't know. I just like the way they look." His hand rested on the page, and I moved it to see what he was trying to hide. The drawing was very plain, just a steel doorframe. The strangest thing about it was that the space outside the frame was shaded, but the inside of the frame was blank, the cream color of the paper. The door was emitting a faint glow.

"Where did you see this one?"

He shrugged. "Nowhere. At least, I don't think so. Sometimes I just make them up."

"What is it, then?" Something about the door bothered me. It gave me the same creepy feeling as the dark, colorless Seal, like it was something I should be afraid of.

"I have no idea," he said. "I try not to question it."

"Well, I'm still impressed." I smiled. "Even if you do only draw windows."

"And doors—don't forget doors."

The crunch of gravel beneath a delicate stiletto heel attracted our attention. Gloria was approaching.

"The concert," Callum muttered, staring at the ground. I was beginning to suspect he didn't like crowds. This didn't surprise me much; he'd been raised in near-solitude, always shielded from the noise and activity of the common people. Public places were bound to make him uncomfortable.

"Your Highnesses, I'm so sorry, but I have to interrupt. Juliana, you need to get ready for the concert, and your valet is waiting for you upstairs, Prince Callum." Gloria eyed us both sternly, as if she was a teacher and we were pupils who had forgotten our homework. "I must insist that you head back inside."

"We're right behind you," I told her. As I rose from the bench, Callum ripped the sketch of the mysterious doorway out of his notebook.

"Here," he said, thrusting it into my hand. "That's for you."

"Oh, Callum, I—" It would have been rude to refuse it, but all the same, I didn't want it. The longer I looked at it, the more unnerving it was.

"I was thinking of you when I drew it," he confessed. "I was thinking about leaving home, and meeting you, and our future, and I . . . It's an allegory. Don't you see? A doorway into the unknown."

Well, that explains it, I thought. Of course I found the drawing unsettling—that door, with its unseen destination, was exactly what I saw when I pictured my own future.

I smiled down at him, knowing what he needed to hear. "I'm looking forward to finding out what's behind that door."

"Me too," he said, with a sincerity that broke my heart. "Me too."

THOMAS IN THE RAMBLES

"This whole thing is a goddamn security nightmare," Agent Bedford griped, coming up to join Thomas on the stage, behind the backdrop. "I hate open-air events." He wiped his brow with a handkerchief. "What's up with you, Mayhew? What're you looking at?"

"Just confirming a position on the Sparrow," he said. He could see Sasha on the enormous North Terrace, surrounded by the guests who'd come for the concert, with Callum at her side. He watched the Farnham prince put a hand on her shoulder and whisper in her ear. She nodded and turned to smile at Callum, her lips coming close to brushing against his cheek. Thomas couldn't tear his eyes away from her. She wore an elaborate headpiece of delicate chains studded with silver thorns that wound their way over the crown of her head, into her plaited hair, and around her neck. It reminded him of her captivity, but she still looked resplendent in it. Sasha and Callum had made their first public appearance together on the Grand Balcony an hour earlier, to the wild cheers of thousands of onlookers and well-wishers. Not everyone in the UCC was enamored of the royal family, but there were plenty who still believed in the power and dignity of the monarchy, and they were overjoyed to see the beautiful couple. And they did look perfect together; even Thomas couldn't deny that.

Thomas closed his eyes and tried to dispel the pangs of guilt and longing that sprung up in him every time he saw Sasha, but he was only moderately successful. *You're a KES agent,* he scolded himself. *Act like it.* All this emotional turmoil was unbecoming of a man in his position, but he couldn't quite banish it. He wasn't just a name and rank; he was a person, too, and it was no longer possible for him to behave like he wasn't.

Since his argument with Sasha a few hours before, all he could think about was her and Juliana and Lucas. He was consumed by confusion and questions and anger, which he'd unfairly taken out on Sasha. She was only trying to help, even if she was wrong. There was no way that what she'd said to him could be true. It was impossible. He knew his brother, and while Lucas had certainly been acting strange the past few months, Thomas was sure it was because he was attempting to regain their father's favor, to rise up in the KES the way Thomas had. Otherwise, why would the General have consented to allow Lucas to take the KES Trials this fall? Such a thing almost never happened. There was one way into active KES service and that was through the KES Academy, from which Lucas had been rejected three times—the maximum number—before giving up. According to KES rules he was ineligible to apply again. That was why he was being so diffident and mysterious; he thought Thomas would resent him for trying to better his situation.

And Juliana—well, it wasn't even worth considering Sasha's claims about her. Perhaps it had been hasty of him to imply that Sasha had developed a romantic attachment to him, that she was jealous, but it was the only conclusion he could reasonably come to. Sasha didn't know Juliana; he did. He knew her better than probably anyone else alive. She'd confided in him. She trusted him with her life. If she'd wanted out, she would've come to him. At least, he thought she would. But even if she had, what would he have said to her? What would he have done?

Still, he felt terrible about how he'd treated Sasha. She hadn't asked for her visions, and she definitely hadn't asked to be brought to Aurora to fill in for Juliana. *He* had done that to her. And it had been clear from the tentative way she'd broken her news to him this evening that she was trying to shield him from the awful truths she thought she possessed. In return he'd accused her, insulted her, hurt her deeply. He'd seen it all on her face, but he'd kept going, because he was afraid. He wasn't used to feeling that way. He'd been surprised by it and hadn't had time to recalibrate, to push it down and deny its hold over him. Sasha would never trust him again. He'd ruined everything that was forming between them, and it was too late to do anything about it.

After leaving Sasha close to tears in the library, Thomas had returned to KES command central, where Captain Fawley, his superior when he was on Protective Service detail, was asking for volunteers to beef up security at the concert.

"I'll do it," Thomas had said, so eager he practically tripped over the words.

"You sure?" Fawley had asked. "Thought you might want to stick close to the Sparrow."

He'd shrugged. "Social event. She's not going to want the hired help standing over her the whole night." He felt guilty abandoning Sasha, fully aware that he was doing it only to get away from her and everything she made him feel, but it wasn't as if she would be unprotected. There was an army of KES agents patrolling the North Terrace, where the cocktail hour was being held, and when the concert began she would be sitting in the front row, easily within range of his stage assignment.

He'd spent all late afternoon watching as Gloria's team set up the chairs and prepared the terrace for the pre-concert event. He'd also gotten a front row seat as a pair of sweaty movers in jeans and T-shirts unloaded the van the Columbia City Orchestra had sent over containing all the instruments and music stands for the night's performance. Bedford had been with him. At some point they were standing near the van as one of the movers struggled to unload a tuba case with a violin case already in hand.

"Can I get a little help here?" the mover asked.

Bedford had shot Thomas a look of disbelief. "He can't seriously be talking to us, right?" He turned back to the guy. "We're KES, man. We've got our own jobs to do."

"Come on!" the guy grunted. "There's only two of us and we're running late."

"Not our problem," Bedford scoffed.

"I'll help you," Thomas offered, picking up the tuba case. "Where do you want it?"

"Mayhew, what the hell are you doing?" Bedford demanded.

"Just trying to be useful," he said, grateful for the opportunity to do something active. Physical activity helped keep his roaming mind in check. With his help, the movers got everything unloaded in under an hour.

But now that the event was about to start, Thomas's entire being was supposed to be focused on watching out for possible Libertas activity. Thomas glanced around the backdrop and saw that Sasha and Callum were making their way to the front row, which meant everyone else would start filing in soon. He thought he saw Sasha notice him, but he pulled his head back in so quickly he couldn't be sure.

You're a damn coward, Thomas told himself.

Soon, everyone was seated; Sasha and Callum were in the front row with the queen and a handful of distinguished politicians. The General had been invited, of course, but he didn't do events like this. He was much more of a behind-the-scenes man. For this Thomas was glad. The last thing he needed was the General's scrutiny.

The orchestra took the stage in silence. Night had fallen, and the only light came from the stage and the aurora whirling high above.

"I'm going to go do a sweep," Bedford announced. "You coming, Mayhew?"

Thomas shook his head. "Gotta keep an eye on Sa— Sparrow." He'd almost said her name. How was he supposed to do his job when he couldn't even get the simplest things right?

Bedford nodded and disappeared into the darkness of the wings as the orchestra struck up their first piece, a dark, fast-paced number that burrowed into his heart like a drill. The strings cried out, driven wild by the cadence of war drums. Thomas recognized the piece; it was called "Revolution," composed in the early eighteen hundreds to commemorate the formation of the Commonwealth.

When "Revolution" was over, the conductor waited for the applause to die down before leading the orchestra into their next piece, a dreamy sonata. Thomas began to relax. Everything was going well; the audience seemed to be enjoying the performance, the orchestra was playing perfectly, and everyone was safe.

There was a crackling noise on his earpiece. "Hey, Mayhew?" It was Bedford, of course.

"Yeah?" Thomas spoke clearly, knowing that the rowan pin would transmit his voice despite the background noise from the orchestra.

"Where'd they put all the instrument cases?"

"What do you mean?"

"The noise makers are all on stage, but where'd they put their houses?" Bedford said. He was trying to sound jovial, but his voice carried a dark undercurrent.

"Back in the van," Thomas told him. "It's parked behind the stage. Why?"

"We've got to stop the concert," Bedford said, serious now. "I'm under the stage and there's a violin case down here."

"Just one?"

"Just one."

Thomas knew what Bedford was thinking—a bomb. It was exactly the conclusion he would jump to if he'd found it. But he had to ask: "Are you sure?"

"No, I'm not sure! Would you like me to give it a little shake?" Bedford cried.

"I'll find Greenberg." Greenberg was the agent in charge, and if the event was going to be evacuated it would have to be on his orders.

Thomas tracked Greenberg to the stage's back stairs, where he was standing guard. "Bedford thinks he found a bomb."

"Where?" Greenberg demanded.

"Under the stage. He thinks we should evacuate the area."

"How does he know it's a bomb?"

"He doesn't, but he found a violin case down there, and all the other instrument cases are in the van out back," Thomas told him.

Greenberg nodded. He put his hand to his earpiece. "Bedford, are you on the mike?"

"Yeah, boss," Bedford said.

"Circle the perimeter and tell me if you see a timer."

There was a pause. "I think there's one . . . Oh, sh—"

"Bedford!" Greenberg cried.

"We've got ninety seconds," Bedford told him flatly. Thomas's whole body felt heavy, like his clothes were lined with lead. There wasn't time to pull in the bomb squad. They'd have to make a run for it.

"Bedford, get the hell out of there now." Greenberg turned to Thomas. "I'll handle the evacuation. You find the princess and keep her safe, you got it? Do *nothing else*."

Thomas didn't hesitate; he just took off running. *Sasha,* he thought as he reached the edge of the stage. The crowd looked up at him, wide-eyed, as a soaring symphony crashed behind him like waves. He counted in his head: *Eighty-five seconds, eighty-four seconds, eighty-three seconds . . .* He had to find Sasha. He had to find her *now.*

Thomas leapt off the stage, landing only three feet in front of her. She stood, surprised and alarmed to see him there. He reached her in the space of a moment—*eighty seconds*—and grabbed hold of her arm, pulling her in close.

"There's a bomb," he whispered in her ear. She froze, but he wasn't going to let her just stand there. No matter what had happened before, it was his job to keep her safe, and he was going to do that if it killed him.

"Hey! What are you doing?" Callum shouted, but when his eyes met Thomas he saw the seriousness in them and backed off. If there was anything the prince understood, it was the importance of letting security do their job. "What's happening?"

The orchestra was so wrapped up in their performance that they didn't notice the action that was taking place right at their feet.

"Let's go," Thomas said to Sasha. It wasn't his job to protect Callum, or the queen; they had their own security details, agents who were coming for them now, streaming off the stage behind him and down the center aisle. Sasha nodded and held tight to his arm as they wound their way through the rising chaos. People crowded around them, voices raised, emotions running high, but Sasha shut her eyes and let Thomas lead her through. They had just reached the end of the lawn when Thomas heard Bedford's voice in his ear—"Thomas?" He looked back instinctively, like Lot's wife sneaking one last glance at Sodom and Gomorrah, and Sasha followed his lead.

One second.

The aurora in the sky was obliterated by a blinding plume of light.

"WHAT ARE YOU DOING HERE?" *she asked, looking up from her book. The matron who had been bringing her meals and cleaning up her room each day since she got to the farmhouse was standing in the doorway, eyeing her suspiciously. The woman had a Libertas patch sewn on to her ill-fitting black button-down shirt; Juliana guessed it must've belonged to a man before, possibly her husband, although she couldn't imagine anyone wanting to get into bed with this dumpy old woman.*

The woman held up a bowl full of purple goop and a plastic poncho. "You're ta have yur hair dyed," she said sharply. She must've been from nearby; her Farnham Country accent betrayed her, with its clipped consonants and gutteral creaks. "Sit in the chair."

"What? I'm not dying my hair, are you crazy?" Her hands flew to her head. She took great pride in her hair, which was a beautiful chestnut brown, thick and straight and glossy. There was no way she was going to let them touch it.

"Shepherd's orders, ma'am," the woman said. She pulled the chair out from beneath the desk and gestured to it. "Sit."

The woman always called her "ma'am," never "Your Highness," something that hadn't escaped Juliana's attention. No one in Libertas felt any compulsion to show her deference. They didn't believe in her, didn't have any loyalty to the Crown. She'd never met anyone who refused to defer to her because she was royalty, and she didn't like feeling powerless.

"Why are you doing this?" she asked, moving to the chair. It was worthless to fight them, she'd learned. They had her trapped in this house, and no one who worked here was even the slightest bit inclined to help her in any way. No matter what they asked, or how hard she resisted, in the end she always had to do as they told her. And now that she'd given them what they wanted, it was distinctly possible—even likely—that whatever they asked was part of their plan to fulfill their end of the bargain. The sooner the better, as far as she was concerned. If she knew the General, he had the KES scouring the country for her, and the KES always found what it was looking for. Eventually they'd find out that she'd been smuggled into Farnham, and then they'd be on top of her. She didn't want to give them the chance.

" 'Cuz the Shepherd toll me to," the woman said. She separated Juliana's hair into several pieces before coating it with the goop.

"Ouch!" Juliana cried. The woman was not being gentle. "I mean, why do they need my hair dyed?"

"Got no idea. Maybe so's it's hard ter reconnize ya wur yur goin'."

"And do you know where that is?" Juliana pressed.

"Course no," the woman scoffed. "Ya think they lemme in on their secrets? I'm just a Second Tier. I follow orders. I dunno plans."

I dunno plans, either, *Juliana thought as the woman continued to tug at her hair.* But someday. Someday I'll have my own plans. And nobody has to know them but me.

TWENTY-SEVEN

I sat in Juliana's bedroom, a coverlet hanging around my shoulders. I was holding a mug of hot tea, but I couldn't bring myself to choke it down. The royal physician—the real one, this time—had patched me up, promising there would be no scar, but my head ached where it had slammed against the terrace when the bomb blast knocked me over. I hadn't mentioned the fact that I'd had another vision to anyone; I'd half hoped Dr. Moss would attend to my scratches instead of Dr. Rowland so that I could confide in someone, because Gloria had no idea about my connection with Juliana, and I wasn't exactly speaking to Thomas. The vision had made something clear to me—they were getting ready to move Juliana. They had a plan, and they were starting to implement it. Soon, she might be so far away that there was no hope for getting her back again. The prospect chilled me straight to the hollows of my bones. If there was no chance that Juliana would return, did that mean I was doomed to stay trapped in her life forever?

"I'm okay," I assured Gloria, who was rushing around trying to make me comfortable, barking orders at everyone.

Shaken as I was, I didn't want Gloria fussing over me; it was only making me more anxious.

"Gloria, calm down," Thomas said. "She's all right."

"She's all right? She's *all right*? And how the hell do you know that?" Gloria demanded.

"Because she just said so." I hid my face in the mug of tea, breathing in its strong jasmine scent. Thomas was riling Gloria up in the hopes that her anger would distract her from her fear; it appeared to be working.

"Haven't you ever heard of *shock*?"

"She's not in shock. You screaming at everybody within a fifty-mile radius might change that, though."

"You." Gloria pointed an accusatory finger at him. "You did this. You brought her here, you put her in danger. This is your fault!"

Thomas said nothing. I could feel his eyes on me, but I didn't raise mine to meet them. I didn't want to look at him. Every time I did I heard his voice in my head, his accusations and his insults, and I got angry all over again.

"You KES won't rest until we're all dead in the ground, will you?" Gloria said, her voice taut. "Frank, Bedford, Sasha . . . you don't care who gets hurt as long as you get what you want."

"I'm sorry about Frank," Thomas told her. From his tone, I could tell he meant it, but I had absolutely no idea what they were talking about. Who was Frank?

Gloria worried her engagement ring between her fingers. She straightened her shoulders. "I don't need your sympathy."

"He was a good agent," Thomas continued.

"I know he was!" she seethed.

"What's going on?" I asked. "Who's Frank?"

Gloria ignored the question, and Thomas chose not to answer it in deference to her. "Your fiancé?" I guessed, noting the way Gloria continued to play with her engagement ring.

Gloria drew in a deep breath. "Frank was KES. He was with the king the day he was shot."

"Did he . . . ?" I couldn't bring myself to complete the question.

"No. But a bullet tore through his spinal cord. He'll never walk again." Gloria closed her eyes briefly, and when she opened them again they were wet with tears.

"Oh, Gloria." I stood, shrugging off the blanket and putting my arms around her. Gloria leaned into the hug, patting my back softly and then stepping back. When I looked at her face, the grief was gone, a mask of professionalism in its place. What was it about the people in the Citadel that made them so adept at doing that?

"So," Gloria said, dabbing at the corners of her eyes. "The question is, how do we move forward?"

"What do you mean?" I wondered.

"Clearly you're not safe here," Gloria said. Thomas nodded in agreement. "We need to remove you from the Castle for the time being, put you somewhere nobody can get to you."

"Like where?"

"The royal family owns several estates up and down the East Coast. Any one of them is safer than the Castle right now, it seems, but we can't take you too far away, with the wedding set for Saturday."

"That's still happening?" Surely with the Libertas threat so high they would rethink the circus wedding in favor of something more private. The treaty didn't need a huge, expensive ceremony to be ratified, only that Callum and Juliana be officially married. Or so I'd gathered.

"It's all planned," Gloria said. "The queen won't be moved. She refuses to be intimidated into canceling."

"Right now the plan is to take you and Callum away from the Castle until Friday evening for the gala. The queen will stay here to maintain some semblance of strength and defiance," Thomas said. "We leave tomorrow morning, so, Gloria, you should help Sasha pack."

"You're going too?" The words flew out of my mouth before I could stop them. I'd been doing such a good job of ignoring him, and I was angry with myself for abandoning the silent treatment so soon.

"Of course," Thomas said. The corners of his mouth twitched, as if he wanted to smile but knew that it wouldn't go over well. "Anywhere you go, I go."

"Right. Your job."

"It is my job," he said.

Gloria narrowed her eyes at us both. "What's happening here? What's wrong?"

"Nothing," Thomas and I barked in unison. He tried to catch my eye again, but I was back to giving him the cold shoulder.

"Where are we going?" I asked, directing the question to Gloria.

"Bethlehem House?" Gloria suggested.

Thomas nixed this. "Too far away."

"St. Lawrence?" I glanced at the painting on the wall. It did look beautiful; I wouldn't mind a few peaceful days in the country if I could spend them there.

"*Way* too far away."

"Well, it needs to be someplace defensible," Gloria snapped.

I had no idea what royal residence would be best, but this did seem like the perfect time to make a request, seeing as we were going to have to move anyway. "Do you have anything with a waterfront view?"

"Actually, yes. Why?"

I shrugged. "Callum's never seen the ocean. If we're going to have to go somewhere anyway, it'd be nice to show him."

"Asthall Cottage in Montauk," Gloria said to Thomas. Thomas's face scrunched up as if he'd smelled something disgusting, but he nodded reluctantly. Gloria turned to me. "It's right on the water. The ocean's still a little cold for swimming this time of year, but we can put Callum in a room that overlooks it, and then of course there's always the private beach."

"It's remote, too, so it'll be easy to keep track of who comes and goes," Thomas admitted. He didn't sound thrilled, but he was on board. "I'll let the General know we'll be moving you there."

He left without saying goodbye.

"I hope you packed your swim trunks, Cal, because we're going to the beach," I said as the door to his bedroom slid open. The cheeriness was forced, but when his face lit up, I didn't have to fake it. It made me happy to see him happy, quite possibly because he seemed to be the only person in the Castle who *was* happy these days.

"Really?" he asked.

"Thomas and Gloria think it's best if we get away from the Citadel for a few days," I explained.

He nodded. "Agent Tyson told me." Agent Bedford had survived the bombing, but he'd been seriously injured and couldn't return to his KES duties yet. From the way Thomas had spoken about it, there was a possibility that Bedford would never be able to serve in the KES again. Agent Tyson was his replacement as the head of Callum's security team.

"I told them we should go to one of the residences by the water, seeing as you haven't ever seen the ocean," I told him. He beamed at me. "And they agreed. So we're going to Asthall Cottage."

"A cottage? But where will all your shoes go?" Callum's eyes crinkled when he laughed.

"It's not an *actual* cottage, Callum," I said, affecting a snooty tone that set him off laughing again. "It's a *manse,* darling, of course." I'd actually been wondering the same thing—Juliana's family owned a *cottage*?—until Gloria showed me a picture of the place. The name might've been humble, but there was nothing humble about Asthall.

Callum put his arms around me, pulling me close, his laughter trailing off. "Is this okay?" he whispered in my ear.

I nodded, figuring it would have to be. Besides, I didn't mind. It felt nice to be held, after the day I'd had. "Are *you* okay?"

"I just can't stop thinking about what happened," he said, pulling away so that he could look at my face. He tucked a piece of hair behind my ear.

"Me neither." I sighed. "I'm so glad you weren't hurt." Thomas had dragged me away so fast I hadn't even had time to see if someone was coming for Callum. I'd spent thirty frantic minutes after the explosion waiting for news of him. I tightened my arms around his waist, remembering the horrible, sinking feeling that came with wondering whether he was dead or alive.

"Same here." He released me and stepped back. "I know you don't like to talk about it, but you have to tell me—did Libertas set that bomb?"

"Thomas seems to think so."

Callum stiffened and turned away at the second mention of Thomas's name, pretending to go through his drawers for stuff to toss into an empty nearby suitcase.

"You pack your own clothes?" I asked in wonder, hoping a change of subject would bring back Callum's cheery side.

"I insisted. Mother never let me do anything for myself," Callum told me. "It's fun."

I shook my head in bewilderment. Packing and unpacking were some of my least favorite things to do, so I was glad to let Gloria take care of it for me. "If you say so." I stood there for a second, feeling like a spare part. "Well, I guess I'd better go see how my own packing is getting along. You're sure you don't need any help?"

"Nope," Callum said.

"Okay then. I guess I'll see you tomorrow morning."

"Juli, wait." Callum looked me in the eye. "I shouldn't even be asking this, but I have to know now or I'll always wonder—is there something going on between you and Agent Mayhew?"

"Why would you even ask me that?" I demanded, tensing.

"I don't know," Callum said, shamefaced. He ran his fingers through his hair, rumpling his curls to hide his embarrassment. "It's just that, when I see the two of you together . . . there's a connection there."

"You're imagining things," I told him.

"Am I? I mean, it'd be okay if . . . well, not okay. It's just that I'd understand if . . ."

"Thomas is my bodyguard," I said firmly. "Nothing else. Ask him yourself, if you don't believe me."

"No, I believe you," Callum insisted.

"Forget Thomas. You're the one I'm marrying," I reminded him.

He gave me a tight smile. "Yeah, but that wasn't your choice, was it?"

"It wasn't your choice, either, but you care about me. Why can't I care about you just as much?" I knew I didn't, but Callum had no idea who it was he cared about. If he knew I wasn't Juliana, he wouldn't give a damn about me, so I didn't exactly feel guilty.

"Do you?" Callum asked. "Look, I know it's weird, that I show up here and act like I'm all in love with you after one day. Believe me, I can see myself doing it, and even *I* think it's weird. But for the first time in my life, I'm finally getting to make my own choices."

"That's a little ironic, considering that you're here because of a choice you *didn't* make."

Callum conceded the point. "I can see my future with you, Juli, and it makes me happy. We're going to have this amazing life together, I just know it. That's what I'm choosing. To not stand in the way of our future. To let myself fall in love with you."

"I'm not there yet," I told him. But that wasn't what was so bothersome about this. My worry was that the real Juliana, the one Callum would actually be married to, would never get there. I didn't want Callum to be miserable for the rest of his life because I had led him on.

"You don't have to be." He smiled a bit sadly. "I just wanted to know if it's possible."

"It's definitely possible." *Anything's possible,* I thought.

3

DAYS

TWENTY-EIGHT

Callum's face brightened immediately upon the sight of the water. "So that's the ocean."

"It is indeed." We were standing at the border of Asthall's sprawling lawn, which was separated from the beach by nothing but a stone retaining wall. I curled my toes in the grass. It felt so good to be away from the Castle, to be barefoot and wild-haired at the edge of the sea. A strong breeze pressed Callum's linen shirt flat against his chest, making it cling to him, a sight I had a hard time looking away from. We'd been forced to send an attendant to buy Callum some clothes in town, once Gloria realized he'd done a terrible job packing for himself.

"It's so . . . big." He laughed at himself. "That sounded dumb."

Sometimes I forget how big everything is. I couldn't help but hear Thomas's voice in my head. I hadn't seen him since we'd arrived at Asthall; he was keeping his distance, though I had no doubt he was watching me very carefully after last night's attack. I was glad not to have to deal with him and Callum at once, but I had to admit to myself that I missed him. Not *him*, but the comforting familiarity of his presence, the way it had been before.

"It's not dumb at all," I told Callum. "Well, what are you waiting for? Go for it."

Callum grinned at me and took off. He plunged feetfirst into the waves, then immediately hopped out. "It's cold!" he cried. "Why didn't you warn me it would be so cold?"

"Because it's more fun this way!" I called back. I ran down the beach to join him, stopping just short of the water.

"Get in here!" he coaxed. I dipped a single toe in just to test it. It was *freezing*.

He kicked at the water, splashing me, and I shrank from the spray with a laugh. "Hey, stop! I'm getting married in a few days, I can't risk hypothermia."

Callum went back in. "It's warming up." He shivered, his teeth chattering.

"Yes, I can see that." His enthusiasm was catching. Eventually, we got used to the temperature, and we played around in the ocean like children until we were exhausted. Then we trudged up the beach and flopped down on our backs.

"Ugh," Callum said, fidgeting. "I think I've got sand down my shorts."

"You were the one who wanted to come to the beach." There was no point in mentioning the circumstances that had brought us both to Asthall. Neither of us could forget them if we tried.

Callum sighed contentedly. "I want to spend every minute of every day here. Let's not go back, okay?"

"Okay," I agreed. "But who's going to tell the queen?"

"Not me! She already hates me."

I stared up at the sky, where a parade of clouds rolled along like tumbleweeds made of cotton balls. "It's a shame you were never allowed to do things like this back in Farnham. I hear the California coast is amazing."

"Yeah, well." Callum buried his fingers in the sand up to his knuckles. "Mother was trying to protect me."

"From what? Jellyfish?"

"I don't know. She never said." Callum turned his head to look at me. "But you can't really protect people from anything, can you?"

"Says the boy who showed up at my door with an armed escort."

"Not like that. You know what I mean. Experience. You can't keep people from getting their hearts broken."

"You think your mother wouldn't let you see the ocean because it might break your heart?"

"No." Callum sighed. "If there's anything I learned from my mother, it's that power makes you just as vulnerable as it makes you strong. People want to use you for it, or take it from you, all the time. She doesn't want that to happen to us. She doesn't want my brothers and me to trust people only to have them turn on us."

"I can understand that," I said. The real Juliana knew the feeling quite well, if Thomas and Gloria were to be believed. Was that what was happening between Callum and me? Was I fooling him into trusting me only to leave him in the end? Maybe so, but what choice did I have?

We were quiet for a while, the breaking of the waves upon the beach the only sound.

"Tell me a secret," Callum requested.

"You tell *me* a secret."

"I asked first."

"I will if you will," I said. I was stalling. I couldn't think of a single secret I was at liberty to tell him.

"Okay," he said. "Here's my secret: I actually fell in love with you back when I was ten."

"What? Are you serious?"

"I saw your picture on one of the press boards. It was of you and your father, I think, at some state dinner. You were wearing a blue dress and your hair was all curled."

"I don't remember that," I said.

"Well, I do," Callum said. "And I turned to my mother and said, 'I'm going to marry that girl someday!' I didn't know what marriage was, really, but kids get funny ideas in their heads and they run with them."

"What did she say?"

"Oh, typical Mother. She said, 'You can't marry her, she's our enemy.' About a little girl! When she told me about, you know, this whole arranged marriage thing, I reminded her of that. She yelled and sent me away." He sat up, brushing sand off his hands. "Okay, your turn. What's your secret?"

I thought about it for a second. "I think the king is trying to tell me something."

"Your father?"

"Yeah. Those things he keeps saying. I'm starting to wonder if he's not trying to communicate with me in some way. He doesn't say that stuff to anybody else."

"Then let's figure it out," Callum said without hesitation.

"What do you mean?"

"Let's see if we can't find a pattern. He said 'touch and go,' I remember that." He picked up a stick and wrote TOUCH AND GO in the sand in a messy, boyish scrawl. "What else?"

"Um, okay, let's see. 'Mirror, mirror.' He says that sometimes. And . . . one, one, two, three, five, eight."

"The same numbers over and over?"

I nodded. "It's the beginning of the Fibonacci sequence."

"What's that?"

"It's this series of numbers that forms a pattern," I explained. "Each number is the sum of the two numbers before it. One and one is two, one and two is three . . ."

"Two and three is five, three and five is eight," Callum finished. "Got it."

"And so on, infinitely," I said. "But he only repeats those six numbers—one, one, two, three, five, eight."

"What's so special about the Fibonacci sequence?"

"It can be applied to all kinds of different things. Analysis of financial markets, computer algorithms. They occur in nature, too, in tree branches and flower petals and stuff. They're sort of like magic numbers."

"Magic numbers," Callum murmured. "Sounds promising. Anything else?"

"Yes! 'Angel eyes.' He says 'angel eyes.' "

"I remember. I thought that was his nickname for you."

I shook my head. "It's not."

"Angel eyes; mirror, mirror; touch and go; and the numerical sequence one, one, two, three, five, eight." Callum rubbed his eyes. "It definitely *seems* random."

"It does," I agreed. "But I don't know that it is."

"What could he be trying to tell you?"

I glanced out at the horizon. "I have no idea."

Then Callum did something completely unexpected; he leaned forward and kissed me.

I was so surprised that I didn't move. All I could think about was Thomas; his face loomed in front of me, the way he'd looked on prom night when he was jumping around on the dance floor. In an attempt to shove away this memory, which hurt more than I wanted to admit, I kissed Callum back, my thoughts racing. Callum placed his hands upon my cheeks and breathed warm air against my cool skin. I wrapped my arms around his shoulders and buried my face into his neck. *I can't do this,* I thought wildly, holding on to Callum as if I was clinging to the side of a cliff. *It's not right. Soon I'll be gone and she'll be back and she won't love him. She won't ever love him, and he'll always wonder what changed. He'll think it's his fault, he'll blame himself. . . .*

This is a betrayal.

"Cal," I whispered, separating myself from him. "I'm cold. Let's go inside."

"Cold?" He gazed at me, confused. We were almost dry now, and it was warm in the sun. "Is something wrong?"

"No," I said with a nervous, breathy laugh. "I just . . . I'd like to put some pants on, if that's all right."

"Um, sure. Yeah, let's go back. It's probably almost lunchtime, anyway."

He took off for the house without reaching for my hand, and I followed at a slight distance, knowing that however hard I tried, I wasn't going to return home without leaving my mark on Aurora.

TWENTY-NINE

Dinner at Asthall was far more casual than it was at the Castle. Back in Columbia City, only the royal family was allowed to eat in the formal dining room, unless we had guests, but at Asthall, Gloria, Thomas, and Agent Tyson were to eat with us as well. Dress at Asthall was also more casual, but that didn't mean Gloria didn't have a say in what I would wear. Tonight I was in a floor-length blue-and-white ikat maxi dress with an empire waist and a draped skirt. It had a long, chunky neckpiece made of dozens of silver chains attached to its fitted bodice, and I wore it with expensive-looking woven silver sandals. Gloria had done my hair herself, in a messy knot at the top of my head. I caught my reflection in a mirror; while the look was more relaxed and beachy, I was still elegant. Gloria seemed pleased with her accomplishment.

"We have a guest for dinner tonight," she told me. It was a deliberately offhand statement, and it raised the hairs on the back of my neck.

"The General?" The words came out in a squeak. I hadn't seen him since the dinner at the Castle when I'd had my allergic reaction, and I wasn't looking forward to trying not to squirm under his gaze all evening.

"Close," Gloria said. "But no. His wife, Alice Mayhew. She lives near here, and she phoned a little while ago, to get in touch with Thomas." Gloria shot me a hesitant look. "You know Thomas is the General's son?"

"Adopted son," I corrected her.

She nodded. "Well, I got the feeling she was fishing and invited her up. It's not exactly standard protocol, but it's not unusual for the princess to extend last-minute invitations to people close to the Crown, and Alice is close—at least through the General." Gloria paused. "I think she just wants to see Thomas."

I shrugged. "Fine. I don't care." I wasn't pleased—I had enough to worry about with Callum and Thomas eating at the same table, and adding the General's wife would only make it worse, especially if there were tensions between her and Thomas—but there didn't seem to be much I could do about it now.

We found the entire group gathered in the parlor adjacent to the dining room. It was easy to spot Alice Mayhew; she was a small, chic woman with a perfect auburn bob and hazel eyes that rested gently on me as I entered the room. Everyone rose from their seats, and Callum came over to take my hand, giving me a kiss on the cheek; any annoyance he'd felt toward me due to our earlier discussion seemed to have dissipated.

"You look beautiful," he murmured, and I smiled at him, grateful for the compliment. There was something about the casual sophistication of the dress that made me feel, for the first time since my arrival in Aurora, a little bit more like myself.

Thomas and Agent Tyson hung back; as KES agents, they

weren't allowed to greet me until everyone else had. Next up was Alice, who smiled at me as she approached and clasped both of my hands in hers. They were cool and soft; a breeze coming through the open window carried her perfume on it, a powdery poppy scent.

"It's good to see you, Your Highness," she said. "It's been far too long."

"It has," I said. "I'm so glad you could join us tonight." I let my gaze wander over to Thomas, who was suppressing a scowl near the back corner of the room. He wasn't happy that his adopted mother was here, but he was working very hard not to show it. I saw it, though, but I told myself it wasn't my problem. Alice seemed perfectly lovely, and I was going to be as polite to her as I was to anyone else.

"Thank you for inviting me," she said, stepping aside to make room for Agent Tyson to pay his respects. Then Thomas approached, and I felt everything inside of me clench. Before yesterday, his presence would've calmed me, but now I didn't know what to feel. He bowed his head in deference.

"Good evening, Your Highness," he said, stiff and proper. I nodded, and he stepped aside.

Dinner was pleasant, all things considered. Neither agent talked much, which I had a feeling was part of the protocol, but the rest of us chattered easily, and by the end of the meal I'd come to like Alice Mayhew a lot. Her lilting voice was like music, and it was soothing just to hear her talk, though all she was doing was telling stories about renovations to the Mayhew home that she'd been overseeing. Every so often, she would look over at Thomas in the hopes of catching his eye, but he kept his own trained on his food. By the time dessert was finished, Alice seemed exhausted from her attempts to get her son's attention, and announced that she was skipping coffee and tea in the parlor and going home early. I offered to walk her out.

She was quiet until we reached the front door, at which time she turned to me and said, "Pardon me for being so forward with you, Your Highness, but I have a question to ask."

This caught me off guard. "Uh, okay."

"You know Thomas very well, don't you?" she asked, searching my face.

"I suppose," I said carefully. "Why?"

"I was only wondering if he's ever spoken to you about me," she said. Her cheeks reddened, but Alice Mayhew was a proud woman and she held my gaze.

"No, I'm sorry, not lately," I told her. Alice seemed so unhappy. I put a hand on her arm in an attempt to comfort her. "Mrs. Mayhew, what's wrong?"

She took a deep breath. "Oh, don't trouble yourself about me. It's only that Thomas and I had a falling-out and I've been trying for a while now to find a way to repair our relationship, but he doesn't seem as though he's willing to forgive me."

"I don't know what you mean." She seemed desperate to talk to someone, and even though I shouldn't have cared, I did. I cared about everything to do with Thomas, unfortunately.

"I did a terrible thing, Your Highness," she told me.

"Whatever you've done, I'm sure it's not something so awful as to be unforgivable." I couldn't imagine this woman intentionally hurting anyone, much less her son.

"It happened right after we got word that Thomas had been accepted into the KES Academy," she explained. "And we found out that Lucas had been rejected for the third time. Lucas was beside himself, and all my husband could talk about was how pleased he was with Thomas, how proud he was to call him his son. I just . . . I snapped. I screamed at Clarence, saying how dare he prefer some boy he'd practically picked up off the street over his real son."

I winced. She nodded, dabbing at her eyes. "I didn't mean it. Of *course* I didn't. I love Thomas, and I would never begrudge him his accomplishments. He earned his place at the Academy, I have no doubt about that. But I was just so distraught for Lucas. He wanted to prove his worth to Clarence so badly. . . ."

"I'm assuming that Thomas overheard you," I said. She nodded.

"They both did. The boys. They heard every word." She took a deep breath. "Thomas walked out of the house that night and he didn't come home. I didn't know where he went or how he got there. I didn't sleep for days, wondering what had happened to him. Later I found out that Clarence had put him up in the Citadel and I asked him to bring Thomas home, but he refused. He told me that Thomas was his own man, and that he would come back when and if he chose. Ever since then, it's been Lucas and I against Clarence and Thomas, but I don't want it to be that way. I want both of my sons."

I could tell from one look that Alice Mayhew was in agony, thinking that she'd driven Thomas away forever because of one mistake. I wanted to put my arms around her, to comfort her, but I wasn't sure if I should. There was the protocol, after all.

"Your Highness?" I turned to see Thomas at the end of the corridor, fixing his mother and me with a stare.

"Yes?"

"Prince Callum is looking for you," he told me.

"Fine. Let me walk Mrs. Mayhew to her moto, and I'll be right in."

"I'll do it. The prince is being . . . rather insistent." There was a sharp edge to his words that told me he was exaggerating about Callum, but I stepped aside anyway. Maybe he wanted to patch things up with his mother; if that was the case, I didn't want to stand in the way of it.

"Good night, Your Highness," Alice Mayhew said with a smile. I could see hope shining in her eyes. "I'll see you at your wedding?"

"Of course," I told her. "Get home safe, Mrs. Mayhew."

She looked me right in the eye and smiled. "You too, my dear."

THOMAS AT ASTHALL

"I'm so glad you've decided to talk to me," his mother said as they walked down the long driveway to where she'd parked her moto. "I want you to know how terribly sorry I am for what you overheard. I didn't mean it, T, I—"

"Please, don't," Thomas said. "That's not why I'm here. I'm going to ask you a question, and I need you to tell me the truth. Okay?"

"Why would I lie to you, Thomas? I'm your mother." Her voice was wobbly, which dislodged something inside him.

"I know," he said gently. "I know you love me. And I'm sorry that I've been so distant since . . . since that night. But I need you to answer my question."

"Of course. Anything. Ask me anything and I'll tell you the truth."

He drew in a deep breath. "When was the last time you saw Lucas?"

Alice thought it over. "Well," she said. "It must've been about a month ago? He came to stay with me for a few days to celebrate my birthday."

Thomas felt another pang. Maybe Lucas deserved to be

the favored son. After all, Thomas had forgotten all about her birthday. "Are you sure that was the last time? He wasn't there this weekend?"

"No, I would remember," she said sharply. "I'm not addled, you know."

He forced himself to laugh. "I know you're not."

"So that was it? That was all you wanted to know?" He could see a buried fierceness rise up within her. Alice Mayhew was not always the sweet, gentle being who had dined with Sasha tonight. She could also be tough and demanding, and all that suppressed intensity was rising to the surface. She wasn't just sad, she was angry. But he didn't have time to deal with it right now.

"Yeah, Mom, that was it. I've got to go back inside now. Are you okay getting home?"

"Yes, I'll be fine." She reached over to press her thumb against the moto door lock, then turned to face him again. "She's a lovely girl, T. A lovely, lovely girl."

He narrowed his eyes. "You mean the princess?"

"Yes, of course," she said, with an inscrutable glimmer in her eye. "Who else?"

When his mother was gone, Thomas stood at the end of the driveway and reached into his pocket, pulling out a blue origami star. Gloria had sent him back for a few things she'd forgotten to pack for Sasha, and he'd seen it lying on her bedside table. Normally he wouldn't have touched anything he wasn't explicitly told to bring, but it had seemed out of place and significant, calling out to him to pick it up and open it. So he had.

Now he opened it once more.

T—I'm sorry, but I can't. I wish I was better, but I'm not. —J

THIRTY

As it turned out, there wasn't much to do at Asthall Cottage after dinner. I ended up playing hearts with Callum, who was extremely good at it and beat me three hands out of four. Finally, I pled exhaustion and turned in for the night. Callum walked me to my room, lingering at the door.

"I like it out here," he told me. "It's so peaceful."

"Me too," I told him. It was such a relief to be away from most—if not all—of the prying eyes at the Citadel.

"When we're married, we should come out here all the time," Callum said. "Every weekend, if we can."

"That's a good idea," I murmured. Briefly, I tried to pretend that I was actually getting married to Callum, that any of his plans for the future might come to pass. It wasn't an altogether unpleasant prospect—if I was going to be forced into marriage, there was no one I could think of better suited to being a husband than the sweet, considerate young prince—but it didn't feel *right,* either, and not only because I was way too young to get married.

He kissed me on the cheek. "See you in the morning."

I smiled. "See you."

He got halfway down the hallway before turning back. "You know what's weird?"

"What?" I asked, hand on the doorknob. It was ridiculous, but I was overjoyed by the fact that all the doors in Asthall had *knobs*. There were no panels, no biometric scanners, no codes to memorize. I could have stayed there forever.

"In a few days, we'll be sleeping in the same bed," he said, raising a playful eyebrow.

I swallowed hard. "Yeah. Weird. Well, good night!" I slipped through the bedroom door and shut it firmly. Kissing Callum was one thing, but sleeping in the same bed with him . . . we had to find Juliana by then. We just *had* to. I did the calculations in my head. Two days. We were running out of time.

"Hey."

I jumped. "Thomas, you scared me. What are you doing in here?"

He rose from where he was sitting, in an armchair close to the window. "I was hoping to talk to you," he said, rubbing the back of his neck.

"About what?" I sat down on the bed and watched as he paced the room. "How jealous I am? And manipulative? Are you here to call me a liar again?"

"Stop, please." He hung his head in shame. "I spoke to my mother, and I asked her when the last time was that she'd seen Lucas. She told me that he came out to her house for her birthday, April eleventh. Except Lucas told me that he'd just gotten back from seeing her *this weekend*. Which means that first of all, he lied, and second of all, there's no explanation for his absence during the time when you saw him in your visions."

I sat perfectly still, not even breathing. I knew where he

was going with this, but I wasn't going to make it easy on him, not after the things he'd said to me.

"And I found this." He held up the origami star. "On the nightstand in Juliana's room. Do you know what it says?"

I nodded. "I saw her write it. Through the tether."

"You were right. About all of it." He shook his head, despair etched all over his face. "She left. She turned her back on us and she left. I thought bringing you here would buy us time to rescue her, but she doesn't want to be rescued. I ripped you out of your world for nothing. I'm so sorry, Sasha. I'm so, so sorry."

"Please don't," I said, tears springing to my eyes. I was so tired, and he looked so sad, that my anger evaporated. "It's all right. If I were you, I wouldn't have believed me, either. She's your friend, he's your brother. I'm just some girl you barely know."

"No, that's not true," he insisted. "You're not just some girl. And you would've believed me. But I couldn't . . . I couldn't bring myself to see what was right in front of my eyes. I didn't want to see that I was wrong, that I was capable of being wrong."

"We're all capable of being wrong," I whispered.

"I didn't want to be. I'm supposed to be better than that; otherwise what was all my training for?" He sighed. "I let you down. You deserve better."

"So do you," I said fiercely. I stood and grabbed him by the lapels of his jacket, pulling him close to me. I could smell the comforting piney scent of his cologne and feel a faint heat rising off his skin; his cheeks and ears were flushed, and he couldn't quite bring himself to look directly at me, as if I was an eclipse, a dangerous celestial event. "You trusted them and they betrayed you. You would never have done that to them."

He stared at me, struck dumb, then took me by my wrists and pressed my hands against his chest. "I'm taking you home," he said, his voice hoarse. He looked as though he'd seen a ghost—he was pale, wide-eyed, trembling—but there was something building inside him, something strong and resolute. I imagined I could see it swirling in the darkness of his pupils.

"What? When?"

"As soon as possible. Tomorrow, if I can manage it."

"Why now? We haven't found Juliana yet." I had a heavy feeling in the pit of my stomach. Shouldn't I have been excited to go home? Wasn't that what I wanted? Yet while a part of me was excited, another part was full of dread.

"I don't care," Thomas said. "You're not safe here. That Libertas bombing . . . if you had gotten really hurt, or God forbid *died,* I would never have forgiven myself. I can't believe there was ever a time when I thought I could justify bringing you here and putting you in so much danger. I can't turn back time and make a different choice, but I can do this."

"How are you going to do it without the General finding out?"

"I don't know. I'll start by asking Dr. Moss if he has an extra anchor, or if somehow he can get me the remote that controls yours," Thomas said. He was growing frantic now, which worried me. I'd never seen him this unspooled before. I was afraid he was going to do something stupid and rash. "I turned it in to the General when we arrived at the Citadel, but maybe Mossie can get it back under the pretense of having to fix it or something . . . I haven't thought it all through yet. But I'm going to make it happen if it kills me."

"No," I protested. "No, I'm not going to let you do that. You'll get in so much trouble."

"Don't worry about me," Thomas insisted.

"How can you say that? How can you—?" The words stuck in my throat. "How can you think I'd go home and leave you to deal with the fallout?"

"You have to," he said. "There's no way for both of us to get out of this, and if one of us is going to get their life back, it has to be you. Don't you see that?"

"I won't go!" I cried, digging my nails into the fabric of his jacket. "Not until Juliana's back. There are other lives at stake here, not just ours. You told me that."

"There's more than one way to stop a war," he told me. "I'll figure something out. You don't have to be part of this. It's not your world. It's not your problem."

"I can't go home yet. I refuse to let you send me back."

"For God's sake, Sasha, *why?"*

"Because," I said in a near-whisper. "I'm not ready to leave you."

The frankness of my admission seemed to catch him off guard, but I was tired of hiding how I felt, from him and from myself. He had a right to know, and I had a right to say it.

The shock of what I'd revealed wore off in seconds, and then I was in his arms. His lips fit perfectly against mine. The kiss was tentative at first, and we were both shaking. He started to pull away, but I grabbed him by the back of his neck and pushed myself up hard against him, tangling my fingers in his hair and letting my tongue graze his top lip softly, sending a shudder down his spine. Thomas held my head in his hands, cradling it like a precious object. His lips roamed the soft planes of my face, pressing against my cheek, my temple, the corner of my eye. He traced the ridge of my jaw with kisses. I arched my back, offering him the smooth skin of my neck to kiss, gasping, breathless, before pulling him back up to meet my mouth once again. The weight of him kept me from floating away, atom by atom, into the universe.

We came apart then, our foreheads and noses touching, as if we couldn't bear to fully separate. We grinned at each other, both giddy with a sense of release.

"What are we doing?" he panted, happily bewildered.

"I don't know," I said. "But I don't want to stop."

"Sasha," he breathed. I loved the way he said my name, like an incantation, like a magic word. "What are we going to do? We're from—"

"I know," I said, nodding frantically. "I know that this can't go on forever, but I also know that I'm not ready to lose you, and tonight I don't care what's right or what's not. Okay?"

"Okay," he said. Then he kissed me again, harder this time, a kiss full of long-suppressed wanting that echoed my own.

In the middle of the night, I awoke to pounding at my door. I rose from a dreamless sleep, untroubled by visions of Juliana, with the imprint of Thomas's lips on my own. I smiled as I went to the door, knowing that there was only one person who could be on the other side.

But when I opened it, I found myself face to face not with Thomas, but with Callum. He was so excited he couldn't even stand still.

"Come on," he said, grabbing my hand and dragging me down the hallway. "I have something I want to show you."

"Callum, it's almost dawn!" I hissed. "Where are we going?"

"Remember when we were talking about those things your father's been saying?" Callum said, charging ahead.

"Yeah?" I rubbed my eyes, shaking off his grip. I was

trying not to betray my annoyance, but it was proving difficult. "What about them?"

"I've been thinking about it ever since, how he kept saying 'touch and go.' It sounded so familiar, but I couldn't place it. Then I woke up just now and I remembered." He stopped suddenly. We were standing in front of a metal door that was out of place in Asthall's otherwise old-fashioned interiors. It was the entrance to the KES situation room, and unlike every other door at the cottage it had an LCD lock. Callum pointed to it. "Look what's written there."

I crouched down and peered at the console. Sure enough, there were three words etched into the metal of the panel's frame. "No way," I breathed.

The label read TOUCH AND GO.

"It's the brand name!" Callum cried, grinning proudly. "These are the same consoles you have at the Castle."

I squeezed his arm. "Good job, Cal! I can't believe you even saw that."

He shrugged happily. "I guess all that paying attention to doors and windows has finally paid off."

"It sure has. How much do you want to bet that one, one, two, three, five, eight is an access code?"

"Could be," he said. "At the risk of sounding ridiculous, this is sort of exciting."

"Although . . ." I chewed at my lip. "Like you said, all the consoles are the same. So the access code could be for any room in the Castle. There are hundreds of them! What are we going to do, go around to every single one and try it to see if it works?"

"I guess we could," he said, less enthusiastic now.

"That might take days. And you never know—it could be the code to a room in the Tower, or anywhere in the Citadel, for that matter. Someone's going to wonder what the hell we're doing long before we get to all of them."

"Okay," he conceded. "But don't you think it's more likely that the room the code opens has something to do with the king himself? If he's trying to give you clues, he has to believe that you know which room, or could at least figure it out."

He was right. The only problem was that I wasn't Juliana. The king's real daughter might have known instinctively what he was trying to tell her, but that would've been just between the two of them. Even Thomas couldn't help with this.

"I have no idea," I said, the thought of Thomas, of the last time I'd seen him, making me woozy. "It's not the code to his room, and anyway, he didn't move there until after his . . . accident."

"The royal bedroom?"

"You mean the one he shared with the queen?" I considered it. "I don't know. Maybe."

"Either way, we need to go back to the Castle," Callum said. "In the morning, first thing."

"That would raise an awful lot of eyebrows." Not to mention that it would attract the General's attention, which I absolutely did not want. But it didn't seem like I had a choice. If the king *was* trying to tell Juliana something, who knew what it could be? What if it was urgent? I'd wasted so much time thinking his exclamations were nonsense. I didn't have a second to lose.

"Who cares? You're the princess, you can do whatever you want."

I gave it some careful thought. "Okay. I'll tell Gloria we want to go back."

Callum took my face in the palm of his hands and kissed me deeply. It took all I had in me not to squirm away, my mind full of strong memories of another kiss. "This is so exciting!" he cried when we separated.

"Shhh, keep your voice down." But I couldn't help laughing. I'd never seen him this animated, not even earlier by the ocean.

But all I could think of was how much I wanted to tell Thomas.

2

DAYS

★ ★ ★ ★ ★

THOMAS IN THE TOWER / 4

"Do you want to tell me what this is about?" Thomas asked. Captain Fawley shrugged.

"I'm just as in the dark as you are, Mayhew," Fawley told him. "All I know is that the General isn't happy. He woke me up in the middle of the night and demanded I get you back to the Citadel as fast as possible."

"And now he's just got me sitting here, sweating it out. Wonderful." Thomas sat back in his chair. To Fawley he might've looked calm, but his guts were roiling. What possible reason would the General have had to send for him last night? He and Sasha had spent several more hours together, kissing and talking. He'd felt more like himself than ever. Then he'd noticed her trying to suppress a yawn and he realized how late it was. She hadn't wanted him to leave, but she needed to sleep. They both did. So he'd seen her to her bed, placing one final kiss on her forehead, and went to his own room, where he found a summons waiting on his mobie. RETURN TO THE CITADEL NOW—DIRECT ORDER FROM HOD. Head of Defense. The General.

It couldn't be good, whatever it was. "I don't know why

he's making you babysit me." They were on opposite sides of a table in one of the interrogation rooms in Subbasement B. Fawley had been tasked with watching Thomas until the General was ready to see him.

"Me neither," Fawley said. "And I don't much appreciate it, to be honest."

"I don't blame you."

The door opened and the General strode through. "Get up, Fawley, and get out of here."

Fawley did as he was told without hesitation. He gave Thomas a look that said *Good luck,* but Thomas knew he'd probably need a great deal more than that.

The General took Fawley's seat and stared at Thomas. "Do you know why you're here?"

Thomas shook his head. "They just told me you wanted to see me."

The General's expression was blank. "You're being removed from active duty."

"What?" Thomas cried. "Why?"

The General continued without hesitation; there was no emotion in his voice. "This punishment is being meted out for gross misconduct on shadow Operation Starling and personal behavior unbecoming of an officer of this realm. Your suspension is effective immediately and of indeterminate duration."

"Gross misconduct? Behavior unbecoming of an officer? What are you talking about? I have a right to know what I'm being accused of, and by who!"

"BY ME!" the General shouted, slamming his fist upon the table. He stood, his chair clattering to the floor, and leaned over the table to get right up in Thomas's face. "I told you when I trusted you with this mission that under no circumstances were you to fraternize with your assignment, and you disobeyed my explicit orders, not to mention your oath to the KES and this country."

Thomas stared at his father with defiance, unwilling to admit his transgressions but incapable of denying them. Everything the General had said was true. And yet he no longer felt guilty. He no longer cared if his father thought well of him, and his only regret at incurring the General's wrath was that it would have consequences for Sasha, consequences he might not be in a position to protect her from.

"You should be grateful I'm not discharging you with disgrace altogether," the General growled. "But if you think you're ever going to see that girl again, you're mistaken."

"What are you going to do to her?" Thomas demanded. He couldn't get Mossie's words out of his head: *He has something special planned for you*. The General *ought* to have discharged him with disgrace—his actions warranted it. And yet he was choosing not to. Did that mean Dr. Moss was right? That the General saw war with other universes on the horizon, a war he expected Thomas to help him fight? Then it hit him, full force in the stomach like a punch: even on Earth, Sasha might never be safe.

"Whatever I want. Leave your gun and your creds with Fawley. You will be detained in your quarters until I decide how you can be most useful to me." He left without another word.

"You're not really going to do this, Fawley," Thomas protested. The Captain programmed a system override into the LCD lock on Thomas's apartment door as Thomas stood watching, quivering with anger. The console turned an alarming bloodred. When the door shut, he'd be trapped.

"I have to," Fawley said, with no trace of regret. Thomas

was bothered by this—he and Fawley had always gotten along, and respected each other, despite the difference in their ages—but not surprised. Two weeks ago, he would have done the same thing. "Those are my orders."

When Fawley was gone, Thomas lost it. So what if he had "fraternized" with Sasha? He was a loyal KES agent through and through, unlike his traitor of a brother, whose crimes were unknown and unpunished. He'd done everything that was asked of him, obediently following orders just like Fawley, even when he disagreed. He'd given his life to the KES, put himself in danger in service of his country, and this was all he was to expect? To be locked in his room like a child without proof or due process? Thomas kicked the metal door with his boots over and over again in frustration, but all that did was leave a dent the size of a golf ball. It didn't make him feel any better. He needed to break something, but everything in the room was metal.

Thomas grabbed a framed picture off his desk, one of him and his adopted family, and threw it to the floor, where it shattered. It was something, but it wasn't enough. He ground it beneath his boot heel, the glass crackling like a bonfire, until the photograph was beyond repair. He didn't care. He wasn't that boy any longer.

THIRTY-ONE

When Gloria came into my room at nine o'clock, I was already dressed, packed, and ready to leave.

"I want to go back to the Castle," I announced.

"You're not scheduled to return until tomorrow morning," Gloria informed me, glancing at her tablet to confirm. "I was thinking you might want to take Callum to the lighthouse today."

"No. I'm going back to the Castle, and I'm taking Callum with me."

Gloria glared at me. "*No,* you're staying here."

"Sorry, Gloria, but I'm going to have to pull rank on you," I said. I was trying to channel Thomas—or Juliana. I didn't even sound like myself, but it couldn't be helped. "There's something I need to take care of back at the Castle."

"*Pull rank?* Sasha, you don't have a rank."

"Yes, I do. I'm the princess. *I* decide where I go and when, not you." I'd been taking orders from everyone else for far too long.

Gloria folded her arms across her chest. "And exactly what is it that you need to take care of, *Your Highness*?"

"I can't tell you," I said. "Only that it's important. Where's Thomas? I need to talk to him before we leave."

"Thomas isn't here. He left at dawn to return to the Citadel."

"What? Why?"

"I don't know. The General called him back and back he went. He's not the 'thing' you need to 'take care of,' is he?" Gloria asked pointedly, complete with sarcastic air quotes.

"No," I said. "I didn't even know he was gone until two seconds ago."

Gloria left to prepare the others for departure, giving me plenty of time to worry. The exhilaration of last night's discovery was all but obliterated by the news that Thomas had been recalled to the Citadel. Something was wrong. Under normal circumstances, Thomas would have come to explain before he left. The only reason he wouldn't do that was if he wasn't allowed to, if . . . *No,* I thought. *It's not possible.*

What if the General knew?

Callum pressed his ear against the door. "I don't hear anyone."

"Cal, that thing is solid steel." We were standing in the hall outside the queen's bedroom, debating whether or not we should try the Fibonacci numbers on the LCD panel. "You're not going to hear anyone if they're in there or not."

"Good point," he said. "But what are the odds? Just try it. See what happens."

"See what happens? I bet you spent a lot of time setting off fireworks in toilets as a kid."

He smiled at me wickedly. "There's not a whole lot to do in a palace, you know."

"Oh, I know." I took a deep breath. "Okay, here we go. Giving this a shot." I placed my hand against the console. It took a second to read my handprint, then went from the blue of being locked to the red of being really, *really* locked.

"Uh, that can't be good," Callum said.

"It's not. Let's get out of here!"

We sped all the way back to Juliana's bedroom. As soon as the door slid shut behind him, Callum turned to me, breathless. "Do you think we set off an alarm or something?"

"Probably." I'd only ever seen an LCD panel go from blue to red once—the lock on the metal box in the trunk of Thomas's moto back in the Tattered City. That one had certainly had an alarm on it.

Callum sighed and flopped down on the foot of the bed. "It's too bad we never got the chance to try the code in the lock."

"It wouldn't have worked. There's no way the king—my father, I mean—was leading me to that room," I said. "It would've been a room he knew I had access to, otherwise what's the point?"

"So what other room do you think it could be? Does he have an office or something?"

"Yes!" I cried. "He does. He has a study. I've been there before." Callum gave me an inquisitive look. "Hundreds of times," I added. Actually, I'd only been there once or twice, for wedding preparations with the queen, but I knew it existed. "There's only one problem."

"What's that?"

"My stepmother took it over when she became regent," I explained. "She's in there all the time. Except . . ." I glanced at the clock on the mantel. It was 3:35 p.m. "She visits with my father twice a day: from nine to ten in the mornings, and three to four in the afternoon. If we go to the office right now, it should be empty."

"Well then," Callum said, jumping to his feet. "What are we waiting for?"

I stared at the console with trepidation. It was blue, of course, and pulsing, waiting for me to put my hand on it. But what if my handprint wouldn't give me access to the study door, either, and the KES was alerted? I'd never gotten a chance to explain to Thomas what I was planning to do, and though we were both back from Asthall I hadn't seen him all day. Gloria promised to make some inquiries, but she'd come up empty. Nobody seemed to know where Thomas was. I couldn't help but agonize over it, but I found some comfort in the knowledge that Thomas could take care of himself. I would see him soon. It was nothing to get hysterical over.

"You're overthinking it."

"What?" *Oh,* I thought with relief. *He means the door.* Before I could react, Callum took my hand and pressed it flat against the console.

"Callum!" I cried, jerking my hand away, but it was too late. The numbered keypad replaced the silhouette of a hand.

"You can thank me later," he said with a smile.

"I'll thank you never," I said, delivering a soft glancing blow to his arm. I punched in the code. *One. One. Two. Three. Five. Eight.* It wasn't until the console turned green that I realized I was holding my breath.

"You should see your face, Juli," Callum said with a laugh. "You look like you're going to throw up. It's just a door!"

"Yeah, well . . . shut up." But I laughed, too. I was being ridiculous. There wasn't anything to fear. It was just a door, and it was opening.

The king's study was empty.

"What's next?" Callum asked.

"'Mirror, mirror,'" I told him. But Callum was already staring straight ahead at the wall, where a long antique mirror with an ornate gold frame was hanging.

"It can't be that simple, can it?"

"I don't think he's trying to trick me," I said, making my way toward the mirror. I felt along its left edge with my fingers but couldn't find anything. I gripped it with both hands and tried to lift it off the wall—it wouldn't move. "It's bolted down."

Callum joined me. "That sounds promising. Here, let me try." But Callum couldn't get the mirror to budge, either. He stood back and gazed at our reflections. "We look good together." He put his arm around my shoulder and grinned.

"Focus." I felt around the right side of the mirror now, searching for the hidden latch I was sure was there. If it couldn't be removed, the mirror had to be hiding something.

Eventually I found it, a button on the back of the frame. I pressed it and heard a small click. The mirror swung forward on hinges, revealing a safe with another LCD console mounted on its door. It was exactly the same as the regular consoles, down to the TOUCH AND GO branding, but this time the keypad was already up, no handprint necessary. I input the Fibonacci code again. The console turned green and the safe was open.

"What do you think we're going to find in there?" Callum asked.

"No idea," I said. I tried to affect nonchalance, but my hands were shaking. Was it possible I was right? It seemed unlikely, but at the same time the only possible truth. "But it's time to find out."

We peered into the safe. It was almost as large as the mirror, and went very deep into the wall. It contained a variety of things: several neat bundles of money, jewel cases stacked one on top of the other, and a tall pile of manila folders. I wondered if Juliana, staring at the contents of this safe, would've known what her father wanted her to find. "Angel eyes" was the last phrase. It could mean anything. It could be a pair of earrings he'd tucked away to save for a wedding gift. But I didn't care much for jewels, and for some reason I believed that the king wanted me to have *information*. I grabbed a bunch of folders and dropped them into Callum's waiting arms.

"Angel eyes," I said. He nodded and sat down on the floor, riffling through the folders. I took the rest and we began our search.

"These are all top-secret military documents," Callum pointed out after a while.

I'd noticed the same thing. Each folder was marked CLASSIFIED in bright bold red lettering, and underneath that there was always a label with the name of the project in blue. We went through them one by one, but none sounded right. CLASSIFIED: OPERATION LARCHMONT. CLASSIFIED: OPERATION PAINTED ARROW. CLASSIFIED: OPERATION LOOKING GLASS.

I paused at the last one. *Operation Looking Glass.* I flipped it open and started skimming. Almost immediately I found mention of Earth. I wanted to read further, but I could feel Callum's eyes on me.

"Did you find anything?"

I shook my head and reluctantly closed the Looking Glass file. "Not yet." I kept thumbing through them but found nothing, and the clock on the wall told me we only had ten minutes left before the queen returned.

Suddenly, Callum leapt up, waving one of the folders.

"I've got it," he said, thrusting the file into my hands. The cover read CLASSIFIED: OPERATION ANGEL EYES. I hesitated, not sure if I really wanted to know what was in it.

"Aren't you going to open it?" Callum pressed. I nodded.

But when I saw what it contained, I was more confused than ever.

All the other files were filled with documents, long, detailed memoranda filled edge to edge with tiny black text. But this folder was empty except for a color printout of a map of the North American continent. The map was dark blue, the landmass clearly outlined in white. There was a thick line that divided the country, just like the map I'd seen in the Tower, marking the border between the UCC and Farnham. The rest of the map was covered in abstract blobs, light blue in color. Some were huge, like the one that hovered right over Chicago; others were smaller, like the ones that dotted northern New York Dominion like freckles. It looked like the sort of thing you might see on the evening news during the weather report.

"A weather map? That's it? *That's* what the king wanted me to find?" I shook my head in disbelief. All that cloak-and-dagger nonsense for nothing. I felt like an idiot.

"Let me see." Callum reached for the file and considered its contents carefully. "Maybe Angel Eyes is some kind of meteorological satellite."

"But who cares about the weather? This can't be it!"

"I don't see any other files marked 'Angel Eyes'—do you?"

He was right. I wanted to go through the Looking Glass file, but it was too dangerous with Callum right there. Whatever happened, he couldn't know about the tandem, about Earth. About me.

I shoved the files back into the safe, slamming the door in frustration.

"I'm sorry you didn't find what you were looking for, Juli," Callum said, laying a gentle hand on my shoulder.

I sighed. "It's okay. Maybe I was just making all this up. Maybe there was never anything for us to find."

"But you were right about the things the king was saying," Callum insisted. "They led us here."

"Yeah, straight to nothing."

"We should probably get out of here. The queen could come back at any second."

"Okay," I said. "Let's go." I hesitated. "Wait, hold on." I opened the safe again and removed the map from the file.

"What are you doing?" Callum looked away in embarrassment as I folded the map in quarters and crammed it into my bra.

"I want to show it to someone," I told him, avoiding his curious gaze. He must've been wondering who that "someone" was, although he probably could've guessed. "Just to be sure."

Despite the disappointment of the afternoon's fruitless search, I was glad to be back at the Castle. I'd loved Asthall, but now that Thomas was at the Castle, I wanted to be as well. I wished I knew how to get in touch with him. I wanted to show him the map and see what he thought of it. At brief moments throughout the day, when I knew myself to be alone, I took it out and looked at it. Something about it struck me as familiar, but for a while I didn't know why, until I realized—this was what Juliana had given the Shepherd. But I was struggling to figure out why it was so important, why it was worth anything to Libertas. I needed to talk to Thomas more than ever; if anyone could shed some light on this mystery, it would be him.

After dinner, Gloria informed me that a new agent, Kline, had been assigned to manage my security detail. My heart fell straight to my toes when I heard this. Something was clearly wrong, but nobody would answer my questions. I kept trying to convince myself that Thomas could handle whatever situation he found himself in, but that didn't make me feel any better.

I turned in early that night, despite Callum's protestations; I felt bad deserting him, but I had a headache and wanted to be alone.

The room was dark, and at first I thought it was empty. Then I caught a sudden movement out of the corner of my eye. There was someone standing out on the terrace. I started to back away, but then whoever it was came through the door and switched on the lights.

"Lucas?" All the muscles in my body tensed. "What are you doing here? Where's Thomas?" Of all people, I figured he'd be the one to know.

"Locked up in his quarters," Lucas said, ambling in my direction with his hands shoved in his pockets. "He's been suspended, you know. Because of you."

"What are you talking about?"

"I'm here to warn you," he said, but there was an edge of malice in his voice, and I knew he hadn't come to me—to Juliana—as a friend. With every step he took toward me, I took one back.

"Warn me about what?"

"The General has it in for you," Lucas said. "He knows all about your little tryst with my brother and now he's angry. That's not what you want."

"Is this how you talk to your princess?" I demanded, my voice trembling.

Lucas laughed. "You? A princess? You've got to be kidding me. Anyone with common sense can tell you're a fake from a mile away. What's your name again? Sandra? Sarah?"

"Don't you dare come any closer," I snarled.

Lucas snapped his fingers. "Sasha! That's it, right?" I seized up, temporarily breathless with surprise and fear. How did he know my *name*? "You look surprised. I don't blame you. Thomas probably told you I'm just some lowly support agent. And he's not wrong. He's not right, either, but then again there's a lot of stuff Thomas doesn't know."

"Like what?"

"Like who was behind Juliana's kidnapping," Lucas said. My eyes widened, and he grinned. "I thought that might get your attention. Let me tell you a little story about Thomas. You probably know that we're not blood related, huh? That he's adopted?"

"Of course I do."

"You know, at first I resented Thomas," Lucas said. "The General already had a son, and yet he had to go and pick up a stray. Like I wasn't good enough or something. But then I *saw* Thomas. I couldn't imagine why the General would choose him. He was small and skinny and always trembling like a little puppy. I figured, hey, this kid's no threat, so I took him under my wing. I loved him like a brother, but then he had to grow up and become a superman. Strong, fast, agile, smart as hell. Suddenly, he was the General's ideal son. Like my father knew something we didn't all along." This last observation was said in a thoughtful way, as if Lucas was truly contemplating the possibility that the General was psychic, of all ludicrous things. This was a trait, perhaps the only one, that Lucas shared with his brother—the secret belief that the General was more than a man.

"So? What does this have to do with me?"

"I'm not finished yet," Lucas said. "Did anyone ever tell you it's rude to interrupt?"

"Sorry," I replied sarcastically. "Continue."

"Thomas has just one flaw."

"Integrity?"

"Exactly," Lucas said. "He's a noble creature. He believes in things. He cares about people. He doesn't want to hurt anyone. I mean, he's a soldier, so he will hurt people, but only in the name of the greater good, and his idea of the greater good is a *little* bit different from the General's. I, however, don't have that problem. So when the General needed to get rid of Juliana, he turned to me."

"*You* kidnapped Juliana?" I was trying hard to sound incredulous, and he seemed to be buying it. But on this next point I was sincere. "And the General was in on it?"

"'Kidnapped' is a harsh word. She went of her own free will. Juliana was infuriated by the marriage with the Farnham prince. I told her that I worked for Libertas, and if she gave them what they wanted, they would help her disappear."

"So you're a traitor," I said evenly.

"I guess that depends on how you define *traitor,*" Lucas said. "I originally infiltrated Libertas on my father's orders. When he told me he wanted Juliana gone from the Castle, I saw my opportunity to win big with the organization's leadership and I took it."

"Why would the General want Juliana gone?"

"Isn't that obvious? Or do you not know enough about our politics to understand? Juliana's the heir to the throne, and in two weeks she'll be the rightful regent. But Juliana hates the General, and she was about to get married, which would only strengthen her position. That meant all the hard work my father put in over the past thirty years, grooming the king to trust and rely on him, was about to go right out the window. He couldn't have that. He needed someone he could control. Someone like you."

"He doesn't control me," I said through my teeth.

"I beg to differ. Anyway, long story short, Juliana isn't coming back, and as long as it's in the General's best interest, you're not going home. I don't know what he has planned for you, but I'm thinking you're not going to like it."

"Why are you telling me all this?" I demanded. "What's in it for you?"

"I'm here to cut you the same deal I cut Juliana," Lucas told me. "Come with me to Libertas, tell them everything you know about the many-worlds project, and they'll help you get home."

"If they don't know anything about the tandem, how are they going to do that?"

"Think of it as an incentive to tell them as much as possible."

"Did the General tell you to get rid of me, too? Why doesn't he just send me back himself?"

"The General is not explicitly aware of the offer I'm making you," Lucas said, dancing around the fact that he was double-crossing his father, which was clearly what he was doing. "He believes I work only for him, but I prefer to think of myself as a free agent. Serves him right, for putting Thomas over me all these years. So what do you say? Are you in or not?"

"I'm not interested," I said. "I'll—"

"What?" He scrunched up his face in a patronizing expression. "You'll tell my dad on me? It wouldn't do you any good. It might get *me* executed in a dark alley, but you'll still be stuck here. Besides, I highly doubt the General gives a damn about anything you have to say. That's just a feeling I have." He put his hand over his heart, as if to mime *feeling*. "You don't have to give me an answer right now, but you might want to decide before Saturday." He strode past me toward the door.

"Think about it," he said with a little wave as the door slid open. "I'll be waiting. Tell you one thing, though. You'll never see my brother again. So I wouldn't let that affect my decision if I were you."

With that, he was gone.

I

DAY

SHE SAT UP BLINKING IN THE *sudden glare of the lights. She'd been asleep for hours, that same tormented sleep she'd been experiencing since her father was shot. She shielded her eyes and searched for a face on the dark figure that had entered her room.*

"Who's there?" she called out.

"It's me." The Shepherd. She should've known. He was the only one who visited her now, except the Farnham country matron. She put her hands up to her hair, which was blond now. She'd looked in the mirror once the matron was finished with her and been astounded by how stark the transformation was. The color brought out completely different features in her face, and she understood why they'd done it. With her hair this color, she was nearly unrecognizable. "Quick, get up and get dressed. We leave at dawn."

"Leave for where?" she asked.

"Columbia City."

"What? No!" Why would they bring her back there? They were supposed to give her a new life. She supposed that would mean she'd have to hide out in Farnham forever, a prospect she didn't relish, but it was far preferable to being dragged back home. "You promised—"

"Don't worry, we're not handing you over to the KES, if that's what you're imagining." The Shepherd took his customary seat on the desk chair, turning it around so that his arms rested on the chair

back. "We have a different plan. But we've had to move up the date. It seems things have not gone exactly as we hoped back at the Citadel."

"Mind telling me what that plan is, exactly?" she asked.

"Of course," he said, smiling his inscrutable smile. "Juliana, what do you know about parallel universes?"

THIRTY-TWO

"Wow, Juli." Callum whistled. "You look amazing."

"You don't look so bad yourself," I told him, reaching up to straighten his bow tie. I was trying my best to flatter and flirt, but my heart simply wasn't in it. I was sick of playing Juliana, especially the Juliana Callum wanted me to be. I had far too much weighing on my mind, and on my heart. My thoughts kept careening back and forth between what Lucas had told me and Thomas's predicament. I had, for a brief moment, actually *considered* Lucas's offer, which revolted me, but I would've been crazy not to. It would be crazier still, however, to trust Lucas and abandon Thomas to his fate, whatever that was, not to mention leave Callum and the queen and all the people who were counting on me. Well, not *me*—Juliana. But at this point, what was the difference?

Gloria had chosen my dress, a long draped gown with a dramatic leather sunburst collar covered in silver beading, and a wide leather belt at the waist. Callum was coordinating by wearing a silver bow tie with his tuxedo. His hand rested at the base of my spine as we stood together in the full-length mirror. I took a deep breath and let it out. Gloria insisted I wear a formal tiara for the gala, so I'd picked out the prettiest one I could find, a garland of wild Sweet Briar diamond roses mounted in silver. It was heavier than it looked and was already starting to give me a headache.

"Can we go back to the beach?" Callum whispered in my ear. I smiled at his reflection in the mirror, but it didn't reach my eyes.

"We're late," I said, moving toward the door. He stayed put. "Cal, are you coming?"

He tugged at his collar. "I don't think I'm ever going to get used to this kind of stuff."

"You will," I assured him. The question was: would I?

"You're late, Juliana," the queen scolded. She was resplendent in a long purple tulle gown, her hair piled high upon her head.

I could hear the low murmur of a thousand voices coming from inside the ballroom. The guests had arrived and were waiting. On the queen's signal, two porters swung the doors open. A great, booming voice announced the queen by her title—"Her Majesty Evelyn, Queen Regent of the United Commonwealth of Columbia"—and she stepped over the threshold.

Then it was my and Callum's turn. The voice, which was coming from speakers placed high above the crowd, declared us as well: "Her Royal Highness Juliana, Crown Princess of the United Commonwealth of Columbia" followed by "His Royal Highness Callum, Prince of Farnham and the Western Territories." My stomach turned at the sight of all the people watching with rapt attention, and for the millionth time I wished that Thomas was at my side.

Callum took my hand and squeezed it. Though I wished he

was someone else, his touch was comforting. We walked into the grand ballroom and the throng of people set upon us.

The good thing about the fact that most of the gala attendees were strangers was that nobody expected Juliana to know who they were. They all introduced themselves, grinning from ear to ear, declaring themselves delighted at the forthcoming union between Callum and Juliana. Callum handled it better than I expected, switching on like a lightbulb and basking in the glow of all the adoration. So much for social anxiety.

After everyone had gotten to speak to us, dinner was served. The banquet table was as long as the room, and Callum and I had to sit at opposite ends, to spread out the honor of speaking with us, so I wasn't able to talk to him. I spent most of the meal looking for Thomas among the group of KES agents patrolling the perimeters of the room, but I didn't see him. Not that I thought I would. I only hoped.

When the meal was over, the dancing began. I wasn't in a dancing mood, but I was forced to spend hours spinning across the floor with an endless stream of male guests. I tried as hard as possible to be cordial and captivating, but my mind kept wandering as they droned on about matters of state I couldn't care less about.

When my last partner finally released me, I looked for Callum in the crowd, spying him dancing with a refined-looking old woman who was half his height. They made a ridiculous pair, and I couldn't help but smile. He was doing his best to charm her, and she was laughing at his whispered jokes. I was about to go over and cut in when someone grabbed me by the wrist and dragged me through a side door into a nearby alcove.

"Hey!" I cried as a door shut behind me. The voices in the ballroom died away completely as the latch caught. I looked around in a panic, expecting to see Lucas or someone even worse. Instead, to my surprise—and great relief—I found myself facing Dr. Moss. He was holding a file folder in his hand, his eyes dramatically big behind the thick lenses of his glasses.

"Dr. Moss, what are you doing here?"

"I'm sorry to have scared you, Ms. Lawson, but I've discovered something very important and I thought I should show it to you as soon as possible," he said, indicating the folder.

"That's all right," I said. "I'm just glad it's you. What do you have there?"

"I finally got ahold of Dr. March," Dr. Moss told me. "I was stumped as to the cause of your problem, but sometimes when Dr. March and I put our heads together, great things occur. For example, your anchor. I couldn't have invented it without him."

I gave the physicist a tight, insincere smile. If I ever met Dr. March, I was going to have a couple of things to say to him. "So? Does he know why I'm seeing the visions of Juliana?"

"He had a theory," Dr. Moss said. He paused, carefully considering his next words. "How much do you know about your parents, Ms. Lawson?"

"What's this got to do with my parents?"

"Possibly everything. Go on, tell me about them." Dr. Moss regarded me with increasing excitement.

"Um, I don't know. They were both physicists. Brilliant physicists," I said with pride. "They died when I was seven, in a car accident. Is that what you mean?"

"Who do you live with now? On Earth."

"My granddad," I told him.

"Maternal or paternal?"

"Maternal. Dr. Moss, I don't understand. Why are you asking me about my parents?"

"Have you ever met *any* of your father's family members? Parents? Siblings? Cousins?" Dr. Moss pressed.

"No. His parents were dead by the time I was born. They were both only children, and so was my dad. His only family was my mom and me. Why?"

"What was his name?" Dr. Moss's fingers worried the edges of the folder he was holding, bending and crushing it.

"George Lawson."

"Did he have any other names?"

"Of course not." Why would my father have had other names? He was a scientist, not a spy.

"Did you know that your father has no analog in this world?"

"Yes," I said. "Thomas said that happens sometimes, that people don't necessarily have an analog in every universe."

"That's true. But there's another possible explanation." Dr. Moss opened the folder. There was a photograph on top, clipped to a handful of documents, parts of which were blacked out. "Is this your father, Ms. Lawson?"

"Yes," I breathed. The man in the picture was unmistakably my dad. "What is this? Why do you have it?" The file read: CLASSIFIED: OPERATION LOOKING GLASS.

"Dr. March and I concluded, after exhaustive analysis of the available data, that the only way in which you could be seeing Juliana through the tether is if you were born with a connection to both worlds," Dr. Moss explained. "And the only way that we know of for that to be true is if you are a crosser."

"What's a crosser?" I demanded. "And why does the KES have my father's picture in one of their classified files?"

"'Crosser' is a term I invented this afternoon to describe someone whose genealogy originates from more than one universe," Dr. Moss said.

"This afternoon?"

He gave me a sheepish smile. "Well, you're the first one we'd ever heard of. There was no official term for the phenomenon, but of course we needed one."

"Of course," I said in disbelief. "Go on."

"In order for you to be experiencing the visions, one of your parents had to have been born in Aurora. It looks to have been your father. His real name was George Anderson, and he was employed as a research scientist by the KES. He was sent through the tandem on a top-secret assignment, to work with Earth physicists in order to sabotage their attempts to develop the many-worlds technologies that we were trying to perfect here at the Citadel."

I shook my head. "That's not possible."

"I'm afraid it's more than possible—it's true. He worked for the KES for several years," Dr. Moss said. "Until he went AWOL."

"My father was from Earth," I insisted. There was absolutely no way he had any connection to this awful world.

"I'm afraid that's not so," Dr. Moss said with regret in his voice. "You see, I knew your father. I didn't realize it when I first met you because he had changed his name, but before he was assigned to Operation Looking Glass, he worked with me in my lab. He was, as you say, brilliant. Beyond his years. I'm sorry to hear that he's no longer with us."

I was crying now, a stream of silent tears pouring down my face, surely smearing my makeup. But I didn't care about that.

"Oh, there, there, dear." Dr. Moss gave my shoulder an awkward pat. "Is there anything I can do to help?"

"No, I don't think so." It was Thomas I wanted, Thomas I needed to talk to. He was the only person I could tell about this, the only person who would understand what it meant and how it made me feel. "I'm sorry, Dr. Moss, but I need to be alone."

I kept thinking about my mother. How would she have felt if she knew that she had married an imposter, an invader from another world who'd come to Earth with the express purpose of destroying her work? Because that was where my parents had met, on a research project at Princeton University.

Unless she knew. But she couldn't have . . . could she? I tried to put myself in my mother's shoes, but I knew so little about my parents that I couldn't imagine how my mother would've reacted to the news that George Lawson, gifted physicist, beloved husband, had been nothing more than an alien from Aurora. And if she had known the truth, had Granddad also known? Was this the mysterious reason why he'd always disliked my father?

"I understand. I should go now. I'm not supposed to be in the Castle, and if somebody sees me . . ."

"Yes, of course," I said. "Thank you, Dr. Moss. For . . . for telling me, I guess."

"You're welcome," he said. "Please take care of yourself, Ms. Lawson."

"I will." He gave me a sad smile, then left the way we'd come, vanishing into the crowds in the ballroom.

I brushed the tears from my eyes. I didn't think I could face the queen or Callum in my condition, and didn't want to. *I have to get out of here,* I thought. I couldn't go back into the party—I was a mess. I didn't want to go to Juliana's bedroom, just in case someone came looking for me.

I could only think of one place no one would find me.

The king's room was dark and cold. The only sounds were the occasional mechanical beeps from the machines that measured his vitals and his own raspy breathing. For whatever reason—perhaps it was my state of mind, or the fact that I now had bigger things to be afraid of than the king's oddities—I felt safer in this room than ever before.

I took a seat and closed my eyes, relishing the silent company of Juliana's father. I wondered what he would make of me. It was obvious from the fact that one of the Operation Looking Glass files had been in his possession that he'd been aware of the existence of parallel universes, specifically of Earth, and that he had been party to my own father's assignment. But had he known about me? Was he aware I wasn't his daughter? A few days ago, I would've said no, but now I couldn't be sure. He'd led me to the Angel Eyes file, even if I hadn't understood. But perhaps I'd been wrong all along. Maybe his mutterings *were* random after all. Had I been so desperate for meaning that I'd manufactured a pattern that didn't exist?

"I found it," I told him, squeezing his hand. "I found the map. Except I don't understand. What *is* it?" But he didn't answer. He never did, and he never would.

I switched on a lamp and picked up *The Odyssey.* I began to read, to tell the king of Odysseus's reunion with his long-lost son.

"'Telemachus,' Odysseus, man of exploits, urged his son, 'it's wrong to marvel, carried away in wonder so to see your father here before your eyes. No other Odysseus will ever return to you. That man and I are one, the man you see . . . here after many hardships, endless wanderings, after twenty years I have come home to native ground at last. . . .'"

THIRTY-THREE

I stayed in the king's room until I was sure the last of the gala guests would be gone. It was almost three in the morning by the time I got back to Juliana's room, but I didn't find it empty.

"Hello, Miss Lawson." The General looked relaxed, sitting on the sofa near the window as if it was completely natural for him to be there. "I was wondering when you were going to show up."

"Where's Thomas?" I demanded. If something had happened to him, surely the General had been the one behind it.

The General's face contorted with thinly veiled anger. "That's none of your concern."

"Then why are you here? If you're going to yell at me about leaving the gala without telling anybody, believe me, you wouldn't have wanted me there," I said. I was too exhausted to argue. He had me, he had Thomas, he even had my father, in a way. There was nothing I could do to fight him. I just wanted him to say whatever it was he'd come to say and then leave.

"That's not why I've come. The queen will be furious, I expect, but it doesn't matter—you're going home."

"What? Are you serious? You're sending me home?" *No!* I thought desperately. I couldn't leave without seeing Thomas at least one more time and being sure that he was safe. But I doubted the General was going to allow me that.

"I told you six days, Miss Lawson, and tomorrow is the last day. I would have thought you'd be elated."

"What about Juliana?" I demanded. "You haven't found her yet."

"Do you really think I don't know where Juliana is?" the General asked. I said nothing.

"They think they're so clever, my boys," the General said. "They forget who trained them. To whom they owe all their skills—even Lucas. I know he turned her over to Libertas when I told him to get rid of her. I don't even mind. She can't tell them anything. She doesn't *know* anything, and if she thinks they're going to help her then she's mistaken. They'll hold her for leverage or ransom as long as they think she's useful, and then they'll find their own way to dispose of her." He brushed his hands together. "Win-win."

So the General didn't know that Juliana had given Libertas the Angel Eyes map. I'd seen the look on the Shepherd's face, and he, at least, seemed to think it was worth the price.

"Where's Thomas?" I asked again.

The General's face grew cloudy. "I told him not to get involved with you. I *explicitly* warned him against becoming emotionally attached. Thomas is a very brave young man, very smart, very skilled, but his heart's soft."

"Then why did you give him the mission?"

"I think that's fairly obvious," the General said. "We have no other agents whose analogs are in your life. Why do you think I adopted Thomas in the first place?"

"Because he's Grant's analog?" That was a risky gamble.

"One of the reasons, yes," the General said. "It was an insurance policy, just in case we ever needed you. You have no idea how thrilling it was to find an Aurora-analog of someone in your life who could actually be molded into a KES agent."

"I barely knew Grant back then," I said. "Even now I don't know him. He could've moved away at any time, and then what?"

"Then I would still have an exemplary soldier who was entirely indebted to me. Besides, it was very unlikely that you and Grant wouldn't grow up together. You'd just lost your parents; your grandfather needed a job, and the university offered him one. And Grant's mother was tenured. Of all of them, he was the best bet, and Thomas has proven to be a very good investment. Until recently, that is."

"What have you done to him?"

"Don't be so melodramatic. Thomas is far too important an asset for me to *do* anything to him. But I couldn't risk keeping him on Operation Starling knowing how he felt about you. He was starting to compromise the mission." He handed me a sheaf of photographs.

"Where did you get these?" The pictures, evidently taken through the curtains with a long zoom lens, showed Thomas and me kissing on my bed at Asthall Cottage.

"I was having you surveilled." He shook his head. "I have to say, I'm disappointed in you. I thought you would be more excited to go home."

"I don't think I can be too excited until I see the strings," I told him. "What do I have to do? Go through with the wedding?"

"There's not going to be a wedding," the General said. "Not if I can help it. I never intended for Juliana and Callum to *actually* get married, although I couldn't tell her that."

"What do you mean, there's not going to be a wedding?"

"Prince Callum is going to have a medical emergency," the General said. "Tonight."

"How could you possibly know that?"

"Because you're going to make it happen," the General said. He reached into the inside breast pocket of his suit jacket and pulled out a small vial filled with an ounce of clear liquid. "He's still awake. He's looking for you, and when we're finished here I'll make sure he finds you. He's worried. He wants to talk. I'll have the kitchen send up a tea tray and you'll pour him a cup. Then, when he's not looking, you're going to slip this into his drink and hand it to him. The solution will do the rest."

"I can't do that," I told him. "I won't kill Callum. You were probably better off keeping Juliana."

"Oh, it won't kill him, I assure you," the General said.

"But it'll make him sick!"

"Hopefully," the General said.

"You're insane! I'm not doing this. Callum is my friend. I'm not going to help you hurt him."

"Actually, you are." The General leaned forward and placed the vial on the table between us. "Because if you don't, you will remain here in Aurora, rotting in the worst prison the Commonwealth has to offer for the rest of your natural-born life."

"Why do you even want to do this? If you don't want him to marry Juliana, why don't you just send him back to Farnham and end this?"

The General sighed. "I shouldn't expect you to understand the delicate political situation we're in. The marriage does nothing for the UCC, because we don't want a peace treaty. We want Farnham. For two hundred years that *family* has been sitting on land that rightfully belongs to this country, and I'm going to get it back. The first step in assuring that

that happens is securing our collateral. Prince Callum *is* that collateral. But I have no use for a hostage who's well enough to be extracted. Not that I think Farnham is capable of such a maneuver, but it never hurts to be sure."

"According to Callum, his mother practically hates him," I said. "What makes you think she won't blow this country to smithereens rather than cooperate with you?"

"Because as much as she may hate him, which I'm not convinced she does, her country loves him," the General said. "If she sacrifices him for her own political reasons, they'll revolt. Libertas will make sure they do. The queen of Farnham likes to pretend they're simply a scourge on the UCC, but they aren't. They operate in Farnham as well, and stirring up revolution is what they do best. She knows she'll lose if she shows her people what a miserable tyrant she really is."

"*She's* a miserable tyrant? What does that make you?"

"A brilliant strategist," the General said arrogantly. "I don't need the love of the people; I have nuclear weapons." He stood up. "I'll leave you to make your choice, Miss Lawson. We have other ways of making sure this task is done, but none of them involve you going back to Earth, so I would consider my offer very, very carefully if I were you."

He strode to the door, confident that he had been victorious over me, the naïve little girl from another world.

THIRTY-FOUR

I picked up the vial and turned it over in my hand. It was the only thing other than the tandem standing between me and Earth—home. And it was so small. Just a flick of the wrist and it would be done. Nobody would ever suspect that I had anything to do with what happened to Callum, and even if they did, by then I would be an entire universe away, where no one could ever touch me.

What was my other option? Disobey the General and condemn myself to a lifetime of imprisonment in Aurora? Either way, Callum's fate was sealed. I couldn't save him, but I could save myself.

I struggled to get out of my dress, ripping it as I pulled it off. The beautiful rose tiara clattered to the floor. I collapsed beside it in tears, panting. After a while, I got up and threw on a pair of pants and a T-shirt, not caring one iota for how I looked.

"Juli?" Callum stood in the door, his voice full of concern. "What's wrong?"

"Nothing," I said, turning from him and wiping my face. My fist closed over the vial. Somehow, I found the strength to smile. It felt unnatural, as though the muscles I needed to do it had atrophied. "I'm fine. Just overwhelmed."

"I'll say." He came in and sat down on the sofa the General had just vacated. "You disappeared hours ago. I was really worried. I thought something had happened."

I shook my head. "No, I just hate crowds. They make me nervous."

He ran his fingers through his hair. "Okay. Well, I'm glad you're all right."

"I am, I promise." An attendant entered the room, pushing a tea cart I hadn't ordered. I nodded my thanks and he left as quickly as he had come. "Do you want some tea?"

"Uh, sure." Callum was bewildered by my strange behavior, and I couldn't blame him. I was acting like a crazy person. I felt crazy, too. Was I really going to do this? *Poison* Callum? Turn him over to the General in exchange for my own happiness? Could I ever be happy back at home, knowing what I'd done, the destruction I'd left in my wake?

"You Columbians and your tea." Callum smiled. "Sorry, I meant that as a joke."

"It was funny." With my back to Callum, I poured us each a cup of tea. Then I uncapped the vial and dumped its contents into Callum's cup. There. It was done. I was the worst person in the world—all the worlds. But I was going home. I hoped desperately that it was worth it.

"Here you go," I said, handing him his tea.

"Thanks."

I took a sip from my cup, but Callum just held his, staring at me with worry in his eyes. "Are you sure you're okay?"

"Yes," I insisted. "I'm fine."

"If you say so." Callum brought the cup to his lips. This was it. The vilest thing I'd ever done was happening right before my eyes. But did it really matter? It was inevitable.

Or was it?

"Stop!" I cried.

He paused, not drinking a drop. "What's going on, Juli? Seriously, you're scaring me."

I put my cup down; it clattered in its delicate saucer. "You can't drink that. I dosed it."

"You *what*?"

"With some sort of poison," I told him. "The General threatened me. He told me that if I didn't do it . . ." I trailed off, hoping that Callum would fill in the blanks with his own terrifying conclusions. I couldn't tell him the full story without explaining who I was or where I'd come from. If I did that, he might never trust a single thing I told him ever again, and I needed him to trust me if I was going to keep him alive.

"You were going to kill me?" Callum recoiled, as if I was a snake. And I was. I knew I was. "Why?"

"Not kill you," I said. "I don't know what it does, but the General said it was going to make you so sick that nobody from Farnham could come get you."

"That's not better!"

"I know, I know. Please listen to me. I couldn't do it. Doesn't that count for something? I don't care what happens to me, I won't hurt you. I panicked for a second and thought I could, but I can't. Never."

Callum was gripping his teacup so hard I thought he might break it. "So what do I do now? I can't stay here."

"No, you can't," I said. "I just don't know how you're going to get out."

"We," Callum said firmly.

"What do you mean, 'we'?"

"You're coming with me," Callum said.

"No, I can't." If I left with Callum, I could kiss any chance of going home goodbye, not to mention any chance of ever seeing Thomas again. On the other hand, it didn't look like staying would increase the chances of either of those things happening. What was the right thing to do? Thomas would've known. *Think like Thomas,* I told myself. *What would he do?*

"Yes," Callum insisted. "There's no way I'm leaving you behind to be punished by that monster. Wherever I go, you're coming, too. We'll get out of here together."

"How can you even say that, after what I did?"

"What you almost did," Callum corrected me. "You couldn't do it. I believe that. I might be nuts, but I still trust you, Juliana. I'm not leaving you, is that clear?"

I nodded. I wished he would stop calling me "Juli" and "Juliana." It was a constant reminder of how many lies I'd allowed him to believe. "It doesn't matter. There's no way out."

"Yes, there is." Callum slipped off his signet ring, the one he'd told me had once belonged to his father, and slammed it, with the stone facing down, onto the little table next to the sofa. Then he did something that filled me with such horror that to my dying day I will never, ever forget it.

Callum picked up his tea and drank it down.

I screamed at him to stop, but by the time the words came out of my mouth he was already setting the empty cup down on the table. He put his ring back on.

"Why did you do that?" I cried.

"Have a little faith," he said. "Just promise to stick with me, whatever you do."

It didn't take long for the poison to take effect. Within a minute, Callum had gone limp and collapsed onto the sofa. I slapped his cheeks, nearly insane with panic.

"Callum! Callum, wake up!" But he didn't stir.

Kline rushed in, roused from his post by the sound of my shouting. "What's going on?" he demanded.

"The prince is sick! Get help, now!" I commanded. He turned on his heel, muttering something into his lapel as he left. *The rowan pin.* Gloria had told me to use it if I ever needed Thomas. Frantic, I cast my eyes around the room for my dress; the pin was still fixed to the bodice. When I found it, I pressed the pin so hard that the needle dug into my thumb, drawing blood.

"Thomas," I breathed, holding it close to my lips. "I need your help."

THOMAS IN THE TOWER / 5

Thomas stared at the ceiling, twisting his KES ring around and around on his finger in agitation. He was lying on his bed feeling utterly useless. It had been over twenty-four hours since the General had banished him to his quarters, and no one had come to collect him. He still had his KES earpiece in, listening in vain for a summons, but when it came it was from the most unlikely source.

"Thomas, I need your help." Thomas started at the sound of Sasha's voice. She was distraught; he could tell just from the way she spoke those five words. Fear flooded through him. Something was wrong. She was in danger, or in pain. He had to get to her.

But how was he going to get out? The LCD screen on the inside of his door was red—no exit. Without thinking, he reared back and punched it so hard the screen broke, stained with blood from his knuckles. He hardly felt the pain. He reached inside the small hole he'd created and pulled out the wiry guts of the console. At least that would disable the lock. Now he had to get the door open.

The towel rack in his bathroom was a thick metal pole that

tapered and turned at both ends. He pressed down on it with all his weight, easily dislocating it from the weak plaster, and wedged it into the small space between the door and the jamb that had been created when the vacuum seal released, managing to force it open about an inch. He inserted the fingers of both hands into the gap and yanked the door with all his might, opening it wider and wider with every attempt, until there was just enough room for him to slip through.

He took off his KES ring and placed it on top of the dresser. After all, it belonged to the KES, not to him, and he didn't want it anymore, though his finger felt naked without it. Then he disappeared through the gap in the door.

At first it looked like there was nobody around, but the General must have activated the motion sensors, because there was a shuffling at the end of the hallway and a young agent appeared, blocking Thomas's only exit. Thomas didn't know the agent very well, but he thought his name was York.

"Agent Mayhew, I must insist that you return to your quarters immediately," York said.

"Get out of my way," Thomas growled.

"I'm afraid I can't do that," York told him. Thomas was right on top of him now, and it was clear to both parties just how much bigger and more intimidating Thomas was than green, uncertain York. "You must remain in your room. General's orders."

Seeing that he had no other option, Thomas did something he never thought he would do—he reared back and punched York in the face. His KES brother fell to the ground, unconscious. Thomas shook out his hand; his knuckles had taken quite a beating tonight.

"Screw the General," he said.

THIRTY-FIVE

Everything happened so fast. One second, I watched Callum slump to the floor, and the next, medics rushed in wheeling a gurney as the flashing lights of an ambulance in the gardens illuminated the room with a pulsing red glow that made me sick to my stomach. I scrambled to my feet as the medics hoisted Callum onto the gurney. He landed with a dull thud, and I actually thought I might vomit.

The paramedics were removing Callum from my room. I rushed after them, pausing only for a moment to take my necklace, *Twelfth Night*, and the Angel Eyes map from the bedside drawer and shove them into my pockets. Whatever Angel Eyes was, the map had been important enough for the king to hide, and I wasn't going to leave it or my own possessions behind for the General to find.

"I'm coming with you!" I cried, following the medics into the hallway. *Just promise to stick with me, whatever you do,* Callum had said. I didn't think he'd said it because he thought he'd need my support. He'd said it because he'd worked something out, and if we were going to escape it was going to be together. I couldn't let them take him away without me.

It was a huge risk, following Callum into an unseen future. I wasn't going to be able to get home now, without the General's help or Dr. Moss's technological resources. Someday Callum was going to discover that I wasn't Juliana, and he wouldn't want anything to do with me. I would be more alone than ever, separated from my home by a quantum veil I couldn't even hope to cross by myself, and from the boy I truly wanted, who I'd abandoned. But this was my choice. I couldn't look back now, and I didn't want to. I couldn't bear to think of it.

The ambulance was parked haphazardly on the circular driveway outside the Castle's grand entrance. The medics loaded Callum through the back. "If you're coming, then get in," one of them said to me.

I climbed in after the gurney. Just as the medic was about to close the doors, I saw Thomas emerge from the ground floor of the Tower and start running toward the driveway, drawn by all the commotion. My heart leapt into my throat at the sight of him.

"Wait, wait!" I cried, but the medic slammed the doors shut.

"This is an *emergency,* Your Highness!" she snapped. "We can't *wait.*"

Thomas reached us a second too late. He flattened his hand against the window and I did the same, imagining the feel of his skin against mine as the ambulance began to move. I watched him through the window as we drove away; he just stood there for a few seconds, frozen, then took off for the shadows of the gardens, disappearing into the night.

The hospital had to be close. There was no way there wasn't one near the Citadel, with all of its important residents, royal and otherwise, and it was unlikely that the General would want Callum at a more distant hospital—he would want to keep an eye on him. But I had no idea what Callum's big escape plan entailed. Was I supposed to be doing something? Surely he would have told me if I was.

My answer came swiftly. We'd only been outside the Castle for about a minute when something slammed into the ambulance, rocking me to the floor. I fell against Callum's limp body as the IV bags dangled above my head.

"Hey!" one of the medics cried, pounding her fist against the wall of the cab. "What's going on up there?"

"I think something just hit us!" the driver called back. A thrill rippled up my spine. Someone was coming. Someone was *here*.

I'd just righted myself when there was another crash, this time from the other side. The back of my head cracked against the metal wall, but I hardly felt it. I checked Callum's wrist for a pulse. He was still alive, but unconscious, unaware of the commotion going on around him.

Two shots fired from somewhere outside and the driver shouted, but I couldn't tell what he was saying. The ambulance swerved wildly, pitching from side to side, before coming to a screeching halt. The medics were both in shock, completely baffled, but I knew what was happening. We were being rescued. I began ripping the IVs out of Callum's arm. The female medic screamed, "What do you think you're doing!" but I didn't stop. I would've dragged Callum off the gurney, too, if I had the strength to manage it.

The back doors swung open and three men dressed in black climbed in. They each held a gun, and I flashed back to what had happened in the Tattered City with the Libertas commandos. What if I was wrong? What if this wasn't Callum's plan at all? What if it was someone else's? A flare of panic shot straight up through my lungs and I found it hard to draw breath.

The medics were easily subdued; as soon as they saw the guns, they backed off. One of the men in black grabbed me and hauled me out of the ambulance. I glanced back to see another hefting Callum over his shoulder while the third kept his gun trained on the medics. There was a fourth, I now saw, dealing with the driver, and a fifth sitting at the wheel of a black unmarked van nearby. They had corralled the ambulance into a small dark alley. I could see almost nothing as the man who held me shoved me into the van. The one who had Callum laid him gently on the floor before climbing in and sliding the door shut behind him. I cringed as three more shots were fired, flinching at the sound of each one. Then the other two men jumped in through the black and the van sped off into the night.

It all happened in less than two minutes.

The men whipped off their masks and started tending to Callum.

"What did they give him?" someone demanded. I was speechless—I didn't even know the answer. He grabbed my fist, wrenching the fingers open; I was still holding the vial. He took it from me and sniffed it, then tasted the rim with the tip of his tongue before opening up a briefcase filled with medical supplies. He tossed a bag of saline at one of the others, who threaded the IV through the existing tap in Callum's arm and hung the bag from a makeshift hook on the inside roof of the van. They riffled through the contents of the briefcase before finding an antidote to the poison he'd taken, jamming a hypodermic needle through the fleshy cap of the vial and drawing its contents into the needle. Then he stuck it in Callum's arm.

"Will that cure him?" I asked. *Please don't die, Cal,* I thought desperately. *Please, please, please don't die.*

"We'll know soon," one of them said. He removed another vial from the briefcase and loaded the liquid into a second hypodermic needle.

"It's best if you're not awake for what comes next," he said. Before I could shrink away, he injected something into my bloodstream.

"What are you doing?" I cried, or attempted to. The sedative overcame me so fast I wasn't able to get all the words out before sinking into a heavy, dreamless sleep.

0

DAYS

THIRTY-SIX

"She's coming around. Juli! Juli, come on, open your eyes." *Callum!* He was alive!

I tried to obey but I couldn't. It was as if each of my eyelashes weighed a ton. I felt a hand on my cheek. I tried to sit up, but Callum pushed back against my shoulders, urging me to settle down.

"Don't worry, you're all right," he said. "Lie back and relax. We're here. We're safe."

"Where's here?" I could open my eyes now, but all I could see was his face. He smiled.

"Home," he said. "Or, at least, my home. Farnham. We're almost to Adastra Palace."

"How did we get here?" The last thing I remembered was being in that van, wondering if Callum would recover from whatever poison he'd ingested at the Castle, and now here we were, both awake, both alive, together. A wave of gratitude washed over me.

"We drove to Buffalo and crossed into Canada, then they loaded us on a plane and flew us straight to Adastra City," Callum explained.

"Those men . . ." The memory of gunshots echoed through my head. I squeezed my eyes shut, trying to erase the faces of the medics who might have been hurt or died so we could escape. So that Callum and I could live. *Kata to chreon.* My debts were piling up, and I was no closer to getting home.

"They work for the Farnham Intelligence Agency," he said. "Basically our KES."

"How did they . . ."

"The ring," he said, flexing his hand. I ran my fingers over the engraved surface of the bloodred stone, thinking of the one Thomas wore, what it meant to him, and what secrets it might hide. "It's a panic button. It called the FIA agents to me. They were undercover in Columbia City this whole time."

"But why?"

"My mother had a feeling something like this was going to happen," he said darkly. "They were there to extract me in case of emergency. I fought her on it, but I'm glad she insisted."

"Me too," I said. I sat up groggily with Callum's support. We were alone in the back of a stretch limousine.

"She's never going to let me hear the end of it now," Callum said. "You should've heard her before I left. 'Don't trust them, they'll kill you as soon as look at you.' I didn't believe her, and I hate, hate, *hate* that she was right. But at least I'm alive. And so are you."

I nodded. "I'm so sorry, Callum."

"Don't be," Callum said. "You're just as much a victim of all this as I am. And look at me. All better." He grinned. "Not a scratch. Well, a few puncture marks, but those'll heal in no time. Girls like scars, right?"

"Sure," I said with a weak smile. "The tinier, the better."

"Well, that's good news, because you can barely even see

mine," he joked. He handed me a glass of water. "Drink this. They tell me you're likely to be dehydrated."

I gulped it down. Dehydrated was an understatement. "Why did they knock me out?"

"They're trained to treat anybody from the UCC as an immediate threat," Callum explained. "They had to incapacitate you. It's protocol. Sorry about that."

"Forget sorry. After what you went through, I think I can handle it."

He smoothed my hair. "We're going to be okay."

"I wish you didn't have to come back here," I said. "I know you hate this place."

He shrugged. "It's fine. I'm just glad we're both living—right now, I don't give a damn where."

Callum put his arms around me. I sank into him, taking comfort in the sturdiness of his body. But now that the sedatives were wearing off, I couldn't get Thomas out of my mind. I could feel his absence like a yawning chasm in my gut. He'd try to find me, I knew he would, but he didn't know where I'd gone. Could he guess? Could he find out? Thomas could do a lot of things, but not if he was suspended from the KES and cut off from all their resources. And did I really want him sacrificing the only career he had left going AWOL to find me? My dad had betrayed his assignment to be with my mom, and look what had happened to them. If Thomas died because of me, I would never forgive myself.

I knew one thing for sure—I couldn't keep leading Callum on. It wasn't that I didn't have tender feelings for him, because I did, especially after what we'd just gone through—what he had *put* himself through partly on my behalf. But there was still Thomas, taking up so much space in my heart, and though in the end I couldn't be with either of them, I couldn't allow Callum to continue to fall in love with the Juliana I was pretending to be.

But that conversation was for later. At the moment, everything was far too uncertain. I had yet to meet the queen of Farnham, and I was worried. Juliana's stepmother sounded easy compared to Queen Marian, and I needed to hold my own against her.

The limo pulled over and the door opened. A man who could've been a KES agent if it weren't for the fact that we weren't in the Commonwealth anymore opened it for us and we climbed out.

I didn't even get a chance to see the outside of Adastra Palace. The windows of the limo had been tinted so darkly that they only gave a vague idea of what the city looked like, although from what I'd seen I could tell that it was less grand than Columbia City.

The security detail that had met us at the car led us silently through the underground garage. "Her Majesty commands that we take you straight to the throne room, Your Highness," the guard told Callum. "She wants to see you immediately."

"I'm sure she does," Callum muttered, so low that only I could hear.

"Cal!" A boy of about twelve came barreling around a corner and slammed into Callum. Callum wrapped his arms around the boy and gave him a fierce bear hug.

"Mother said you weren't coming back," the boy said. "She said you'd gone to live with the enemy forever."

"They're not the enemy, Sonny," Callum said. "Well, not all of them. This is Juliana."

"Pleased to meet you, Your Highness," Sonny said, bowing his head a little and reaching out to take my hand. When I gave it to him, he kissed it. "Welcome to Farnham."

Callum gave me a sideways glance, struggling to keep a straight face. "We're well trained here."

"I can see that." I smiled at Callum's little brother, impressed by his gallantry. "Hello. It's lovely to meet you, Your Highness. Can I call you Sonny?"

He shrugged, blushing, both elated and embarrassed by the attention. "She's nicer than I thought she'd be," he said to Callum.

"Then you don't know her yet," Callum teased. I made a face at him, and he returned it. God, I was glad he was alive.

"Let's go see Mother," Callum said to Sonny. Now it was Sonny's turn to make a face.

"Rather not, thanks," he said, ducking out of Callum's embrace. "It was nice to meet you, Your Highness."

"You can call me Juli," I told him.

"Nice to meet you, Juli!" he called back as he disappeared around the corner from whence he came.

"*He* gets to call you Juli after meeting you for two seconds?" Callum said in mock exasperation. "Unbelievable."

"What can I say? I like him better," I said. Callum tugged on a strand of my hair and smiled. Then he sighed.

"Come on, Mother awaits."

He led me into a cavernous room that was empty but for a throne at the far end. A woman was sitting in it, tapping her heel against the marble in agitation. She was surrounded by a half-dozen bodyguards, all of whom were stiff as rods. It didn't inspire a lot of confidence.

Queen Marian stood as we entered and watched as we crossed the vast distance between the door and the throne. Callum fell to one knee at the queen's feet.

"Hello, Mother," he said. "May I present—"

"Yes, yes, I know who she is," the queen said. "Stand up, Callum." She leaned forward as if to examine him, taking his chin in her hand and tilting it this way and that like she was mapping it. "I see there's been no lasting damage from your exploits."

"It would appear that way," Callum said. There was a slight wobble in his voice.

"No thanks to you," Queen Marian said. She was talking to me. She turned to her bodyguards and summoned them forward with a wave of her hand. "Take her to the Hole."

"What?" Callum jerked up in alarm. "No, you can't do that. She's here with me! She's my fiancée!"

"Not anymore," Queen Marian said. "I've had quite enough of this whole royal wedding business. It's very clear that the General never intended for the two of you to marry, or for the peace treaty to be signed. I know how to proceed."

The bodyguards seized me, one at each arm. "Wait!" I cried. "You can't do this!"

"She helped me escape, Mother," Callum protested.

"No, dear, my agents helped you escape," Queen Marian said. "Take her to the Hole and throw her in a cell with that other piece of UCC filth. I'll decide what to do with them later."

The bodyguards dragged me away. I struggled against them, doing all I could to resist, but it was futile. They were far stronger than me. Blood rushed to my face; I could barely hear Callum over the thump of my heart in my ears. He was screaming for his mother to reconsider, but Queen Marian was unmoved.

After pulling a sack over my head, the bodyguards took me down a seemingly endless flight of stairs. After a while I stopped fighting them. We reached the bottom of the stairs and proceeded down a long hallway before we finally stopped. I heard a metal key turn in a metal lock and a set of metal bars creak open. Then I was on the ground, the heels of my hand scraping against the rough cement floor. One of the men whipped the sack off my head, and I found myself in a large cell, harshly lit by fluorescent lighting in the ceiling. I turned sharply and watched them slam the bars shut. I reached up and grabbed them, hauling myself to my feet and banging my palms against them.

"Let me out of here!" I shouted. "I haven't done anything wrong!"

"It's useless," a voice said. "They won't listen."

I turned slowly, not quite believing my ears. Against all odds, *Thomas* was sitting on the lower level of a metal bunk bed, his head hanging in defeat.

"Oh my God," I cried, rushing to him. I knelt before him, my hands on his knees, but he pushed me away.

"Who the hell are you?" he demanded angrily. Then he recognized me. "Hey, I know you. You're . . . you go to my school."

"Grant," I breathed. "I can't believe you're here."

"Yeah, well, neither can I," he said, lying down on the bed. After a few seconds, he popped back up. "Wait, what are *you* doing here?"

That other piece of UCC filth, Queen Marian had said. I remembered something Thomas had told me about Grant. They suspected that he'd been taken into Farnham by Libertas and traded for something, that Queen Marian thought he was Thomas. I didn't know how he'd gotten into Farnham, but at the very least it seemed as though the last part was true.

"It's a long story," I grumbled, falling into a cross-legged position on the floor.

"I've got time," Grant said.

So I told him everything, from the tandem to the analogs

to the peace treaty between Farnham and the UCC to Libertas to the arranged marriage between Callum and Juliana. He was silent for a while after I finished. I was afraid I'd scrambled his brain.

"So you're saying that we're in a parallel universe? Where there are people who look exactly like us but are not us?" He shook his head. "That's crazy, Sasha, you know that, right?"

"I'm not crazy," I told him. "Hello! Look where you are. This is not normal."

"You've got that right," Grant said. "And you're saying I ended up here because my . . . what'd you call them?"

"Analogs."

"Right. I touched my analog and that's why I ended up here?"

"Basically, yeah."

"Okay, but that doesn't explain why a bunch of armed thugs grabbed me off the street and brought me here," Grant said.

"Libertas," I said. "They thought you were Thomas. Your analog. They traded you for something. Do you know what?"

He shrugged. "Not a clue. I was knocked out for most of it. I woke up in here and I haven't been able to get a single answer out of anybody."

"That's not a shock." Now that all the adrenaline had drained from my body, I was overcome with fatigue. My stomach growled. "Do they feed you in this place?"

"Sometimes," Grant said. "I've been hoping this was all just a very vivid nightmare. Now it's looking like not so much."

"Sorry," I said. "Believe me, I wish it was."

"So now what?" Grant asked.

"I honestly have no idea."

THIRTY-SEVEN

Days passed. I kept hoping Callum would find a way to get me out of the Hole, but he never came. I found it hard to keep track of time. Our cell had no windows, and we could only make rudimentary guesses about time of day based on when our bodies told us to sleep and wake up. We'd been fed five times since Queen Marian had her guards throw me into the cell with Grant, but none of them would speak to us, let alone tell us anything useful.

"I can't believe this!" I cried, slamming my hand against the bars as yet another guard walked away after delivering our meals.

"You'd better eat," Grant advised. "That soup is barely lukewarm, and it's no good cold."

"I'm not hungry."

"If you don't want it, can I have it?" Dinner consisted of one small bowl of soup and a hard roll that Grant was trying to soften by soaking it in the broth. It was definitely not enough for a guy like him to subsist on; I was so full of rage I couldn't bring myself to eat.

"Go ahead," I said. I sank down against the bars and tucked

my knees under my chin. "I just can't believe I went from one prison to another. This is the biggest load of crap. I'm sick of this place. I want to go home." I looked up at the ceiling, which was covered in mold. "Do you hear me? *I want to go home!"*

Grant sighed. "Sasha, stop it. I did exactly what you're doing for like three weeks. Nobody's listening."

"I'm not giving up," I told him. "I've gotten out of worse jams than this before. I'll get us out of here, too." The truth was, I'd gotten out of those jams with help from other people, mostly Thomas. But I couldn't just shut down under the weight of hopelessness the way that Grant had. The only time he ever became animated was when we were fed; otherwise he was as motionless as a stone, sleeping or pretending to sleep as I lay awake thinking up harebrained schemes to get us out. There had to be a way. There just *had* to be. That was what I kept telling myself, anyway, but the longer Grant and I remained locked in the Hole, the more I accepted that Callum wasn't coming. I couldn't even allow myself to hope that Thomas would. Still, every once in a while I let myself believe. This was one of those moments.

"Hey, you come up with a plan, I'll help you," Grant said, his mouth full of my bread. "I'm just saying. It doesn't look great."

"Yeah, I know," I said. "I know."

On the third night—or maybe it was the fourth—of my incarceration, I awoke to the now-familiar sound of the cell doors sliding open. I sat up, wondering what fresh hell awaited me, but it was too dark to see anything until the motion sensors on the fluorescent lights caught whoever had entered the cell and flickered on.

"Sasha?" Grant whispered.

"Grant?" I inched over to the edge of the bed to peek out at the intruder.

"No," the voice said, sounding a little bewildered. "It's me."

Thomas.

I leapt off the top bunk and threw myself at him. He caught me and held me tight. "You're here," I said happily, for the moment forgetting everything else. I buried my face in his shoulder, squeezing my eyes shut to keep from crying, but a few tears slipped out anyway. "I thought I would never see you again."

"Not a chance," he said, smiling against my cheek. "It took me a while to figure out where you were—Farnham's a big place, but some of my connections in Adastra told me you might be down here. No wonder they call it the Hole. It's awful."

"Sasha, who is it?" Grant rolled out of bed and stood up, squinting into the lights. It took a few seconds for him to register exactly who he was looking at, but once he did his face contorted into an expression of blind fury. *"You."*

"Grant, wait!" But he didn't listen. He might not even have heard. Without pausing to think, Grant lunged for Thomas, and in the split second when his fist connected with Thomas's jaw, Grant vanished into thin air.

"Grant!" I cried. Thomas fell from the force of Grant's impact, clutching his face, and the ground rumbled beneath us, throwing me to the floor as well. We watched in horrified shock as the door to the cell slammed shut, locking us in.

"What the—" I couldn't even get the entire sentence out.

"The disruption event," Thomas said gravely. "You remember what I told you?"

It took me a second to figure out what he was talking

about. The disruption event. The physical event caused by the ripple created when mass traveled between universes. It had knocked the door loose and caused it to close. We were trapped.

"And here I thought I was coming to the rescue," Thomas said, prodding his jaw tenderly. "I should've known he would do that. It's not the first time."

"I did tell him about the analog problem," I said. "Maybe he did it on purpose."

"I brought this for him," Thomas said, drawing something out of his pocket. "I was going to send you both back. The ungrateful bastard."

"The anchors!" I cried triumphantly. "Thomas, we can get out of here. You put on the anchor and we'll go back to Earth."

"Bad idea," Thomas said.

"Why?" My face fell. I was desperate to get out of Farnham, he had a solution in hand, and he was telling me we couldn't use it?

"I didn't expect us to stay here," Thomas explained. "I didn't map this place. I have no idea what it corresponds to on the other side. We could end up anywhere."

"But anywhere is better than this," I protested. Wasn't it? And if not, then what had happened to Grant? Worry dropped into the pit of my stomach like a stone.

"Oh really? How would you like to land *in the foundation of a house*? Or maybe you'd prefer to end up under the wheels of a moving moto?"

"Okay, you made your point," I grumbled. I propped myself up against the wall, too tired to stand.

"Sasha, what happened back there?" Thomas asked. "Why did you run?"

"The General tried to force me to poison Callum," I told Thomas. "He said he was going to keep me in Aurora forever—in a place just like this, I assume—unless I did what he said. He said he'd send me home if I did it, but I couldn't. I told Callum and he arranged for an extraction. Apparently he had undercover agents in Columbia City the whole time."

"That was smart of him." Thomas hung his head. "I'm sorry, Sasha. I didn't know."

I shrugged. "It is what it is."

"No, it isn't. This is all my fault. I never should've brought you here." He kneaded his brow with his fingertips.

"Stop it, Thomas. Let's just forget about that, all right?" I leaned my head back against the wall and sighed. "How did you get here?"

"Just because the General cut me off doesn't mean I don't still have my own ways of getting things done," Thomas said. "Dr. Moss was able to get his hands on the remote that controls your anchor, plus an extra, and smuggled me out of the Citadel. Then I used my connections to get here. Took me longer than I would like, but I did it."

"I guess that means you're officially fired, huh?" I noticed he was no longer wearing his KES ring.

"Yeah, I guess it does."

"I'm so glad you're here," I told him. I laid my head on his shoulder and closed my eyes. He took my hand and squeezed. I shivered; the cell was always cold. Thomas took off his jacket and wrapped it around my shoulders. I put it on and snuggled up against him. All the talk of analogs and anchors reminded me of something—I'd never had a chance to tell Thomas about my father and his connection to Aurora.

"I found out something else," I said. "Back at the Citadel. About the tether."

"Really? What?"

"Dr. Moss came to see me at the gala. He said he consulted with Dr. March and they think—"

"Hold up. Dr. March?"

"Yeah." I searched his face. "What? What's wrong with Dr. March?"

"Oh, nothing," Thomas said offhandedly. "Except I'm pretty sure he doesn't exist."

"What?"

"Mossie is a genius, but he's also a little, you know." Thomas whistled and whirled his finger in a circular motion around his temple. "He talks about Dr. March all the time, but I've never met the man, and never met anybody else who has. I hate to use the word 'delusion,' but . . ."

That was disturbing, but it didn't change the fact that Dr. Moss had a genuinely possible hypothesis about why I could see Juliana through the tether. "Dr. March or no Dr. March, he had a breakthrough. He says that I can see through the tandem because I have a connection to Aurora."

"What kind of connection?"

"My father was born here."

Thomas's eyes widened in surprise. "Are you sure?"

I nodded. "He showed me the file. Apparently my father was one of the research fellows in Dr. Moss's lab at the Citadel a long time ago, before he was drafted into the KES for an assignment. On Earth."

"What kind of assignment?"

"Do you know anything about Operation Looking Glass?" As soon as I asked the question I knew he did.

"Yeah," he admitted. "I've heard of it, but I don't know much about it other than that the KES sent a couple of agents to Earth in order to sabotage the efforts of scientists in your world from developing the many-worlds technology."

"My father was one of those scientists," I told him. "Until he went AWOL and, I guess, married my mom and had me."

"Wow. That's news to me," Thomas said. I stared him down. He held his hands up in surrender. "Seriously, I didn't know. I would've told you if I did."

"I believe you."

"So how are you feeling about all this?"

"Lied to," I confessed. My whole life I'd had this image of who my father was, and now all of that was gone. I couldn't even guess at what was real and what had been made up. "But it's stupid to feel betrayed by someone who's been dead for almost ten years. Right?"

"I don't think there's a statute of limitations on that particular emotion," Thomas said.

"I keep wondering if my mother knew. Or Granddad. And if they would've told me someday." I paused. "You don't think Operation Looking Glass had anything to do with their deaths, do you?" I had my own suspicions, but I was desperately hoping Thomas would assure me that my parents' accident was just that—an accident.

Thomas's face darkened. "I think anything's possible when it comes to the General."

I bit down hard on my lip, drawing blood. Still chilled, I shoved my hands into the pocket of Thomas's jacket and, to my surprise, found something inside. I pulled out a clump of withered, drying flowers—white roses and a bit of baby's breath, precariously attached to a white elastic band.

"You have my corsage?" I asked, puzzled. Thomas nodded. "But I threw it away back in the Tattered City."

"I rescued it," he said. "It was the only thing I had from . . . us, in your world. I guess I didn't want to let it go. I meant what I said to you that night on the beach. It was the best night of my life, being with you; it was the one time I really felt like myself. Ironic, huh?" I nodded, pulling him in for a soft, lingering kiss.

"Thomas," I whispered. "That's very romantic, you know?"

"I know," he said with a wry smile.

Then I remembered something. I pulled the Angel Eyes map out and smoothed it over my knees. Thomas leaned over to get a better look. "What's that?"

"I'm not sure. I thought you might recognize it." I told him how Callum and I had found it, and how Juliana had given another copy of the map to Libertas. "Why would the king want Juliana to see a weather map? And what the hell would Libertas need it for?"

"This isn't a weather map," Thomas said, examining it closely.

"Really? Then what is it?"

"No idea. I've never heard of this operation before." He put his arms around me and held me tightly, pressing his lips to my forehead. "I'm glad you ran," he said into my hair. "Even if it meant we had to end up here. At least we're together."

"I am, too," I said, getting choked up again. "I didn't want to leave, but I just didn't know what else to do."

"I understand." He pulled back a little to look down at my face. I smiled at him sadly. A great cloud of uncertainty hung over us. Would we ever make it out of here? And even if we did, what then? I would go back home, but would Thomas come with me? Or would he stay in Aurora, his home universe? It didn't feel like he belonged in Aurora. It felt like he belonged with me, wherever I was. But it wasn't my choice, and, in a way, it wasn't his either.

For the moment, though, none of that mattered. He bent his head and kissed me deeply. I kissed him back. We kissed each other, sinking deeper and deeper into an unfathomable ocean, straining toward infinity.

THEY DIDN'T HAVE TO GO TO *Columbia City, after all, which was just as well. There'd been some problems at the Farnham-UCC border, and not even the Shepherd, who appeared to have more connections than a revolutionary could ever dream of, was able to get clearance to pass into the Commonwealth. There was trouble brewing again. Nobody told her what, exactly, but she had to believe it was the General's doing.*

The Shepherd had told her about the girl, the one who wore her face. Sasha, that was her name. Sasha from Earth. A parallel universe. She'd listened slack-jawed as they told her what her "new life" would entail. She'd never in a million years imagined that in order to be free, she'd have to take over someone's identity, but there was no turning back now. The plan was set. Libertas had no way to transport her through the tandem, so they were going to rely on the universes to do the heavy lifting. All they had to do was bring her to Sasha, and after several days of searching, they'd found her—in Farnham, of all places.

She couldn't go alone. She needed someone to help her sneak into the Adastra Palace Prison, or, as the locals called it, the Hole. She expected the Shepherd to do the honors, but instead they'd sent him. *She supposed it was fitting. He was the one who'd brought her out of the Castle, and he would deliver her, as promised, to her new life.*

She knew what she had to do when she arrived on Earth: she had to go to the police and tell them that her name was Sasha Lawson, that she was from Chicago, Illinois, and that she had no memory of the last two weeks. When they asked her about Grant Davis, she was to tell them she didn't know where he was. And then, after the furor died down, she was to slip quietly into Sasha Lawson's life until she was eighteen. Only then would she be truly free. But it didn't seem too bad, considering how many years she'd already waited.

It wouldn't be long now.

THIRTY-EIGHT

They're here.

The thought rang through my head as I opened my eyes, waking from a deep sleep. Thomas and I were crammed together on one of the beds; we'd curled up close to each other, my head on his chest, his knees bent and sort of hanging over the edge. In spite of that, I'd slept better than I ever had since I came to Aurora. I'd been shy at first, as we crawled into bed exhausted, wondering what it would feel like to have him that close, but the moment I settled in next to him and his arms wrapped around me, I felt calm and comforted, or at least as calm and comforted as I could feel while I was trapped in a dark, cold dungeon in an alternate universe. I'd drifted off to the sound of Thomas's light, soft breathing, warmed despite the chill by his nearness. We didn't speak, letting the silence envelop us, feeling as though we were the only two people in the world and wishing, at least in part, that it could always stay that way.

But we weren't alone anymore. I knew they were there before I heard them, but as I struggled to sit upright, my limbs still tangled with Thomas's, the door to our cell slid open, emitting a loud, animal squeal as it was dragged along its rusty tracks. Footsteps echoed off the stone walls.

"Isn't that just adorable."

Thomas's eyes flew open, and he leapt to his feet while I scrambled after him. He turned in the direction of the voice, his hand darting reflexively to the shoulder holster he wasn't wearing, to grab a gun that wasn't there. The lights, which had shut off long ago, snapped on, but not before I realized that there were two people in the cell besides Thomas and me, not just one. It took me a moment to recognize the voice, but when I did, I knew we were in trouble.

Lucas was pointing a gun at us. "Don't move," he said. "Stay right where you are."

"Since when do they let you carry a gun?" Thomas asked. His tone was calm and even, but I could tell from the way he was standing—straight as a pole, shoulders tensed, using his body to shield me—that, unarmed, he was at a terrible disadvantage and he knew it.

"At least I have a gun," Lucas said.

Thomas jerked his chin toward Lucas's companion. "Who's your friend?"

The girl revealed herself, stepping out from behind Lucas and shoving back the hood that covered half her face. "Hey, T," she said, her mouth curling at the edges in a wry, sad smile. She was blond, but in all other ways, she was me.

You're never prepared to meet your analog. It's a situation where knowledge does you absolutely no good. Even if you understand what they are, that they're not *you* but that they are *real,* it doesn't stop you from thinking you're losing your mind. For a second, it's like you're floating; you lose all sense of space and time, and everything else disappears except them and you. Your nerves start humming like tuning forks, and your vision goes blurry at the edges. You start to hope you're crazy, because the only alternative is that you're not.

I stared at Juliana. She stared back. Neither of us was willing to speak, or capable of doing so. The silence in the room was so oppressive that I sagged in relief when Thomas finally said something.

"What are you doing here?" he demanded. "Juli, for God's sake, where have you been?"

"Didn't you get my note?" she asked.

"Yeah, I got it," Thomas snapped. "It was . . . concise."

"I meant it," she told him, with a hint of desperation. Juliana was disheveled, her eyes wild, and in her normal-person clothes, with that hideous bleached hair, she looked nothing like the princess from the photos and paintings that covered the Castle walls, nothing like the image I'd seen in the mirror when I was pretending to be her. But my soul recognized her even as my eyes did not. Did she even know or understand just how much we were connected?

"I'm sure you did."

"I'm sorry I couldn't live up to your lofty expectations," she said, her voice trembling. "I couldn't stay there. He would've killed me. You know he would."

Thomas's jaw tightened, but he didn't bother asking who she meant by "he." We all knew who she was talking about. "I asked why you're here."

Juliana glanced at Lucas, so we turned our eyes on him as well. He affected surprise. "Oh, is it my turn to talk?" He nodded at me. "We're here for her."

Thomas used his arm to block me. "I'm not going to let you lay a hand on her."

"Don't worry, we'll leave her intact," Lucas said. "All Juli's got to do is touch her and my work here is done."

"Touch me?" A horrible realization struck me. *She's going to use me to pass through the tandem.* I glanced down at the anchor around my wrist. As long as it was activated, I was stuck fast to Aurora and nothing could dislodge me. If Juliana touched me now, she would be sent to Earth, not me.

She's going to steal my life.

"You can't do that!" I cried. "You can't take my place!"

"Why not?" Juliana snapped. "You took mine."

"Because I was forced to! You can have it back, I don't want it. I want to go home."

Juliana hesitated, and I could see that she was conflicted. "Please," I begged. "Don't."

"I won't let her get close enough," Thomas assured me. There was a pause as he and Lucas sized each other up; then Thomas darted forward like he was going to try to take the gun from his brother, but even I could tell they were too far apart for that to actually work.

I shouted at Thomas in warning, but it was too late. A shot cried out in the cell as Lucas pressed the trigger of his gun. Juliana and I both shrieked, identical sounds from identical mouths that lingered in the air long after the ring of the bullet bursting from the chamber had lost its echo. Thomas clutched his right shoulder and stumbled backward, narrowly missing me as he fell to the ground and cracked his head against the wall.

"Thomas!" I screamed, dropping to my knees. My hands shook as I pressed them against his wound, trying to staunch the flow of blood. He winced, sucking air through his teeth in pain. I followed Thomas's hateful gaze to his brother; Lucas's face was white as paper and he was breathing heavily. Juliana stood immobile with shock.

"Touch her," Lucas commanded, his voice shaking, but Juliana didn't move. He swung around and pointed the gun at her, only inches from her temple. *"Do it now, Juliana!"*

She stumbled forward, and I was sure that she would collapse, but she didn't. She crouched down in front of me, and I shrank back until I hit the wall. With Lucas training a gun on me there was nowhere to go.

"I'm sorry it has to be this way," Juliana said, her eyes meeting mine. I stared unfeelingly back at her, bracing myself for what was about to come. I felt weightless and numb as she closed in on me, reaching out to touch my face, tentatively, as if she still didn't believe, after all she'd seen, that I was even real. My fingertips itched with adrenaline. The air crackled with electricity and smelled like an approaching storm. I wondered just how much this was going to hurt.

Out of the corner of my eye, I saw Thomas reach into his pocket.

"You don't have to do this," I told Juliana. She hesitated. For a split second I thought she might reconsider.

"I'm sorry," she repeated. She sounded like her heart was shattering, but I felt no sympathy. She was a coward and a traitor, if not to her country, then to Thomas, and through him to me. I had no pity for traitors. "I can't. I wish I was better, but I'm not."

I glanced down and saw that in his hand Thomas held a small black rectangular device. As Juliana extended her hand to make contact with my skin, Thomas's finger hovered over the remote's solitary button. Our eyes found each other and I knew what he was going to do.

"Get your own life, Juli," he said with great effort. Then he pushed the button and deactivated my anchor.

* * *

The space around me expanded and contracted, stretching out infinitely in an infinite number of directions. Time no longer seemed to exist. The scene in the cell receded from me at an extremely high velocity, and I felt as if I was being pulled apart atom by atom.

Then, like the flame of a candle, I was snuffed out.

EARTH

THIRTY-NINE

I was awake, but I couldn't move. My body felt like one giant bruise. At least I was breathing. The air was sweet and clean, and smelled like . . . home. *This will pass,* I told myself, to keep from panicking. It was just the kickback from going through the tandem.

I waited for it all to drain away, and while I did I thought of Thomas. I'd known, in those last few seconds, what he was about to do. He'd decided that whatever unknown fate awaited me back on Earth, it was better than having Juliana steal my life. *My life.* The one I'd been born into. The one I missed so much I ached for it. But I ached for Thomas, too. I didn't want to imagine what was going to happen to him, but I couldn't help it. If Juliana and Lucas didn't kill him, they would certainly leave him in that Farnham jail cell to rot. And what then? What would Queen Marian do with the spy she'd caught, especially when she saw that the princess she thought she had in custody had magically disappeared? Nothing good, I was sure of that.

Oh, Thomas, I thought. Tears rolled down my cheeks, dripping off my face and soaking my hair.

And what about Callum? What would become of him now that the wedding was off, the treaty broken, and the Juliana he knew nowhere to be found? And the war that was sure to come. How much of Aurora would be left standing once it was over?

Eventually I found that I could move my left hand, then my right. I rested until I had enough strength to open my eyes, to sit up and look around. I was in a vast field filled with the shoots of some kind of grain—corn, maybe? So I hadn't landed in the foundation of a house after all. I wished I could let Thomas know I was all right, but that was impossible. He would have to live without knowing what happened to me, and I'd have to live without knowing what happened to him. This was the part of love I hated, the pain of losing the person you wanted to keep more than anything in the whole world. All the worlds.

I sat there for a long time, too weak to stand, too turned around to know where to go when I did manage to move. My hands were crusted with dried blood from Thomas's arm; the anchor I'd worn around my wrist now lay scattered in pieces close by. Not knowing what else to do, I drew my knees up to my chest, buried my face in them, and wept. Like a child I wept.

As the sun rose over the horizon, I saw a figure coming toward me, one that I would recognize anywhere. Except it wasn't him. It couldn't be him. It would never be him. But it was someone. Someone I knew. Someone who understood at least a small portion of what I'd been through, because he'd been through it, too.

"Grant," I said as he approached. My voice was hoarse, my throat as raw and sore as the rest of me. I wanted to cry at the sight of him, but I'd shed all the tears I had.

"I was hoping I'd find you here," he said, helping me stand. "I knew it was a long shot, but I thought, maybe . . . I don't know."

"I'm glad you came," I said. "I'm glad you're all right."

"Are *you* all right?" he asked.

I shook my head. I didn't think I'd ever be all right. Not in a million years, not in an infinite number of lifetimes. But I had to go on. I couldn't give up. Thomas had risked his life to return me to mine, and I wasn't going to waste it.

Grant nodded. He got it. I was grateful for that, at least. "What do we do now?"

I gazed out at the horizon, at the sun climbing in the sky. "Let's go home," I said.

So we did.

NOT THE END; ONLY THE BEGINNING

ACKNOWLEDGMENTS

Thank you to my family, my friends, and everyone who has dedicated time and energy to making this book the best it can be, particularly my agent, Joanna MacKenzie, and my editor, Françoise Bui. I'm incredibly grateful for the advice and/or enthusiasm offered by Emilie Bandy, Alex Bracken, Mary Dubbs, Kendra Levin, Ari Lewin, Eesha Pandit, Nicole Rodney, and Kim Stokely, all of whom read drafts along the way. Special thanks go out to Cambria Rowland, who styled Sasha like a boss, and Sarah Hoy, who designed *Tandem*'s beautiful cover.